IMPERILLED

KRISTINA FREER

Imperilled
Copyright © Kristina Freer 2021

All rights reserved.

No part of this book may be reprinted or reproduced or utilised in any form or by any electronic, mechanical, or other means, now known or hereafter invented, including photocopying and recording, or in any form of storage or retrieval system, without prior permission in writing from the author.

If you would like to share this book with another person, please purchase an additional copy for each recipient.

ISBN: 9798713701291

First paperback edition
Some names and identifying details have been changed

For my parents, Zygmunt and Maria.

I hope this book will be a legacy to them both, and the brave Polish people who endured so much. I also hope that the world will take a lesson from the horrors of the time and that History teachers will impart the truth of the Soviet occupation of the Polish Eastern Borderlands so the like of this will never be repeated.

FOREWARD

Until she was in her eighties, my Polish mother never spoke of her 1940s wartime experiences. Occasionally there would be a reference to some distant part of the world far removed from her origins which she never embellished and which left me perplexed.

There was never any mention of relatives, apart from an ancient Uncle in Western Poland, emigrating to America in 1911, long before she was born. When asked why I hadn't any grandparents, like all the other kids, she would simply say, 'They died during the war.' I just assumed they buried them in eastern Poland where they lived before war broke out; like most teenagers, my past was not at the forefront of my priorities, and I never pried.

When she moved in with us, she began reminiscing about her life as a girl. Deep wonderings in uncoordinated fragments emerged, which meandered from here to there and made no sense.

When I delved further, an astounding story emerged, delivered in snippets, according to her flashes of memory. I scribbled down everything in an exercise book, intending later to do something with this jumble of reminiscences.

Sometimes, she would grab the biro and draw a shaky map or correct my spelling of a place visited.

Eventually, I began compiling her thoughts into chronological order, piecing together the jigsaw that was her life story.

After five years, my first draft was complete. I asked for the opinion of a highly respected teacher who felt that it was a story that should be told in schools. She encouraged me to join a writers' club to hone the final draft.

My mother's story could never be a hundred percent accurate, given her declining memory and passaging time, but extensive research has allowed me to describe the destinations she visited. With the help of authors' licence I could imagine conversations between her and those she loved, bringing her story alive. Everything else is true.

Having taken so long to carry out such a mammoth task, I sat with her and read it. Tears pooled in her eyes, and she said, 'Ahh child, why are you bothering? It was such a long time ago; no one will read it.' She died before I could publish it, and it is my silent regret she never lived to see it in print.

INTRODUCTION

The Kresy may be worlds apart from the luminescent ruby stars installed atop the Moscow Kremlin, light years away from the world of power – but it's on its deadly radar.

It is a land of mists and swamps where elk and bison roam its vast primaeval forests. This tranquil backwater, on the eastern edge of Poland, is dotted with wooden farmsteads. Cockerels crow, farmers toil, and girls, like Marisha Glenz, spend their days in meadows herding their father's cows.

If you think this a place where nothing ever happens - think again.

IMPERILLED

PART ONE

1

10TH February 1940. Ignacy Glenz's farmhouse. Pre-dawn.

I stumbled and tripped; my nightmare getting worse. I was being dragged across the kitchen floor, cold steel against my head. I kept telling myself wake up, wake up but opening my eyes the truth dawned; this was no dream.

The Russian soldier of the Soviet Secret Police grabbed my hair and forced me against the wall. 'Stay quiet or I shoot.'

I struggled to breathe. Everyone knew Stalin's henchmen carried guns and shot anyone they wanted whenever they chose. For Christ's sake, why didn't I recognise who he was in those leather jackboots and peaked cap? 'Tatta! Help me!' I cried out, but what boomed in my head escaped as a squirming whimper.

My father's plea ripped through the air. 'Tovarisch, please – my daughter wasn't escaping – she was shutting the door. For God's sake, man; it was a stupid mistake.' He rubbed his neck and ran his hand through his hair. 'She's fifteen year's old; she's just a child.'

What? A mistake? My chicken's eggs in the

box on the shelf above the stove were hatching. He'd left the door open and the snow was blowing in; the cold would kill them. I had to shut it yet one glance at my mother's face said enough, and the way she kept wringing her hands, repeating 'Jesús María', left me in no doubt my family was in trouble, I just didn't understand why. I writhed and struggled, but Peaked Cap grabbed my wrist, spun me about and pointed the barrel of his gun at my chest.

'Silence!'

His lips were mean, the sort that only parted in a cruel smile, and his words, in Russian, flew faster and louder. I could see no humanity in his eyes.

Things were grim enough without my mother riling him further, but whatever he said detonated her fury. He turned his pistol on her and clenched my arm so hard I squealed.

My father moved a step closer and splayed his palms. 'Tovarisch, please – is such violence necessary? Let go of my daughter's arm, I beg you. She's done nothing wrong.'

The Tovarisch ignored him, but his lethal stare was piercing.

Cowering beside him in my nightgown, my bare feet were turning numb in the melting snow he'd tramped into the house. I flinched when he spoke and his saliva spattered my cheek. His breath stunk of garlic and nicotine and I turned away, trying to hold back the vomit. All the while, the Black Madonna and Child watched over us from the picture frame high on the chimney breast wall. In desperation, I sent up a silent prayer. 'Mother Mary, save me.' Mustn't let him know I'm scared.

Boots crunching on snow announced more trouble as two figures poured over our threshold. With rifles at the ready, the points of their bayonets glinted in the lamplight. They looked scruffy, muffled to the ears against the cold, with only their scarlet armbands marking them as militia.

Peaked Cap flicked his head. 'Search!' They dispersed in the opposite direction, hunting for bedrooms at the back of the house.

My brother, Karol, staggered out first, groggy with sleep. 'What's going on?' He raised his hands when he felt the militiaman's rifle at his back.

Gerhard, my eldest brother, and his wife, Lodzia, stumbled out next, trailed by the other militiaman with his rifle at the ready. Lodzia was gripping their little daughter on her hip, trying to pacify the crying child. 'What do these people want, Gerhard? Why are they here?'

'Silence!'

Shocked, Gerhard turned, took her arm, and drew his little family closer. 'I've no idea.'

The militia now turned their rifles on Bookiet, my German Wolfhound snarling on his belly beside my feet, having barked himself hoarse.

My scalp prickled. Dear God, please don't let

them shoot him. How will I round up the cows on my own?

Mother beckoned, her voice cracking with fear. 'Marishu, come to me. It's alright, child.'

'No, Mama, he'll shoot me.'

'No, he won't.' She met the Russian's eyes and held his gaze without wavering. 'Enough of this madness. Please let go of my daughter's arm. She meant only to shut the door.'

A moment later, Peaked Cap flicked his head. 'Shift.'

Fear, relief, and the stench of his breath proved too much; I spewed up the previous night's supper all over him, threw out my arms, and took off wailing for the safety of my mother's embrace.

'Bitch!' His lips pursed in an ominous line, and he looked as if he might strike me, but swiped his coat and jaw with a heavy uniform sleeve instead.

'Hush, shush. It's alright now. You should have stayed upstairs.' Mother planted a sturdy kiss on my forehead, then grabbed me hard by the elbow and pushed me behind her for safety.

Peaked Cap stunk – and his expression showed it. Unable to conceal his disgust, he opened a sealed brown envelope. 'Family Glenz – six of you and a child – we have orders to search your house. You are Ignacy Glenz?'

Father nodded.

'Answer me! Ignacy Glenz aged fifty two?'

'Yes, yes, I am he.'

'And you are Anna Glencova, aged fifty two?' He glanced up at Mother.

'Why ask if you already know?'

Under duress, my father placed his arm around her waist. 'My wife Anna, our daughter Marisha, our younger son, Karol, the elder Gerhard, his wife Lodzia and our grandchild, Ella. Satisfied?'

'Shift.' The swarthy militiaman lifted his rifle and with abrupt motions corralled us all into a group.

Peaked Cap prowled around in measured steps. 'You,' he said, 'keep your eye on them, and you,' he said to the scruffy one, 'come with me.' He turned to us. 'No talking. After the search, you will have half an hour to pack your chattels.' He sifted through his paperwork and read out a Decree of Deportation.

'Dear God!' Mother crossed herself and repeated it twice more for good measure.

A worrying sign, I feared. I didn't understand much of it – but it was an act of expulsion that prevented us from continuing to live in Poland, though he didn't make the reason apparent.

'Half an hour – what are you talking about?' Fear flickered behind my father's eyes. 'Where are you taking us?'

'To safety.'

'Don't worry – we're safe right here in our own home. And why the guns – we've done nothing wrong?'

'You ask too many questions, Ignacy Glenz.'

'Wouldn't you if someone forced their way into your home in the middle of the night and terrorised your family? We're not going anywhere.'

'Shut up! It is not a choice. You are Polish elite – you are enemies of the people.' His mannerisms suggested he was no longer prepared to tolerate my father's questions. He gestured to the scruffy one, and the pair of them tramped upstairs while we waited in silence.

Returning empty-handed, they disappeared to ransack the downstairs rooms.

The swarthy one jerked his rifle and ordered us to back up against the wall. We stood there in our nightclothes while Bookiet barred his teeth and inched towards him on his belly

I could stand it no longer. 'Will the blacksmith's family who live on the farm near Sciapanki be leaving too?' I saw my mother's puckered brow urging me to shut up, but I needed to know. Wanda was my best friend, and her brother, Jusio, was my sweetheart. However, the door flew open, the other two returned, and left my question unanswered.

Peaked Cap turned to my father. 'Sit down, Glenz. You need to make a list of what you'll be taking. You will travel by train, so we allow you only 500kg.' His lips twisted into a sarcastic smirk. 'And as much money and jewellery as you Kulaks (wealthy peasants) have.'

My parents turned to each other, and Father shook his head in despair. We were ordinary, diligent farmers, as were all the Polish families around here who struggled to eke out a living. We weren't rich.

'Pack bedding, kitchen utensils, warm clothes and enough food for a month. We also permit axes, small saws and sewing machines.'

Father glanced sideways at him and raised a brow. 'A lot of things for one month?'

'What about my bicycle?' Karol asked.

'Not allowed.'

He was about to protest, but Mother silenced him with a scowl and a curt shake of her head.

'Well, Glenz?' Peaked Cap was impatient.

Father pulled out a chair and sat down. He clenched his jaw, lifted the hem of the cloth and reached into the drawer for pencil and paper. 'Remind me again where you said you were taking us.'

'To safety. That is all you need to know.'

2

We were all in the grip of silent panic as chaos and confusion descended.

Peaked Cap ordered my father to remain seated, and towered over him with his pistol. He glanced at his wristwatch to remind us all we were wasting precious time. He had said half an hour – he meant half an hour.

Lodzia thrust Ella into Father's lap. With the list forgotten, whatever lay in reach was crammed into swag bags which she and Gerhard had formed out of bed sheets. They dragged eiderdowns and pillows from bedrooms and bound them with twine, while the two militia thugs trailed around after them to ensure they didn't flee through a bedroom window.

Scurrying around, I threw back curtained screens in search of what? To my surprise, Mother had kept every misshapen, wonky wicker basket I had ever made.

She wobbled on a chair, unhooking the cured sausages that dangled from the rafters, hurling them into my wicker hampers, along with any other ingredients that came to hand from the pantry. 'Karol, make yourself useful, son. We'll need pots and pans.'

When she'd stripped the rafters and pantry shelves, she stood with one hand on her forehead, the other clutching her hip. 'We need vegetables, Ignacy. This amount won't keep the seven of us fed for a month.'

I glanced in the proving pans above the stove where Mother's bread dough, that looked so plump and smelled so enticing last night, had collapsed. Lifting the perforated lid of the box where my chicken's eggs incubated, I received an angry and urgent peep, peep, peep from a bundle of blonde fluff announcing it had arrived. Another little beak was also pecking its way through its shell, and I didn't know what to do. 'Tatta, can we take these with us?'

'Leave them, child. The cold will kill them.'

It seemed so cruel; my chicks would die if I took them, and they would die left behind without anyone here to feed them. I replaced the lid and turned once again to my father, but he was speaking to Karol who was dashing around, his arms full.

'Fetch a sack of potatoes, carrots, and beets from the piwnica, son.' Father had already explained to Peaked Cap there was an outside cellar where we overwintered root vegetables.

Karol dropped the plates on the table, the pans on the floor, and turned for the door, but Peaked Cap barred him and wafted him away with his pistol. 'No one leaves the house.'

Mother paused from her dashing around. 'Karol! Pack your things. We haven't much time.

Take nothing we don't need.'

With one strike, Peaked Cap had deprived us of our behaviour and doomed my chicks. I felt doomed too. I snatched some candles from the basket and reached for the picture of the Madonna and Child.

'No frippery,' said Peaked Cap.

I cast him a defiant glare, opened my mouth to argue, but Mother stopped me. 'Marishu, go and pack, and bring your pillows and eiderdown.'

Striking a match, I cupped my palm around the flame and brought it to a candle. I made for the rickety stairs and scrambled up so fast that melting tallow scalded my hand, but I ignored the pain. Amid the swirl of dust motes in the attic, I grabbed Lodzia's red pigskin holdall and upended it, not caring what dropped out.

Stalin's henchman had trashed my tiny bedroom in the cockloft. I owned little enough as it was, but what was mine I cherished, and he defiled my personal space. I threw the bag on the bed, lit the lamp from the candle flame, and flopped onto the rumpled eiderdown. Surveying the mess, I scooped up the pile of clothes dragged from my drawers and stuffed them into the bag. What space remained I filled with my watercolours, a box of family photographs and my World Atlas, which I could read on the journey.

There were shouts, slams and bangs throughout the house, and Mother's voice carried upstairs. 'Marishu, what are you doing up there? Make haste; we're ready to leave. This instant. Did you hear me?'

'I heard you.' Dragging my eiderdown from the bed, I grabbed my pillows and closed the holdall.

Stepping out onto the landing, I caught my father, out of earshot of the Ruskies, talking with Mother. He said, 'The way those three are behaving, it wouldn't surprise me if we never see this place again.' Mother agreed with him and said that was why she worried about the food situation. They looked up when the floorboards creaked and said no more.

It had stopped snowing when I stepped out onto the porch, but the wind that had been blowing down from Siberia all winter knifed through the hood of my coat. The familiar trace of pig manure hung in the air, and the tin bath that lived on the hook outside our kitchen door sparkled diamond-bright with frost. My parents' words haunted me. 'Never come back?' How could this be true? Why? The possibility terrified me, threw me off balance; it was unthinkable that I would never see Wanda and Jusio again. No! My parents had to be wrong. This was my home. I didn't know anywhere else.

The blue light of the moon shone on the roofs of our farm buildings and the line of poplar trees beyond. A loaded cart stood nearby carrying our essentials; its horse, motionless.

I was unsure how I felt about this train journey. Of course I would go anywhere my parents led, but the thought of stepping into the unknown scared me because trains were not for people like us. Sometimes I loitered by the tracks in Zhabinka and watched them pull out of the station, imagining all their unknown destinations, leaving my father to barter over a heifer or two he had brought to market. This was my world; it was safe – except now it wasn't. Why wouldn't Peaked Cap tell Tatta where he was taking us?

All around me startled chickens sat on upturned pails and wheelbarrows, watching us leave. Szatan's lusty crowing didn't help either. They would freeze if no one shooed them back into the henhouse.

I watched the Scruffy One grab a squawking hen, its wings flapping in terror. He held it upside down by its feet, placed his thumb under its throat, clicked its head back and the hen flopped, no longer struggling, its brain and spine severed. He flung the carcass onto the cart, no doubt thinking about his dinner later, and saw me watching. His eyes dared me to say anything. I didn't, but that chicken was ours – it was coming with us. It was our food.

Somewhere on the farm, a door swung back and forth on rusty hinges, smacking against a wall. We brought all our animals indoors to overwinter, and they were sitting in their straw-cushioned sheds that Tatta had reinforced with an assortment of nails, screws and wire. Only the cattle enjoyed the luxury of a brick cow shed – made from bricks Karol and I had shaped by hand; it took us ages.

I yawned so hard that my jaw almost locked. At this hour, in the middle of winter, I was fast asleep. All this commotion distressed my cows; I could hear their sombre dirge rising from the cow shed. It was like a funeral cry, and it upset me. Who would do the milking? What was about to happen around here that demanded we abandon our home and animals with such speed?

Within minutes everyone was piling out of the house. Lodzia was on the cart, entertaining Ella with her little rag jester, jingling the bells on its pointy hat.

Mother stepped down from the porch, crying. She had never owned a coat but swaddled herself in layers of thick shawls. The warm woollen leg-bands she had wrapped around her feet and legs were visible between the hem of her sturdy long skirt and the tops of her valenki, and she had knotted multiple floral woollen headscarves beneath her chin.

Karol appeared, carrying something strung up in a sheet. He smirked to himself as he placed it on top of the cart. I knew what it was; it was his precious bike. It lived in his bedroom to ensure I wouldn't use it – as was often my fancy. It was a wonder the Soviets hadn't noticed, but I didn't snitch.

Gerhard staggered out with Father's box of shoemaking paraphernalia. Why is he bringing that thing, I wondered? Surely our boots won't wear out in a month.

Peaked cap and the Swarthy One followed Father out and pulled the door shut.

'Come on, kohanie,' Tatta put his arm on my shoulder, and gave the house one last glance as if saying goodbye. 'Time to leave.'

With that glance, I knew that my parents had lost everything they had ever possessed.

So began our 9km trek to Zhabinka Railway Station. In that dead hour, everything felt so weird. In my head it was like a dream – but the truth was we were leaving.

Peaked Cap gave the signal – the Scruffy One slapped the whip – and the horse moved. Bookiet, eager to begin his adventure, trotted alongside.

'Clear off!' bellowed Peaked Cap, but Bookiet jumped onto the cart, his legs splayed to maintain his balance.

The Swarthy One grabbed him by the scruff of his neck and flung him to the ground.

Bookiet whimpered, yelped and scrambled to get to his feet.

Mother and Lodzia spun around.

Before anyone could do anything, the Swarthy One aimed and fired.

I heard the rifle crack – then an instantaneous, pitiful yelp, and I watched

Bookiet's blood seep into the snow. My hysterical screams echoed into the night, but my father gripped my arm. I wanted to run and help my dog and strained to escape his grasp, but he tightened his hold. I glanced into his eyes and saw the pain there, but he drew me into his arms and held me tight.

'Leave him, child. Perhaps it's best this way; he didn't suffer.'

'Yes, but I saw his leg twitching He needs us.'

'He's dead. Come on – leave him. It's no use.'

I couldn't stop wailing. None of it made sense. 'Why did they have to kill him?'

'Because they are evil.' He ran the heel of his hand across his cheek, glared at the Ruskies, and turned away. 'Poor Bookiet, but you mustn't dwell on it. He's gone.'

This nightmare was getting worse. Fear mixed with grief in my belly and I stumbled ahead with my father's arm around my shoulders. However, it didn't stop me feeling anything but loathing for these odious brutes.

Mother, Lodzia and little Ella sobbed. Gerhard and Karol walked in seething silence on the opposite side. The other two followed the cart; the militiaman with his rifle slung over his shoulder on a piece of string, and Peaked Cap with his pistol at the ready. Who were they planning to shoot next, I wondered?

3

Five minutes down the lane, I paused and glanced back. Bookiet wasn't following, and our home appeared more forsaken with each step we took. Everything I had ever loved and everything I had ever known was there. In springtime, it was a haven of apple blossom, nesting storks and croaking frogs. Now everything had changed. My dog was lying injured in the snow, his precious life ebbing away. He trusted us to rush back and help him, but we couldn't. We had to abandon him because of these killers. I hated feeling like this.

The moon reflecting on the snow had transformed the countryside into a forbidding icescape. As it slipped down into the western sky the profile of our farm stood out against the moon, our poor animals trapped in their sheds and abandoned to starve. A tiny light glowed at my bedroom window, imploring us to return. Too late, I thought, I forgot to snuff out the lamp.

All at once, the protective blanket of my entire world was being ripped asunder, and I realised my life would never be the same. I couldn't bear it and turned away, my childhood over.

No one spoke. The cart's squeaky wheel tolling the minutes like a death knell, the odd snort from the horse, and the occasional sob were the only indications this nightmare was a reality.

At the corner where the three lanes met stood a massive wooden cross, surrounded by silver birches which were almost invisible beneath their cloak of snow. I always believed it was there to protect us, but it wasn't defending anyone – neither Bookiet nor us. What was the point of it? So furious did I feel, and so full of hatred, that if I had an axe, I would have hacked it down. Better still, if it landed on the Soviets and smashed them into hell.

Ploughed land, that now lay dead to the world beneath its shroud of snow, accompanied us to both sides of the lane. My father's face was expressionless, his cold tobacco pipe clenched between his teeth.

'Tatta, do you really think we won't ever be coming home? I mean, something must have made you say it. You can tcll mc; I'm grown up now.'

He removed his pipe, put his arm across my shoulder and gave me a reassuring hug. 'Of course, we'll be coming home. Before you know it, I'll be sowing those fields with grain. You'll be grazing the cows down by the stream and making more of your wonky baskets.'

'Will I? Will I, really?'

'The Soviets are taking us to safety because

the Nazis have invaded western Poland. There's a chance they might move east. Stop worrying. You're such a little worrier; it's not right for a child of your age.' He gave my shoulder another hug as if all this was normal.

'Yes, but what about my chicken's eggs, they were already hatching? What will happen to them?' When I looked into his face he had no answer, but his eyes were glistening. 'If the Soviets planned to return us, why did they have to shoot Bookiet? He could have come with us. Why the guns? Why are they so aggressive? None of it makes sense.'

'Because they know that stubborn old farmers like your mother and I would refuse to leave our homes and our animals. We'll be back soon enough, and all this will seem like a distant dream.'

My parents weren't stubborn farmers though. We may not have been as well to do and elegant as the folk who lived in Zhabinka with their fancy clothes, but my father never rested. His hands were calloused, veiny and toil-worn, his fingernails permanently ingrained with muck from his fields. He did whatever needed doing, and he made sure we never went without.

I yearned to cling to normality, yet even as the mass of the Little Forest loomed ahead, it seemed like an alien place – a place no longer for me. From spring to autumn for as long as I could remember, Wanda, Jusio and I picked berries and mushrooms there, as did all the children unless the gipsies arrived. Sometimes we would come across their hooped vardos encircled in a clearing, while their horses grazed nearby, their dogs yelped, and Bookiet eyeballed them and barked, itching for a fight. Poor thing; he wouldn't be doing that again – or chasing rabbits.

We would run home to spread the news and everyone took in their washing because there was a prejudice against the Polska Roma that they were thieves and the men were rogues. Sometimes the first sign they had arrived was smoke curling from their campfire or the distant sound of their fiddles carrying on the evening breeze while they entertained themselves around the camp fire. The next day the women, in long skirts, with fringed shawls tied about their waists, appeared bare foot and uninvited in our kitchen. They peddled gold and silver work, then stole our eggs while their menfolk traded horses. Mama could never afford to buy jewellery, but instead bought red ribbons for my hair, then fretted lest they cast evil spells over our family.

Last year, Jusio slipped his hand into mine. I still remember that tingle – that divine sensation it sent up my arm and flooded my brain – it was a sense of such giddy excitement. Where was he now, I wondered? Had the Soviets already marched him and his family to Zhabinka Station too? I hoped that he would wait for me on the platform so I could tell him what they had done to Bookiet. I craved a hug and fresh reassurance that everything would turn out fine, because what was happening here and what the grown-ups were telling me didn't sound hopeful.

By the time we reached the outskirts of town, snow clouds had besieged the first rays of dawn and deepened my desolation. The unknown day broke sullen and overcast, and the wind rose again, whipping the hems of our coats like bed sheets on a washing line.

The railway lines through Zhabinka connected Warsaw, Brest and Moscow, and the buzz on market days hung over the tiny town as the dawn chorus hung over the Little Forest; it was a lively place.

We tramped along Kirov Street, the magnificent station building already in sight. Today, however, there was no easy banter. I could see no men of commerce delivering bolts of cloth to their tailors, no rough-and-ready farmers herding livestock to market, joking with their counterparts as was the style of the common man. Instead, a grim procession of carts, and sledges choked off the station's approaches, the cart horses restive, sensing panic.

Apart from a few early risers, and those whose slumber the commotion disturbed, it felt as if the towns people had kept themselves to their homes. Perhaps they feared that by association, we hapless country folk would taint them with our fate. I saw terror flash through a man's face before he disappeared behind the door to his dwelling. Other residents peered from behind half-drawn curtains, perplexed by the constant line of tumbrels that crept past their abodes. Perhaps they were questioning when their turn to sit atop such a cart might come.

I recognised two customers out and about who often purchased Mama's eggs and cream, and Lodzia's spun linen thread. They didn't acknowledge any of us, preferring to deny any affiliation like Peter thrice denied Christ. It made me wonder what chance we had if our people had already condemned us for a crime we hadn't committed? I felt like a leper in my own country.

The Scruffy One spotted a vacant space beneath a banner of Stalin and jerked the reins so hard that his semi-feral Konik reared and almost toppled the cart with Mother, Lodzia and Ella still on it.

My brothers and I sent up a mighty roar, and Father rushed forwards to help the idiot control his horse. What a sight greeted us!

Wet, grey flakes were now falling out of nothing, and a dreadful air of oppression hung over the station. The wailing of human anguish was everywhere. Fear stunk. The NKVD was in control, their blue caps visible amongst the shabby, dun-coloured Red Army uniforms, whose soldiers were barking orders to defenceless citizens. 'Out, collect your belongings. Get in the queue!'

Babies were crying. Frightened mothers

herded their children, and dragged the smaller ones upright by the arm when they stumbled, in case they fell beneath the feet of those following. Grandparents, confused and fragile, shuffled behind, carrying their few possessions.

Friends and relatives were arriving, but soldiers allowed only those singled out for deportations near the station. They thrust food parcels into the hands of loved ones, hugged them and cried, refusing to let them go as they bid them farewell. All the while, soldiers shooed them away, lest they stepped beyond the demarcation lines. I cast about for Jusio and Wanda, but there was no sign of them or their family.

I felt my heart quicken. I tried to blot out the wailing and helped my mother and Lodzia climb down from the cart, while Father and my brothers removed our luggage. There were people, baskets, bags and bundles everywhere.

'What's this?' Karol hoisted the dead chicken out by its feet.

The Scruffy One snatched it from his grasp. 'That's mine.'

I snatched it back. 'No, it's not. It's ours. I saw him kill it, Tatta.'

The Scruffy One tried to get it off me, but I gritted my teeth and held it fast.

'Let him have it,' Father said.

I released my grip on the hen and the Scruffy One slapped it back into the cart without looking me in the face.

The NKVD Agent who arrested us handed our details to another Peaked Cap and rejoined his other two underlings. The three of them drove off somewhere – no doubt to arrest another family and murder their dog.

It occurred to me that these goings-on were not just one or two families travelling to safety. This was mass evacuation on a vast scale. Militiamen herded people like us to the backs of queues. Armed guards watched to ensure no one escaped and fired shots in the air to deter those too terrified or foolhardy to remain. Soldiers everywhere marshalled recent arrivals. When our turn came, Father gave our surname and address.

However, it wasn't until we passed through the station building, saw our transport, and watched how the Soviets were treating the Poles – that the magnitude of our fate hit us. At that moment it was as if we saw into each other's minds and shared each other's fears.

'Jesús, Maria.' Mother clasped her hand to her cheek as Karol slipped his arm around her shoulder and gave her a protective hug.

'Dear God, so it's come to this.' Father took my hand and clasped it in both of his.

Gerhard picked up Ella, placed his arm around Lodzia's waist and drew her close. Ella gazed over his shoulder; her eyes perplexed and sucked her thumb.

It was not the train that alarmed me, but the type that awaited us. Seeing the windowless boxcars and long, metal flues protruding through the wagon roofs, I knew what they expected of us – but was trying to deny it. It wasn't just me. This was not the train in which normal passengers travelled; not the ones I had seen leaving from here.

A freight train, suitable for the mass conveyance of livestock, waited for us in a siding beyond the main tracks as an unbroken line of faded, rust-coloured wooden trucks snaked into the distance and disappeared. Attached to the front end of it was a massive locomotive – facing east. The open doors of the wagons revealed the gaping black chasms beyond, as one by one, the Soviets forced terrified people to climb in, to the point where a tight mass of standing passengers gazed back at us.

A bearded old man raised his stick to the heavens, looked skyward and in a loud voice cursed Soviet Russia, bloody Stalin and the lot of them, calling on God to mete out divine retribution for their ill-treatment of him.

One soldier shoved him, and without the support of his stick, he slipped and fell on the crusted ice. My hand flew to my mouth. From the uproar, it looked as if he had broken his leg. Despite him screaming in pain, the soldiers dumped him onto a wooden stretcher and slid him into the wagon as if he were a lump of bread dough dispatched from a flat spade into the oven.

Within the range of a guard, I turned to my

father in anger. 'Tatta, did you see what those fools did to that old man?'

'I did, kohanie.'

Mother dragged me closer and peered into my face with a maddening frown. 'What is the matter with you, Marishu? Do not anger these people. Do you want a bullet in your head? Have you already forgotten what happened at home?'

Father picked up two sacks. 'Boys, we need to take our baggage to a separate goods wagon towards the front of the train.' There was a moment of panic while my parents separated food and bedding from the rest of our belongings.

'Wait here for us, Anna, or we'll never find you.'

'Hurry, Ignacy – please hurry.'

4

'Shift!' The guards herded us to the end of a queue, at the front of which the dreaded NKVD were processing the columns and counting out people for each wagon as we shunted forwards. However, the menfolk, returning from the goods wagon, their faces anxious, threaded through other groups to rejoin their families, thus muddling up their figures. It was chaos.

There was no means of escape. It was now time for us to climb in. I couldn't breathe; my bowels felt loose. It was only a train of sorts, but I felt the panic of a doomed pig facing a glinting blade.

Lodzia was fast turning mutinous and directed her fury on the soldiers. 'Did you not hear me? I said there are seven of us – not four! We are waiting for our menfolk to return from the goods wagon.' Her words were slow and precise, as if she were addressing a bunch of idiots.

They ignored her.

'God, are they thick or what?' she said through clenched teeth.

'Jesús, Maria, they won't know which wagon we're in.' Mother craned her neck towards the front of the train, and stubbornly refused to oblige, but a soldier clamped her arm and tried to steer her.

She slapped him off viciously. Her voice was suddenly deep, as if it belonged to a man. 'Get your dirty hands off me. I am waiting for my husband and sons.'

She received a shove in the back with a rifle butt for her defiance.

Little Ella, utterly bewildered, started wailing until Lodzia scooped her up and held her tight.

Shocked by their brutality, I seized my mother's arm. 'Mama, come on! We have to go!' I glanced towards the front of the train, but there was still no sign of my father or my brothers. I went first, but the wagon stood high above the ground, and the foot of the ramp was unstable. Someone grabbed my hand and helped me up. It was Zygmunt from the neighbouring farm. He and Gerhard were best friends. It was such a relief to see him; at least he was someone I knew. Once aboard, I took Ella while he assisted Lodzia.

From the loud conversation between the soldiers and my mother, she might have known arguing was pointless; yet still, she resisted and refused to board. They had no time for dawdlers; one after the other, our food hampers flew, spilling their precious contents over the filthy wagon floor.

I yearned to smack their stupid, ignorant

faces, but crouched down to pick up the food, and heard my mother cry out in pain. My anger turned to relief when I spotted my father and brothers running towards us. I waved and shouted for them to hurry, and Mother and Lodzia shouted too.

The moment they arrived, the soldiers barred their way and diverted them to the next wagon. However, my brothers had already helped Mother on board and were themselves climbing in amidst the vocal displeasure of some inside who protested they were over-crowded as it was. They told them to get off – the ones shouting the loudest being the stuck-up old boy wearing the homburg in the corner, and his fat wife with the gold tooth.

'Please allow my father on,' I shrieked, my panic rising.

'We stay together,' Tatta shouted. 'Get out of my way, my family's in there.'

A cry from the next wagon distracted the soldiers. 'On your knees!' A civilian was trying to escape.

Karol and I threw out our hands and heaved our father on board. When the soldiers turned back, he had already disappeared amongst the other passengers.

Were we expected to travel cooped up like this? The boxcar resembled a stable on wheels with a massive sliding door, and two open metal grilles at roof height for ventilation. Even our horses had the luxury of being able to stretch out in comfort.

People and sleeping children already crammed the shelves at opposite ends of the wagon. We would probably have to travel overnight standing up like this. I cast about for somewhere to sit down, but there wasn't any space on the floor either. People stood or sat huddled on their suitcases or hessian sacks around a tiny stove in the middle of the wagon which struggled to chuck out any heat. It was inhumane; we wouldn't treat our animals this way.

I heard the sounds of slowly turning wheels, of the sliding steel doors beyond our wagon, the thuds, the bangs, the shouts and the cries. A moment later, it was the sound of the rollers running along the track of our wagon. A soldier rammed the door shut, taking with it our light and our liberty. A scraping thud, and an enormous iron bar slid into its loop. Another over-stuffed wagon was ready to roll to God knew where; we hadn't yet been told our destination. There must have been over seventy people caged in here. I knew we were all going to suffocate. I hammered on the door and tried to force my fingers into the gap at the edge, but it held fast.

My father squeezed out from the mass of bodies and pulled me away from the door.

I flung my arms around his waist. 'I've got to get out, Tatta. I can't breathe.'

'Calm down and inhale. It's alright –

everything's alright.'

But it wasn't alright – I needed air. What had happened to us all? How could my life have changed so swiftly?

Zygmunt offered his space on the top shelf, and passengers moved out of my way as I clambered up and snatched at the iron bars like a mouse desperate to find an escape hole. The cold metal felt good against my cheek, the snowflakes and freezing air calmed me. Neither was I alone in my misery; children were crying, grown-ups banging on the walls begging to be let out; the din was unbelievable. I picked up grim snippets of conversation between my brothers and Zygmunt, but they made no sense – what a culmination to a ghastly night.

5

Amid the strangers were the dim but familiar faces of people from surrounding farms; the Tomalas and the Powiecki family – and there was Sasha Chorwat with her brother and two little boys.

My panic attack had abated and I climbed down to rejoin my family in a compact space beside a screened area. There was a vile stench coming from behind it, and it was making me retch. Impatient to discover its source, I flung back the blanket to see a passenger squat over a hole hacked out of the floorboards. It was hard to know who was more embarrassed – he or I. He clutched his dropped trousers in his fist, as he aimed for the opening – and missed.

Gagging, I let the blanket drop and turned to my mother in disgust. 'Oh God, I could never use that hole; I'd rather die. Have you seen it, Mama? I want to get off.'

'Hush, he can hear you. Honestly, Marishu, it serves you right for being nosey. How do you expect people to relieve themselves if the Soviets won't allow anyone to leave the wagons?'

I slumped down onto my folded eiderdown.

'Don't worry. Hopefully, we'll be there soon.'

'Yes, Mama, but where are they taking us? *Why* are they taking us?'

'To safety.'

'Huh, so why are they treating us like prisoners if they're so concerned about our welfare?' The not knowing was the scariest thing. Then everything crystallised. The signs had been there since that Sunday the previous September when the Soviets invaded Eastern Poland. So, this is what those leaflets meant by, 'The Soviet Army has come to protect the proletariat from their masters in Poland.' Is this how they were doing it? They were protecting the White Russians and other ethnic minorities from us? We were harmless, Polish people living peacefully in our own country? What had we ever done to them, other than try to help them and bail them out when their harvest failed because most of them were lousy farmers, too fond of the cherry vodka? These people were our friends, our neighbours, our school chums, and the Soviets had to shoot Bookiet to prove – what? That they were more powerful than us? Was this some sort of Soviet joke? If so, they had a sick way of showing it and I despised them even more.

I couldn't understand how something so cataclysmic could happen to us in an instant. Yesterday we were happy, going about our daily lives. Today we were incarcerated in a cattle truck – robbed of our freedom.

I went over and over it in my head, trying to

piece together the events that had led up to this. What was I doing on that Sunday last September? Nothing special; the same as I had done every other Sunday throughout the year.

Wanda called for me on the way to Zhabinka. Summer was ending and our cornfields looked magnificent in the morning sun; their kernels were hard and dimpled, their stalks already turning brown. I remember Tatta saying he had known nothing like it; it was the best harvest we'd had since moving here. Our small granary overflowed with assorted grains ready for milling, the barn was full of straw, and in the kitchen garden Mama struggled to harvest the bumper crop of vegetables that ripened all at once, so that Tatta and Gerhard had to load the cart and transport much of it to market in Zhabinka.

I knew then that Jusio was 'the one for me' and Wanda had her eyes set on a boy in church, whom she yearned to see again. We larked about all the way to Zhabinka, carefree and happy – raising our faces to the sun, arms outstretched. I even performed two cartwheels, landed on my head when my elbow gave way, and we both howled with laughter when I collapsed in a heap in the dirt.

Everything changed after we left the church after Mass an hour later. Columns of enormous metal contraptions clattered over the cobblestones and headed straight at us. Someone said they were Soviet tanks, but we were no wiser never having seen one. The sight overjoyed the White Russians and they cheered them on as if they were saviours. Some even offered bread and salt in the traditional expression of Slavic hospitality, others waved leaflets that littered the street.

We shrank into an alleyway and watched lorry loads of infantrymen following – callow men who stared at us from beneath their helmets. We watched them trundle by and wondered where they were all headed.

When they were all gone, I grabbed a handful of leaflets, and we ran much of the way home to tell our parents.

Arriving breathless and holding my side with the stitch, I remembered my father trying to calm me, but I could see alarm in his eyes. When I asked what the leaflets meant; who were the proletariat and who were their masters in Poland, he said the Byelorussians were the proletariat, and the Poles were their masters. It stuck in my mind at the time because of the horrid way it made me feel. I didn't care to think of myself as different from other members of the community into which I had been born. Those leaflets were whipping up feelings of discord.

Father told me not to worry. He screwed up the leaflets and said that sort of thing was irresponsible, but soon after the Soviets had ensconced the NKVD in villages and hamlets all around us. The local militia carried out inventories of the inhabitants of every house.

Wanda moaned they had destroyed all Polish language books at school, and they now devoted their studies to Soviet propaganda. Banners of Stalin hung everywhere and they were told to spy on their parents and report any signs of revolt. Naturally, everyone was livid they were being controlled in this way and expected to conform to the new rules. On whose say so?

Oh yes, and it upset Tatta because they replaced the zloty with the rouble and equated its value. He was such a placid man, but just before Christmas they abolished the zloty altogether, and it was the first time I saw him steaming angry. He said our savings were now worthless! The Soviets had decimated the economy and the country would never recover. Then all fell silent – until last night - or so I thought. Unlike the adults, I never paid much attention since we lived in the middle of nowhere and I spent most of my days alone in the meadows with my cows. I was more interested in Jusio and Wanda.

I looked around the loaded wagon. Time dragged. Mother was talking to me, but I wasn't listening.

Everyone was polite and civilised, but now the whole wagon roiled with exasperation. Karol glanced at his watch again. Six hours later, and we were still at Zhabinka.

Little Ella, cold and hungry, didn't understand what she was doing here, and neither Gerhard nor Lodzia could find the right words to explain it.

I stood and climbed out of the pile of limbs almost on top of me and went to stare through the knothole I had found in the wooden slats.

'They're still bringing families, and they're taking them down to the far end of the train,' I said to whoever was listening. The waiting was driving me mad. I kicked and thumped the wagon wall. 'Let us out of here!'

'Come away, child,' Mother patted the space beside her, 'why distress yourself. Sit down. The train isn't full yet, and I think you'll find we won't be going anywhere until it is.'

'When will that be?'

'Well, I don't know, do I? You ask some silly questions.'

I turned around, slid down the wall, and flopped onto the floor beside her, my knees raised, knocking them together in an agitated fashion. My thoughts turned to the Swarthy One who shot Bookiet. There was something familiar about the way he walked. He had better watch his back because when we returned I would get my revenge; I was sure he was a local Belarusian, or one of the Jews who were always scrounging favours from Tatta. Oh yes, I would track him down and teach him a lesson – one he would never forget. He would learn that people like him couldn't go about killing other people's pets. Neither could the Ruskies go around confiscating people's farms and imprisoning them in these stinking wagons as if we were subhuman. Hatred was not an emotion I had ever savoured, but once tasted, I decided I liked the flavour. I didn't know yet what his punishment would be, but I had thirty days to dream up something sufficiently vile and then we would be back. But would we?

'Do you have to do that? Keep your knees still,' Karol complained. 'You're getting on my nerves.'

'What?'

'Keep your knees still.'

I wasn't even aware I was doing it. 'I might if I had somewhere to put them.' Oh, God, this was purgatory. Trying to blot out the constant noise and stench was impossible. Passengers complained there were not enough shelves on which to sit, and the floor was no place for luggage which rightfully belonged to the goods wagon.

Small children who had so far viewed it all as one big adventure, were now fractious because of the lack of fresh air and mental stimulation. They misbehaved, taxed their parents' nerves and everyone else's tolerance. Babies were cold, hungry and needed changing.

Father pushed himself to his feet, 'Come on, boys – let's see if we can make some floor space.'

The distraction pleased me. Everyone helped, pushing luggage under shelves, stacking suitcases against walls, making space for all who were standing to sit on the floor – but not enough to lie down.

It wasn't just our lives that had turned upside down, so had my stomach. I could eat a scabby goat. I knew we should have brought that murdered chicken with us. At least there was a stove here we could cook it on.

A row was brewing between a man and two women. The wagon fell quiet, and everyone listened.

'Bloody irresponsible,' the man snapped. 'The stove's not here for your exclusive use. Other people need to heat food too.'

One of them lashed back at him. 'Well, think on, because I'm not depriving my children of food, and if we use up all the coal then fine, just fine. It's up to the Soviets to supply more. They should try being jammed up like herrings in a barrel for hours on end.'

Gradually, people lit candles and torches and brought out food. The stench from the hole was off-putting, but everyone was too hungry to care. Most were asleep by the time the grey light beyond the grilles turned to darkness. The rest fidgeted and tried to arrange themselves on the floor in the most comfortable positions, which, as I discovered, was impossible.

I put my eye to the knothole once more. The station was quieter than it was when we arrived, everyone imprisoned in their wagons. Across the tracks, swift-slanting snow lashed against a string of insipid electric light bulbs that swung in the wind. I saw soldiers patrolling with rifles, guarding the train. I heard cries of distress from newly arrived civilians. Diminishing numbers of those imprisoned were banging on walls demanding release until too exhausted to bang any more.

Sleep eluded me. When I dozed off, the man in the homburg in the corner awoke me with his intrusive snoring. All night long, someone needed to use the toilet hole and climbed over us with a lit candle or torch. By morning, the area around the hole was a disgusting mess.

6

Two days passed and our train remained bolted and static at Zhabinka.

We crouched together, freezing and frightened, our eiderdowns pulled tight over our hats and coats. Watching Lodzia trying to remove her earrings with stiff frozen fingers, I offered to help.

'Thanks,' she said, 'I've got to get them off. The metal shaft through my earlobes conducts so much cold that my ears throb down to the drum. Oh, the pain!'

I paused when I heard the enormous metal bar being raised from the door, and my hopes soared, but it was just the guards delivering pails of boiling water. They had no intention of freeing us. The metal bar clunked back into place, and there we sat, caged in this minuscule space barely able to breathe.

On the fourth day, something was happening.

Wagons shunted together, wheels and couplings clunked, and the engine blew off steam with a whistle. My father and brothers, their feet apart, braced themselves against the shelf and the door as the train hauled its mighty weight and lumbered out of Zhabinka Station. That is how our journey into the unknown began; we were on our way, but no one had yet informed us of our destination?

Departing our homeland without being able to see it generated a gamut of emotions. Many cried, some sang hymns, others prayed – caressing each rosary bead between their fingers.

I neither cried nor prayed. I had my eye to the knothole again, watching the familiar landscape pass by as the train gained momentum, rattling over joints in the rails.

An hour into our journey, our transport drew into Arancycy Station and the engine shut down.

I scrambled to my feet and pressed my eye to the knothole. 'There are lots of soldiers on the platform, Mama, and they've all got rifles. What do you think it means?'

'They're going to shoot us,' Karol said.

Throughout the wagon, what began as a ripple of hope that we had reached our safe destination, swelled into an urgent torrent of desperation to get out. Everyone surged towards the door.

Soldiers removed the metal bar, and our entire wagon was as an angry ant's nest in our zeal to get off; everyone scuffling and pushing before a shot rang out and shocked us all into silence.

I faced our captors down on the platform, and my jubilation of moments ago fizzled out at the sight of their trained rifles. We were not free.

An NKVD officer appeared at the door. 'Six of you to fetch soup, six more to fetch kipyatok, and another six to carry bread.'

When it arrived, I looked down at the few noodles that floated around in my bowl of lukewarm water, then over at Mother. 'Am I supposed to eat this?'

'Don't complain. We don't know when we'll get any more. At least it saves the food we brought with us.'

With our meal consumed, night fell. The commotion outside told us more Polish civilians were being brought to fill the other wagons.

A shrill whistle and a blast of steam announced our departure two days later. Our transport coiled away from the station, yet the perennial question remained – to where?

Hour after monotonous hour we jostled from side to side, listening to the chuckuty-chuck of wheels passing over the tracks, to mothers trying to explain to cold and hungry children why they shouldn't cry.

I sat down beside Mother on the floor, the draught from the toilet hole whipping up around my legs, and I pulled my eiderdown closer. My father slid down the wall beside us and we sat in silence in our tiny girdle of space.

'Where are they taking us, Tatta?'

'If only I knew, kohanie – I am so sorry; this is all my fault.'

'Why? It's not.'

'It is, Marishu. I should have realised what was happening the moment the Soviets set foot on Polish soil.'

'Yes, but how could you have known?'

Mother sighed – a recent habit she repeated often. 'I suppose your father didn't want to see the worst in people. You know what he's like.'

'Nothing wrong in that, Anna. But, I admit, the signs were there. Some Byelorussians began settling old scores, robbing Polish farmers of livestock....'

'Yes, then we heard rumours they murdered quite a few,' Mother added.

I spun around to face her. 'I didn't know that! Are they going to murder us?'

The next day we crossed the border into the USSR.

I noticed our transport never stopped at the larger stations, but rattled through as if Stalin's henchmen were ashamed to allow their citizens a glimpse of their depraved and hideous secret. Approaching the larger towns, those on the top shelves thrust their hands through the iron bars and shouted for help. Some threw out their names on scraps of paper or banged on the walls with saucepans, shoes and fists, anything that made a noise, pleading for help. No one heard us; no one knew we were here; it was as if we were invisible.

If our train stopped at city stations, it was

always in sidings well beyond the platforms, and when I put my eye to the knothole, what a shock I got. Transports rammed with human cargo occupied the many tracks alongside ours – tear-stained faces pressed against the bars of the boxcars – everyone shouting for help.

These were the days when guards delivered pails of soup and boiled water to each of the wagons. There was never enough to go around. Often there were days with no food or water at all. Those on the top shelves scraped snow from the wagon's roof and sills, and we had to eke out what remained of the rations we had brought with us.

We continued northeast, the cold hammering into us from all sides.

I shrank back from the metal door and listened to the wind as it forced its way through the slats and added to the ice forming on the walls. The pounding of the wheels was endless. On and on our transport ploughed, through snowstorms and blizzards, the din booming in my head. The noise grew louder than before, and my wretchedness increased with each second that passed. I no longer measured my misery by the minute – each instant of having to endure these conditions was indescribable. Even though my parents tried to buoy my spirits, I sensed we would never return home. The Soviets would never take us this far to safety.

Two weeks into our journey and the train

began decelerating – again. It was the same routine. 'Where are we?' people asked. Then the usual answer from the kids on the top shelves, either, 'Nowhere – empty plains' or 'a station'. Everyone knew 'empty plains' meant we were in for another long wait. A 'station' buoyed everyone's spirits; meaning bread, soup and boiled water and, if we were lucky, a few shovels of coal for our stove. However, it was a very long train and every wagon needed fuel, as did the engine. But what did it matter when only those nearest to it gained any benefit? The cold was now affecting everyone's health and many were suffering, particularly the youngest and the elderly.

Smaller children cried incessantly the further north we travelled, but it was more than crying, rather it was a desolate sobbing that came from sensing their parents had lost all hope.

There was a concern for an old woman who sat propped against the pile of suitcases. Her family fussed around her, and other passengers tried to help. Everyone spoke in low, grave voices.

It occurred to me I never knew either of my grandparents; they remained in western Poland when my parents moved east. It hadn't mattered before, but now it did. They visited once when I was five years old, but I didn't remember them, and now they were dead. As for our relatives who remained in Upper Silesia, they were going about their daily lives unaware of the disaster that had befallen us. I resolved to correspond with them the instant we returned; they might even invite me to visit. I had never written a letter before, but the thought empowered me. It was a plan; something that took my mind off the dreadful thought we might never return.

Today the guards opened the doors and allowed us out to stretch our limbs for the first time since leaving Zhabinka.

It was so bright. I recoiled and squinted; the light was unbearable. My eyes watered as I tried to focus. Blinking, I gazed out over endless snow-covered plains; there was nothing out there. Land and sky moulded into one as if all colour had drained from the world, barren, sightless and Godless. There was no danger of escape; our captors could afford to be magnanimous.

Everyone looked crumpled as they slid out into virgin snow: men in their homburgs, farmers in caps and grandmothers in headscarves, even the elegant woman in the fur coat and Cossack hat. I realised neither class nor decorum mattered anymore because we were now all the same. Soon the snow around our transport turned deep orange with urine.

'I won't be long,' I told Mother and shrugged off my eiderdown. With so little to eat, my digestion was all over the place, and I hadn't had proper toileting since leaving home.

Dropping from the wagon, I crawled under its belly, slid down the bank and found a spot away from the others. Within moments an even more intense cold penetrated my clothes, chilling both blood and bone. Squatting here, I felt an overwhelming sense of emptiness. I could see the entire length of the train in both directions, resting on its tracks like a vengeful dragon curving far into the distance. In the silence, the wind skimmed the light surface from the snow, obliterating our transport from view as it moaned across the plains from one empty horizon to the other. Where are they taking us, I wondered; the thought never left me.

I heard it then, a muffled caterwauling mixed with anguish that knew no consolation, and it came from all directions. People were bringing out their dead. Corpses were being lowered from wagons and slid onto people's shoulders to lie in their snowy graves.

Mesmerised, I couldn't look away as they tried to bury them in the frozen ground beside the tracks. The best they could do was to cover them with snow.

Guards moved from wagon to wagon and cleared out any dead whose loved ones refused to let go. They threw them out like so much carrion, not stopping to watch them roll down the railway bank. Mothers clung to their lifeless children until dragged from them, too numb to protest.

Our transport moved off. Two days later, another station, another bowl of soup and a crust of bread. Who could survive on such slops?

Once the guards were sure there was no

chance of their prisoners absconding, they allowed us off the train to buy or barter for what little food was available at the few tiny stations we approached.

Vast forest accompanied us on both sides of the track now and had done for the past six days. It was even colder. Was there no end to this nightmare?

Occasionally, we pulled into a siding and waited – just waited. Our food was all gone, and hunger gnawed at our insides. When the guards opened the doors, we were in the middle of nowhere. Where could we run to or hide? Sometimes we saw a cluster of weather-beaten farm buildings, a ramshackle hamlet or the faded blue dome of a desecrated church. Soviet Supply transports passed by us at speed on the main track, heading to wherever they were heading. Some speculated they were heading for Finland, others said for the White Sea, but no one knew for certain.

The distance between these remote stations seemed never-ending, but the train was slowing again. At the first opportunity, Karol and I jumped out of the wagon, our weak legs wobbling as we landed, grabbing each other's arms to regain our balance. Armed guards stood by the train and funnelled us towards the waiting locals who had brought kettles of soup and black bread, hoping to make a few kopeks. No matter how swift we were, as we approached the nearest crone, she gave an apologetic toothless smile; the soup was all gone. She held out the last piece of blackened bread in consolation.

Karol proffered a coin, and I took the bread, trying desperately to hide my disappointment.

Others who had got off the train in search of food returned with bizarre tales that our transport was now much shorter. They saw guards detaching wagons full of passengers. Karol and I were so hungry; we hadn't noticed. However, if this were true, such hysteria only added to everyone's paranoia. When would they abandon us to freeze to death?

7

OH, FOR PITY'S SAKE! The train was slowing yet again.

I stirred; this was pure torture. Tatta told me the ultimate cruelty was being forced to leave our country without an inkling as to the destination, or how long it would take to arrive.

Mother was leaning against Father's shoulder, her mouth agape, her eyes shut. She was never plump, but was now so thin that for a moment I thought she was dead. With an upwelling of dread, I shook her hard. 'Mama, wake up!'

The urgency in my voice awakened the rest of the family. But she opened her eyes. 'What is it?'

'Nothing. We're stopping again.'

She sighed. 'Ahh, what's another stop?'

She was doing this so often these days, but then, the whole wagon was now a sea of anxiety and hopelessness. It reeked of it when people whispered their fears, or spoke aloud, worsening with every passing day. Sputum-riddled lungs rattled throughout, and it was difficult to sleep.

Mother sat up and glanced around. 'Listen to those poor souls; we'll all be dead before we get to wherever they're taking us. Dear God, why are they doing this to us?'

Moments later, with much juddering and slamming of buffers, the train stopped with a backwards jerk. Voices of protest cried out. In the dimness, I saw the mass of bodies sprawled at angles throughout the wagon. No one stood – they hadn't the energy – just a vista of eiderdowns with protruding heads. My father and my brothers propped up against each other's backs; Lodzia and Ella curled together for warmth. No one was asking, 'Where are we?' No one cared anymore.

Soviet troops walked the length of the train removing door bolts. 'That's it. You've arrived.'

Frightening thoughts surged through my mind. So, this was it, the safe place. The door to our wagon rolled away and watery sunlight flooded in. I gazed out at the weathered grey bones of an old station building and was unprepared when my eyes came to rest on half a dozen four-sided carts lined up against the wall. Four were empty, but corpses filled the other two; arms and legs spilling over their sides. They resembled overloaded hayricks on wheels after a bumper harvest. I leaned into my father's chest, my eyes brimming with tears, 'Tatta, I want to go home.'

'Don't look. The Soviets are useless fools; they should have removed those bodies.'

'Where have they come from?'

'Died on the last train, I should imagine.

They've not had time to empty this one.'

I couldn't see the slightest sign of remorse on the Soviets' faces.

No longer intimidated by their captors, a brave soul demanded, 'Where have you brought us?'

'Kholmorgorki, Plesetsky District, Arkhangelsk Oblast.'

'What for?'

'We will resettle you in one of the forest stations, and there you shall live. In the meantime, you will stay here. No one is to leave the train. Is that clear?'

A hum of protest rose from inside and Lodzia stood up. 'Why this far? If this is your idea of safety, we were safer at home! We demand you return us to Poland! This instant!'

'That is impossible. You are all political settlers; an unreliable element – enemies of the people. Don't worry; you will get used to it. If you've got any dead, bring them out and stack them on those carts. If you can't manage on your own, get someone to help you. Now!'

Sobbing, the bereaved relatives of the dead woman, who had been leaning against the suitcases, obeyed and passengers shifted out of their way to make space for her family's pilgrimage to the cart.

'Did that man mean we have to stay here forever, Tatta?'

'He did.'

'I knew it! What about our animals? They'll

starve.' Oh God, and what about Jusio and Wanda, or if Bookiet had recovered? He might be outside our house pining for us. I couldn't imagine what was happening at home. Had all my chicks' eggs hatched? Then I remembered Chopin, my ginger tabby, who shot behind the dresser when Peaked Cap forced his way into our kitchen. He must still be there. Those poor little chickens. 'Where are we, Tatta?'

'Why don't you have a look at your atlas?'

Fumbling in my bag, I opened the atlas at the page I thought most likely to be our destination. I located Moscow, and with no concept of distance, having only ever travelled as far as Kobryn, I felt sure it was somewhere around there. 'I can't find it. It's nowhere near Moscow.'

'Then try a little further north.'

My fingers reached up to Vologda, but there was still no sign of Kholmorgorki.

'Here, give it to me,' he took the atlas, and I watched his finger ride up as far as the White Sea. 'Here we are, Kholmogory, and a little further down is this God-forsaken place, Kholmogorki.'

I took the atlas and my eyes roamed around the location. First there was Archangelsk on the banks of the colossal Severnaya Dvina with its mammoth tributaries, spewing into Bay of the White Sea, then down to Kholmogory, and along the railway line to where our transport now stood. Realising we were just outside the Arctic Circle, I traced the route back to Moscow, then to

Kobryn, before my finger stopped at Zhabinka. My God, I thought, closing the atlas, we're at the end of the earth!

The NKVD compiled an inventory of the living. A few hours later, we received our first food in days. Mother told us to keep some back for later.

I stood at the open wagon door eating my bread when I saw something moving. It seemed to emerge from that implacable wall of forest on the horizon. As it drew closer, I realised it was a posse of horses and sleighs, with girls and boys some no older than I was at the reins, their horses playful, arching their necks in the sunshine.

The NKVD gave orders for parents with young children, the elderly and the infirm to make ready for onward transportation. 'The rest of you will remain here; it will be your turn tomorrow.'

Lodzia and Gerhard fell into this group. Their driver was a stunning girl aged about twenty. Her skin was the colour of alabaster, and her nose and cheeks glowed salmon-pink from the cold. She slipped off her mitten to remove wisps of dark reddish curls that had escaped her fur ushanka and had blown across her eyes.

She mesmerised Karol. While Gerhard went to collect their bags from the goods wagon to load onto her sleigh, he pretended to absorb himself with her horse, which was dropping its head, or flipping it high while the girl patted its neck.

Wary of horses, I kept my distance. Tatta's beloved Bay, Gniady, was a brute. Sensing my fear, he never missed the chance to give chase, sending me indoors in terror. However, every one of these horses was eager, interested and alert – not as if I would ever rub their noses or get anywhere near the things; it was best to stay away from their scary teeth and their hind hooves.

The girl introduced herself as Natasha and taking her hand, Karol, his blue eyes sparkling, kissed her fingers. 'And I am Karol Glenz.'

Sensing the chemistry and the girl's coy body language, I thought, 'Oh, not another one.' My brother had left behind a host of broken hearts in Zhabinka, and already the girls here were falling for him.

'Is it far to this forest station?' Lodzia asked. 'How long will it take? My husband wants to know why can't the rest of our family come with us now?'

'We haven't enough sleighs, but we will be back, and you will see them tomorrow. As for how long – about 12km. Maybe six hours or more, depending on the weather; the snow is deep. Even now, some will have to walk.'

The guards were manhandling the passengers who were suffering from cramp, chucking them into sleighs. Family members were being torn apart. There was much sobbing, kissing and hugging, wondering if they would ever see their loved ones again. Everyone stood to observe the convoy as it set off east across the empty snow-covered terrain, heading for that implacable wall of forest on the horizon.

It was so cold we all scurried back to our wagons. Night fell, and with all the children gone, I found space on the top shelf. The chattering calmed, and people settled to sleep. My eiderdown offered little warmth without the additional body heat of those who had left. For a moment I forgot my hunger, thirst and misery and looked up at the sky through the iron gratings, stunned by the beauty of the mass of stars sparkling in the blackness until sleep consumed me too.

It was still dark when I awoke. Lost in the remnants of a dream, I forgot where I was for a moment until the sound of sputum-riddled lungs reminded me. I hoisted myself onto my elbows and gazed through the bars. Dawn was breaking over the forest, and the sky was changing. Blurred masses of grey were giving way to oranges and pinks, and beyond the forest the first rays of the sun thrust through the trees casting biblical rays across the snow.

My parents and Karol were on the shelf below, I leaned over the ledge. 'Are you awake yet?'

'We are now, thanks to you,' Karol replied. 'What do you want? Go away.'

'I'm hungry.' Anxious now to be on our way,

it disappointed me when nothing happened.

My parents spent hours engaged in conversation with the Powiecki family'. Why did grown-ups find politics so interesting and never involve me? The guards delivered pails of boiling water mid-morning, but the door remained bolted until they came again with bread and soup, at which time they left it open.

'Eat your soup, but save the bread,' Mother urged. 'We'll need something to sustain us later.'

How golden were our wheatfields, I mused as I stuffed the remaining piece of bread into my pocket? None of us had ever known hunger at home. Perhaps there was more food at the forest station.

The horses and sleighs arrived to collect us in the afternoon, and there was Natasha again, heading for Karol.

'She's offering to take us on her sleigh.' His eyes were bright, his voice eager. 'I'll fetch our things from the goods wagon. Why don't you go back inside; it's too cold out here.'

Unbelievable; he doesn't lift a finger at home. I was looking forward to the sleigh ride until I realised I would have to walk; thanks to Karol's bicycle. That, together with Tatta's large box of shoe making paraphernalia and Mama's sewing machine, not to mention the rest of our things, there was no space for either of us; the sleigh was hardly a large one.

I was livid. 'Leave it behind, Karol, because

I'm not walking!'

'I'm not leaving this. It's mine.'

'And where do you plan to ride it? The snow's a metre deep!'

'It won't always be snowing.'

'Hey, you two stop it!' Our father had to intervene. 'Leave the bike here, Karol. You and Marisha can't walk. It's twelve kilometres to the camp. Ask a guard if you can collect it later.'

'I am not leaving it behind; it's all I have left. Look, other people are forming a queue; if they can walk, so can we.'

'Oh, let him take it,' Mother couldn't stand arguments. 'Just keep to the compacted track where the sleighs have been.'

Well, she would say that. Karol was her favourite, and I was my father's.

The train left the moment all wagons were empty, and our convoy set off following the route of the previous day's procession with nothing in sight but distant borders bounded by that thin line of trees.

An hour into our journey out of nowhere a white purga caught us mid-way between Kholmorgorki and the forest. All at once, we found ourselves amidst clouds of wind-driven snow, which spun up into the sky and returned to earth as a swirling whirlwind. The icy wind surrounded us, lashing a million razor-sharp crystals into my face. The cold penetrated through my clothes to the very marrow of my bones. I twisted every which way as I tried to shield myself from the onslaught, but so utter was my exhaustion, so grave my hunger; it was difficult to muster the will to keep going.

I veered into a snowdrift, and Karol dragged me back, yet still, the convoy pressed ahead.

The temperature plunged further still as the light faded, and the snow sucked at my long coat. Trickles of sweat stung my eyes and blurred my vision, but I ploughed on trying to keep pace with Natasha's sleigh. It was becoming increasingly difficult to lift my knees out of the snow in places.

An hour later, the storm blew itself out and left the world becalmed. The moon, full and bright, welled up from behind the trees and illuminated our path. Driven through midnight forests, we blundered forward into the haze of our own spent breath.

A rough track hacked out of the trees drew us inside and swallowed us up, so from the outside world, it would seem as though we never existed. No one would find us.

After a few more hours, the trees began thinning. Some grew tall and fine, but occasionally the woodland became reedy.

Just as I felt I could go no further, our convoy stopped on elevated ground. Natasha turned around and pointed to a settlement camouflaged by snow. 'Down there is Vodopad, and there you shall live.'

The horses snorted, and no one spoke as

everyone contemplated their futures. Coils of smoke rose from chimneys, snagging and jerking in the wind, a frozen, alien place – our home. I tried being adult about it, but I didn't know how I felt about living in a village when I had spent my entire life living in the middle of nowhere. Moonlight shone on what looked like water, so a stream, or a river, maybe? My first instincts were that I would hate it, and I yearned to return home.

8

We moved downhill, and the convoy gathered around a sizeable shack where Natasha got off the sleigh. 'This is the administration block. Remember where it is. You will need to come here in the morning.'

I wondered how I could remember anything when snow blanketed the whole site. The rooftops reminded me of clusters of oyster mushrooms, which grew stalkless on the dead wood of the deciduous forests back home. The crowd became noisy and animated, but the snow muffled all the sound, and was so thick I worried the whole settlement might collapse beneath its weight.

Natasha paced about, lest her circulation froze. 'Sorry for the delay. We're waiting for people to come and take you to your quarters. Someone's gone to the community centre to fetch them. They shouldn't be too long. You are so lucky, compared with what happened to us.'

I thought I had misheard. Lucky – after everything we had endured? I didn't think so.

'Do you and your family live here, Natasha?' Father climbed off the sleigh to join us. 'Or are you free to leave?'

'For our sins, we're prisoners like you.'

I wondered what those sins might have been, but Karol seemed keen to monopolise her attention. 'How many people live here?'

'Apart from us Ukrainians, we've collected about seven or eight hundred, but we were expecting many more. There were quite a few corpses at the station. At least the poor souls saved us another trek to Kholmogorki.'

'What will they do with those bodies?'

Natasha shrugged. 'I very much doubt they will bring them here as our cemetery's about full. Unless we start another, they'll probably bury them in shallow graves until the frost thaws in spring and then give them a deeper burial.'

How matter of fact she is, I thought, how unaffected by the dead who might be a parent, a child or a sibling, whereas I was a bundle of anguish just watching one dead woman being removed from our wagon. Natasha was a few years older than me, but seemed mature beyond her years.

'What is this forest station, Natasha?' Father asked. 'I presume it's logging?'

'We're not allowed to say. The Kommendant will tell you more in the morning,' she gave a wilted smile, and looked around. 'It isn't paradise, but you will get used to it.'

I felt another stab of terror. Get used to what? I hoped these people would hurry because my wet coat had frozen into a plank.

'Where do you and your family live?' Karol

pried.

'Our quarters are behind yours, at the forest edge.' She was about to say more, but a cluster of lamps flickered and a reception committee appeared, one of whom, holding a document, called out names in alphabetical order. Natasha returned to her sleigh.

'Dobry Vecher,' the toothless babushka escorting us, spoke in Russian.

'Good evening,' we replied, and the sleigh moved on.

'We were thinking you weren't coming,' she said. 'We've been expecting you for three weeks, but we kept the stoves in your cabins going night and day. There's nothing worse than the cold.'

I couldn't agree more and could barely wait to get into our quarters. I envisaged the blazing log fire, the warm and comfy bed, and a clock ticking slowly on the wall. I felt such a rush of gratitude that these Ukrainians were so kind to us – so different from the Soviets.

Mother said, 'Spasibo' – 'thanks.'

'You should thank us; you are the lucky ones.'

There it was again – we were the lucky ones.

All the cabins were long and low, so probably very spacious. Some we passed had faint lights glowing at the windows, but I couldn't see in because of the frosted leaves obscuring the glass.

We arrived at our abode – Number 20. It lay almost buried beneath a snowdrift which extended over the eaves, and only the footprints on the steps belied it was empty.

'There are eight rooms per block,' said the babushka, 'four from the back door, four from the front. Make sure you use the right steps because eight families live here.'

I went first and followed the babushka into a small corridor with four doors leading from it.

'Your family have two rooms; your son and his family are already in the first one. This one's yours,' she said, stepping into the room and briefly shining her lamp around.

Mother and I peered in, but the poor lighting made it difficult to see it in much detail. The smell of damp, burning wood hung in the air, but at least there would be warmth. With a sinking feeling, I realised I wouldn't be getting own my bedroom.

By this time, Natasha, Karol and my father had unloaded our baggage into the little hallway, and Mama and I rejoined them to watch Natasha and the babushka leave.

'You must come to the administration block at ten in the morning,' said the babushka. 'The Camp Kommendant will tell you more. Dobroy nochi.'

'Good night,' we called back and watched her climb onto the sleigh. She and the lamp disappeared, and everywhere was black, save for the glow from the stove.

'Candles, I didn't pack candles,' Mother panicked.

'Yes but I did.' I fetched my holdall and upended it on the table, thankful now I had snatched them in my mindless haste to help my parents pack – along with my mother's precious onyx carriage clock; a family heirloom passed down to her by my late grandmother.

Father lit the wicks from the fire and held them aloft so we might better inspect our new home.

'Is this it?' Karol snorted. 'Surely, we're not expected to live here!' He half turned, 'Our chicken shed was better furnished than this!'

We gazed up at the ceiling, and down at the wooden floor and walls. Whoever built this shack had stuffed the gaps between the logs with moss to keep out the wind. A lamp stood on the table. Mother gave it a shake, but it was empty. In the twilight I thought their faces looked like those of ghouls arrived newly from hell, huddled together for safety while we all awaited Satan's arrival.

'At least there's a heap of logs in the corner,' Father rubbed his temple. 'This is grim.'

Gerhard arrived at the door bearing his lamp aloft. 'I thought I heard voices; we were wondering when you'd arrive. Lodzia and Ella are asleep in the next room.'

'Then don't wake them,' Father shook out our bundle of eiderdowns. 'We're all desperate for sleep. Have you been waiting up?'

Gerhard glanced at his clothes. 'No, I sleep in these; it's bloody cold.'

'Have you got proper beds?' I asked.

'No. Wooden slats, same as yours; bit stingy with the straw.'

'Alright son, go back to bed. We'll see you in the morning.'

We abandoned everything, wrapped ourselves in our eiderdowns, collapsed onto the slats and instantly fell asleep.

9

Something had woken me up. I lay watching the last of the logs collapse into ash before it dawned on me where I was. Vodopad. The room didn't reek like the cattle wagon, but smoking tallow hung in the air and two of the candles were now flickering stubs. At least it was an improvement not to have a knee in your back, a foot in your face or strangers crowding you, although I wondered how long I could cope with sleeping on rough wooden boards. Karol and my parents were still asleep. Thank goodness we all had some wholesome flesh around our bones to cushion the hardness.

What was it that had disturbed me? I couldn't remember; perhaps a dream, but it was enough to invoke alarm. No! There it was again! I just felt it! I tried to swipe it off, but it had scurried over my cheek and disappeared down the back of my neck.

In the light of the one candle still burning I saw bugs, some the size of thumbnails scurrying over me, making themselves at home in my hair, sucking the blood from my scalp and flesh. I screamed, threw my eiderdown in the air and shot off the slats. 'Mama, there are bugs in here.'

I bent over, threw my hair over my head, ruffled through it with my fingers and did a weird little stomping dance, which I hoped would immediately shake and brush them off me.

'Shush. You'll wake the whole shack.' Mother got off her slats, picked up my eiderdown, shook it out and looked around. 'They seem to be everywhere.'

'How do we kill them!'

'Calm down. How can we?'

Bugs! I hadn't accounted for bugs. I thought I had done so well keeping a grip on my emotions this far, but this was one ask too many. I slumped back onto my slats, bent over, my hands dangling between my knees, and sobbed. How could I ever sleep in peace again in this lousy dump when I knew they would eat me alive? After everything we had endured – now this.

Father threw back his eiderdown, stood up, circled the room and inspected the walls. 'Hmm,' he said, 'can't see much in this light. They're bark beetles. They've had me too.' Turning his attention to coaxing the fire back to life, he poked around the ashes to find a glowing ember, to which he added some dry kindling from the pile of logs by the door. Within minutes he had skilfully brought it to life.

I tried to help fuel it, but the top logs were new and still wet.

'Bring them from the bottom of the stack, child. The only way to destroy bark beetles,' he said, 'is to set fire to this shack. Pity whoever built it didn't think to first strip off the bark.'

Karol, now awake, slapped his neck and ran his hand through his hair. 'Huh, our safe haven.' He attempted to stamp the bugs out, but the blighters just scattered. 'How can anyone live like this?'

'Don't bother son; they give off a disgusting stench when you squash them. I'll see if they'll move us to a clean shack – if they have any.'

I stood at the window in search of daylight but saw only ashen clouds congealing over the camp.

Mother lit another candle from the one remaining flame. 'You'd have thought they could have left us with at least some paraffin in that lamp.'

I hoped that our next room might have more furniture because apart from these wooden slats for beds, there was just a crude table with a wonky top. Where were the chairs, the shelves, something in which to wash up? Apart from a stove set into the wall serving our room and Gerhard's, there was nothing in here.

I longed for my thick palliasse, the feel of Mother's rag mat when I swung my feet out of bed, net curtains at the windows, dried lavender hanging from the rafters – and what had we got? Bugs!

Lodzia arrived with Ella a little later. 'Gerhard's trying to shave. I hope he doesn't slit his throat. Trouble is, there's nothing flat on which to stand the mirror. It keeps toppling over on the table, but he insists we try to maintain as much normality as possible.'

'I'm growing a beard,' Karol announced. 'At least it'll keep my face warm.'

'Lodziu, do you have more furniture in your room?' I asked. 'This one's beyond basic.'

'No, it's identical to this.' She headed for the swag bags, 'are we going to unpack these? We might as well try to make ourselves at home.'

Mother stopped her. 'Kohanie, Ignacy said he's going to ask if they can move us to another shack, so there's no point yet. We're all bitten.'

'So are we.' Lodzia uncovered her arm in solidarity. 'We've already asked. Everyone we've spoken to is the same. The entire camp is lousy. Oh,' she said, noticing Karol's bicycle leaning on the wall beneath the window, 'was that allowed?'

'No, it wasn't.' I glared at him with icy patience. 'Neither was his accordion, but he still brought them. If it wasn't for his stuff, we might have got a ride here on Natasha's sleigh, instead of disappearing up to our waists in snowdrifts.'

'Well, Gerhard brought his guitar,' Lodzia said, affecting a look of puzzlement. 'Ah,' she said, picking up the onyx clock, 'I'm glad we didn't leave this behind. Where shall we put it?' She settled on the windowsill, and there it sat, a potent reminder of our past lives. In here, it looked like a new hat on an old scarecrow.

Before ten, Mother reached for some of her

shawls and handed half to me because my coat was still wet. 'I suppose we'd better see what this Camp Kommendant has to say.'

'Yes, but what about finding a shop, Mama? Shouldn't we go there first – we need food?'

'We'll find one later.'

'Yes, but…'

'It's always, 'yes but' with you, kohanie. I'm sorry, this time it's important we go to the meeting, so we know what's going on here. We'll fetch the food later. They've been expecting us, so it's not as though they will run out soon.'

Gerhard joined us, his face looking as if he had done battle with a hawthorn bush.

Setting out, we met other families from nearby shacks. Cold, hungry, despondent, dishevelled and bitten; everyone headed in the same direction to line up under the Soviet diktat.

The Camp Kommendant came out, flanked by three NKVD cronies. A cursory look around, he stared at us with dead eyes and launched into his speech, but had the good grace to pause while those of us who understood Russian translated to others.

'My name is Kommendant Ivanov.' He turned to the man on his right, 'and this is Vice Kommendant Smirnov, Head of Security, amongst other things. If you have any issues about anything, Vice Kommendant Smirnov is your first point of contact.'

'The name of this 'settlement' is Posiolek

Vodopad. It is a corrective labour colony, and we have brought you here so we can re-educate you into earning your living by honest toil.'

Spontaneous laughter and jeering erupted from amongst those who were farmers.

Decent working men, including my father and my brothers, needed no lectures about honest toil from a pen pusher like him.

Various voices from amongst the crowd rose in challenge. 'Rubbish! Nonsense! Toil? What do you know about hard work?'

Undaunted, Ivanov continued. 'You will earn your living in the forest, and you will abide by the basic tenet of socialism, which means he who does not work does not eat. The settlement staff will be your instructors.'

His speech then slipped into some received socialist liturgy, which washed over my head with its 'munificence' whatever that meant, of the great Soviet government and how we should be 'grateful' – ha, grateful, 'for its generosity'... I switched off.

Unbowed and defiant, someone called out, 'Then feed us. We're starving here.'

'You will receive payment for your work, and you will buy your food in the settlement shop and the cantina. Comrade Szefczuk who runs the commissary will do everything possible to satisfy your needs. You will find both him and his wife very helpful.

'Today is a free day to allow you to settle into your dwellings and become acquainted with the

Posiolek. Tomorrow morning, those of you aged sixteen or over will start work in the forest. The Station Headman and his staff will assign you your tasks.' He was about to leave but stopped. 'For those of you who may contemplate escape – let me assure you, you will fail. Vast forests, swamps and the estuary of the immense Northern Dvina surround you for thousands of kilometres in every direction. Also, a myriad of lesser tributaries criss-cross the entire region and are major rivers in their own right. You will never find your way out. The NKVD will shoot you if you succeed.

'Although there are no physical barriers to keep you here, I have to warn you the forests contain many dangerous animals, every bit as hungry as you are, so unless you relish being eaten alive I would advise against it. All of you will spend the rest of your lives here. You will get used to it.'

There was no opportunity to protest, or to ask questions. Having delivered his death sentence, he turned away and he and his henchmen filed back into the admin shack.

That was it; we would never get out of here alive.

Father raised his brows, said nothing, but removed Ella from his shoulders where she had been sitting throughout, and set her down on the ground. Gerhard rubbed his temple, took a deep breath and gave Lodzia a grim smile who – after a moment – looked away. Karol stared ahead without blinking, perhaps thinking life might be quite pleasant here if he got to know Natasha better. Mother said, 'And may God help us all.'

'According to Natasha, there's a river down there; the Vaymuga.' Lodzia cleared her throat and infused her voice with a firm note of optimism as if she hadn't heard anything that man had said! 'It's where we'll draw water when the snow melts; then we must drag it back to the shack.'

I thought – yes, no doubt that'll be my job. I tried to blot out our future but it was too bleak. We had no future. I couldn't cope with the very thought of it. Even though I had suspected the truth, this was worse; I didn't want to believe it. It was as if I was defying fate to prove me wrong, but it was still a shock uttered from the lips of the man in charge. Now, somehow, I had to blot out our non-existence from my mind, or I would go mad just thinking about it. And what of poor little Ella, so young, so innocent? What was there for her to look forwards to; absolutely nothing? I took her hand, and said, 'Shall we play a little game?'

'What shall we play?'

'I know, we'll see who can breathe the deepest to get all the stinky stuff from the train out of our lungs, and then we'll see who can hold it the longest without going giddy and falling over.'

'Good, idea, sis,' Karol said, 'fall over and break your leg; that's all we need.'

I abandoned the game. 'Come on, we'll go to the shop instead,' I said to Ella.

'Can I have chocolate?'

'After what we've been through, you can have anything you like, my little angel.'

The crowds broke up, and we set off towards the river. The air was sharp, and it stabbed my lungs; the silence as pure and serene as the wintery blanket that covered the shacks on either side of us. Across the Vaymuga, gazing back at us, ancient forests stood brooding and motionless.

Then from out of nowhere came the muffled tones of a balalaika, and a beautiful voice singing, Kalinka. It was such a happy little song, and so unexpected that Karol started whistling. Before I knew it, I was singing along. However, I stopped when all those memories surged to the fore – those evenings we spent around the fire at home, Bookiet at my feet, his snout resting on his paws. Tatta would hold his well beaten up fiddle to his chest, plucking and caressing the strings with his bow. Beside him, Karol would sit with his accordion, and Gerhard with his guitar, stamping their feet, while Lodzia and I clapped to the escalating tempo and Mama sat knitting. Such sadness then enveloped me thinking of the loss of our perfect family life.

We followed the music to the community centre, where the words, KRASNY UGOLOK (Red Corner), on a banner outside invited us to partake in Sovetskij Soyuz (Soviet Union) on

Saturday night. What sort of labour camp was this? It confused me. In one breath, the Kommendant was telling us this was a prison where we would spend the rest of our lives – next we came across this! How odd.

Indoors, beside a table on which sat an old gramophone playing a scratched record, a Ukrainian woman stood leaning on her broom handle, singing to an invisible audience. She stopped when we entered, and her lips parted into a half gummy smile. 'Dobrey Utro.'

'Good Morning,' I said, and my family nodded.

'Please, carry on,' Mother insisted, 'it was beautiful; you could have been an opera singer.' But the woman stood and watched while we sauntered around, leaving the record hiccupping over the scratches.

Karol continued whistling and his fingers reached out to a piano keyboard that resembled a mouthful of rotting teeth. 'Needs tuning,' he said.

I noticed there was a makeshift stage here. Oh, so perhaps they put on theatrical performances like the one at Kobryn, to which my parents had once taken me. Odder and odder – things were looking up. Earlier I saw there was a school besides the admin shack, which meant the place wasn't full of older people.

The cleaner gave another half-gummy smile when we left and carried on crooning and sweeping. Somehow I felt pleased that she had sung something cheerful instead of picking some mournful lament. Here were these forgotten people, living in this terrible place, yet somehow they had recreated fragments of their former lives for themselves. Odder still, the Soviets had allowed them to do it.

We stepped out into the snow and bumped straight into the Powiecki clan – all twelve of them – searching for the shop, as were the rest of the camp. They were in Shack 23.

Alongside the community centre was the bolnica – the surgery. It was empty and locked.

'At least we have a doctor,' Mother said.

'They wouldn't waste a doctor on a place like this,' Lodzia said. 'There's a quack cum medical student, and one of our own nurses from Poland. Her name is Irena and she has already volunteered to help out.'

'Is there anywhere for washing clothes,' Mother asked, 'or do we have to collect snow and heat water?'

'No. There's a banya over there,' Lodzia pointed to another snow-covered shack. 'It's a communal area for doing laundry, and there's a steam bath for personal hygiene. We went yesterday after we'd been to the cantina.'

We popped in to have a look while passing, and when I saw everyone scurrying around naked trying to hide their genitals, I thought, 'you won't catch me in here!'

Karol continued whistling, and I was getting fed up with trudging around after everyone.

'Who cares about washing? Where's this shop? I am starving.'

Ella tugged at Lodzia's hand. 'Ciocia (Auntie) Marisha said I could have chocolate. May I please?'

'We'll see.'

We found the shop backing onto the river; the bakery built on behind it. It was a dark, fetid place, lit by a solitary paraffin lamp rigged over the counter that illuminated only the empty, bug-infested shelves behind it. It wasn't a place anyone would want to linger in or shop. I was hoping to step into a warm, welcoming place infused with the aroma of baking bread, but it was as cold inside as out. Neither could I see any sides of pork, kielbasa or other cured meats hanging from anywhere, no vats full of butter or baskets of eggs. There wasn't anything, except a barrel with a lid on it standing beside the counter. I turned to Mother in alarm. 'Mama, I told you we should have come here first. There's nothing left!'

Comrade Szefczuk appeared from out the back and stood listening at the counter, on which stood two sets of ancient scales.

Ella placed her hands on the edge and pulled herself up to peer over the top. 'I can have chocolate.'

Everyone ignored her.

'Give Comrade Szefczuk a chance to refill the shelves, kohanie; I'm sure everyone's been stocking up after so long without food.' Mother readjusted Ella's knitted hat as if the fact there was no food was normal. 'We must have exhausted the poor man.'

'What you see is what you get. There is no more,' Szefczuk said.

'Yes, but...'

'I've got pearl barley, flour and fish, and you won't often see fish in here, I can tell you.' He brought out the pearl barley, and a small sack of flour from beneath the counter, then went through to the bakery and came back with three dark loaves, which he placed beside them. 'We bake at two in the morning, so if you're not here early, you'll miss out.'

'Have you any meat?'

'Meat? No.' He half laughed. 'Well – we get a reindeer if the Nenet's are passing this way, which isn't often.'

Mother reached for her purse. 'Right – I'll take whatever you've got.'

'One fish or two?'

'May I have seven?'

Szefczuk lifted the lid from the barrel, and the stench hit us.

'Phoar.' I backed away. 'I'm not eating those! They stink.'

'Suit yourself. We've been waiting for three weeks for you to arrive.'

'Are they salted or smoked?' Mother asked.

'Brined.'

'Perhaps if I gave them a good boiling,' she gave him a hopeful smile as if by doing so, it would change these stinkers into flying fish, but then changed her mind. 'Perhaps I'll just take two then.'

He slapped the fish on the counter. 'Nothing wrong with these.'

Mother cleared her throat. 'What other things do you stock?'

'We don't. Once it's in, we sell it. We get some Halva and tobacco, but us Ukrainians like it, so we have first picks,' he gave a brief nod, 'which, after everything we've been through, I think is fair.'

'Is that all?' Lodzia exchanged worried glances with Mother.

Szefczuk drew a lengthy breath and stared, his patience waning. 'When the boat comes upriver from the Magazine at Permilovo later in the year – when the ice melts – there's more choice, and we sometimes get clothes, but it's never much.'

'What about cloth? Do you ever get any fabric?'

'The odd bits; and it's always cotton percale if we do. This place is a hard-labour camp. Everyone's up to their necks in snow and mud; there isn't much call for silks and satins if that's what you're after.'

'No, I was thinking more about felted wool. My husband makes valenki, and I wondered...'

'Forget it.'

'It's alright, Anna, I've brought plenty with me.' Father said.

Szefczuk regarded him as if he were a little deluded. 'I doubt you'll have time to make boots. Sleep is all you'll be wanting after a day's hard labour in the forest, believe me.'

I watched my parents exchange glances. 'What about milk, eggs and vegetables? Where do we buy those?' Mother steered the conversation back to food.

'At our kolkhoz – if they're willing to sell you any. Turn left out of here. Follow the river to Kenga; it's not far.'

'Kolkhoz?' Lodzia said. 'This is a bizarre labour camp.'

'Nothing bizarre about it. We Ukrainians run the kolkhoz. We've been here since the 1930's, and we created it like we created the community centre and the school and everything else you see around here. Left to the Soviets there would be nothing here but toil and death. After all these years, it's still us and them. At least this latest Kommendant is half decent. Not like the last bastard.'

Everyone fell silent, before Mother said, 'What about paraffin, where do we get that?'

'From here.'

'Oh, good, may we have some, please?'

'You need to bring your lamp.'

So that was that! I had to carry the slippery, unwrapped fish. I always got the rotten jobs. It smelt vile, and I hated the way people were looking at me, thinking it was me who stunk.

Karol said, 'Right, Gerhard – where's this

cantina?'

'Down there. See that queue snaking out of the door? There's another river beyond it; the Levashka. Make sure you don't get it muddled up with the Vaymuga, otherwise you'll get lost.'

I stopped dead. 'I-am-not-walking-any-where-else-with-this-stinking-fish. My hands are freezing. It's gone right through my mittens.'

Father said, 'I think we'll give it a miss today, son. Let's go back to the shack.'

10

'Thank God I saved those two pieces of pork fat I brought from home.' Mother set about preparing something to eat. Chopping up a substantial piece of the first slab, she rendered it down, while Father cut up the bread. 'I can't believe a shop catering for a camp of this size carries no stock. What are people supposed to eat?'

'Don't forget, there's the cantina,' Karol said. 'People probably take their meals in there.'

'Meals?' Gerhard half laughed. 'Don't expect any Bigos, or meatballs in sour cream with mushrooms. You'll get soup – if that's what you call it.'

Barely able to contain ourselves waiting for the fat to melt down, we all fell on the frying pan, ravaging its contents with our bread, soaking it up, sprinkling it with salt and devouring it with such zest. Heavenly pork fat from our own pigs – it tasted like nothing else on earth.

I savoured the last mouthful and turned to Mother, 'Please, Mama, do more.'

She glanced at what remained of the first slab and turned to me with apologetic eyes. 'As much as I would love to, kohanie, I think we should pace ourselves until we see what's in the shop tomorrow.'

'I'm still hungry,' Karol said.

'We're all hungry. You must wait for the fish soup.'

Gerhard was already on his feet. 'Come on; we need to stock up on firewood.'

Father delved into his box and twisted two screws into the walls diametrically opposite each other, in front of the stove, and strung up a line of twine. 'We'll need somewhere to dry our clothes. I'll put up some shelves too; there's no shortage of wood.' He threw my wet coat over the line and went to rummage in his box.

Mother reached for the enamel bucket and handing it to me said, 'Here, child, fetch some snow. I need water.'

Scooping snow from the porch, I returned and plonked the pail on the table. 'I'm off to have a look around.'

'Then go to the shop and get some paraffin for this lamp.' She reached for her purse. 'Don't wander far or you might get lost, and keep away from the forest. It's full of wild animals, remember?'

'I will,' I promised, reaching for a dry pair of mittens. Once outside, I turned and headed in the opposite direction. Walking past the admin shack to where we arrived last night, I wondered whether I should believe all that stuff about not being able to escape. Nothing gobbled us up on the way here. The Soviets were controlling us with fear. I didn't intend spending the rest of my days in this place. There was a trail through those trees somewhere, and it shouldn't be difficult to find. But then, I thought, a hungry bear was more likely to attack a lone girl than a convoy, so – perhaps not.

Standing here on this slight incline, it was icy cold; cold beyond anything I had ever encountered. I listened to the wind moaning, watching the treetops swaying in vigorous harmony to its tune, and turned around to see whether there was another way out of here, but a dense wall of forest surrounded me. It stretched unbroken to the horizon and I realised the noose now encircling us was as deadly and as sinister as the cattle wagons that brought us here.

Walking back towards the shop, I paused for a while at the edge of the Vaymuga to gaze at the vast expanse of water, frozen solid at the bank and halfway across. Only the middle part progressed sluggishly, relentlessly, as if determined to get as far away from this place as possible. Perhaps in the summer in a boat, when the ice had melted, I could too. But where would I get a boat? Even if I did, I didn't want to join the Divina and find myself washed up in the White Sea. I couldn't leave, anyway; not without Mama and Tatta. I would never survive alone.

Snowflakes began falling onto my cheeks, and I brushed them away, not realising how cold I had become. Squalls of icy wind gusting across the river drove me into the shop to buy the paraffin, and I scurried back to the shack. Setting the lamp on the table, I removed my mittens and stretched my hands to the fire. 'I bumped into Alfred Powiecki. He told me Sasha's little boy is sick. She's in the same shack as them. Poo, that fish soup stinks!'

'Did he say what was wrong with him?'

'No, except it was Mieczyslaw.'

Mother drew a lengthy breath. 'He was in our wagon, unsettled all the way here. The little mite must be starving. Perhaps the poor girl couldn't get any food at the shop. I'll take her some pearl barley.'

Gerhard and Karol returned with arms full of branches, and a visitor.

Natasha stepped into the room, and Karol – no longer crestfallen, his voice vibrating with elation – said, 'Mama, Natasha drove the horse and sleigh yesterday. Do you remember?'

'Of course.'

Natasha's gaze travelled to the pan on the stove. 'I shall get in trouble if they find me here. They don't encourage us Ukrainians to socialise with the Poles, but I wanted to see if you have enough food.'

'Kohanie, it is a feast compared with what we had before. I'm making fish and barley soup. Won't you sit down and have some? We never had time to thank you yesterday; it's almost cooked.'

'No, no, I must go. Thank you, but save your food, you'll need it.' She glanced back over her shoulder as she went through the door. Karol followed her.

'That's kind. I like her, but why did she tell us to save our food, Mama?' The bleak mood which crowded in on me at the shop now threatened to overwhelm me. Perhaps there would be no more food on sale – ever.

'Don't be daft Marishu,' Mother wiped her hands on a cloth. 'She's smitten with our Karol, and he with her. Haven't you seen the way they look at each other?'

'So, you've noticed it too.'

Our second visitor, Vice Kommendant Smirnov, barged in, violating our privacy, intruding on our conversation as if part of the family. There were no bolts on the doors, no polite knocks, no apologies; neither did he remove his cap.

'Hmm, cooking already.' Smirnov picked up the little carriage clock, looked it over and set it back down on the window ledge. 'Nice.' His eyes roamed over Karol's bicycle propped against the wall beneath, but he made no comment. 'And an accordion! Who's the musician?'

'Both my sons play,' Mother answered.

He turned to face us. 'I see you have already made yourselves comfortable and have acquainted yourselves with the layout of the settlement?' He didn't wait for a reply, and his manner was blunt.

'This shack is lousy with bark beetles,' Mother said. 'I would hardly call it comfortable.'

He flipped his hand, his voice sparking with sudden annoyance. 'Ah, what are a few bugs? You will get used to it.'

Hmm, well – what do you know? I was feeling vengeful and yanked up my sleeve to reveal multiple welts, then pulled away my scarf to give him a look at more on my neck. I scratched my head for good measure to the startled look on Mother's face warning me I had gone too far, and an ill-concealed smile from Father in support of my bravery.

Our plight seemed of no consequence to Smirnov; he changed the subject. 'I trust we can look forward to seeing you at the dance at the club on Saturday night?' It was a command, not an invitation.

A dance! Good heavens, things were looking up, but Father sauntered up to him and I could feel the tension humming through the space between them.

'I'm sure you didn't bring us here to entertain us. Did you want something, comrade?'

'Ah, it is a pity you feel this way. We expect all prisoners to join in with the community spirit of the camp, and you too will abide by the rules. In the meantime, I'm here to tell you what's going to happen to you.

'You, you and you,' pointing to Father, Gerhard and Karol, 'will work in the forest felling trees. You will work ten-hour shifts, but you will have to leave an hour earlier to arrive at your poloska (workstation) on time.'

'And how shall you pay us?' Father clamped his pipe between his teeth, struck a match and lit the mahorka. The smell of tobacco mingled with the stench of fish and the room smelled even worse. Drawing on it, he allowed the smoke to escape slowly, shrouding Smirnov's face.

He ignored the insult, pursed his lips and wafted it away. 'It depends on how hard you work. We base production on 'norms'. If you meet your 'norm' you will each receive eight roubles. If not, it could be as little as two roubles per shift, and it will penalise the complete team.'

'Two roubles for a ten-hour shift?' Father stared into the man's eyes, and half laughed. 'Tell me, how I'm supposed to feed my family on that?'

'What about the girl, Marisha, is it? Is she sixteen?'

It surprised me Smirnov even knew my name, but then his documents told him all he needed to know.

'Fifteen and a half, if you want to be precise. According to Kommendant Ivanov, I understand she's exempt from work until her sixteenth birthday.'

'When is that?'

'Not until October.'

'What difference will a few months make...?'

'I said, no!'

A belt of fear squeezed my gut to the point I hardly dared breathe. Did Smirnov honestly expect me to chop down trees? The only time I had ever wielded an axe was when I chopped off that poor chicken's head. Mother needed it for the pot and the headless bird had chased me across the farmyard, its wings flapping. Mother said it was just its nerves, but I vowed never to lay a hand on either chicken or axe again.

'You may live to regret it. It would mean another ration of bread.'

'No, I forbid it.'

Mother sat down beside me, placed her arm on my shoulder and rubbed my arm. 'October's a long way off yet, Marishu. Don't worry, child.'

Having delivered his news, Smirnov left us to absorb it.

Slaves – prisoners? We were all pawns in some giant Soviet chess game. Our lives were at the mercy of the hand that moved us – and no one in Poland knew where we were. No one would ever rescue us because they hadn't a clue where to search. How did we end up in such a dangerous situation where the Soviets had stripped us of everything we owned, our liberty and even our hope? A sudden wave of despair drove me to get up and stand by the window where only the view whispered there was a free world out there – one of which we were no longer a part.

Father removed his pipe and stared at nothing in particular, 'In which case, I think it would be useful if we each had an extra pair of valenki. There's nothing worse than going out in wet boots. We'd better make a start on them today. Marishu, come and let me show you how to cut them out and stitch them to make them waterproof. I won't have time to do much if I'm working all those hours.'

Did my father have any inkling we might come to such a place? At home, Mother was often boiling the woollen cloth that Lodzia had woven to reduce it to the felted consistency required and I was familiar with the process. I didn't mind cutting them out, but I didn't relish waterproofing them. Father always went a step further to ensure everything was as robust as possible and firmly stitched the soles and vamps with tar-covered twine to which he attached strands of hogs' hair to further waterproof them. Was it any wonder at the state of his poor hands when all he wanted was to ensure we were all adequately shod?

The fish soup was ready, but ravenous as we all were none of us wanted to be first to try it. I watched Mother with ladle poised and gave her a dubious look. 'What if it poisons us all?'

She sniffed it and drew back sharply from the pan. 'Well, I suppose you have to ask yourself why that barrel was nearly full. If everyone was as hungry as we are, why didn't they snap them up?'

'I can't believe this,' Gerhard said, 'we're all starving, and now we're getting picky over a bit of smelly soup.'

'Well, you eat it then,' Karol replied. There was a nasty, brief silence. 'I'm not eating it. 'Do more pork fat, Mama; I'm starving.'

'There's no bread left, kohanie. I'll make some plain pearl barley soup, but you'll have to wait a bit longer. Marisha, fetch some snow.'

11

To my surprise, Natasha returned in the evening.

She and Karol sat together on his slats as if joined at the shoulder, their arms and legs brushing against each other's, often gazing into each other's eyes.

Gerhard and Lodzia joined us. Mother fussed around, preparing coffee made from the roasted barley, which she had brought from home, and I sensed her discomfort when she had nothing more she could offer our guest. Oh, how I longed for some of her poppy-seed cake and doughnuts.

Even allowing for our natural interest, Natasha must have felt awkward being the centre of attention of every person in the room; like a curio in a shop window. We were keen to know all about her and about Vodopad.

Father raised his palm, 'Now then – one at a time. Tell me, Natasha. Everyone's been quick to tell us we're the lucky ones. Seems an odd thing to say. How so?'

She regarded him in a moment of puzzlement. 'Because you had shelter to move straight into – with fires burning. We kept them burning for you, so you didn't have to endure the same fate as us.'

'What was here?' I asked.

'Nothing. The river and the forest. We got off the train at Kholmogorki, as you did, and the NKVD led us here in mid-winter, on foot, carrying whatever they allowed us to take. There were no horses and sleighs to greet us – except for them to ride on.

'Everyone ploughed through deep snow – then they abandoned us on the river bank – well over a thousand of us. Young, old, children, babies, and cripples. Most of the elderly and cripples perished before they got here.

'Once we arrived and people realised what was happening, they rebelled and tried to follow the NKVD back through the forest to the railway line. But they shot them.'

'Dear God,' Mother remarked. 'And this is the *safe* place?'

'We were just as frail and malnourished as you are. All of us huddled together in the forest under the stars, with a ferocious gale raging across the river and no food.'

I didn't know what to say. Our journey was grim enough, and I moaned all the way here; was still moaning.

Natasha raised her eyes to the bug-ridden roof to stem back the tears, blinked, but some escaped. She seemed annoyed she couldn't control her emotions and brushed them away with her fingers. 'We had to build massive fires. We kept them going night and day.'

'Why did they bring you to this spot?' Father

asked.

'We later learned this was a designated area for logging operations. There's another gulag in Permilovo, thirty kilometres south of here. The sawmills are there. The river network around here is ideal to feed it with logs. The NKVD Commander from Permilovo originally oversaw our work, but we have our own Kommendant now. Ivanov is a decent man. Compassionate, but nobody's fool. If you play fair with him, he will do what he can to help. If you don't, then you take the consequences. He is by no means a walkover, and the others are very strict.'

Gerhard said, 'Szefczuk told us you built this entire settlement?'

'Every log and splinter is down to our toil. Those first nights were the worst, dark beyond darkness; grey mornings, frozen corpses laying all around us.'

This conversation was turning into something I wasn't expecting. I thought it would be a meet and greet – getting to know you sort of an evening, but what Natasha was describing was scaring me.

'These forests are teeming with dangerous animals,' she said. 'They must have known that. How did they expect us to protect ourselves? We had no weapons other than our own axes and saws.' She raised her brows and stared at the floor. 'It was brutal. I tell you, there is no reasoning with a hungry bear.'

'Bears?' My eyes widened.

'Oh, yes, brown bears, wolves, wolverines. You wouldn't believe what's out there.'

Affecting a look of curiosity, Lodzia asked, 'Well, how did you survive, if you had no food or shelter?'

Natasha perched on the edge of the slats, ramrod straight, gripping the wood. 'Our priorities were to make massive fires and keep them going night and day. Fallen trees lay everywhere; the men dragged them out, and youths and young children kept the fires stoked, while the rest of us built crude shelters – like igloos – to get out of the wind and the snow. As soon as we had some protection, everyone set about either collecting uprooted trees or chopping down fresh ones as fast as we could; men, women, teenagers, even ten-year-olds like me. We needed to build something permanent, or we'd have frozen to death; many did.'

Her tears were falling as fast as she spoke. 'You've no idea of the heartbreak. People were losing their loved ones, small children, babies, yet they swallowed their grief and carried on chopping the blessed trees.

'Then some NKVD officials arrived from the sawmills at Permilovo and insisted we use the logs to build them an administration centre before anything else.

Muttering astonishment, Lodzia shook her head, 'My God, and what did you eat?'

'We, well we...' agitated, Natasha cast about, her eyes coming to rest on her worn boots. She looked as if she was losing ground and couldn't see how to fight her way out of it.

Our curiosity aroused, there was no going back. Karol gave an exasperated laugh, 'Come on then; it can't be *that* bad. You can tell us.'

Natasha looked stricken, and after a while, her eyes filled with tears again and her voice wobbled as if she was trying to hit the right note. 'I suppose you might as well hear it from me because you'll hear it from someone else; all the Ukrainians were guilty.' Absorbed with sudden concentration, she raised her head and said, 'We ate the corpses.'

There was a collective gasp, as if she had simultaneously winded us all.

My repulsion welled, I didn't know what to say and glanced sideways at Karol, who was giving Natasha a long, considering look, as if he wanted to say something, but changed his mind. I wondered how he was feeling about her now, knowing she was a cannibal.

In the well of silence that followed, we all slowly averted our gaze from her to the stove and listened to the logs crackling.

Why did she have to tell us? Had it not been for Lodzia goading her, she needn't have. Perhaps it was something she was desperate to get off her conscience. There was no point discussing it with other Ukrainians; they were all complicit, and frankly, I was wondering – who was the more dangerous, a hungry bear or this beautiful girl sitting in our midst.

Lodzia shuddered. 'Ugh, human bodies?'

Natasha threw her a protesting glance, and her incomprehension showed in her face. 'We had to. They left us here with no means of survival. These people had already frozen to death. What else could we do? It wasn't as if we had purposely killed them. If *we* didn't eat them, then the wolves and bears would have. I'm sorry; it's not something I wish to discuss. I'm not proud of it.'

I was about to ask if they cooked them first, but my father must have read my mind and his forbidding glare stopped me before I opened my mouth. I wasn't being flippant. I needed to know the practicalities in case Szefczuk ever ran permanently out of food. Life up here was clearly brutal and all about self-preservation. We could so easily find ourselves in her situation.

Letting this pass, he threw on another log and stood to watch the flames devour it. 'It's alright, child, you don't have to apologise to us.' His expression urged us all not to pursue it.

With an indulgent smile to show he understood, Gerhard broke the silence, 'Where did you come from, Natasha?'

'Krym, near the Black Sea. The Soviets brought us here in 1933. It was a ten-year sentence. In three years' time, my parents will have served their time – except there's only my mother and myself left.' She gave a hollow laugh, 'but where will we go? The Soviets have taken our homes, our lands, everything, so, we're condemned to staying here unless I marry a Russian from outside of the camp, and we move away to wherever he lives.'

'They let you do that?' I asked.

'I suppose it all depends on his connections. Kommendant Ivanov is more compassionate than the last. He's prepared to listen. Not that anyone's done it yet; who are we going to meet from out there?'

Mother said, 'Szefczuk told us there was a kolkhoz here. Tell me about it.'

'We Ukrainians created it, like everything else. Never expect the Soviets to take the initiative.' Looking as if she was more able to face us, Natasha took a lengthy breath, raised her brows, and stared at the floor.

'When we realised this would be our permanent home, we started pushing him with our demands. We put forward the logic of raised production figures if he agreed, so he went along with the experiment. He even produced a clapped-out record player and some scratched records from somewhere. Later, an ancient piano arrived. They're in the Community Centre.'

'We've seen them,' I said.

'Things got a little easier when we started the kolkhoz, and we no longer had to rely so much on the boat coming upriver from the Magazine at Permilovo. Winter is the worst because, as you saw, the Vaymuga freezes for months and the shop is almost empty. We persuaded him we needed a cow and a bull we could breed with, some chickens, and some seed potatoes. So now we have milk, eggs and vegetables – and six cows and a bull!'

'Wow,' Lodzia said. 'There is hope here, then.'

'Oh yes. Ivanov didn't provide ordinary cows that would have frozen to death. He did his research and got us Kholmogory Cattle that were bred in this region. There is nothing like this at the gulag at Permilovo; that one's a proper penal colony. I pity them.'

'Natasha, tell us about your family,' Mother said.

Her question unleashed another torrent of emotion, and she sobbed. 'Forgive me. I am so sorry.' She brushed away her tears with the heel of her hand and sniffed back her dripping nose. 'Tatta, my twin brothers and my little sister perished within a year of arriving here.' She looked on wistfully. 'We were such a handsome family, but the Soviets destroyed us; they just – destroyed us. That's Communism for you.

'One day our world turned upside down. Our government, whom we trusted to give us a better life, took everything we'd worked for – complain – and they shoot you.'

'It sounds much like our situation,' Father said. 'What horrendous crimes did your family commit?'

'None. We were in the way. They called us kulaks. Stalin despised farmers like us who believed in private ownership – rather than Communism. He believed in collectivisation. He wanted us to hand over all our food to the government, and he wanted our land, but didn't want to pay us for it. Long story short, there were massive famines in Russia in the 1930s. Millions starved. Those with land like us, who rebelled, they banished to gulags. This is how Russia treats its people; our country has degenerated into this. They shot the Tzar and the Bolsheviks took over, and now we have Stalin and his henchmen. These people have total control over our lives.' Once Natasha had finished her diatribe, she fell silent, leaving us deep in thought.

Father looked pensive as he built up the stove for the night. Having talked well into the evening, he said, 'I think we'd better turn in; it's an early start for us in the morning.'

Natasha stood up. 'Thank you for the coffee and for listening to my woes. You are the only people from the outside world I've been able to tell. It's been therapeutic.' She glanced first at Karol, then at the rest of us. 'Please don't think badly of me. I'm not an evil person.'

Karol reached for her hand. 'Come on; I'll take you home.'

'Well,' said father, after they'd left, 'that was grim. In which respect, I suppose we really should consider ourselves the lucky ones.'

12

What was that? I opened my eyes and listened. The embers flickered and glowed.

Someone was in the hallway outside our door.

'Davay podvigaysya! Get moving! Make your way to the Artel in half an hour.' Someone was rounding up the workers. At home, this was Szatan's job – except he had the brains to let rip just before dawn, and there was no sign of that beyond the window.

I felt Karol's feet move near my head as he shifted position and tried to get comfortable on his slats, but he didn't wake; he never did. I must have fallen asleep before he returned last night from seeing Natasha home. Hungry beasts hadn't mauled him after all then. All this scaremongering about the forests teeming with voracious animals was just a ruse to dissuade us from escaping.

Father roused himself, lit the lamp, and started banking the stove. Just as quickly, Mother threw on a shawl, turned up the lamp and reached for the bag of flour and a bowl.

I propped myself onto my elbows. 'What are you making, Mama?'

'Pancakes – of sorts. Fetch some snow and

then tell Gerhard and Lodzia to come here for their breakfasts.' She went over to shake Karol. 'Come on; it's time for work. Wake up, or they'll throw you in the Black Hole?'

Karol murmured something and turned over.

'Get up then.'

Still half asleep, I stuffed my feet into my valenki, pulled my coat tighter, and stepped out of the shack onto the freezing porch. Damn, all the clean, untrammelled snow now lay beyond the steps. Trust it to be down there. The wind seized my plait and whipped tendrils of hair about my face. Dragging the hood of my coat over my head, I hurried down the steps and scooped a pail full of it.

One by one, lights in adjoining shacks began reflecting against the snow as the Ukrainian did his rounds. I stood and paused for a moment, gazing at the night sky. I missed Jusio and Wanda so much. Where were they now? Tatta said he thought they were still in Szpitali. Unlike our family, they rented their farm. It was the land that Stalin was after.

The icy wind stunned me awake, and I scurried indoors, banging on Gerhard and Lodzia's door as I passed. But they were already up, adding more layers of clothes over those in which they slept. I left the pail on the floor by the table and dropped onto my slats to examine my latest batch of bites. After the nightmare journey here, I hoped I might get some sleep, but the

NKVD made sure the entire camp was awake.

Mother scooped the last of the damson plum butter out of the pot which she had brought with us and spread the pancakes with the most gossamer of films. Lacking milk and an egg, they were nowhere near as delicious as those at home, but it was food. If only there were more. The saucepan with the cold fish soup waited on the table, yet still no one dared eat it. Lodzia lifted the lid and sniffed. 'What are we going to do with this?'

'Eat it, I suppose,' Father said. 'It is food after all, and if Natasha can eat dead bodies, then I'm sure a bit of smelly fish won't kill us. Besides, I'm still hungry.'

'Oh Ignacy, what a thing to say.' Mother prodded the soup, took a sip and pronounced it edible. 'It doesn't stink so much when it's cold. You could leave the fish and eat the pearl barley. It's a shame to waste it.'

'For goodness sakes!' Gerhard picked up the ladle, slopped it into a bowl and ate it cold.

Father and Karol finished it off, and all three then headed for their first day in the forest.

'I hope it doesn't make them ill,' Mother peered through the window after them. 'How will they find their way home at night? It's so dark in the forest, and there are no roads.'

With the men gone, the day yawned ahead of us. Wearing two jumpers and a cardigan, I threw another log onto the stove and set to work on the valenki while I listened to Lodzia reading a fairy tale to Ella.

Enchanted, Ella took the book from her and traced her finger over the Snow Queen's silver gown and ermine cape. She stared for a while at Kai being whisked away into the night on her sleigh pulled by two flying horses. 'Where is she taking him?' she asked.

Lodzia made dramatic eyes, and her expressions were such that they filled her child with awe. 'To her snow palace in a frozen land.'

'Where's that?'

'They call it Spitsbergen; it's *very* close to us – near the North Pole but the Snow Queen travels *all over* the world with the snow.'

A shadow passed across Ella's little face. 'There's a lot of snow here. Will she take me away too?'

Lodzia slapped shut the book and put it aside. 'No, kohanie; it's just a fairy-tale; it isn't true.'

'Yes it is.'

'Now you've frightened her,' Mother said. 'You shouldn't be filling her head with such things. Some of those fairy tales are frightening.'

'It's not the fairy tale, it's this damned place. Even I can sense the oppression.'

'She's three and a half. She can't sense anything.'

I could see a row brewing and put down my work. 'It's six-thirty; do you think the shop's open yet?' I said, already wiping the tar from my fingers. 'Szefczuk said they bake at two. It won't hurt to be first there.' Anything was better than this horrid job.

Lodzia buttoned-up Ella's coat, pulled her little hat over her ears and stuffed her hands into mittens.

'You're not taking her with you,' Mother said. 'Leave the child here.'

'The fresh air will do her good, as will a change of scenery.'

Instead of jumping into the snow from the top step, Ella walked down and looked about. 'Mama, will you make me a snowman – a big one? Please.'

'Not now, kohanie; we need to fetch the food.'

'Please.' So urgent was her need, she wouldn't stop until Lodzia promised.

'We'll both make one when we return; how's that?'

Ella agreed.

To our dismay, a lengthy queue had already formed outside the shop.

The stars were bright and clouds scudded across the moon. 'Makes you wonder whether they've been here all night,' Lodzia said. Ella nagged her further about the snowman, forcing Lodzia to snap, 'I don't want to hear another word about this blessed snowman; do you hear me? I wish now I'd left her at home with Mama.'

We wrapped our arms around our bodies and stamped our feet to keep warm, but I was feeling optimistic; perhaps Szefczuk had got fresh supplies.

Once inside the shop, the queue snaked back and forth on itself three times, but the shelves were already empty.

'We're too late!' Lodzia was livid.

'Lodzia, is everything alright? You seem very strung up today?'

She stared back at me. 'It's not alright. Nothing's alright and never will be. We're all starving – and look at this place. Empty. Gerhard's panicking. He said if he, Tatta and Karol don't get some proper food soon, they won't have the energy to meet their norms. Then where will we all be?'

We drew nearer the counter, and I could see Szefczuk slicing and weighing out the bread. He worked at a snail's pace, careful not to give away too much as if every precious crumb had a currency. His wife was helping – a comely Ukrainian woman with rotten teeth, which she revealed when she spoke. Each of her slices was wonky, thinner on top, working down to a wedge at the bottom.

Szefczuk reprimanded her each time the scales thumped against the base. 'Cut straight, woman!' We heard him shout. However, I hoped we would get her slices because they were more generous than his.

The constant queuing bored Ella and she made her displeasure known, tugging at Lodzia's coat to ensure she hadn't forgotten her snowman.

'Mama hasn't forgotten,' I reassured her, before Lodzia dragged her, protesting, to the cantina for soup, where another lengthy queue awaited us.

When we returned to the shack, Karol's bike had disappeared and Mother was in a state.

'Smirnov and another NKVD came to fetch it. They said they banned it because it was a means of escape. When I protested, Smirnov told me to shut up – Karol should think himself lucky they didn't throw him in the kartser and made him do solitary confinement. They picked it up and walked off with it. It's the one thing he treasured above all. Why couldn't they have taken his accordion instead?'

Because you can't pedal that thing, I thought, and almost laughed, but stopped myself.

Darkness fell and the passing hours had Lodzia and Mother wringing their hands, glancing at the clock. It was now seven at night, fifteen hours since the men had left for work.

'I wonder if they've got lost,' Lodzia said.

I too had been gazing out of the window earlier, watching the sky changing from dusk to blackness, darker to the east, and lighter to the west.

'Dear God, Anna.' Father stumbled through the door half an hour later followed by my brothers who were too exhausted to speak. They could only stagger to the slats and slump down.

'Come on, get those wet clothes off,' Mother tugged at Father's coat, and Karol kicked off his boots. Lodzia marshalled Gerhard back to their room to change, and I hung up the wet coats and stood the boots beside the stove to dry.

Gerhard paused at the door, 'That's a fine snowman standing guard outside.'

'I made him, Tatta,' Ella boasted, 'to look after us all.'

'I think he's protecting her from the Snow Queen dragging her off to her winter palace,' Mother said.

He turned to Lodzia, 'Who the devil's put that frightening thought into her head?'

'It comes to something when you can't even read your child a fairy tale without her turning paranoid.'

It was then that Karol noticed his bicycle was missing. He stared at the wall, then at Mother and back at the space, before he turned around and scanned everywhere else.

'Smirnov took it,' she said. 'He said they didn't allow them.'

'How dare he! I want it back.' He got off his slats, ripped his coat off the line, and everything else fell off.

'Sit down, son. He threatened you with the Black Hole and solitary confinement if you made a fuss. It's not worth it. It's only a bicycle.'

'It was mine! He had no right.'

'Here, eat your dinner.' Mother set the

109

warmed-up soup before him.

'Where have you been working, Tatta? Was it far to walk?'

'Ahh kohanie, they took us deep into the forest, across the Levashka River, over a shaky bridge. They piled it high with tree trunks stacked on the riverbed, and a raft-like contraption that started on one bank stretched across the logs and finished on the opposite bank. It was a bit nerve-wracking, not to mention dangerous, I can tell you.'

'Is there anything else to eat?' Karol set the empty plate on the table and looked at Mother.

'I've nothing to give you. Didn't you get anything at lunchtime?'

'Huh, a horse and cart arrived with a vat of soup. It was like eating washing up water. It's not substantial enough. We need meat – vegetables – eggs, anything but this.'

'The forests are a mess,' Father said, 'overgrown with brambles, fallen trees everywhere – not as straightforward as they try to make out. How did the girls get on at the shop? Has Szefczuk restocked the shelves?'

'There was nothing to buy; they came back with just the bread.'

'I promise you, Tatta, we were in that queue at a quarter to seven, but it seems everyone who's too young or too old or sick to work, got there before us. I'll make sure we're there before them tomorrow.'

13

Look at the state of my hands, I thought, staring at my tar-covered fingers. I sat on my slats by the table on the folded eiderdown cushioning my tender backside as I worked on the valenki. No more queuing for food; there could be no more distractions. Mind, if Szefczuk refused to accept Lodzia collecting all our rations, I would have to rethink my day.

With my tongue peeping between my lips, I focused on getting the stitches as close together as possible. My efforts were turning out well. It was vital I completed my part by the weekend so Tatta could take over and finish them off.

I had lost all sense of time when the door flew open, and Lodzia entered the room dressed in her coat and pulling on her sheepskin hat. Ella trailed behind her with her rag jester, the little bells on its tri-cornered hat tinkling. 'Where's Mama gone?'

'To the Banya. Why?'

She patted her pockets for her purse. 'I'm going to find this kolkhoz; see if I can get some milk and eggs, or perhaps a spent hen, although I doubt they'll have vegetables at this time of year. We can't exist on soup and bread. Can I leave Ella with you, kohanie? I'll be quicker on my own.'

I glanced at the clock and wished I could go too. It was early afternoon. 'Why don't you wait until tomorrow and we'll go together?'

'I'll be there and back in an hour.'

Lodzia had always been stubborn, I thought; level headed, but headstrong, and there was no point arguing. 'Szefczuk said you turn left at the shop, and follow the river to Kenga,' I called after her.

'Yes, I know where it is; I won't be long.' She turned at the door, lifted the wicker basket to show she intended to return with substantial purchases and gave a fond smile.

I returned to the messy job of attaching hogs' hair to the tar-covered twine. 'Good luck,' I called after her, but Lodzia was already passing by the window.

More than an hour later, I paused from my shoemaking and placed my hands on the small of my back. I stretched, glanced at the clock, then down at Ella sitting quietly beside me, and wondered if Lodzia had bought a fowl.

When Mother returned two hours later, I was instantly on my feet, wiping my hands on a damp rag. 'Lodzia went to the kolkhoz to buy milk and eggs, Mama. That was over three hours ago. She said she would only be an hour.' I reached for my coat, shrugged into it and grabbed an extra knitted hat to wear beneath my hood.

Mother too glanced at the clock. 'How far

away is this kolkhoz?'

'I don't know, do I? When have I ever been there? Szefczuk said it wasn't far.'

'Then perhaps she's bumped into Natasha or one of our old neighbours, and she's sitting at theirs having a natter. You know what a sociable little chatterbox she is. There's must be a simple explanation.'

'I doubt Lodzia's at a neighbour's, Mama. She set out to buy milk and eggs and she was determined to get them. Anyway, she wouldn't be with Natasha; she lives at the back of us near the forest and the kolkhoz is in the opposite direction. Sczefczuk said to follow the river to Kenga. I'll go and look for her.' I tied a scarf around my neck and pulled it up to cover my nose and lower face.

'Look where? Don't be so silly, Marishu, Lodzia has her head screwed on the right way around. Don't you worry about her.'

I turned and yanked the scarf away from my mouth. 'Mama – it'll be getting dark soon; what if she's slipped and broken her leg or hip? She'll soon freeze to death.' At this, Ella let out a wail, and I grimaced, regretting my careless words.

Stepping out of the shack, I headed first to the cantina, hoping Lodzia might have called in, but there was no sign of her. Passing the shop, Szefczuk said he hadn't seen her either. Two teenage girls, who were playing records at the Krasny Ugolok, looked up when I entered and shook their heads. No one in a green coat had been there since they arrived.

I was now half running, half walking along the riverbank, calling Lodzia's name to baffled glances from the odd passer-by.

Some way past the community centre where the shacks of Vodopad ended and the forests began, the Vaymuga curved away from me. Another river, which I took to be the Kenga, joined it from my right, with what looked like two smaller flows leading off it, their banks delineated by obscured shapes, presumably brushwood. They confused me.

I paused and wondered if Lodzia might have crossed one of these smaller rivers, mistaking it for part of the bank. The covered snow made it impossible to tell where solid ground ended and the water began. Was she already floating beneath the ice?

The flat, angry mass of forest rose all around me. I returned to the empty path. The silence was all-pervading, and I continued walking some distance, not knowing if I was heading in the right direction. Szefczuk said turn left out of the door and follow the river to Kenga; it wasn't far. But what did he mean by 'far?' Up here in the land of unending forests, distance stretched into infinity.

Pausing at the edge of the trees, I called, 'Lodzia, where are you?' The trampled path ahead suggested recent use. Were some of these tracks hers?

A man was approaching. He was wearing a

padded jacket over padded trousers, his feet clad in a pair of valenki, and a shapka ushanka pulled well down over his ears. His face looked gaunt; eyes sunken as if he were a ghost, but his mode of dress differed from the Polish style.

'Have you seen a young woman in a green coat wearing a sheepskin hat and carrying a wicker basket?' I asked. 'She was looking for the kolkhoz hoping to buy food.'

The man lifted the flap from one ear, and I repeated my plea.

He shook his head, turned and lifted his stick. 'No. See those shacks down there? The first one's mine. If she'd been looking for food, that's where she would have knocked first. I see everyone coming and going.'

In the distance, stood three indistinct shapes, but it was difficult to see. Everything was white, grey and brown. I gazed into his faded blue eyes, 'Is the kolkhoz down there?'

'It is, but she's not there; have you tried the community centre or the cantina?'

'I've checked both – and the shop – but there's never any food; Szefczuk told us we could buy milk, eggs and vegetables from the kolkhoz if they will sell some.'

The old man half laughed. 'Not at this time of year. We have barely enough to feed ourselves. Try in the summer. There may be more to share.'

'But we're all starving. We get a small ration of soup and a wedge of bread that's supposed to last all day, and the workers get little more. We'll die if we don't get more food.'

He shrugged. 'We've been here since 1933. They left us in the open air with neither food nor shelter. Think yourself lucky.'

I changed the subject. 'But what about my sister-in-law; she has a small child; won't you help me find her?'

'Where? You've already looked in the obvious places unless she's visiting neighbours.'

I was already shaking my head. 'No, she was looking for food. Do you know these forests?'

'Huh, who knows any forest in Russia? It's one never-ending forest. Carry on, and you'll end up in Finland, or the White Sea – if you make it that far. Only stupid people venture out in such places when they don't know where they're going.'

'So she must have taken a wrong turn somewhere. Please help me look for her; she's been missing over three hours.'

He looked at me as if I were demented and splayed his palms. 'Look where? Don't you understand – she could be *anywhere*.'

'Well, if you say the kolkhoz is behind you,' I cast about in exasperation, 'what about if she veered in this direction? Where does this track lead?'

The old man shook his head. 'Into the forest. Look, take my advice, and go home before it gets dark. You're endangering yourself; you will never find her.' He had already lost interest and was walking away.

I wished Tatta was here. He would know what to do, but it would be dark before he returned from work. I couldn't abandon her. Wouldn't I be desperate for someone to find me? I stood alone on the empty track. The wind swept across the river, catching the powdered snow, lifting it here and there. I was sure now Lodzia had taken a wrong turn, and I knew where it might have happened – where those two rivers converged back there.

Backtracking, another path veered to my left, and I followed it, the trees thin and reedy, the Vaymuga visible to my right. Lodzia could have come this way, and it was easy to see how she could have got muddled. 'Lodzia,' I called again. 'Lodzia, are you there?' I pulled my hood away from my ears and listened before I ventured a little further into the forest.

Calling her name, I carried on searching, as much for a body as her cries for help. I skirted around the trees in as straight a line as I could, avoiding the brambles and thicket that grew everywhere. The wind came as a wall, only to open up and allow me passage through, curling around me, urging me on. It wasn't long before I became uncomfortable having come this far. I stopped. Cupping my hands, I yelled again. 'Lodzia, are you there?' I listened, and shouted louder, but heard nothing. I half turned and called in another direction – still nothing, and yet again in another direction. Nothing. It was as if my words were bouncing back at me.

A wave of panic engulfed me when I turned around. I could no longer see the Vaymuga. My heart quickened as I spun a full 360 degrees and tried to regain my bearings. Snowflakes were blowing into my face; oh no, it was snowing again. It wasn't ordinary snow either, here it poured out of the sky like an upended bag of goose down.

My breath rolled from me in short, frosty puffs, as I stood to wonder how to get out of here. I tried to remember how many times I had turned around, then headed back in as straight a line as I thought I'd entered the forest, but floored trees which hadn't been there before, lay spread across my path. Many of them had soil clods around their splayed roots; the craters they left behind, filled with snow, pine needles, cones and debris.

I didn't know whether to veer left or right; the trees were pressing in on me from all sides. I turned around once, and then again. They all looked the same. I plunged through a gap and stumbled on, thinking I was heading back to the river. With my view choked off, I felt tiny and muddled, as would a lost child amongst a crowd of strange legs, my hands cold and painful.

Panting frozen breath, I picked my way through the thicket and then stopped because it looked different again from this direction. The forest was thick and oppressive here. I turned once more, my arms flaying, and my head craning up to the chink of light at the top of the trees, I had absolutely no idea where I had come from. I stumbled on; heartened when the trees grew sparser but, as quickly, they were denser again. No good looking at the ground; the snow had already hidden my tracks. The sound of rushing water somewhere made me listen more keenly. However, it wasn't water; it was more of a crashing sound when the wind shifted and dislodged snow from the treetops, sending it plunging to earth.

My fingers were going numb. In a spasm of panic, I cupped my hands and bellowed, 'HELP.' It was then I remembered Natasha's warning about watching out for swamps and wished I'd taken the old man's advice and gone home. I felt vomit rise in my belly knowing I'd done wrong, but I hadn't a clue how to remedy that, and it wouldn't go away.

The light was already diminishing and patches of shadows were forming everywhere. I caught my foot and crashed into the snow, scratching my face on undergrowth as I went. Winded, I rolled over onto my back.

I lay for a moment, gripped with fear. Saucer-eyed, I listened to the sounds of the forest, to the sighs and fidgets of the wind. The howl of a wolf pierced the semi-darkness, and I wondered if it had already smelt my fear and was summoning others to join in the waiting feast.

Sobbing now, I scrambled to my feet. A litany of incoherent whines and pleadings mixed with saliva dribbled from my lips as I blundered forwards; my nose ran, and I couldn't see where I was going through my tears. Confused, and incapable of logical thought, I pressed on, the cold biting into my bones, but I knew I had to keep moving or I would freeze to death.

The wind rose, howling through the trees as if wailing for the dead. My muscles ached with the effort of pushing on, and I felt the sweat trickling down my chest and back, soaking my garments. Was this how it felt to die? The heat seeped into my fingers, while frigid air pressed against my sweaty outer clothes; I knew I'd had it – no one would ever find me now.

Branches slapped back into my face, and I slumped against a tree to catch my breath. My eyes darted around at the sight of the mounting darkness and my body now trembled with cold. I had no idea how long I had been walking, or if I had been going around in circles. It would be so easy to lie down and stop fighting.

In moments of silence, I could hear the blood throbbing in my ears. The snow had almost stopped, and sometime later the gale blew itself out, taking the clouds with it.

The heavens were full of stars; those in the east where the sky was darkest were vibrant, almost pulsating with energy – those in the west still faint pinpricks.

I dragged the heel of my hand under my nose and almost missed the fleeting memory that came unbidden. The other day, when I was looking out of the shack window, the sky to the west was looking lighter than in the east. The Vaymuga lay to the east, yet my instinct beckoned me towards the light. I was still aware enough to know I had to follow the darkest sky and the brightest stars, even though I was becoming too weary and wanted to rest; above all, I needed to pee. I sniffed away my snot and tears and blundered forwards into the encroaching night.

Was I hallucinating or had I stumbled finally upon a wide snow-covered gash in the forest? Was this a river?

The moon rose beyond the trees, but I didn't recognise the landscape; no shacks, no people, nothing other than the sounds of the forest, the mournful animal yowls. It had to be the Kenga River upstream – or was it the Levashka River, which joined the Vaymuga on the opposite side of the camp? Perhaps I had stumbled on the mighty Northern Dvina?

I looked up at the moon. What was it telling me? Nothing. I was too cold to think about its significance. Which way, which way should I go? I turned left and stumbled along what I assumed to be the riverbank.

The moon shone brighter now. What was that ahead – shacks? Yes, they were shacks, but they didn't look as if they belonged to Vodopad. There were only three of them and a more significant building beyond.

I staggered to the first one, banged on the door, and passed out on the porch.

14

I was lying on a straw paillasse and the room was warm. My first thoughts were, I'm still alive. Where am I?

I didn't recognise my surroundings: two chairs, a crude cupboard with shelves, and a curtain at the window, strung up on a piece of sagging twine. My coat was slung over a rope near the stove, and my valenki stood drying beside it.

A voice said, 'She's woken up.' Three people came over to look at me.

I didn't recognise the man and the woman, but the third person I had seen somewhere before; it was the old man in the fufaika who told me to go home on the riverbank. I struggled to my elbows. 'Where am I?'

'We take it you didn't find your sister-in-law then?' The woman went away and returned with a bowl. 'Here, drink this.'

I put it to my lips and, for the first time in weeks, savoured the warm, heavenly taste of milk. I drank without pausing until it was all gone, wishing for more.

Lodzia! Reality dawned, and a dreadful feeling of calamity lodged in my gut. I was her only hope of survival and I had messed up. No one would find her now. When I recalled how close I came to the howling in the forest, I assumed if the wolves hadn't already ripped Lodzia apart, probably a massive brown bear had loomed up behind her. I prayed she hadn't seen him first, but if she had turned around, I felt sure he would have felled her with one swipe of his claw. Poor Lodzia would have been lying there terrified, looking up at him, trying to push herself away on her bottom, while her feet scrabbled ineffectively against the ground, shrieking as it bit hard into her flinching leg. No one would hear her screaming for help – and she would know it. I buried my face in my hands and could bear it no longer. Now I had to break the news to my family; and how was I supposed to do that?

The woman sat looking at me with compassionate eyes.

'Where am I?' I asked again?

'At the kolkhoz in Kenga,' said the woman. 'My husband found you slumped against our door.'

'How long have I been here?'

'Hours. We thought you were dead.'

She and her husband looked younger than the old man. She wore a bright green woollen headscarf emblazoned with garish roses, pulled well over her forehead, almost swamping her thin face. With her hands in fingerless gloves, she tightened the knot beneath her chin and I noticed she had the bluest, kindest eyes. Her husband's face was swarthy and reflected a life of toil and tragedy, haggard almost, his two front teeth missing. A piece of string held up his well-patched trousers, but his smile was warm.

Swinging my legs off the bed, I put them on the floor, wondering if they would support me. 'I have to go. I am so sorry I've put you to all this trouble and thank you for your kindness.' I needed to be at home; a major tragedy had befallen my family. Right now the burden was all mine, and it was too heavy for me to carry alone.

The old man said, 'Do you know where you're going in the dark? It's nearly seven o'clock. Why don't you stay here until someone comes and claims you?'

'Thank you, but I've got to get back and tell my family what's happened. If you could lend me a lamp and give me directions.' I had to get home before my father and brothers returned from work. I didn't want them having to turn out again to search for me when they were exhausted and famished.

'You'll end up back in the forest,' warned the old man. 'Come on; I'll walk you back as far as Vodopad. Think you can make your way home after that without getting lost?'

'But you're old. I couldn't ask you.'

He smirked. 'I'm 55 years old; not exactly ancient.'

To me anyone over thirty looked ancient, yet I was grateful. 'I couldn't ask it of you.'

'You're not asking. I'm offering,' said the old man. 'After seven years I know this area; you don't. My name's Vasily, and these are my neighbours, Boris and Roza.'

Vasily walked me as far as the first smoking chimneys of Vodopad, and I left him with a promise to visit again.

He talked all the way about their arrival here in 1933. I caught snippets of how the Soviets had treated them, and he repeated much of what Natasha had already told us, omitting eating the dead. Even after all these years, he was still burdened with that need to tell someone – to try to make sense of what had happened to them as if I had the answers. My mind was elsewhere though. I was trying to plan the kindest, most sympathetic way of breaking the news of Lodzia's death – for Gerhard's sake. My brother was such a decent man, and I didn't want to hurt him, but there wasn't one. However, by the time Vasily and I parted, I had framed what I intended to say in as compassionate a way as I could.

The muffled sound of music filtered out from the Krasny Ugolok, and I couldn't resist stepping inside for a few minutes to warm my hands and feet by the fire and to practice my speech. Every time I thought of Gerhard, I felt sick. This would devastate him; he adored Lodzia, and she adored him. Never in my life did I think I would have to deliver such dire news.

Two girls standing by the gramophone were

swaying in rhythm to a baritone singing 'Ey Ukhnem', the evocative song of the Volga boatmen, but it did nothing to lift my spirits; the reverse – I felt more depressed. They looked at me and nodded when I entered, but didn't speak.

I sat by the stove and thought of what happened. Had I tried hard enough? The trouble was, there wasn't even a body to bury; a grave to visit – and little Ella – she was so young. How could I tell her that her Mama wasn't ever coming back? I decided to leave that to Gerhard.

Feeling warmer, I pulled on my mittens and strode out along the footpath, passing the homecoming workers. The closer I got to the shack, the more my stomach coiled with dread. With leaden steps, I climbed the two treads into the shack and opened the door to our room.

My entire family turned and stared back at me – except there was no Lodzia. My father and brothers were there, still wearing their wet work clothes, Ella clinging to Mama's leg, and there was a vast empty Lodzia shaped space.

No one spoke, but then Mama rushed over, shouting, 'Dzieki Bogu, Dzieki Bogu,' Thank God! She scooped me into her arms, pushed back my hood, and ran her hands over my cheeks as if disbelieving I was real. 'You've scratched your face. Where have you been, child?' She kissed the top of my head and refused to let go. 'We all thought, well, we didn't know what to think; you went rushing off.'

I forgot my speech, and blurted it out, 'I

couldn't find her, Mama. She's dead.'

Gerhard splayed his palms and was about to speak, but I silenced him. 'I am so sorry, Gerhard, I've searched everywhere, the cantina, the shop, the *Krasny Ugolok*, the kolkhoz. I kept calling her name. I even thought she might have fallen through the river ice. The people at the kolkhoz hadn't seen her either. Believe me; I did my best; I couldn't have done more.'

Once it was out, the relief was immense. It was no longer my burden. I looked at each of their faces, but none of them seemed that concerned. I frowned and would say more, but Mother stopped me.

'Lodzia isn't dead, kohanie. She's out there looking for you. She's been searching for you since she got home, which was about half an hour after you left to search for her.'

'Not dead!' I was incredulous. 'So where was she?'

'With Natasha – all along – but you were too headstrong to listen. She bumped into her on the way to the kolkhoz and Natasha told her not to bother; the Ukrainians have barely enough food to see themselves through the winter.'

I was angry now, 'That must have taken the best part of half a minute – then where was she?'

'When Natasha found out how hungry we all were, she took Lodzia back to her shack and gave her some of their potatoes.'

My father and brothers moved out of the way so I could see the small pile of potatoes on the table.

The door burst open, and in walked Lodzia. 'She's nowhere. God knows what's happened to her.' And then, 'Marishu! *Where've* you been?'

I couldn't speak. I still thought I was staring at a ghost.

Lodzia came forward, 'Ahh kohanie, you had us *so* worried; I've been up and down that river bank God knows how many times. I've been in and out of the *cantina*, the *banya*, the *Krasny Ugolok*. I came back here to see if you'd returned, but you hadn't. This almost unhinged Mama. So, I went out searching again. Where've you been?'

'To the kolkhoz looking for you!'

'But I didn't go to the kolkhoz. I bumped into Natasha on the way...'

'Mama told me. So, where did you go once you'd got the potatoes?'

'Nowhere. Natasha made some Russian tea, and it was so deliciously sweet, we got chatting. When I was about to leave, her mother came home so I couldn't rush off; I stayed a while longer. She told me some interesting things.'

'And I thought you were dead!'

'No, I was drinking tea.'

'Chatting! Drinking tea! All this time!' I was almost shouting, my nostrils flaring. 'I thought you were in that forest somewhere, and the bears had got you.' I almost added, and I nearly died there looking for you, but I didn't give her the satisfaction. 'Why didn't you come and tell us where you'd be. Didn't you think we would worry?'

'Kohanie, you ought to know me well enough by now; I would never venture into any forest if I didn't know my way out of the other side. Besides, I knew you were absorbed with the valenki.' She searched my face and saw the scratches. 'You didn't go into the woods looking for me, did you?'

'D'you think I'm *that* daft. I slipped and fell on the ice and landed in a bush.'

Father came up, took my coat, glanced at the scratches, but said no more. 'This is dry, so you didn't come to any harm. So where were you?'

I removed my mittens and unwound the scarf from around my neck. 'If you must know, I've been drinking warm milk with Vasily, Boris and Roza in their cabin at the kolkhoz. I had a good look around at first; no one had seen you, so there seemed little point in carrying on. I knew you would turn up sometime. They were kind. They've even asked me to visit again.'

'That's all right then,' said Karol. 'We were about to look for you. I'm starving; what's for dinner?'

'Oh,' Lodzia said, turning, 'we have potatoes now. I told Mama to make some potato pancakes. We still have some flour and pork fat left, don't we, Mama?' She turned to me, put her arm around my shoulders and led me to the table, 'You'd like some nice potato pancakes, wouldn't you. Marishu?'

Is that all Lodzia could think about; a plate of potato pancakes? She had no idea of the sacrifice I'd made for her. Well, it's the last time I would martyr myself for anyone. Nor would I forgive her. Ever! I ignored her. From now on; let her stew.

'Listen, I have news.' Lodzia carried on as if nothing had happened. 'There's a postal service here. Natasha told me Alina Zadarnowska is in the Kommendant's employ, and she takes letters to the station at Kholmogorki. She goes on horseback – by herself, there and back! How about that?'

'So? What's it got to do with me?'

'Everything, Marishu – it means you can now write to Wanda and Jusio and tell them where you are.'

I pretended I didn't care, but oh God, could this be true?

Much happier now, Mother started grating potatoes for the pancakes. 'So tell me about this Vasily, Boris and Roza. Did they tell you anything new?'

'I can't remember now.'

'But you must have talked about something; you were there long enough.'

'Oh, they were telling me about when they first came here, the same things as Natasha told us.' I had to figure out how to get my hands on some paper and an envelope. Lodzia most likely had some, but I had decided I wasn't speaking to her anymore.

'Right then,' Tatta said, 'Lodzia, if you are going to be out somewhere for longer than you say, please come back and tell us so we don't worry, and we know you're alright. And you, Marishu, promise me never to go haring off on wild goose chases.'

'I didn't, Tatta, I was with Vasily, Boris and Roza.' I'm sure he didn't believe me.

'Whatever. But imagine if you hadn't been – for example, what if you *had* got lost in the forest – we would never have found you? Would we?'

I avoided his eyes. 'No. I promise.'

Lodzia, wanting to make amends, swiftly brought the promised writing paper and envelope. 'Here you are. Come on, we'll write it together.'

I shrugged her arm off me. 'I'd prefer to write it alone.' I didn't want her looking over my shoulder while I was pouring out my heart to my beloved. I wanted him to know how I truly felt about him, and I couldn't write a love letter with Lodzia's critical eye watching over me. It would be too embarrassing.

'As you wish.'

15

Sitting on my slats with my World Atlas on my knees, the blank sheet of writing paper resting on top, I gave the matter some thought before I started. I had never written a letter before – any letter, let alone a love letter. I addressed it to Jusio. Wanda was too young; she wouldn't know what to do. Jusio would. No doubt he would share the news with her – but this letter was important. It was a matter of life and death – and with this, I would save my family's life. I licked the lead in my pencil and started writing.

My dearest, darling Jusio,
I'm not sure what the date is, but it must be the middle of March. I am writing this in the hope you and your family are still in Sciapanki, and this letter reaches you. I miss you so much it makes my heart ache. It's awful – and Wanda too.

I suppose you want to know what happened to us all — one minute we were there, the next we had disappeared. The Soviet Secret Police came to our house and arrested us in the middle of the night on 10th February and loaded us onto the most appalling, smelly cattle trucks at

Zhabinka Station. There was no food or sanitation, and we had to relieve ourselves in front of everybody into a hole in the floor. The stink was unimaginable....

Oh dear, this letter wasn't going quite how I'd intended, but there were other things Jusio needed to know. Ah well – I only had one bit of paper, so I made my handwriting smaller to get it all in.

They kept us imprisoned on this train for maybe three weeks – not sure because all the days were the same, little food, and often no water. When we arrived here, just outside the Arctic Circle, they threw us off the train and made us walk through dense forests for hours to this ghastly camp.

Jusio, this is important – could you tell as many people as you can about what's happened to us, because we are all starving here and they're working us to death in the forests. Send this letter to your relatives back in western Poland because they will know what to do about it, and they may help us or send someone to save us.

Could you go over to Szpitali and see if Bookiet's still alive? The NKVD shot him on the way to Zhabinka, and we left his body for dead on the track before you reach the Little Forest. I saw his leg twitch a bit, so he could still be alive and scavenging somewhere.

I hate to beg, but if you can, please send

food. Kielbasa would be perfect and a slab of pork fat. Two pieces, if your mother can spare them because they don't last long and all the food we brought with us has gone. All they give us is a slice of black bread and thin soup made from a few fish heads, a bit of pasta and dead beetles when they drop in from the rim of the vats or the roof of the cantina. The shop is always empty, apart from some stinking fish nobody wants.

I wanted to escape as soon as I got here, but today I got lost in the forest, looking for Lodzia, and now I have lost my nerve.

Please write to me soon, because without you I have no hope. You are my future. All my love, your little zaba. x x x (Little Frog – his nickname for me)

I kissed the three kisses at the bottom of the page, and slipped the letter into the envelope. Let's hope a brown bear doesn't gobble up Alina Zadarnowska before she manages to post this, I thought.

Clenching my teeth, I scratched my head with tar-covered fingers until my skull ached. It had crusted over, and we hadn't even been here a week. I would soon be bald at this rate.

'Look at my fingers, Mama,' I held up both hands the next day. They were becoming more stained with every needle-full of twine I used. 'I should be at the Banya getting clean; not here.'

'Then go, kohanie; you don't have to push yourself like this.'

'How can I when I see Tatta wrap his feet in rags and stuff them into wet boots? I've got to get them finished!' Everything about this place irritated me. Being trapped in this room was like a prison within a prison; I wanted to be out in fields minding my cows. The boots needed completing by tomorrow – it was Tatta's day off, and he wanted to work on the soles. Then I'm done with it, I vowed. These are the first and last batch of valenki I shall ever make.

'Give them a good scrub, and they'll soon look like a baby's bottom,' Mother sat beside the window, darning socks, straining to see to get the wool through the eye of the needle. Lodzia had gone to collect the food rations hours ago and left Ella with us.

She returned distraughtly. 'Mama, I've just heard that Sasha's little boy died yesterday.'

Mother set down her darning. 'Dear God, is it Mieczyslaw? Why didn't someone come and tell us? The poor girl – I must go to her.'

Lodzia left the food on the table, scooped up Ella, hugged and kissed her, swaying back and forth.

Mother reached for her shawls, mumbling, 'The poor mite, his little life snuffed out.' Louder now, 'He might be the first, but he won't be the last. You mark my words: The Angel of Death is hovering over this camp.'

'Wait! I'll come with you,' Lodzia set Ella

down.

I felt Sasha's anguish, her helplessness, as she must have watched her son die – as I had watched my Bookiet die. I jabbed the needle angrily into the matted wool and pulled the thread through the other side. Unexpected tears flooded my eyes and brimmed over my cheeks.

Not long after, Mother and Lodzia returned grim-faced.

I wiped my hands on a rag. 'How was she?'

'I can't imagine. Her brother has buried him at the side of the shack beneath a heap of snow for the time being. He promised to dig a deeper grave in summer when the ground is softer.'

'Yes, but won't the bears or wolves sniff him out and dig him up?'

'If they do, they do. What can anybody do in this backward place? At least she still has Jan, but he doesn't look long for this world either.'

Six hours later, my father and brothers trudged in exhausted from work.

This death had affected me so severely, I could contain myself no longer, 'Tatta, Sasha's little boy has died. It was Mieczyslaw.' I needed his reassurance this wasn't about to happen to any of us – that it wouldn't happen to me.

It seemed reassurances were not his to give. He placed his hand on my head and drew me gently to his chest. 'The poor little chap.'

Hearing this, I felt even more vulnerable.

Gerhard went to his room to change, and Father and Karol tossed their wages on the table.

Tatta said, 'I'm sorry, Anna, this is all there is. It doesn't make any difference how hard we work; the equipment's always breaking down.'

'They expect us to work in razor-sharp gales to meet their lousy norms,' Karol added. 'If you ask me, Mieczyslaw's better off out of it.'

I noticed he wasn't his confident, chirpy self. He changed out of his wet clothes, ate his bread and soup, sat down in front of the stove with his accordion, and started playing, Hey Sokolyi – Hey Falcon. He always turned to music when he was feeling unhappy, and played until a more pleasant mood returned, but tonight he played and played until Tatta told him to stop; it was time to sleep.

'Aren't you seeing Natasha tonight?' I asked. 'Have you two fallen out?'

'No, we haven't. Mind your own business.' He put away his accordion, climbed onto his slats and pulled his eiderdown over his ears.

It was snowing hard on Sunday morning, obscuring the window and further dimming the room.

Tatta turned up the lamp and inspected my handiwork. 'You've done well, Marishu,' he clipped me fondly under the chin. 'This stitching is nice and straight -- and close together.'

I smiled. I was desperate for a good wash, but there was no point venturing out to the banya in this weather. Instead, I sat and watched what he did next. I had come this far in my shoe-making career, I thought I might as well learn how he made the soles and insoles using tree bark, cushioning them with cut up pieces from one of my mother's woollen shawls.

'At last,' he said, 'they're finished.' He gave a pair each to Gerhard and Karol and took the last one for himself. 'Now we can step out like kings to chop down their lousy trees.'

I almost cried. As tired as he was, Tatta still managed a stab at humour. I looked down at my ruined hands and decided it had been worth it. Then I picked up the scissors and hacked off my plait. I was sick of bugs nesting in it. I was sick of everything. Sick of all four of us being cooped up in this small room. I was used to my own bedroom, to our big kitchen, to wide open spaces; not being corralled in this cell.

Gerhard and Lodzia joined us later, and Mother threw up her hands in despair, 'See what she's done to herself?'

I wondered now if I had been too hasty. No one said I looked either more beautiful, or better, but the plait lay on the table like a severed limb – evidence of my recklessness. 'What's the matter with everyone? It will grow again.'

Karol laughed. 'You look like a tomboy. Oh, and try using the Banya more often; you stink.'

* * *

Three weeks passed and still no reply from Jusio. I didn't know what to think.

We sat eating our dry bread and Karol said, 'Bit grim at the Krasny Ugolok last night. Someone told us a girl called Dorota Malinska had died.'

When no one spoke, I said, 'We didn't know the family, did we?'

'No. The place was dead anyway. Natasha and I only go there because there's nowhere else to get out of the cold. Wish we hadn't bothered. Morbid.'

They must have made it up again, but I didn't pry. 'Did they say what she died of?'

Karol got up from the table. 'She starved to death.' He looked down at Gerhard and our father, 'Come on, let's go. Another day in bondage beckons.'

I watched them leave. All three were wearing their new boots, and I felt a quiver of satisfaction.

With the boots completed, there was no longer any need to stay indoors and I left with Lodzia to collect the bread and soup, but nothing had changed.

'Are we to spend the rest of our lives queuing for food?' she said. 'I still can't believe they have reduced us to this.'

Dire news coming up the line cut short her moaning: Oleszkiewicz's son died last night. There was more – his mother was six months pregnant.

'Oh no, poor woman. What's the point of bringing another child into this world? Into this misery?' Lodzia said, agreeing with the woman in front.

I tried to agree with her, tried to feel sorry for them, but with each subsequent death, I seemed to grow shorter on compassion.

When we returned to the shack, Mother was throwing wet washing over the rope above the stove. 'I suppose you've heard then?'

'Oleszkiewicz's boy? Everyone's talking about it.'

'Didn't I tell you the Angel of Death was hovering over this place?'

16

Vice Kommendant Smirnov's unannounced arrival in our room the following Sunday startled us all. I hated the way he and that Ukrainian, who stuck his head around our door every morning, felt they had the right to invade our privacy without knocking. Neither did I like anyone leering at me.

His manner was unapologetic, almost chirpy. 'Well now,' he said, 'Apart from your son here who has already graced our establishment with one of our long-time 'residents' – Natasha is it,' he stared directly at Karol, 'we haven't seen the rest of you at the Krasny Ugolok. You should go. You should enjoy yourselves after a week's work; make the most of the camp's hospitality.'

Father stood up, moved closer and towered over him. 'Comrade, you make this place sound like some spa in the Tatra Mountains. It is a corrective labour colony, as Kommendant Ivanov made clear when we arrived. I can assure you, all anyone wants to do after a week's toil is to sleep. Besides, two close friends lost their young children, thanks to your camp's 'hospitality'. It would have been disrespectful.'

I knew my father fostered an offhand

attitude to what Smirnov thought – I'd overheard an unguarded comment he made to Mother. A little voice in my head screamed, 'No, Tatta, hold your tongue,' but secretly I was egging him on.

'Oh, well, I am sorry for their loss but these things happen.' His tone was courteous at first, but he soon became officious. 'However, it is important all prisoners join in with the community spirit of the camp's hospitality. Perhaps your two sons might be so good as to contribute with some live music – maybe encourage some dancing. It is not a request; this is an order. Do I make myself clear?'

'Prisoners? According to whom?'

'Comrade Stalin.'

My father's manner was curt, and he was already holding open the door. 'We'll see. And thank you for your concern.'

Gerhard said, 'Are we supposed to be touched by his phoney interest in our welfare? Dancing? Where does he think we are? Cinderella's ball?'

Father said, 'No doubt the low morale is affecting production levels, and it's worried Ivanov and his cronies. These deaths have badly upset everyone.'

'Well, I'm not playing my accordion for him or anyone – other than for Natasha and me,' Karol said.

'The trouble is, Karol, the only way the Soviets can maintain discipline is to enforce rules which you break at your peril. I suppose in some respects we're lucky to have landed in a hard-labour camp that's amenable to its prisoners. We have the Ukrainians to thank for that. I've heard of men serving time at Stalin's pleasure in Magadan and Vorkuta, and I doubt the camp Kommendant at either would tolerate anything like this.'

'Wait a minute,' I said. 'How did Smirnov know Karol was there with Natasha? Is he spying on them?'

'Marisha has a point; why would Smirnov be interested? It isn't anyone's business who you see. I don't know – perhaps you should go. Mama and I will stay behind and look after Ella. He already thinks we're a rebellious bunch.'

'Are you going to the Ugolok tonight or not, Marishu?' Lodzia was getting ready, plaiting her hair and winding it around her head in a coronet. Despite all the mud and poverty, she still managed to look elegant.

I glanced at my hands. 'No, you two go. I can't get this muck off. Anyway, I haven't anything to wear. I've lost so much weight that nothing fits.'

'Nonsense.' She fished around in her things for a belt. 'Look, choose whatever you want to wear, then put this around your waist and you'll look fine. Come on, it will do you good. I'll do your hair. It needs a bit of a trim as it's lop-sided. And don't worry, Jusio will write as soon as he can.'

I supposed she was right, but God, did I miss him? It was like a dull ache that never went away. Delving into my bag, I brought out my best dress; my first shop-bought garment that I had lusted over in a shop window in Zhabinka for weeks. It was white muslin and the loveliest thing I had ever seen, with its balloon shaped sleeves embroidered with flowers between two rows of red braid from shoulder to elbow. I nagged Mama into buying it for me, even though she couldn't afford it, and planned to wear it on my sixteenth birthday with my first pair of pretty bootees – which I had been hoping she would buy me nearer the date. In doing so, I knocked the lid from my box of photographs, and Jusio's face stared up at me. I brushed my finger against his lips and sighed, 'And now you will never see me in it, my darling.'

'You're lucky,' Lodzia said as she snipped away at my hair with Tatta's large scissors. 'It might be short, but you have waves.'

And it's even shorter now, I thought, as I looked down in alarm at the remains of my tresses scattered over the floor.

Lodzia stood back to admire her handiwork. 'I like it. It frames your face; emphasises your cheekbones, and your eyes look larger and bluer.' When she had finished, she gave me the hand mirror. 'Here, look at yourself.'

Staring back at me was a lousy complexion

and an even worse haircut. I looked like a pixie gone wrong. Wearing this dainty dress, with my beaten-up calf-length boots, and blackened fingers, I looked a fright. A dress like this needed pretty shoes and my long dark hair tied up in a red ribbon. Why had I chopped it off? I slapped the belt around my waist and cinched it in, but who was I supposed to impress? No one. Jusio still hadn't replied to my letter, and no food had arrived.

Karol laughed when he saw me and picked up his accordion. 'See you there.'

I stuck out my tongue at him.

'I hate this idea of having to play at Smirnov's insistence,' Gerhard reached for his guitar. 'How that man notices everything – I wish now I'd left it at home. He's also coerced Zygmunt into bringing his violin. If Smirnov insists we be there and play, then he will hear us loud and clear. Zygmunt has a plan.'

Lodzia shrugged into her coat and kissed Ella goodnight. 'What sort of plan?'

'You'll see.'

'Perhaps it will be like the old times playing in village halls back home,' Lodzia said. 'People need to cling to some sort of normality.'

'But this isn't normality, Lodzia. This is the 'new' normality'. We have no choice but to get used to it.' I slipped my arm through hers and we headed for the Krasny Ugolok. Pausing when we reached Sasha's shack, we gazed at the mound of snow beside it. How I hated having to pretend we were having a wonderful time when Mieczyslaw's little body lay frozen 60 centimetres beneath the surface, covered with a flimsy branch of Spruce.

Onwards we trudged, our boots crunching on snow. A brisk wind blew across the Vaymuga, but the night was clear, the sky dappled with stars. I pulled my scarf higher over my nose and face and put my head down.

Gerhard and Karol joined Zygmunt on the dais cum stage. I pushed back my hood and unbuttoned my coat. It surprised me to see how full the place was. Smirnov had done an excellent job bullying people to attend. Everyone was discussing the deaths, expressing their sorrow and concern over the parents' inability to give their children a decent burial.

A record was playing on the gramophone. The singer's voice had slowed to a deep dirge and nearly stopped, then someone wound it up again, and it went at it, ten to the *tuzin*, like a budgerigar, before it got stuck in a groove and someone had to thump the table. How depressing it all was.

I continued looking around, hating being here, but then I saw a boy standing by the stage staring at me with an expression I had never seen before. He looked a little older than I was, perhaps around twenty, and he was taller than me. Even though four girls surrounded him, I stared back. And in that moment of looking back into his face, something inside me moved. I could feel the heat rising to my cheeks. My breathing became shallow and my heart pumped faster. We gazed at each other for a moment or two, but it was a moment or two too long. It wasn't what strangers did. I couldn't look away, and when he did – I almost groaned.

After a moment, I turned and tugged Lodzia's sleeve. 'Who's he over there?'

'Where?'

'Don't look now, but he's over by the stage with those four girls.'

'I've no idea, but I'll find out if you like.'

'No, you mustn't,' I whispered. 'He mustn't know I like him.'

'Oh, for heaven's sake, what's the matter with you? I'm not that daft.' Lodzia was un-wrapping the shawl from around her head and shoulders. 'He's looking at you again.'

I couldn't resist turning around and giving him a coy smile before lowering my gaze.

'Anyway, I thought you were pining after Jusio.'

I felt a fleeting pang of betrayal, but these fresh feelings were so exciting that the urge to keep looking at this boy was uncontrollable.

'Well?'

'He didn't write.'

She gave me a searching look. 'Now, that's not like Jusio. He's one of the kindest, most thoughtful boys I know. I suppose you sent him your address. Anyway, don't be so impatient;

there's a war on.'

I stared back. 'Address?'

'Ahh, Marishu....'

'I never thought. I've never written a letter before, have I? There's never been a need. Anyway, I had other things to tell him; urgent things he needed to know so he could help us.'

'No wonder he hasn't replied. You are such a scatterbrain. Write to him again tomorrow.'

'Yes, yes, but what about him over there? How do I get an introduction? How did you meet Gerhard?'

'We met at the church hall in Zhabinka. He came over and asked me to dance.'

'Yes, but I can't just walk over and ask him, can I? He might think I'm forward. Who do you think those girls are?' All four were beautiful, and I cursed myself again for hacking off my hair.

'I don't have a clue. Hey look – Smirnov's arrived.'

The room fell silent. Everyone turned to stare. Even though the gramophone was still playing, my brothers and Zygmunt struck up on stage. However, instead of playing a Mazurka, bidding everyone to dance, they launched into Idje Sen (I'm going to sleep). Everyone knew the lullaby, and began humming in tune, louder and louder, and louder still until the humming blotted out the music and it felt as if everyone was shouting. No one took to the floor; no one was smiling, making it clear they were here only at puppeteer Smirnov's behest.

I spun around to look at the stage, but my brothers and Zygmunt were no longer playing; they were humming along with the rest.

When I looked back, Smirnov had gone, but the gorgeous boy was walking towards me.

I held my breath. Me? He's coming to me! I opened my mouth to speak. But Damn! He'd only come to turn off the gramophone hiccupping behind me, stuck in a grove. I hadn't even noticed. I tried to step out of his path. He stepped the same way. I stepped to the other side, and so did he. 'Sorry,' I stammered.

He fixed me with his eyes and smiled – just that. He lifted the arm from the record, closed the lid, then walked off toward the four girls.

I turned and looked at Lodzia 'I thought he would speak to me.' I felt so stupid; I was sure I was blushing.

Lodzia whispered, 'He's still looking.'

I glanced over my shoulder. Yes, he was looking, but not at my face – at my boots. Oh God, he's looking at my boots! What must he be thinking? They don't go with this dress. When I looked up to face him, he grinned.

He grinned at me!

He gave a tiny nod, and I couldn't work out if he found my boots amusing, or he liked me. Or if he was grinning because he'd never seen such a frump; too polite to laugh out loud, as Karol had.

'Get over yourself, Marishu. Everyone here's wearing valenki.'

The lullaby ended, replaced by a Polka.

Natasha arrived, stamped snow off her boots, unwrapped her long scarf and joined us. She glanced over at the stage, twiddled her fingers at Karol and blew him a kiss.

I leaned against the wall and watched couples taking to the floor. I'd never done the Polka, so it was as well no one asked me, not that anyone would, the way I looked. I glanced over towards the boy. He was leaning against the wall with both hands behind the small of his back, one knee bent, his foot propped against the wood. A girl was speaking to him, and he seemed absorbed in what she was saying. Who was she?

The next dance was a waltz, and my heart quickened. I yearned for him to ask me. I could do the waltz. Lodzia taught me last year. One, two, three, one, two, three – we did it in a straight line all the way from the house down to the pigsty and back, until I got the hang of it. I sighed. He was wasting time. If he didn't make haste, the music would end. It ended.

Natasha said something, and I turned around to reply. They were playing yet another waltz, and Lodzia was making urgent facial expressions at me.

Before I asked what she meant, I felt a tap on my shoulder, 'Will you dance with me?'

The adrenalin rush made the hairs on my face and neck stand on end, and an unexpected gush of desire consumed me. It was the boy. I fell into his arms. Like a buffoon, I smiled and spoke at the same time and it all came out gibberish, unrecognisable even to me, but he didn't seem to care. Instead, I concentrated on my steps; One, two, three, but there was no music, no tempo when Lodzia taught me to dance, and I trod on my boots. I felt such a twit. What must he think?

He threw back his head and laughed, grabbing me tighter about the waist and did a twirl. Oh God, Lodzia didn't teach me how to twirl; but I managed to stand upright. He had such beautiful eyes; they mesmerised me.

'Do you have a name?'

'It's Marisha.'

He made a nodding motion as if he approved. 'Mine's Stefan. Where are you from?'

'Szpitali. We have – we had a farm. It's about 9km north of Zhabinka and you?'

'We lived on the outskirts of Kobryn.'

'And is your father a farmer too?'

'My father worked in forestry. They brought me up on a farm, but he's a forester; and so am I.'

The waltz was ending, and I hoped my brothers wouldn't play anything where I could make a bigger fool of myself, but they continued with another waltz and I sent up a silent, 'Thank you, God.'

Stefan's hand moved up to my shoulder blades, drawing me closer, his other hand clutching mine to his chest, our foreheads touching.

'I like your hair,' he said, 'it's – different. It

emphasises your eyes.'

'Thank you! I agonised over cutting it off for ages,' I fibbed.

Time seemed to stop and we kept on dancing the waltz, irrespective of what was playing. When the music ended, we remained entwined on the floor waiting for the next dance, but that was it. Lodzia came over and tapped me on the shoulder. 'Come on, bed time.'

Stefan held my hand, letting my fingers slip through his own. 'I enjoyed tonight. Will you be coming again?'

'Yes!' I blew him a kiss and hurried out into the night after Lodzia, Natasha and my brothers. Blowing him another illicit kiss, I threw my hood over my head, and turned away, feeling totally brazen. This had to be the most exciting night of my life!

17

Even the bark beetles didn't bother me as much.

Stefan Novak. His named rolled off my tongue. He was nineteen years old. He told me that he and his sisters hadn't wanted to be there either, but Smirnov was most persuasive. They were his sisters! I could have kissed him. I wished he had kissed me.

I climbed off my slats and rummaged in my bag for my atlas. Leafing through the pages, I reached the town of Kobryn. My parents once took me there; it wasn't far from Zhabinka, and I wondered why fate had to bring us both to this place to meet each other.

Then Lodzia walked into the room and shattered my daydreaming. 'Here,' she said, handing me a sheet of writing paper and an envelope. 'I thought you'd need these. Jusio cared for you, you know, but judging by last night, I don't suppose you're bothered now.'

'Ah yes, thanks.' I was ashamed to admit since meeting Stefan, I hadn't given Jusio a second thought.

'I'm going to fetch the bread; are you coming? I'll go for the soup later.'

'You'll be waiting all day; she doesn't want to

get up this morning,' Mother said. 'I don't know what the matter with her is.'

I didn't want to queue for rations. It was so enchanting to lie here reliving every moment of last night. 'Could you fetch ours too, Lodziu – the ration book's on the table. I'd better write this letter.'

'A boy danced with her last night.' Lodzia tutted and left.

I closed the atlas, rested the paper on top, and sat for some time deciding what to write. I'd lost that yearning I'd had for Jusio, and it seemed to have disappeared overnight. Well, not even overnight – faster than that. It vanished the moment I clapped eyes on Stefan. I was sorry my feelings could change so quickly, but that's how it was. I started writing,

Hello Jusio,

I have an apology. Since I hadn't heard from you, it occurred to me you might have replied, and enclosed your letter within the food parcel itself. In which case, the postmaster, either here in Kholmogorki or back in Poland, had eaten my kielbasa, taken the pork fat home to his wife, and disposed of your letter. Now I realise you wouldn't have known where to send it because I omitted to include our address. I apologise if I worried you...

I stopped writing for a moment and wondered in which area of the forests Stefan was working; perhaps he was near my father's workstation. I thought of his powerful arms wielding the axe, his forearm brushing sweat from his brow. Oh yes, where was I? I continued writing:

We are staying at Shack 20, Posiolek Vodopad, Kholmogorki, Archangelsk Oblast, Russia.

Did you find Bookiet's body, and what has become of our farm and the animals? Is anyone feeding them?

I doubt I shall ever see you again because the camp Kommendant told us this is where we shall die, which, judging from our diet, won't be long coming. Three children have perished in the last couple of days. We are all so hungry, and the boat from Permilovo can't get to us with supplies until the river ice melts. Please send food; anything will do; kielbasa and a big slab of pork fat, two if your mother can spare them. But if you write, send the letter separately from the food.

With Best wishes, Marisha.

There, done. I placed the letter in the envelope, feeling awful having to beg from the boy I had betrayed with my feelings for another, but why waste the opportunity to remind him about sending food? I thought about my actions and then sealed the envelope, ready to give to Alina Zadarnowska to post later.

My next problem was figuring out how I would get to the Krasny Ugolok tonight because I doubted my parents would allow me out alone. I didn't know if Stefan would be there. But what if he was? I was anxious he might think I was snubbing him if I didn't turn up.

Mother said I could go only if accompanied, and I had to be home by nine o'clock sharp. I had already asked Karol if I could tag along with him and Natasha, but he told me to get lost. Lodzia was my only hope, so I had better be kind to her.

She returned much later with the bread, left it on the table and stretched out her hands to the stove. Once she had thawed out, she said, 'I'm off to pick up the soup. Coming?'

'Yes, why not!' I reached for my coat. 'I need to take this letter to Alina Zadarnowska,' I said, but I waited until we were almost at the cantina before I broached the subject.

'Lodzia, would you come to the Ugolok with me tonight? I so enjoyed it last night, and I have no one to go with.'

She half smiled. 'No kohanie, I want to spend the evening with Gerhard; I haven't seen him since five this morning.'

'Oh, please.'

'No. Sorry. Ask Karol.'

'I already did; he said he'd prefer a septic toe to dragging me along with him and Natasha.'

'It's the boy you danced with last night, isn't it?' She tilted her head to one side, 'You think he'll be there? Marishu, don't you think you're a little young to be getting into romantic entanglements?'

'No! I'm fifteen and *three quarters*. Some girls in Poland marry when they're sixteen.'

'I'm sorry; I can't come with you. I want to be with Gerhard.'

I dug in my heels. Lodzia owed me. I had a mind to resort to moral blackmail and tell her the truth about the day I got lost in the forest. I refrained; even I wouldn't stoop so low. Neither could I defy my parents. Anyway, Lodzia would tell Mother the truth, and then she would worry each time I stepped out of the shack, thinking I got lost in the forest. Back in Szpitali, I would have opened my bedroom window and shimmied down the Wisteria with no one noticing, although I'd never had reason to do so.

What I needed was a girlfriend of my age. Mama wouldn't have any objections, and I knew how to get one. It crucified me to think Stefan would be at the club tonight. What if he met someone else?

After collecting the soup, I made an excuse to help Mother with the laundry at the banya, but I had a cunning plan. What I intended was to go to the steam bath, even though I detested sitting around naked. I noticed last time there were girls of my age there who were still too young to work, and I had struck up a conversation with a girl called Krystyna Ceglowska.

There was no sign of Krystyna, and I found myself by Mother's side scrubbing the family's laundry. It meant staying in tonight, but my hands looked better for it.

Success! Two days later, Krystyna was at the steam bath. She even suggested I join her and her sister at the Ugolok that evening, and I flew home to tell Mother I had someone I could go with and, I was already squeaky clean. I had never smelled so nice since I arrived.

What to wear? I hadn't anything new, and couldn't wear the same dress as on the night I met Stefan. Everything else hung off me. Strange, how I'd never bothered about clothes in the past; throwing on anything which came to hand.

Picking through Lodzia's clothes while she was out collecting the rations, I found two garments which would suit.

My sister-in-law was happy to make a loan of her clothes, and Mother could hardly object to me going out with my girlfriend. However, she said, 'Why can't you and Krystyna visit the club in the afternoon, instead of in the evening? I don't like you going out at night.'

'Because her eighteen-year-old sister has to work during the day, and she likes to go out later.' I amazed myself with my quick-thinking duplicity; what lies wouldn't I tell to see Stefan again. 'But it's an excellent suggestion, Mama,' I added, 'I suppose I can still go with Krystyna in the afternoons when we're bored.'

With all obstacles banished, wearing Lodzia's pale green dress, cinched in at the waist,

I set off to meet Krystyna. I felt such excitement at the prospect of seeing Stefan again; I was almost giddy with it.

He wasn't there when we arrived, but a few other youngsters were, including the Ukrainians. The scratchy records on the gramophone, which had got on my pip on Sunday night, didn't even irritate me tonight.

Karol and Natasha arrived at a quarter to eight. They both acknowledged me, but sat alone elsewhere. Stefan still hadn't come. I felt sure he would be here soon and kept glancing at the door each time someone entered.

The evening wore on and I was becoming paranoid; perhaps he'd found someone else and taken her elsewhere – like where? The cantina was the only place I could think was warm enough, but who would want to sit in that smelly hole all evening?

I'd argued with my parents to allow me to stay out until nine-thirty, but if Stefan didn't get a move on, my time would be up. They only allowed me some leeway because Karol could see the argument turning into a row, and intervened, promising he would keep his eye on me.

Each time the door opened and shut, it fanned my despair with a freezing blast of air, until I accepted Stefan would not show. The whole evening fell flat, and when I saw Karol pointing at his wristwatch. I bid Krystyna and Alina goodnight and walked back to the shack feeling empty.

'Did you have a pleasant time, kohanie?' Mother asked when I walked through the door.

I took off my boots and stood them beside the stove to dry. 'Yes, it was good,' I fibbed. 'Krystyna's fun. It's good to have a friend again.' I wasn't lying because it was true, and I missed Wanda.

Sensing I was feeling glum, Lodzia said, 'Was the boy who asked you to dance there tonight?'

'Who? Oh, him. No, but it was still a good evening.'

'Listening to scratchy Russian records? Never mind, he'll probably be there on Sunday night. People in the bread queue and at the cantina have been asking if Gerhard, Karol and Zygmunt would play again – so we're all going. The boys can't disappoint them.'

I had never known time to drag so slowly.

I felt a little crazy. Stefan was all I could think about; I didn't even know if he liked me that much. Because he didn't dance with anyone else all evening probably meant nothing, and I was reading far more into it than there was. Here I was allowing him to consume my waking thoughts. But was he thinking about me?

18

Sunday arrived, and I was ready two hours before it was time to leave.

I wore Lodzia's dress again and promised to make myself a shorter, more flattering pair of valenki. It meant I would muck up my hands, but this last lot of grime was wearing off, so it was a sacrifice I would make.

Lodzia kept smiling at me. 'He'll be there. Don't be in such a rush – trust me.'

How could she read my moods so well? Lodzia was twenty three and married; how could she be so sure?

The place was already full when we arrived, and my brothers and Zygmunt were warming up on the dais.

I took in the room at lightning speed, but I didn't see him. I saw his sisters, but not him.

Lodzia touched my arm, and I spun around. Stefan was standing beside me.

He said, 'Hello, Marishu.'

His eyes had a way of creasing and lighting up when he smiled, and all the nerves danced on the surface of my skin. 'Stefan, I didn't think you'd be here tonight.'

'I was here on Monday night, waiting, but you didn't come. I was also here on Tuesday and Wednesday.'

'My mother wouldn't let me out on my own.' It sounded so lame.

'It's because she cares.'

On stage, Karol led the music with a waltz. He knew it was the only dance I knew and smiled at me when I looked up at him in amused surprise.

'Shall we?' Stefan said, and I took his hand. His touch sent the most disturbing sensation through me, and I melted into his arms, resting my cheek against his and feeling as if we belonged together. We waltzed around the floor, and when we reached the stage, I caught my brother's eye and whispered, 'Thank you,' realising for the first time that Karol sort of cared about me too; as much as any brother could care about a pesky little sister.

The evening ended, and I felt almost bereft we were about to part, but Stefan accompanied me home – along with the rest of my family in tow.

'I need to know where you live,' he whispered. 'I can't risk losing you again.' He also insisted on meeting my parents. 'I want them to know I'm no ogre, and no harm's going to come to you.'

My feelings oscillated between flattery, embarrassment and gratitude.

I wanted him to kiss me, but Stefan seemed

to have other ideas.

My parents were both surprised and pleased as he made himself at home on the slats. I observed the way he rested his forearms on his thighs, fingers intertwined, relaxed in their company, explaining his father worked at the Artel sharpening saws and fixing wheel spokes and things.

Father said, 'Well I never, so Novak's your father! I like him. He's a good man.'

Stefan didn't outstay his welcome. He said, 'Thank you for allowing me to see your daughter home. I hope you won't mind if I call on Marisha again.'

He stood up, and I was at his side, showing him out. We stood in the little hallway, and he pulled me closer but said nothing. It was dark and cold out here, and I couldn't see his face, but I felt his breath on my lips as they brushed against mine, almost like a butterfly fluttering.

'Better go,' he said. 'Can I see you tomorrow?'

My arms were around his waist, and I reached up to kiss his earlobe. 'Yes, please.'

'See you at seven-thirty.'

The next day, I said, 'Mama, can I use your sewing machine? I want to alter my clothes to fit.'

'Ahh, kohanie – let me do it.'

'No, it's alright; I know just how I want them.'

She dragged the table closer to the slats, and

I heaved the machine on top.

'He's a thoughtful boy. Are you seeing him again this evening?'

I dumped my clothes onto the slats bedside me and altered each one. Good job Mama taught me how to sew and make clothes. 'He's coming for me at seven-thirty. I want to wear something different; I can't keep borrowing Lodzia's clothes.'

'Does he have siblings?'

I was concentrating on my sewing; I needed them to fit where they touched, to show off my figure. 'He's here with his parents and four sisters: Nina, she's twenty two, Zofia's twenty, Olga's fifteen, and Rosalia who's thirteen. They're all so pretty, but Stefan told me they thought my hair was nice, and they might have theirs cut too.'

'Who knows – you might have started a new trend.'

My fingers on the handle, I propelled the wheel around as I whizzed down another seam. Snapping the thread with my teeth, I stood up and held the skirt against my waist. 'That's better. Did I tell you Stefan's a forester? They lived on a farm near Kobryn.'

'And what about Jusio?' Mother asked.

There was that flutter of betrayal again, but I thought no, Jusio was a childhood crush. Stefan's the one for me. 'I've written to Jusio and asked him to send food. Stefan said his mother's written to relatives in Western Poland too. Don't you think it's wonderful Alina Zadarnowska's brave enough to travel to Kholmogorki station every day to collect the post? You'd never get me on a horse. Stefan rides too, you know.'

* * *

Sundays were best because Stefan was mine from morning till night. We always made for the cantina first for our plate of fish-head soup, a slice of bread and a mug of sweet Russian tea.

Today, floating amongst the fish heads was a cube of potato and some shredded cabbage. 'Oh, look!' I lifted the evidence with my spoon.

Stefan hunted around with his spoon. 'I've got a few noodles and a dead beetle. I bet Smirnov and Ivanov don't eat this *guvno* – shit.' He finished first and stared at his empty bowl, still hungry.

'You should've eaten the beetle.' I was hungry too. 'Try not to think about it, because I have plans for today. I will take you somewhere special.'

He half laughed, 'What here, in Satan's playground?'

'Wait and see.'

Smelling like herrings, we stepped out into the face-slapping cold and I led him down towards the river.

'We're not going to the Club?' he put his arm around my shoulders, and I put both of mine around his waist, my head resting against his chest as we kept walking.

'No – you'll never guess.'

'To work, then? I take this route every morning.'

'Not to work.' I smiled to myself; this would be such a surprise.

We left the shacks of Vodopad far behind, and Stefan said, 'Someone told me there's a trail through the Kenga forests. If you keep going, it takes you to the railway line, well south of Kholmogorki, and you can jump on a freight train. Imagine, Marishu – we could escape, and no one would see us. We'd be on our way before they found out. We have to find it.'

'Are you serious?'

He stopped walking, but his gaze was earnest. 'Would I joke about something like that? Think about it. Once we're free, we can make our way back to Poland and alert the authorities to what's happening here. It's the only way we can help free our families and all these other people here. We are their only hope.'

'But Stefan, there are no Polish authorities left in Eastern Poland; Stalin's invaded it. Tatta told me that Hitler bombed Warsaw, so they've carved up the country between themselves.'

'We head further west, then.'

'And live on what? It's impossible; we're trapped here forever.'

'No, look, if we can just reach the railroad and jump a train, we'll be in Moscow in no time. There will be plenty of food down there. It's a city. I can trade my watch to get us by.'

I was unsure. We had no money; no food and I was reluctant to leave my family. 'A trail, you say? I never found one when I got lost. I have never felt so terrified, Stefan, I thought the bears would get me.'

'What on earth were you doing in the forest?'

'Looking for Lodzia. She was going to the kolkhoz to buy food, but she bumped into Natasha, and she told her not to bother; there wasn't any. So, while I was risking my life searching for her, she was sitting at Natasha's drinking tea. She doesn't know what happened to me, and my parents still don't know the truth of it. And you must never tell them.'

He stopped walking, stared at me. 'So how did you get out?'

'I've no idea, but that's why I've brought you here; I want you to meet my friends: Vasily, Boris and Roza. I collapsed outside their door and they saved me. I'd be dead now if it wasn't for them.'

'Collapsed? Marishu, promise me you will never, ever venture into a forest if you don't know your way out of the other side.'

'Oh, don't worry. I promise.'

'Marisha!' Vasily threw open the door. 'You're not still looking for your sister-in-law? Come in, come in. Let me fetch Boris and Roza. It's a rare day we get visitors, I can tell you.' He hobbled off to the next shack and hobbled back. 'Is this your fellow?'

Vasily made tea. Boris and Roza arrived soon after. I smiled at Stefan when they fussed around, insisting we sit on the only two comfortable chairs in the room. They wobbled, but the feather-stuffed cushions were luxury.

Studying Stefan, Roza said, 'I approve of your fellow.' Then after a momentary silence added, 'Is your brother still seeing Natasha?'

It surprised me. 'I didn't know you knew Karol.' I noticed the looks Roza exchanged with Boris and Vasily. 'Why, what is it? Why shouldn't Karol see her? They love each other.'

They said no more. 'Please, is there something I should know?'

Vasily drew a lengthy breath, 'It's like this, Marishu – Natasha – well, they betrothed Natasha to another.'

Was he serious? 'So why is she never with him? Who is he?'

'He's the boatman who brings supplies upriver from the magazine in Permilovo. His family live in Vologda.' Boris tapped the side of his nose. 'Between you and me; I think it's the mother's doing; She makes sure they get extra rations.'

'And she intends to marry him!' I went cold. 'Who else knows about this?'

Boris shrugged. 'Well, all the Ukrainians; everyone who knows Natasha; there are no secrets in this place.'

'Does that include Vice Kommendant Smirnov?' I remembered he made some comment about Karol when he bullied us into going to the club at that time.

'Of course, Smirnov would know,' Roza said, 'Smirnov knows everyone's business in this camp; it's his job to know.'

'And when's the wedding, or haven't they set a date?'

Roza said, 'Well, we Ukrainians will have served our sentences soon. Then we will be free to stay or move away. Vasily, Boris and I will live out our days here, as will many others. You see, we have nowhere else to go, the Soviets confiscated our land, but Natasha has the chance of moving to Vologda to live with his family. She will have the chance of real freedom.'

Vasily said, 'Her fiancé isn't a prisoner like us. Someone in his family has clout. So, we think he might wangle it for her to move out sooner if she wants. Her mother is keen they marry, so she can go with them, and who can blame her?'

I cast my mind back to the day we arrived when Natasha admitted to cannibalism. She also mentioned something about getting out of this place, only if she married someone outside the camp. How I wished I'd asked more questions. 'Please,' I said, getting up, 'could you not mention this to any of the Polish community? It would destroy my brother, and it might not come to anything; you see, Natasha adores him.'

Having said our goodbyes and promising to visit again, we waved and continued back to Vodopad.

'Stefan, you must promise me not to mention a word of this to anyone. Promise.'

He raised his hands. 'Nothing to do with me.'

19

'Spring's on its way; the river ice is melting.'

Stefan and I had reached the meander in the Vaymuga and watched its moving centre flowing more swiftly and carrying pancakes of ice along with it. The banks, which froze overnight, were becoming slushy on sunnier days, heralding the end of the crippling winter that took so many lives.

We sauntered alongside the riverbank, as we always did on Sundays, but hadn't returned to see Vasily, Boris and Roza since the day they'd let slip the shattering news about Natasha and the boatman.

Stefan didn't seem bothered about the weather; he was interested in finding this trail through the Kenga forests. The trouble was, in whichever direction we struck out, rivers and tributaries got in our way. My atlas showed the deltas, estuaries, major rivers and their tributaries, but no secondary branches, even though they were of significant size.

In our private moments, when we discussed our escape route, he was against heading northwest to Kholmogorki. It was where we had arrived and was too open, with too many NKVD on patrol. He favoured following the Vaymuga south, then picking up the railway line at Samoded-Permilovo, but the Kenga River flowed into it from the north – and there was no bridge over either of them. 'We could always swim across,' he joked.

'Forget it. I can't swim. Anyway, I'm scared of water. Oh look, Stefan! There's a boat heading here; at last – food. Do you think it's him; her betrothed? What did Roza call him, Valerik?' I tried to get a better look, but he was still too far away.

'I've no idea. Shall we go back to Vodopad?'

'Could we? I wonder what he's delivering.'

We listened to the boat spluttering its way up-river and getting closer. 'It's a wonder it doesn't sink,' Stefan said. 'Is there anything in Russia that isn't decrepit?'

When we arrived at the shop, Szefczuk was already helping him unload. Valerik was tall and ugly, his bearded face swarthy – nowhere near as good-looking as Karol. He was ancient too, about forty years of age, and I wondered what Natasha saw in him – or perhaps she didn't. Ugh, imagine kissing something like that!

The boatman dragged a barrel down the plank, and between them he and Szefczuk shuffled it into the shop.

'Oh God, not more stinking fish.'

He returned to the boat, and threw six bundles of fufaikas onto the riverbank, followed by other provisions in sacks.

'We need food,' I said. 'Why doesn't he bring us something nice to eat?'

'No, this is excellent. People also need clothes; I need a jacket. Some haven't any proper boots. You could earn some decent money if you made valenki for this lot.'

'We haven't enough fabric.'

'They would have to bring their own. Come on, hurry. We need to alert our families to be first in the queue. Seriously, there's one redeeming factor about this camp – Kommendant Ivanov allows people to make money aside of work – like the couple who dig out the shit pits, and the girl who takes the post to Kholmogorki. He has the right attitude.'

'Only because he hopes to keep us here until we all drop. Anyway, that couple only collect the poo because they want to nourish their allotment so they can grow the biggest spuds.'

'Yes, but each shack pays them to get rid of it. Don't you see – they're making money? Do you suppose Valerik will stay overnight at Natasha's place? She won't be expecting him. Should we warn her; otherwise he might catch her with Karol?'

'No, Stefan, we mustn't. You promised.'

'Karol's got to find out sometime. Wouldn't it be kinder to put him out of his misery?'

'No! It would not! Let's see how Natasha gets herself out of this one; she should have been honest with him from the start.'

The sounds of 'Hey Sokolyi' greeted us when

we arrived on the steps to our shack. 'Oh dear, Karol's home.'

'I wonder if Natasha's with him?'

'I doubt it. This is Karol's attempt to cheer himself up. He always plays it when he's got something on his mind. I bet she's dumped him.'

The entire family were sitting around the stove, but there was no Natasha. Karol put down his accordion.

'Marishu come and sit down, you too, Stefan. We have terrible news,' Mother said. 'Smirnov's not long left. They are transferring your father to the saw mills at Permilovo. He leaves tomorrow.'

I was on a different wave length, expecting Karol to be heartbroken. 'What? Samoded-Permilovo?'

Stefan nudged me in the ribs.

'Why, do you know where it is?' Lodzia asked.

'Nothing other than the train passed through it on our way here. How far is it?'

'Thirty kilometres south of here,' Gerhard said. 'Smirnov's been doing the rounds looking for someone who's good with their hands. Someone good at fixing things.'

'And your father had to pipe up he was.' Mother shook her head at his stupidity.

In his own defence, Father said, 'I know, but I thought he wanted someone to help at the Artel.' He turned to Stefan, seeking support. 'Your father's always snowed under with work; perhaps he could put in a kind word for me?'

'Can't you get out of it?'

'No, lad, I leave in the morning. A guard will deliver me there, but then I have to walk back if I want to get home. None of us Poles are allowed to use the train.'

'What are we going to do?' Mother cried. 'It's so far away. Your father will only be able to come home once a month. How will he manage without us?'

'I'm worried how you will manage without me!'

This was not at all what I was expecting to hear – Smirnov breaking up our family. How would we know if Tatta fell ill? Who would wash his clothes or queue for his bread?

Father said, 'Permilovo's too far to walk there and back in a day. I wouldn't even have time to eat and visit the banya. But if I worked non-stop each weekend, and saved up my free Sundays, I could make the journey once a month, spend two days here with you, and walk back. That way I could pick up a fresh change of clothes and make sure you had enough money to buy food.'

It was only later after Stefan went home; I thought to ask. 'Aren't you seeing Natasha tonight, Karol?'

* * *

Was it only four weeks since Tatta left for Permilovo? The place seemed so empty without him here. I knew Mama was getting worried because we had run out of money and were relying only on Gerhard and Karol's wages, which never stretched far.

'How much did you get?' I asked Lodzia when she returned from the Ukrainian quarter after selling my box of watercolours and brushes. There was always something they fancied or needed. Tatta told me it was a waste of time bartering. Since the Soviets devalued the Zloty, the Polish currency was almost worthless.

'Ten kopeks.'

'Is that all! I would have been better off keeping them.'

'Why? You haven't any paper, so what's the point – you will never use them.'

Worse, Mother told me the one-year-old son of our neighbour, Alfred and Lucia Powiecki, just died. I wondered if the ground was yet soft enough to bury him; what happened to my compassion? And what of Sasha's little boy – and Oleszkiewicz's child; then the other five children, all dead in quick succession, never mind the grownups. No one ever seemed to die in Poland, but here death seemed akin to the June fruit drop.

* * *

Icicles like the swords of Damocles hung from our cabin roof. They were dripping faster now and the low arc of the sun began to melt the snowy blankets on neighbouring roofs, honeycombing the upper crusts before it dipped below the horizon and everything froze again when darkness fell. Mama told me to be ultra-vigilant when passing the shacks not to get a spike in my head or get buried beneath an avalanche.

Thank God Tatta is due home today, I thought. I missed him so much; the place wasn't the same without him. Krystyna was unwell, and the day yawned ahead until Stefan came to collect me this evening.

I slumped onto the slats with my atlas, and my fingers retraced the route home. I revisited the haunts of my past, and my heart was sick for losing it all. Tatta told me to have hope. 'No war lasts forever,' he said. However, being trapped in a place like this, it was easy to say and much harder to endure.

He still hadn't returned at seven-thirty, and everyone sat around looking worried until Stefan arrived.

'Some months have five weeks,' he reminded us. 'Are you sure he didn't mean that – instead of returning every fourth week?'

Mother said, 'I remember him saying, 'I'll come home once a month.'

'So do I,' Lodzia affirmed. 'I remember it.'

'So where is he?'

Stefan said, 'Which route would he take – the way they brought us from Kholmogorki station – or through the Kenga forests?' He and I exchanged swift glances. 'I mean, I think I heard one of the Ukrainians mention there's a quicker route.'

'Who knows?' Gerhard got up, threw another log onto the stove and paced about the room. 'I expect he would follow the route they took him, but you say there's a track through the Kenga forest? Hmm, interesting.'

We sat and watched as the log took hold and flared into life, none of us able to offer a solution until Mother squeezed the bridge of her nose and said, 'So we don't even know which way to head in search of him.'

Dawn broke earlier these days, and the morning air wasn't as razor-sharp as it was when I left the shack with Lodzia to collect the bread. The wooden steps from our porch were black and saturated, and patches of grass peeked through the melting snow.

I raised my face to the sun, however feeble it was, grateful for the small mercies I could call my own.

We reached the front of the queue where Mrs Szefczuk was slicing out her uneven wodges of bread, and her husband was looking on – tutting as usual. I did a quick flit over to her side when the queue split at the counter.

'Well, it's young Marisha,' she said. 'We haven't seen you in here in a while.'

Lodzia said, 'No, she's always got her head stuck in that atlas of hers, dreaming of distant lands with her new love.'

'You have an atlas? I've always wanted an atlas. Another year and we'll be free; then the universe awaits.'

'Not if you keep giving away all the bread,' Szefczuk muttered. 'Cut it straight, woman!'

She ignored him, turned to Lodzia, and took her ration ticket. 'Have you planted your potatoes yet? It's time.'

Kommendant Ivanov allotted all Polish prisoners a small square of empty ground at the edge of Vodopad. When the boatman came up from Permilovo, he brought seed potatoes to encourage us to grow our food. The Kommendant did everything in his power to persuade his charges to put down roots and make a go of things here, even offering beetroot, cabbage and gherkin seeds for us to plant. His gift was a hard row to hoe. The land was full of tree and bramble roots that first needed clearing.

We returned to the shack, and I picked up the spade Natasha lent us. 'Come on, Mama, let's go to the allotment and see if we can plant the potatoes. Mrs Szefczuk said it's time.'

'No need, kohanie; I've already driven the spade into the soil beside the shack. It's still too cold and wet and they'll rot.'

Removing my coat, I rested the spade against the wall. 'I can't wait until summer. Roza told me the forest teems with berries and mushrooms. Imagine it, Mama – proper food.'

'Yes, if only we could get some fat. I wonder

why Jusio didn't reply. I can only assume the Soviets confiscated your letter – or their house.'

'Mama, I was thinking – with Tatta working away, I should start work earlier. Why wait? What's three or four months and I know we need the money, because I overheard you talking to Gerhard.'

'Kohanie, enjoy what's left of your childhood. We'll manage.'

'Yes, Mama, but I'm not a child. I'm almost sixteen and I want to help.'

'We know you do, but no. Tatta and I won't hear of it. It's crippling work.'

20

Karol returned from work, eased off his valenki, left them where they stood, and slumped down on his slats. 'They're transferring me to Volosne tomorrow. It's where they stable the bulk of the horses.'

Mother, perplexed by the sudden change of routine, said, 'Why? Is it far? Will you be able to return to Vodopad at night? Or will you have to stay over?'

'I'll try; I want to be with Natasha. They've chopped down a load of trees, and they're building new shacks and a cantina by the stables. It might have to be just once a month. Pity I haven't still got my bicycle.'

'Bit sudden,' I said. 'Are they sending just you, Karol, or other people too?'

'Just me. My overseer said they need an extra worker to collect the sawn logs from the workstations and send them downriver to the sawmills. I suppose it beats felling them.'

'Yes, but there's a stable at Vodopad. Why can't you use one of our horses?'

'There aren't any spare. They're all being used.'

This meant we had even more pressing

needs. We were struggling without Tatta's weekly wage and now we might not have Karol's. Lodzia wasn't working because she was looking after Ella. Mama was exempt because of her age, and she never owned a coat so couldn't work in winter, and I was too young. It meant we would all depend on Gerhard's wage to keep us until Tatta and Karol returned at the end of the month.

'You see, Mama, it's even more reason for me to start work right away. I could ask if they'll put me with Gerhard's team as he's already one short.'

All three replied in unison. 'No!'

With Karol gone, I sensed trouble when Natasha's mother arrived at our shack the following day, asking for Anna Glencova.

Mother, oblivious to Natasha's shocking secret, smiled, her hand outstretched, 'How nice to meet you. Oh, I can see now from whom Natasha gets her beautiful eyes. She's such a stunning girl.'

Lodzia, who had met her previously, seemed delighted she had dropped in to see us and was all welcoming smiles.

Natasha's mother did not reciprocate the cordiality, determined to get to the point. 'You know my Natasha's betrothed, don't you?'

I listened in silence, and realised from her hostile attitude I should have spoken sooner, but it was too late now.

For a fleeting moment, Mother peered at the woman to see if she was jesting. 'Since when? She and Karol are in love! Anyone can see that.'

'Ahh, it is infatuation. His handsome face has turned her empty head. Even if they were in love, what sort of future would she have with your Karol? In this place? None. Marrying is her one chance to get out of here and enjoy a normal life. I forbid her to come here again. And if she comes, you are to send her away. Is that clear?'

Mother sat down, patted the empty slats beside her and beckoned Natasha's mother to join her. 'This is news to us. Won't you sit down? I'm sure we can talk this through. Who is she betrothed to?'

Natasha's mother remained standing. 'He is a Russian. You wouldn't know him. His family live in Vologda and that is where they will live when they marry – in Vologda – with his parents.' Rebuffing any opportunity for discussion, she turned at the door, 'Remember, if she comes here again, you are to send her away.'

Not prepared for a fobbing off, Mother hurried after her, 'You can't leave us with a blow like this. What do I tell my Karol?'

'Tell him what you like; that's your problem.'

'So, what does this 'Russian' do for a living that will give your Natasha such a grand start in life?'

She jerked her head back around the door as if she were about to announce some grand profession. 'He's the boatman who brings supplies upriver to Vodopad when the ice melts. My Natasha used to help him unload the boat when she was a teenager; it's how they met. Now they're engaged,' she repeated to ensure everyone understood the gravity of the situation.

I said, 'How is it that Natasha can leave Vodopad and get married, and we can't? And if she can leave, why doesn't she take Karol with her? They adore each another.'

'Even if she could, which she can't, what sort of life could he give her? He has no money, no property. Where would they live? Just because Valerik is a boatman doesn't mean his father is without influence. He owns the boat that brings the supplies from Permilovo and he is in the Government's employ.'

I couldn't help myself. 'From the state of it, it's a wonder it doesn't sink?'

Natasha's mother flashed me a withering glare. 'Unlike you, we've almost served our sentences. They class you as enemies of the people.' With that she turned on her heel and left.

Mother closed the door and leaned against it. 'Poor Karol; he'll be heartbroken. How are we going to tell him? I'd never have thought Natasha would have kept something like this to herself. I liked her.'

Lodzia said, 'I don't know how she finds time to see this betrothed. She's always with Karol. Where is Vologda anyway?'

I reached for my atlas, although I already knew it was on the line from Moscow to Archangelsk. I had been exploring every possibility of returning to Poland since Stefan suggested escape, but we were so far from home that the task seemed insurmountable. There was still the problem with leaving my parents behind. Escaping was no glib stab at freedom because I knew that abandoning them would mean I would never see them again – and as much as I loved Stefan and wanted to be with him forever, I wished I didn't have to choose.

'Now what are you daydreaming about, Marishu, have you found this Vologda yet?' Mother asked.

'Yes, it's south of Permilovo.' I snapped shut the atlas and returned to my thoughts. What would I do if Stefan demanded I choose between him and my family?

* * *

Another month passed, and there was still no sign of my father.

Mother threw up her hands and paced about the room, 'He must be ill. What other explanation can there be?'

For a while, no one spoke until Gerhard voiced the inconceivable, 'Or dead.'

'Someone would have let us know – wouldn't they,' Lodzia said? 'I mean, what would they have done with his body?'

Images of Soviet guards throwing corpses off the cattle wagons on the way here, leaving them for the wolves to eat, loomed large. 'If I knew how to get to Permilovo, I'd go to him. We need to know; it's the not knowing…'

'Marishu, forget it. You would never find your way through the forests and then we would have lost the pair of you. It is out of the question.'

Gerhard and Lodzia agreed with Mother. 'Terrible idea.'

Stefan said nothing, but I could see the cogs turning behind his eyes; no doubt thinking of escape.

I felt as if they were all ganging up on me. 'Yes, but if I asked Kommendant Ivanov for help first, perhaps he'd take pity on us.'

'Pity? All Ivanov has to do is ensure he works everyone into the grave, and prevents them from escaping before they keel over,' Lodzia said.

Gerhard agreed. 'You heard his welcoming speech – dangerous animals, swamps, rivers. Natasha told us the same; the woods are teeming with them. Forget it, Marishu; I know you adore Tatta, we all do, but it's a terrible idea.'

'So, you're suggesting we do nothing? He might just be hanging on there for one of us to reach him; he needs us. I know he does. I can feel it. At least let me ask Ivanov. He lets Alina Zadarnowska go to Kholmogorki – and nothing's eaten her – so why not let me see what's wrong with Tatta? You won't let me work. I've got the time.' I cast about the room. 'Well?'

'Alina goes on horseback – not on foot; you're afraid of horses.' Lodzia held my gaze, 'Anyway, we haven't got a horse.'

'Karol could go,' Gerhard said. 'His camp's full of horses.'

'And how do we get to him?' Lodzia replied. 'He comes home only when his clothes are filthy enough to stand up on their own. I don't know why Natasha's mother doesn't get the message; she doesn't want to marry Valerik. She told me so. Why else would she keep hanging around here, hoping to see Karol?'

Nothing was resolved. My family wouldn't allow me to even try; they refused to discuss it. My waking thoughts, and throughout the weeks that followed, were always of my father. How could I think of anything else when I knew he would have returned to us if he were able?

I sometimes recognised the shadow of those people who first boarded the cattle trucks with us at Zhabinka, so stout and robust, now yellow with scurvy, shuffling along – old before their time.

Gerhard told me that bouts of lethargy beset even the fittest in his team. Their eyes filled with pus, their legs burnt with intermittent pain until they had to stop working, and their limbs shook. There was no chance they could meet their norms, and it was affecting his entire team's performance. It was a parlous state for anyone to find themselves and there was no telling who scurvy would next attack.

'By the time the fat man slims, the thin one has long since died,' had always been my father's mantra. I was becoming obsessed each time someone mentioned illness, checking myself for symptoms of scurvy and looking for any signs of it in the rest of my family. Tatta might also be suffering. That scared me the most.

I had to go to him. I was sure if I could just explain to Kommendant Ivanov I needed to take my father a change of clothes, and we worried about his health, he couldn't refuse. Everyone agreed Smirnov was a bastard, but Kommendant Ivanov a reasonable man. It was a two-day trip, but I would promise on my life to return. My one worry was Stefan might insist on coming with me, using it as an excuse to escape but I couldn't keep this from him. I had to make him understand my family were my priority right now.

On Sunday we were picking berries in the woods along with the rest of the camp. Someone said it was illegal, but the lure of fresh fruit was irresistible and Smirnov and his other NKVD spies couldn't be everywhere at once checking up on everyone. For me, it was a risk worth taking.

A cloud of mosquitos, flies and midges feasted on our flesh as we feasted on the berries, finding their way into our eyes, ears and noses. They teemed around the riverbanks and in the forests, around boggy areas where blueberries glistened in the summer heat.

Yet the yearning to savour fruit outweighed the nuisance, as I spotted a mass of cloudberries – those large, golden-yellow blackberry-like fruits, so juicy and so delicious.

The forest hummed with life, its dirt path illuminated by the sun, and I plunged deeper in. 'Stefan! Over here – look, I've found some huge cloudberries.' My basket was brimming already and I had eaten my fill, but couldn't resist one last plump one. Reaching out for it, I disturbed another cloud of midges, sending them into a feeding frenzy on my skin.

Stefan picked a berry and popped it into my mouth. 'Shall we take some of these to Vasily, Boris and Roza?'

The juice hit the back of my throat, making me cough as I spoke. 'There won't be enough for us. Can't they pick their own?'

'Ha-ha, Marishu. I'm not saying we give them all away. Come on; they're not far.'

Our hosts were as cordial as ever, delighted with their gift, and it was good to return their kindness.

Stefan, flopped out in a chair, took a sip of tea. 'We used to collect these in the forests in Poland; and mushrooms.' Changing the subject, he said, 'Tell me, is there a trail through the Kenga forest leading to the railway line?'

'There is lad. It's the old track some of us Ukrainians used to reach the sawmills at Permilovo,' Boris said. 'Probably overgrown by now. Why do you ask?'

Aha, I thought. That's why he wanted to come here, but Stefan was so transparent.

'Oh, one of my friends tried to escape on the strength of some rumour. He got lost. Lucky for him he found his way back. I told him, if there were such a track, wouldn't Boris and Roza have escaped years ago?'

'Ha, and go where?' Roza said. 'Stefan, it is easy being seduced by thoughts of freedom, but there's nowhere you can go where the NKVD aren't waiting for you. Never underestimate these ruthless people. Here,' she cast about at the bleak poverty of it all, 'here at least we can live. We have the Kolkhoz, and we're mostly self-sufficient nowadays. We have the community centre. Life's hard – but where isn't it in Russia? Winters are crippling and the summers are short, but Vodopad is the only home we have.'

'We weren't thinking of escape.' I came to his rescue. 'My father is working at the sawmills in Permilovo, but he never returned as promised at the end of last month. We're *desperate* to know what's happened to him. My mother is making herself ill with worry. Roza, *please* – would you show us this track? I know I was lost three months back, but if Alina Zadarnowska can navigate a track to Kholmogorki, then so can I.'

Their expressions were impassive. Boris said, 'Kholmogorki is 12km from here; the sawmills are over 35km.'

Only Roza understood my urgency to see my

father. 'It's a very long way, Marishu. You will have to stick to the banks of the Kenga as you travel through the Kenga Forest. Never deviate; there are no shortcuts. The river is your guide. At the other end of the forest you will come to a wide, open plane which we call reindeer country. Remember where I told you the leaves of the silver birches are spotted red? You keep walking straight till you reach the Moscow/Archangelsk railroad.

'The railroad bridges the Kenga river. It's a single track and there are no handrails. You will need to climb onto the railway line, walk south along it, then jump get off on the opposite bank. Now you are about a third of the way there.

'Next, you will follow *only* the railway line all the way to the station at Samoded-Permilovo. The NKVD will stop you. So, you must ask Kommendant Ivanov for a Pass. Tell them you want the sawmills, and they will either arrest you, or direct you to the railway spur which leads to the Permilovo sawmills.'

'Why should they arrest me if I have a Pass?'

'Because you are a child,' Boris said.

'I'm nearly sixteen!' I bristled. So, the sawmills are not in Samoded-Permilovo?'

'No, no, Marishu. They are further east, beside the Vaymuga River. That's where they remove the logs from the water. The railway spur is used to transport the sawn timber to the main Moscow/Archangelsk railroad.'

'With respect, it isn't a journey for a girl on

her own, and especially not one with your navigational skills.' Boris's eyes remained unblinking; neither was he joking.

'Don't worry. Marisha won't be alone. We'll leave next Sunday,' Stefan said.

'You will push it getting there and back in a day, lad.'

'Then I shall ask Smirnov for a day off.'

'And decimate everyone else's norm's for the rest of the week?' I said.

I didn't relish making the journey alone, yet I had to leave right away. Delaying another week could be fatal for my father's condition. Even if Kommendant Ivanov agreed to let us both go – which was doubtful – they wouldn't allow Stefan an extra day off work.

We said our goodbyes and made our way back to Vodopad.

'Stefan,' I said, 'Please understand I have to do this alone; I can't wait until next Sunday. I stand a better chance of being released from the camp unaccompanied. We don't want Ivanov thinking we're escaping, because that's what he will think.'

'Then at least take Lodzia with you. Your mother won't let you go alone.'

'Lodzia has to queue for food. Besides, she wouldn't leave Ella behind with Mama for two days.'

'Why not? She's her grandmother! No, I won't rest knowing you're out there alone in the forest.'

'And I won't rest if I don't go to Tatta. It may already be too late. I have to do this, kohanie; please understand. No one will stop me; I've made up my mind. But first, I have things to arrange.' I made enormous eyes at him and said, 'Don't worry, I shall follow the river bank.'

21

I stepped down from the porch into a dense mist that had swallowed the Vaymuga and concealed the forest beyond. Absorbed into the throng of workers, we headed for the Artel. Last night Stefan had worked himself up into such a state of worry that I would get lost, that he insisted he at least accompanies me partway to his poloska, at which point we would part and go our separate ways.

In my baskets were clean clothes for my father, and the spoils from selling my World atlas to Szefczuk's wife: two loaves of yesterday's bread, a packet of Halva (Tatta's favourite sweetmeat) tobacco for his pipe, and two bottles of water, their necks stuffed with rags.

Stefan and I arrived simultaneously from different directions. He took me in his arms, kissed me, gazed into my eyes and down into my baskets. 'I couldn't dissuade you then?'

'I suppose there's no point telling you not to worry, but I'll be fine. How many times have we walked that riverbank? I promise I'll stick to it. I'll be back before you know it.'

'Yes, but we've only ever walked a short way and turned back.'

'Stefan, I'm stronger than you think. I can do this,' I said, averting his gaze.

He took a lengthy breath. 'Have it your way. At least let me help you with those baskets.'

The sun was already lighting up the sky beyond the treetops as we walked towards the river. Pausing for a moment on the bank, we watched a flock of snow geese fly past, enveloping us in a cacophony of dat, dat, dat.

With the shacks of Vodopad behind us, the work teams veered north and disappeared into the forest, but Stefan held back. He took me into his arms, and we kissed goodbye. 'Why won't you let me come with you?'

'No, Stefan. How many times, for goodness' sake! Smirnov will throw you into the Black Hole, and it will affect everyone's wages. Think about it, how can they meet their norms with a man short? Go on; I'll be fine.'

'I love you.'

'And I love you too. Now go.' I watched him trudge off, hands in his pockets, but he kept looking back before the forest swallowed him.

The rising sun burned off the mist and a vivid world returned. I strode out along the old pathway keeping to the riverbank, the drone of insects all around me. When I reached the point where it flowed into the Vaymuga, I stopped and watched a rusting boat moving upriver from the Magazine at Permilovo to the shop here in

Vodopad. No doubt Natasha's intended was at the helm.

Setting off again at a steady pace along the bank of the Kenga, the tangle of long grass, nettles and wildflowers ravelling around my boots made walking difficult. This part of the river was familiar; we had often walked this way, but never much further. Passing beyond that point was strange. I sensed a fleeting awareness of losing grip on my courage but ploughed on into the unknown.

To my right, and beyond the river to my left, the mighty forests rose into a dome of brilliant blue. I wondered, but only briefly lest I lose my nerve, whether this was the spot where I emerged into the open having got so lost searching for Lodzia.

The track narrowed and brambles latched to my shawl. Releasing myself, I almost missed an abundance of shrubs with great, ripe, fleshy berries that grew to my right. The temptation to pluck them was too great to resist. My half-empty food basket beckoned, and I could imagine my father's face when I turned up with such delicacies.

The forest was alive with birdsong, butterflies, minks and squirrels, but I was ever alert for the sound of something more sinister, jittery when something rustled the undergrowth nearby. Still, I dived in. Several-hundred-year-old spruces and larches looked down on me from a significant height, but I kept on plucking; a laden branch here, and another there. Mosquitos and midges feasted on my flesh, but I was too pre-occupied to care. However, I was wiser this time and kept the river in my sights.

The sun was nearing its zenith when I reached the forest edge. I presumed this was the reindeer pasture Roza mentioned where Stalin murdered his priests, and the leaves of the birches are said to have soaked up their blood as testimony to his barbarity. There was no sign of the Moscow to Archangelsk railroad. Nor were there any reindeer.

My baskets were full, and my legs ached. I slumped down in the shade of the nearest tree, ate some berries, and guzzled an entire bottle of water, not realising how thirsty I was. Keep to the river, keep to the river, I kept telling myself. You'll be alright. This is no time for wobbles.

I got to my feet and pressed on. At one point, I wondered if I had gone wrong somewhere. Where was this railroad? I needed to cross the Kenga otherwise I would never reach Permilovo.

And there it was; the river crossing. Today there were no raucous, metallic shrieks announcing a train's thunderous approach. There was a deafening silence.

Water terrified me, but I swallowed my fear and walked along the tracks. The Kenga flowed beneath me and headed off in another direction. No more meandering river and forest with things to watch to keep me absorbed. I had another vista; a man-made gash through the taiga, kilometre after kilometre of unending sameness I had to conquer. I pressed on, heading south, the quietness growing deeper until I could hear the steady rhythm of my breath from within.

Roza said this point marked over a third of my journey. I kept walking, and walking in a straight line, my brain turning numb, my limbs aching, my baskets getting heavier. I reached that level of exhaustion that equates to lunacy. If only I could give my limbs and my mind a rest; but there was no choice but to keep going.

At last, there it was in the distance – the silhouette of my destination. If Tatta was still alive and frail, he would never have made it to the river crossing, let alone back to Vodopad.

Four NKVD were approaching. My breath quickened; my stomach tightened. My parents were there before dealing with Peaked Cap in Poland, but this time I had to face the bullies alone. I reached in my basket for my pass, lifted my chin and explained my mission, pretending to be much braver than I felt.

They checked my baskets and directed me to the railway spur which led to the sawmills at Permilovo and told me to follow the track.

Where was this sawmill? I thought it was just a brief journey from the settlement, instead my aching legs swallowed up the kilometres.

I arrived in the late afternoon, exhausted and

hungry. They had electricity here, and the place thrummed with noise.

After asking several people if they knew where I could find Igancy Glenz, I panicked because no one had heard of him. After doing a full circle, I found the administrative office, and they pointed me to the far end of the yard where my father was working.

Everything was in motion as I headed off, unused to such noise. Polish girls about my age were retrieving logs from the river; others were stacking them. Nearby, men were cutting wood for building materials. At speed, other groups were loading them onto freight wagons.

My baskets felt even heavier now. I set them down and paused for a moment to regain my strength, watching the workers shovelling wood cubes into wheelbarrows. Others were moving to and from the generator, returning with empty ones to collect more fuel.

I picked up my baskets. After some searching, I found him, although it was a moment before I was sure it was my father. He was never a portly man, but oh his face! Emaciated and bearded, his sinewy arms grappled with some old component on an industrial-sized saw. When he coughed the phlegm in his lungs rattled and rasped.

'Oh, Tatta, what's happened to you?' I rushed to him, stopping short to make sure it was him.

'Marisha, you came.' His eyes, now sunken, pooled with tears. 'Oh, child, you have no idea how good it is to see you.'

I tilted my head, blinking back the tears. 'How are you, Tatta? We've been waiting for you to come home. Mama is so worried.'

'I can't.' Even his voice was weary, 'I am so sorry, but I no longer have the strength. It's too far. I've been so worried about you all because I haven't been able to get money back to you. How are you managing?'

I threw myself into his arms and sobbed. 'You mustn't worry about us; we manage. Lodzia has been selling some of our things – she's good at it. Oh, Tatta, they must let you come home; you're not fit to work.'

He gave me a wry smile. 'How can I? They say they're short of mechanics and the chainsaws are always breaking down. Everything is so dilapidated. It's a full-time job keeping it all going.'

'I don't care. You must see the doctor and let him see you're unfit for work. You can't go on like this. We'll see him tomorrow,' my voice gained speed, 'we'll see him together. I'll explain – this is why I'm here.'

'Marishu, there is no resident doctor in a place like this. Even if there were, there's no time, I have to keep working.'

'No doctor? But how do people manage?'

'They either recover or they die.'

I could see it was where my darling father was heading. 'I've brought you bread and these berries, and look, some tobacco,' I took a loaf out of my basket, handed it to him and watched in alarm as he dropped the spanner and fell onto the food.

I stayed with him until he finished work and returned to the shack room he shared with three other men. It was a mirror image of the bug-infested one at Vodopad, except it was messy, smelled of dirty bodies and clothing and lacked a woman's civilising influence.

We went to the soup kitchen together and he offered to share his rations. I refused, although I was ravenous. 'You need all the food you can get, Tatta.'

He insisted, so I ate a little and shared some of his tea.

'Is there a shop here?'

'There is, but there is nothing left to buy when I get there.'

'So, what do you eat?'

'Soup. I'm allowed two plates full, but not having time to queue for bread, I've persuaded the counter staff to sell me an extra portion.'

'Yes, but, Tatta, there's no goodness in this stuff.' I was livid. 'They should never have sent you here on your own. I'll go to the shop tomorrow. I'll not give up. Do you have a ration card and some money?'

He nodded.

'Then I will buy you food, and you will eat it. I am not leaving here until I know you're better fed.'

'But, kohanie, Mama will worry about you.'
'Mama knows where I am.'

I spent the night at the camp, squashed up on my father's bed, listening to the other three men coughing. It was no rest, and I awoke exhausted and hungry.

In the morning, he polished off the bread, changed into his clean clothing and removed his money from his pocket, 'Marishu, go to the shop, get yourself something to eat, and take the rest home and give it to Mama. It's my wages. I was beside myself worrying about how to get it back to you.'

'No, Tatta, you need it for yourself.'

'I'll get by until Saturday. I have enough.'

Home? – Our one room in a shack crawling with bugs. But Tatta wasn't talking about the quality of the furnishings, he meant the people he loved, and those who loved him; nothing else mattered. He left for work well before six, and I headed for the shop and bakery, before seeking the camp Kommendant.

I took the bread to my father where he was working, because a starving mouth would have gobbled up his loaf before he returned to his shack room at night.

'Tatta, put this bread somewhere you can keep your eye on it.' Then I handed him the packet of Halva. 'This is a special treat for you.'

He stared down at it, bemused, and held it

out to me, 'Halva? But you've already given me tobacco. No, kohanie, you take it.'

I closed his other hand around it. 'It's your favourite.'

'I can't take this. What will you eat? He looked up at me. 'How did you get this?'

'I sold my atlas to Szefczuk's wife.'

'Kohanie – your atlas! That was your favourite book.' Hope left his face. Then he tore into the Halva. As he chewed, saliva frothed at the corners of his mouth, mixing with tears flooding down over protruding cheekbones.

I wrapped him in my arms. I never believed a miserable piece of sweetmeat could cause such joy.

When he'd cried himself out, he looked at the Halva again and into my eyes. 'Don't worry about me, child, human life is worthless in Russia; people are replaceable. They think more of their horses; there are fewer of those.'

I swiped away my tears, 'Listen, Tatta, from now on, I shall visit you every two weeks. If Kommendant Ivanov trusts me to keep my word, I'm sure he'll let me come and see you again. He seems a reasonable man. And I shall tell him you must come home; you're not fit to work. I lifted my fist and shook the money he gave me. 'And I shall bring you better food; there's more choice in the shop now summer's here and the boat visits Vodopad.'

'No, kohanie, it's too far....'

'Shush, Tatta. I will see you in two weeks and

no arguments.'

He looked into my face, 'Have hope child; never lose hope. Just remember that.'

I walked away, looking back as he stood watching me and eating his Halva, until he was a tiny blob, and then I reached the camp gates. Oh God, now I had to get back to Vodopad. Tatta wouldn't last much longer if he didn't get more food and some rest, and if I didn't get something to eat soon, neither would I.

22

I set off for Vodopad, dreading the journey, knowing how long it took to get here, but my baskets were lighter, my walking unhindered. Mid-morning, a freight train lumbered past, shattering the peace, heading north toward Archangelsk.

Reaching the bridge over the Kenga, I stood mid-track to survey my route, the glare of the sun pooling a shadow at my feet. Everything looked different from this angle, but the river was my guide. I crossed the caribou plain at a brisk pace because I needed to get through those woods before darkness fell.

In the forest, where the trees bordered the riverbank, the old rutted path veered inwards. It seemed its curve was more pronounced, and I was heading further into the woods. Was I on the same path as before? The Kenga was still visible to my right, and I kept clear of the swamp like vegetation and rotting trees in my way, watching where I put my feet. Then I stumbled across a patch of arctic raspberry bushes – those delicious, thornless fruits that grew close to the ground. God, I was so hungry, that I picked and ate, my fingers turning purple, the juice soaking into my skin. There were more over there, and I stripped the bushes bare.

Back to the rutted path, I hurried on my way. The birds had ceased to sing now, and little by little my eyes adjusted to the spreading gloom. I shouldn't have stopped; I wasn't going to get through the forest before dark and my footsteps became more strident.

A canopy of stars freckled the sky beyond the Vaymuga when I reached Vodopad. Valerik was still here; his boat moored behind the bakery, but I was too physically and mentally exhausted to wonder what he was still doing here. All I craved was sleep but there was a huge, white horse tethered outside our shack. Was Karol stupid enough to filch a horse from Volosne? He had to be.

I opened the door to our room, and Stefan, unable to contain his anxiety, rushed forwards and swept me into his arms, 'Thank God you're safe.'

His body felt so good. 'Ahh, kohanie, why aren't you in bed? You have work tomorrow.'

He released me for a moment to allow my mother to envelope me in her comforting arms,

'Poor boy, he's been so worried since you left. We all have. How was your father?'

'Frail.' I reached into my pocket. 'He wanted you to have this.'

'But what about him?'

'He's paid on Saturday, and he has enough

till then. Is that horse out there your doing, Karol?'

'Don't you start. Yes, it's mine, and no, I didn't steal him; I borrowed him.'

Mother said, 'Natasha turned up at Volosne today looking for him.'

'Natasha? But that Valerik and his boat are still here.'

Karol's body tensed, and he turned away towards the window so I couldn't see his face.

'She and her mother are leaving Vodopad tomorrow,' Lodzia said.

I gave Stefan a look of disbelief, doubting Karol's overseers had suddenly turned benevolent. Easing off my boots, I said, 'Did you pinch that horse, Karol?'

He turned back and stared at me. 'I asked to borrow it so I could bring Natasha back to Vodopad. Satisfied?'

I wondered why she couldn't have walked rather than make him take unnecessary risks.

Changing the subject, Gerhard crouched in front of me. 'What about, Tatta? You said he's frail? But he's still working?'

'I barely recognised him. How could a human being deteriorate so fast in nine weeks?'

'We have to bring him back to Vodopad.'

'There's no chance. I spoke with the camp Kommendant at Permilovo, and he said it was out of the question; he couldn't spare him.'

'Then I shall go and fetch him,' Karol said.

Exhausted as I was, I glared at him. 'You

know Karol; sometimes you say the stupidest things.'

'Why? I have a horse. Where's the problem?'

'Come on, Karol, I know you mean well,' Gerhard said, 'but you can't just ride into another camp and abscond with one of its prisoners. They'll shoot the pair of you. There has to be another way.'

Mother agreed. 'Gerhard's right, Karol. Let him speak to Kommendant Ivanov. We need to do this through him.'

'I'll go and speak with Ivanov,' I said. 'It'll show him I kept my word. I haven't fled and abused his trust, and having seen Tatta personally, I'm concerned about his health.'

Karol scoffed at my suggestion. 'Huh, I've begged them to allow me to return to Vodopad, although God-knows-why they refuse to listen. I'll go and fetch him. Who's to know? People are dying all the time. For all they care, he might be dead in a ditch somewhere. It'll save them having to dump his body in the river.'

'Don't be so stupid, Karol! You don't know the layout of the camp. Where are you going to look?'

'I shall go on Sunday; on his day off. He will either be at the cantina or queuing at the bakery. Don't you worry, I'll find him.'

Feelings were running high. Lodzia placed her calming hand on Karol's shoulder. 'Leave it to Gerhard, Karol; we have to deal with it from this end.'

Stefan and I said our goodnights in the porch, and I returned to my family. My last words before closing my eyes were, 'Gerhard, promise me you'll leave Kommendant Ivanov to me.'

23

I was awoken by a disturbing dream which was fading fast. When I finally came too, Karol had gone, Mother sat darning socks, and the horse was staring at me through the window.

'Is that thing still here? Where's Karol?'

'Down by the river.' She lifted the needle to the light to re-thread it. 'Poor boy, he's gone to have it out with this boatman – as if that will do any good. It crucifies me to see him so unhappy.'

'Has Lodzia gone to fetch bread?'

'Hours ago; we let you sleep.'

'What time is it?' I stuffed my feet into my valenki, gave the horse a wide berth, and hurried down to the Vaymuga. Karol was leaning against the back of the shop, smoking a roll-up, one ankle crossed over the other, the empty boat tethered to a tree stump beside the riverbank.

'Did they let you borrow that horse, Karol?'

'What do you think? None of them do favours for anyone unless there's something in it for themselves, and they think they won't get caught. I had to bribe the overseer. Don't worry. He's not the NKVD; he's one of the Ukrainians.'

'Yes, but a horse, Karol. Does he wield that sort of power or did he first ask permission from the NKVD?'

'Neither. I told him I'd be back last night. I thought Natasha and her mother would be gone by then, but she's still here. That tells me she doesn't want to go.'

'You *fool*. Let her go.'

He took a drag, blew out a plume of smoke and stared out across the river. 'I can't. I love her, and she loves me. It's that witch of a mother.'

'So why are you hanging around here?'

'I'm waiting for her betrothed to get into his boat and bugger off back to Permilovo. There are some home truths he needs to know. He won't be bothering her again after he hears what I have to say.'

'But your overseer must already know you haven't returned. He'll have assumed you've escaped on the horse, and already snitched on you. He's responsible for it. You're both in big trouble, Karol. They'll shoot the pair of you.'

Natasha and her mother appeared carrying enormous wicker baskets, heading for the boat. Her betrothed, with a sizeable hessian sack slung across his back, staggered behind them.

Karol flicked away his cigarette stub, pushed himself away from the wall and faced Natasha, his expression imploring her to rethink.

She set down one of her baskets, rested her hand on her belly, and gazed back at him with a look that said, if only life could be different.

The hairs on my face stood on end and I turned to face him in astonishment.

Her mother grabbed Natasha's arm and pulled her towards the riverbank.

She held back, 'No, Mama, please, just let me gaze at Karol's beautiful face one last time.' She tilted her head; her lips moist and tremulous parted a little, her eyes brimming with tears, and gave him the loveliest smile.

I grabbed his arm. 'Karol, don't do this to yourself.'

He kept looking at her, willing her to stay while her mother dragged her away. Natasha gazed back at him, trying to disentangle herself from her grasp.

'Get a move on!' Valerik snarled.

This was such a shock. I left him then; he didn't need me here. Instead, I headed to the Administration building to ask permission to speak to Kommendant Ivanov.

He was yet to arrive, so I arranged myself in the middle of the steps outside the cabin and waited. He would have to ask me to shift to let him in.

The rusting boat was pulling out into the middle of the river, and I tracked it until it disappeared from view. The Vaymuga, the road of the forest, looked stunning in summer; unlike in winter when it dragged by, its banks frozen halfway across. Now it moved with a vibrancy I had never seen, the surrounding forests nourished by melting snow, vivid and alive. Poor Karol. At least nothing so horrid would ever happen to Stefan and me.

He was back at the shack when I returned, making ready to leave for Volosne – Natasha lost to him forever, and I knew, in that moment of loss, his world must have collapsed. How could he bear it? He pulled me to one side, 'Look, Marishu, not a word about – you know – the baby.'

He looked deep into my eyes, and I knew he meant it.

'I don't want anyone to know.'

'Did she come to Volosne to tell you she was pregnant?'

He nodded. 'It's why her mother wanted to get her married off so fast, pretend it's Valerik's baby. My child.' He shook his head, 'I can't bear it. I thought if I told him she was pregnant with another man's child he wouldn't want her. But I didn't get the chance.'

'What a mess; I am so sorry, Karol.'

'Not half as sorry as I am.' He kissed our mother goodbye and left the door swinging on its hinges.

Stefan called for me as usual at seven-thirty. 'Fancy a walk?'

'I think I've walked enough, don't you? Let's go to the club instead. I went to see Kommendant Ivanov this morning, see if he can help bring my father home.'

'And?'

'He was waffling. Said it will take time to get him transferred back here. They have to hand over all the details, make lists – it wasn't his decision. If the saws need mending, they need mending. It was all excuses. I don't think he has any intention of doing anything.'

'So, what happens now?'

'He promised to write to the other Kommendant. It was the best he could do. It takes time to find a replacement mechanic. Meanwhile, they're working Tatta into the grave. It's not only the chainsaws that are decrepit, but the conveyers, the transformers – everything keeps breaking down; he fixes one thing and something else stops working. We have to get him back home somehow. He gave me some money, so we'll perhaps be able to buy him some better food the next time I visit. I'll stay with him an extra day each time to ensure he eats more.'

'You're not going again?'

'I have to, Stefan. He has no one to help him collect his rations, no one to wash his clothes. I plan to go every two weeks if Ivanov lets me; even if it's only to boost his morale and take extra food. I'm sure you'd do the same for your father.'

'And you're prepared to do this? All that way? Alone?'

'I've done it once; I can do it again. Fear is just a state of mind.'

Stefan let the matter drop. 'Did your mother tell you, Sasha's brother has escaped?'

'No. How?'

He stared at me as if it were obvious. 'He up and went; he followed you out of the camp. Sasha reckons all these deaths freaked him out. Simple as that.' He clasped my hands. 'We could too. If you reached Permilovo, why can't we? We just have to walk out of here and follow the Kenga.'

'Yes, and the NKVD were waiting. I had to show my Pass from Ivanov before they'd allow me to go to Tatta's camp. It terrified me I can tell you. Being interrogated with a gun stuck in your ribs is no fun. Once was enough, twice too often.'

'But the NKVD are only patrolling stations and towns. We can by-pass those.'

'Stefan, don't you understand? There is no cover. The railroad is just a wide-open gash through the terrain. Stations are open places; you can't hide there or in the forest. The only way is to jump a moving train and it's too dangerous. Anyway, I can't leave right now. Please try to understand.'

He took a curt breath, raised his brows and stared into the distance. 'And I respect you for that, but...'

I sensed his disappointment and dreaded the thought he might ask me to choose. 'You could always go alone,' I suggested.

'Are you serious? I love you. I could never leave you here. What would my life be without you?'

24

The dreaded day arrived; my sixteenth birthday. Smirnov wasted no time summoning me to hard labour.

All visits to my father had to stop right away and none of us knew what to do. Kommendant Ivanov failed to return him to Vodopad, and the cruel Russian winter was setting in. The berries, mushrooms and brined fish I had been taking to Tatta nourished him and helped keep him alive, but now we all knew that without those – and adequate rest – he would not survive much longer.

The snowstorm last night had left a white, silent world. Violent eddies of air swept down between the shacks, throwing drifts against anything in the way, camouflaging trees and the river bank. Mother swaddled me in so many scarves that I could barely turn my head.

It was nearly five o'clock and Gerhard was impatient, waiting for me on the porch step. 'Are you coming or what?'

Lodzia waved us off. 'Good luck, you poor thing. Hope they put you in Gerhard's brigade. Fingers crossed.'

Mother stood by, looking worried.

'I doubt it,' Gerhard said. 'My brigade is already a foursome.'

Raising my hand in farewell, we headed off to the Artel. The fresh snow had not yet crusted, but the sky threatened more snow. Stefan waved and wished me luck as he made off with another group. I had visions of working next to him on an adjoining poloska, and we could perhaps meet up. My other assumption that they would place me with Gerhard or another established brigade was also wrong. I was part of a fresh one. There were four of us. Luiza, subdued and bereaved – the eldest at twenty eight, who had lost her remaining child the previous week; Rysiek, an over-zealous teenager, singled out as the brigade's feller, and Helenka, who was about the same age as I was. We were all novices.

The overseer first drove home the prize of meeting our 'norms', and the consequences of not doing so, which he spelt out to us in a way we all understood: 'If anyone of you cannot meet your 'norms', we will cut the wages of your entire brigade. And remember, he who does not work, does not eat.'

Norms, flaming norms; I was already sick of the word. Luiza mumbled something about, 'Good – and the sooner we're all dead, the better.' I didn't know if I should comfort her or abandon her to her grief.

With our production targets drummed into our heads, we set off deep into the forest, our journey eased by the compacted path of snow provided by those who had gone before. Stefan's party headed in the opposite direction.

The overseer led the way with his lantern aloft. We followed in single file, listening to the sounds of our laboured breathing and the distant call of wolves.

By the time we reached the Levashka River, streaks of orange slashed the eastern sky beyond the treetops. I froze. It never occurred to me we had to cross water. The overseer went first and the other three followed. I remained. This rickety bridge must be the one my father described, supported on three enormous log stacks piled onto the riverbed. There were no handrails, and the surface was uneven and icy. Beneath it, the river rampaged on its journey to join the Vaymuga.

Having held up everyone for long enough, the overseer threatened to throw me into the Black Hole if I didn't make haste. Aware of the others egging me on, I stepped onto it, but all I could think was, damn, I'm scared. My legs were flagging. I held out my arms to maintain my balance, blocking out all sound, aware only of my breath labouring in and out of my lungs at gasping intervals. I put another foot forward, concentrating on finding a plank, rather than a gap or a chunk of ice. The relief I felt on reaching the other side was immense.

Onwards we trudged through the trees, our passage lit by rays of sun too weak to warm. Arriving at our poloska, which was a chunk of the forest no different from the rest, the overseer exposed the extent of our site and told us to await our instructor. Experienced brigades toiled on nearby workstations, watched over by a guard, snug in his long woollen coat and peaked cap. Working at a hastened yet practised pace, trees were coming down everywhere.

There were places where bonfires were burning, and I assumed it was so workers could thaw themselves out if they became too cold to work, but no one was dawdling; there was no time to sit, smoke a cigarette or to take in the scenery. Work was progressing at an alarming rate. We had already crossed areas of bald landscape where it seemed as if a swarm of termites had chewed their way through the forest.

At our feet lay a dead tree, its massive splayed roots protruding like the petrified claws of a giant prehistoric bird. I swept the snow from its trunk and sat down. Are we expected to chop this lot down, I wondered; the task seemed insurmountable. 'What do we do about these fallen trees,' I asked? Many lay strewn across our site; others leaned higgledy-piggledy against the branches of neighbouring trees.

Assuming responsibility, Rysiek said, 'Take them down first, I suppose. We can't get at the other trees until we get these dead ones out of the way.' He smiled to himself. 'I think we're lucky, we won't have any problem meeting our norms. All we have to do is saw these up and stack them.

What a doddle.'

Our optimism was short-lived when the instructor arrived.

'First,' he said, 'not all trees are equal. Your job is to select only the best trees for felling. Old ones, such as these,' he kicked the one on which I sat, and I shot to my feet, 'are of no use. At some point, storms have toppled them and they are already in the process of decay. They are fit only for firewood, and you should first move them out of the way. Time spent removing these does not count towards your norms.

'The 'Dziesiatnik' in charge of production will be round later in the afternoon to measure what you have produced. Here,' he said, handing Rysiek a candle and some matches, 'I presume you know how to build a fire? There are plenty of rotting trees. Build it slowly. If it goes out, go to one of the other poloskas and light a branch from theirs.'

We watched him walk away to another workstation, and I turned to Rysiek, 'So, this will be a doddle will it?'

We set to work. This morning's fresh covering of snow was a nuisance, but nothing a young, vibrant team like ours couldn't handle. We had 'norms' to meet – no point dallying. However, as I soon discovered, the snow concealed rocks, undergrowth and brambles, and my knitted mittens offered no protection when the thorns pierced my flesh and soon became sodden. Removing the leaning trees also presented problems. Somehow, when shaken or hauled, they fell in all directions, and we had to get out of their path. Dragging those, even partially trapped beneath others, was much harder than we ever imagined.

'God, I'm sweating.' I removed one of my scarves and threw back my hood.

Rysiek sawed up one of the fallen trees. 'Right, let's drag a piece each to that clearing over there, and I'll make a start on the bonfire.'

'No, look, let's leave the fallen trees for the time being,' I suggested. 'I think we should make a start on chopping down some fresh ones. Otherwise, we'll never meet our norms.'

Rysiek thought about it, agreed, and as the feller of the brigade, he set about hacking away at the wet wood of a healthy tree, in a V formation as the instructor had shown him to do. He didn't get far before he needed a rest. We girls came to his rescue, and with frozen hands, we finished what he had begun, oblivious to a guard who, with arms akimbo, stood watching our performance on the sloping ground nearby. It was only later that I spotted him.

Soon the mighty fir was whooshing to the ground, sending up a flurry of snow as it landed. Helenka and I hacked off the branches; Luiza marked off the lengths and set about sawing them into logs while Rysiek dragged the branches to the clearing to make a start on the bonfire.

Half an hour later, I went to see what was

keeping him. He'd lost the candle and was messing about, moaning he had to fetch more burning branches from another bonfire and they kept going out before he got back – what a drip!

I helped with some small piles of rotted bark and soon a grand fire was warming our cheeks.

'Come on; let's get more dead trees,' Rysiek said. 'We need to build a good wigwam of them.'

That took up most of the morning. I looked about in dismay; we had done so little. Only the bonfire was doing well.

Rysiek and Luiza began arguing over the length of the tree trunk he felled because he'd taken the simple route and started chopping it at knee height, rather than at the roots. Now Luiza was left with two proper lengths, and another 'bit,' which was too short for the 'norm' and of no use. They would pay us only for two bits instead of three.

I listened to the exchange before Rysiek got the hump and took himself off to a nearby poloska to see how to do it. Luiza and I made a start on chopping down another tree, while Helenka thawed herself out by the fire.

'We have to expose the roots first,' I shifted snow away from around the base with my boot. Once we had a clear run at the trunk, we began hacking at it with our choppers. Tatta never told me it was this hard.

Luiza straightened up, holding her back. 'These axes are no good; they're blunt. We need a crosscut two-man saw. We'll never reach our 'norms' with these primitive things.'

'Yes, yes, alright.' I continued chopping. 'We'll ask for one tomorrow. Meanwhile, we'd better get on with it.' I gave a mighty thwack; my axe jammed in the trunk and wouldn't budge. Swearing under my breath, I straightened and ran the back of my hand across my forehead. 'Where's Rysiek? He's supposed to be the feller. This is his job, not ours.'

Luiza was hacking away from the other side. The tree creaked, tearing and rasping as it leapt off its stump, twisting to one side. We watched it topple as it made its way to the ground, heading straight for the bonfire where Helenka watched transfixed.

'Helenka, move! Get out of the way. It'll hit you!' Shouting, gesticulating, running sideways, we watched it thump onto the bonfire, sending up a flare-up of sparks, just missing her.

When Rysiek returned, all four of us spent the rest of the day removing fallen trees in readiness for a clear run tomorrow. That was the total of our day's achievement: two felled trees, one sawed into three pieces – one too short and therefore useless, the other left smouldering on top of the bonfire and a chaotic jumble of uprooted trees crisscrossing the forest floor. It was a disaster.

It was already growing dark. No point starting on another tree today. Exhausted, I sat down beside the bonfire and waited for the

Dziesiatnik to arrive to measure our day's production. We had worked so hard and knowing we had made no inroads into our norms, I wanted to cry. Now I understood why my father and my brothers were so obsessed with achieving their norms. With a lurking dread, I realised this would be my life forevermore. I couldn't bear it.

25

They disbanded our pathetic team and put me to work with an experienced brigade out Volosne way, near where Karol was working. Being a worker, they allowed me extra soup and bread rations, enabling me to share the bread with Mother. Sometimes I crossed paths with Karol and he would give me whatever money he had to take home to help.

The toil was relentless. By the start of November, I had developed leg ulcers on my left shin and calf, just as Sasha's little boy had before he died. I knew the consequences, but kept quiet because I was now the primary food provider for my mother and myself and only cared about meeting my norms.

Karol refused to return to Vodopad because the memories were still too raw, but showed his face once a month to collect a change of clothes. I was acting like a conduit getting back money to the family, but now my visits to Permilovo had stopped, and without Tatta's wages, we were struggling. My money was crucial to our survival. I could not afford to fall ill.

One morning, I was late for work. I had overslept and Mother, who worried about my declining health, had encouraged me to rest. Incensed, I leapt off my slats because my absence meant my brigade would not achieve their norms today let alone the punishment the overseer would mete out to me. The prospect of doing a week of solitary confinement in the Black Hole terrified me.

Ignoring Mother's pleas, I hurried off into the forest, hoping to God that Mr Demczuk would still be there in his boat to ferry me across the river. There was a rickety bridge further upstream, but it took longer to reach, and I was late enough.

Reaching the river, I saw him on the opposite bank, tying the boat to a tree, about to leave. I put two fingers into my mouth and gave a piercing whistle.

The moment he arrived, I jumped in and he began taking me across. To my horror, it leaked. The faster Demczuk rowed, the heavier the boat became, and the slower it went until his oars were going around like windmills, and the only place we were going was down.

With the water now lapping fast around my ankles and fearing we would sink and I would drown, I jumped overboard and dropped to the bottom of the river.

I remembered coming up and thrashing about for air before I went under again. Then it all went black. The next thing I remembered was floating and feeling a firm grasp around my windpipe as Demczuk, himself a weak swimmer, dragged me out of the river and laid me on the bank. When I opened my eyes, he was nearby on all fours, coughing his heart out.

The minute I could walk, we staggered back to Vodopad, drenched and freezing, and fell through the door.

'Jesús, Maria!' My mother threw more logs onto the stove and it flared into life.

'Your daughter, Mrs Glencova,' Demczuk said with ill-concealed fury, 'jumped overboard. She almost drowned and took me down with her.'

Mother thawed him out, lent him some dry clothes and that was the last I saw of him or his crummy boat.

It was when Mother stripped me of my soaked clothes and put me into something dry that she spotted my leg ulcers.

'Jesús, Maria! How long have you had those?'

There was no time to answer. She disappeared out of the door, calling for Lodzia to come quickly and look.

Raising myself off the slats, I looked at my leg.

'Come on, get near that stove and dry your hair. You have to go to the Bolnica. These are what Sasha's Jan died from.'

'Don't tell her that,' Lodzia said in alarm. 'You'll frighten her.'

'How is your general health?' the quack asked

after he had inspected my leg. He didn't look too concerned; perhaps he wasn't.

Was he stupid or what? I looked away.

'Answer the doctor, kohanie,' Mother said. 'He only wants to help you.'

Sucking in a lengthy breath, I said, 'I feel listless all the time. I'm prone to bouts of exhaustion. My legs and my muscles ache, I am starving all the time and I look like a walking skeleton. Apart from that, I feel just tickety-boo.'

Mother said, 'I am so sorry, that's teenagers for you.'

He cleaned up my leg and applied warm candle wax to each sore. 'Keep these dry. You won't be able to work for at least two months, maybe longer. I recommend plenty of rest and some nourishing food.' His gaze turned away as he recognised the absurdity of what he had just said.

'How can I not work? I have to work! I am a breadwinner – apart from my brother – and he's working away at Volosne. My other brother has to provide for his wife and child. They moved my father to the camp at Permilovo, and the last time I saw him, he was almost dead on his feet.' I spoke faster and faster, then burst into tears.

'What can I give you, child?' Mother said as we walked back to the shack. 'If only we could get you some berries, but it's winter.'

'Don't worry, Mama. I shall soon be dead and then I won't be a burden to anyone.'

'Please don't talk like that, kohanie, you are not a burden; I just feel so guilty that I can't give you proper food.'

I turned to her. 'Mama, this is not your fault. My God, don't you think I haven't noticed you sacrificing your rations so that Ella could have more? It's this God-forsaken-hole. They've got us all here, trapped like spiders beneath an upturned glass and each time one of us dies they flick away our bodies, and there are less and less of us, and yet we still have to toil in their damned forests and meet their bloody 'norms'.'

'I've never heard you swear so much.'

'Because this place is enough to make anyone swear. How can I live my life, Mama? Stefan and I want to get married, but we can't. Where would we live?'

'Married!'

'Yes, married. We love each other very much. But what's the point, Mama? Tell me, because I am at a complete loss to understand. What right had the Soviets to rob us of our freedom? I want to be free. We're human beings, not their slaves! What futures have we? We'll all be dead soon; me quicker than the others. They've already ruined Karol's life. No wonder he can't stand the sight of this place.'

We returned to the room we now called home, and I lay down on my slats nursing my tears, utterly miserable. 'I'm, sorry Mama, I'm no use to anyone, am I?'

Lodzia returned from the Banya with our washed clothes. She looked down at me wallowing in my misery and smiled. 'Hey, it's good that you don't have to work, Marishu. The rest will give you time to recover. Think yourself one of the lucky ones.' She picked up a saucepan, 'I'm off to the soup kitchen now.'

I felt worse because I realised that Mama and Lodzia would insist on sharing their food ration with me. Mine was still available at Volosne. It was bad enough that fate had denied me the right to earn my measly eight roubles – if we met our norms – but they would now cut my bread ration to a minuscule 800 grams a day. I would receive only one plate of soup and never recover my health. Far from feeling lucky, I faced the shattering truth that I was now one of those on the downward spiral towards death. It was inevitable. The Soviets had total control over my life. No one escaped.

I looked at my soaked clothes drying on the line over the stove and asked Mother if I could borrow her thickest shawl.

'Now where are you going?'

'To the cantina at Volosne, to eat my soup and get my bread.'

'Report to them here that you can no longer work. They will transfer your rations to Vodopad.'

'No, Mama, my rations will be smaller. As long as I can walk, I shall go. At least I can bring some bread home for you.'

'But you are ill, kohanie. You need to rest. Anyway, the boat sank.'

'Don't worry; I shall cross the river by the rickety bridge further upstream. I won't even have to pass my poloska so no one will see me. It will take me longer, but I don't care.' I looked at my mother's once beautiful face, now shrunken with hunger, and knew I was doing the right thing.

'But, kohanie...'

'Mama, I am not an invalid – yet. I can still walk. I got up for work this morning, didn't I? And if I hadn't jumped into that river, I would still be sawing their lousy trees.'

26

My plan worked for three days.

Although I received a larger food ration at Volosne – until they discovered my duplicity – I still had to pay for it. Without a wage at the end of the week, I would have no money left. I would have no option but to transfer my food ration to Vodopad and exist on the paltry portions of a non-worker. The other disadvantage was that I would no longer see Karol when he needed to give us money. Too bad; he would have to return to us more often. Natasha was long gone; he couldn't grieve after her forever.

Returning home with the last portion of bread for my mother, I knew something was wrong when I passed the window to our darkened room. Perhaps we had run out of paraffin. I felt a stab of guilt for not being here to fetch more, leaving her to sit in the dark. But she was missing, and the room was cold.

Setting down the bread, I lifted the lamp, surprised to find it half full. It was so unlike her to let the fire die down, but the last log had collapsed into cigar-like ash. I had to tickle the embers back to life with twigs before it retook and I could bank it with logs.

Someone holding a lamp passed by our window, and snowflakes bounced against the light. I rushed to the door, but it wasn't Mama returning. Everything seemed wrong; why was she even out in the dark – in this weather? I stood alone in the empty room, and I was afraid; she had always been there for me – it was something I took for granted.

Once satisfied I had rescued the fire, and the flames were coursing up the flue, I went next door to Lodzia's room and found her asleep on the slats, her arms entwined around Ella, who was barely visible beneath her eiderdown.

Having barged in, I tiptoed out again, but too late – Lodzia awoke with a start. 'Sorry, I must have nodded off. Is Mama back yet?'

Cold fingers of fear clutched at my heart. 'No, what time did she go out?'

'I have no idea. She wasn't here when I returned with the soup at about one o'clock.'

I moved forward into the room again, 'I'm worried, Lodziu. The fire is almost out, and the little clock's gone.'

Lodzia rose and reached for her shawl. 'I never noticed the clock. She glanced at her wristwatch. Where could she be?'

Mama never went anywhere when it was snowing. She didn't own a coat, and even her thickest shawls were as nothing against the Russian winter, but she was out now.

I ran from room to room asking each of our neighbours if they had seen her, but no one had.

I ran to the nearby shacks – still nothing. Most of them were still at work. With mounting alarm, I returned to our shack expecting to see her sitting on her slats, but she had still not returned.

'Well?'

'Nothing.' I fought back my tears and told myself that there had to be a logical explanation. The shop, the cantina, the club, the banya, every possibility drew a blank.

'You don't think she may have gone in search of Tatta? She was saying only yesterday he might be dead by now and wondered why they hadn't returned his body, but they never do, do they? What's another corpse to the Soviets?'

My mind refused to make sense of what Lodzia was implying. Mama didn't know the way there, and she was too frail to make such a journey. 'But it's madness.'

'Yes; it is madness; even I wouldn't be so stupid unless I wanted to end it all.'

'End it?' The thought hadn't occurred to me. 'But why would she want to do that? She adores us all, especially Ella.'

'Because she can't live without Tatta; they were devoted.'

Dear God. All this was my fault. Had I not been so pre-occupied with my savage lust for a bigger chunk of bread and an extra plateful of soup, I might have been here to stop her. I slid my palms down my cheeks as reality dawned; I could never forgive myself if anything happened to my darling Mama.

*

The lateness of the hour had turned the sky into inky blackness when Alina Zadarnowska came tearing into our room, shouting her head off that Anna Glencova had collapsed near the river on the path leading to the Kolkhoz.

She was babbling something about Mother wanting to accompany her to Kholmogorki earlier in the day, wanting to sell a clock, but she dissuaded her.

I grabbed my coat and the lamp and fled with a strength I thought had long since deserted me. Alina Zadarnowska ran after me, but I was too fast for her and it was snowing mercilessly. 'Where is she? Where is she?'

She caught up, out of puff, barely able to catch her breath. 'There, there,' she pointed.

Slanting snow drove into my eyes, and I could barely see. 'Mama!' Oh God, she wasn't moving. 'Here, hold this,' I thrust the lamp into Alina's hands. Mama was curled up in the snow. I was already crying as I put my cheek to her lips, but they were cold. I felt the pulse in her neck. It was faint, but still there. 'She's almost frozen!' I put my hands beneath her arms and tried to lift her out of the snow, but it was hopeless. She was a dead weight, and I found my energy sapping. 'Don't just stand there, give me a hand then.'

Alina wedged the lamp in the snow and came to assist, but we could only drag her into the middle of the path.

'Mama, wake up, wake up!' I patted her

cheeks, rubbed her hands. 'Help! Somebody, please help me!'

People returning from work sidestepped her – others paused to look, but continued on their way, too exhausted, hungry and cold to care.

After several attempts, Mother opened her eyes and gave me a feeble smile. 'Leave me, child. It's no use. Go home.'

'I'm not leaving you, Mama,' I pulled her into my arms and cradled her to the warmth of my chest, while Alina searched for a strong man to help us. But there were no strong men.

'There's some money in the pocket of my skirt. I sold the clock to Boris and Roza. Take it and go home; it should last you a while.'

'But why, Mama, and in this weather!'

'Because I wanted to put a stop to your daily visits to Volosne. There's enough money here to get you some more food from the shop. Don't worry; it's too late for me.'

'But there *is* no more food, Mama. It's winter.' Knowing this, I felt even worse. 'You mustn't give up. Please, stay alive – for me. How will I live without you?' I rubbed her hands, tried to revive her circulation.

Amongst a crowd of workers returning from the forest, Gerhard heard the commotion. As exhausted as he was, he slid his arms under Mama's body and carried her home.

'Is she still alive?' Lodzia spread her bedding beside the stove, and I provided the pillow.

'Just.' Gerhard laid her down, unsure what to

do next.

Lodzia reached for the soup pan and stuck it onto the stove to reheat, while I rubbed and patted Mama's hands and legs, watching her face all the time.

She groaned when the blood reached her extremities. Gerhard moved her away from the stove and laid her on her slats. 'What were you thinking going out in this weather with just a few shawls? Are you mad?'

'I know, I'm sorry, but I needed to sell the clock.'

'Then why didn't you ask Lodzia to do it? She wouldn't have minded.'

'Ahh, I don't know. Lodzia's always so busy queuing for food; she has washing to do and Ella to look after. I assumed I'd get more for the clock if I took it to Kholmogorki, but that Alina wouldn't take me. So, I went to see Boris and Roza instead. On the way back I slipped and fell; I think I've broken my ankle and my hip.'

'I wouldn't have minded going, Mama,' Lodzia said.

Guilt pestered me still. This was all my doing. I should have been here, pulling my weight, helping Lodzia; not embarking on six-kilometre treks through the forest in search of food.

Everyone fussed and fretted, relieved to do so. Gerhard examined her ankle and hip, prodding and poking, ripped up a tablecloth and bound her foot. 'I think it's a bad sprain. Fortunately, I think your hip is just bruised; you have no fat to cushion your bones.'

The door opened and Karol appeared just as I said, 'Mama, please don't criticise Alina; had it not been for her, you would have perished out there.'

'My boy!' Her eyes lit up the moment she saw him, my rebuke forgotten. She stretched out her arms and he bent down and kissed her.

'Why would you have perished, Mama?'

'Ahh, ignore them; it was nothing.'

'Nothing, huh? Look at the size of your foot,' Gerhard said.

'I know, I know, I'm a silly woman, and I won't do it again. At least I got a good price. We need the money.'

Clearly Karol hadn't a clue what was going on here in his absence. 'Any news of Tatta?'

Mama said, 'I think he must be dead. And if he survived, what use would he be to the Ruskies in his state?' There was wistfulness in the way she said this, as if she had already accepted his death before she knew for certain. 'I want his body back. We need to bury him.'

Karol took himself off to the banya to get clean and remained subdued; he was still missing Natasha. We ate our usual bowl of soup and a slice of bread, while our father's absence hung between us. He had always been such a massive presence in our lives in every way; now the void was unbearable.

On Sunday, Karol whispered something to Mother just before he left for Volosne, and she reached into her pocket and handed over the proceeds from selling the clock.

* * *

A week later when Stefan called for me, he was not alone. Pushing open the door, he said, 'Look who I found outside.'

From out of the shadows stepped Karol, supporting Tatta. He could barely walk, his gentle features suspended between joy and relief.

All of us were instantly on our feet.

'Dear God! Ignacy!' Mama hobbled to his side, slid her arms around his torso and lowered him onto the slats nearest the stove. 'I thought you were dead.'

Tatta rested his forehead against Mama's cheek, his eyes glistening with a serenity that was gratitude.

Too stunned to speak, I gazed in astonishment, elated beyond belief to have Tatta back with us, yet mortified by the ramifications of what Karol had just done. When I last spoke with Kommendant Ivanov, he assured me he was still doing all he could to get Tatta transferred to Vodopad, but these things took time, sometimes a very long time. Sometimes it was impossible. Now that Tatta had morphed out of the blue, how would we explain his presence? Karol had dropped us all in it, and our entire family was now in trouble.

Mother said, 'How did you do it, son?

'I used the money from the sale of the clock to bribe the Ukrainian who let me borrow the horse to bring back Natasha.'

'And he allowed you all this time off?'

'It cost me, but it was worth it. He's a decent sort – despises the Soviets as much as we do. I left early on Sunday before it was light.'

'Yes, but how did you find Tatta at the sawmills?'

'He was in the bread queue; it was either there or in the cantina.'

'And what if he wasn't?'

'Then I'd have knocked on every door, declaring I'd got the wrong shack.'

'And no one saw you leave?'

'Probably, but we didn't look suspicious. I tethered the horse in the woods at the back of the sawmill where it wouldn't be seen, and once I'd found Tatta, we went back to his room, collected his eiderdown, rolled it up tight and left the rest of his clothes behind. They were filthy anyway.

'The place isn't guarded; people are moving around all the time. Once I'd got him on the horse and swaddled in his eiderdown, we just upped and went.'

'What have you done with the horse?' I asked.

'Left him outside.' Karol got to his feet. 'I plan to leave early. Meanwhile I need to get him inside somewhere, or he'll be stiff by morning.'

I stared in disbelief, 'You fool. Someone will

see it, and think it's one of ours. They'll lock it in the stable, and you'll never get it back.'

'No, they won't; he's between the shacks.'

I turned my back to the family so Tatta wouldn't hear. 'Karol how are we going to explain this when Kommendant Ivanov sees Tatta back here? How are we going to reinstate his food rations at Vodopad? We are in such trouble.' All we needed now was a dead horse rotting outside our shack because none of us would have the strength to move a great lump like that.

'Who cares? Tatta would have been dead by then. Just tell him that the Kommendant at Permilovo released him; he knows we've been trying to get him back for long enough. Who's going to argue? Ivanov won't know; he'll think the other Kommendant did as he asked. At least he's alive.'

He was right, of course. 'Meanwhile, where do we put this horse?'

Karol stared at Gerhard. 'I thought I might put him in your room.'

'Don't be so ridiculous,' Lodzia said. 'I'm not sleeping with a horse!'

'No, no, I thought we could all move into this room for the night?'

Gerhard said, 'I'm sorry Karol, it's out of the question. Take him elsewhere.'

I reached for my coat. 'Come on Karol; there must be somewhere else we can put him.'

Stefan, who had been listening to this

throughout, shot to his feet. 'There's space in the Artel, but I haven't got a key. I shall have to tell my father, but he won't be pleased.'

'What about putting him in the club then? There's plenty of space in there.'

'Oh yes, and he'll shit all night. That, Karol, is an idiotic idea. How will you explain that away? Horses make huge turds; you can hardly mistake them for a rat's dropping.'

Stefan's father was not best pleased either. 'I want him out of here long before the workers turn up in the morning,' he kept saying. 'I mean it, Karol; otherwise, we will all end up in solitary confinement.'

Karol left for Volosne very early. 'I'll be back on Sunday,' he promised, but before he left, he took Mother's hand, placed some money into her palm, and curled her fingers around it. 'There's still plenty left.'

Exhausted by the excitement of having Tatta back, and worrying about how I was going to explain his presence to Kommendant Ivanov, I lay awake all night. He had to believe me because Tatta needed his rations reinstating at Vodopad.

I was waiting for him when he arrived, but refused to set foot inside the Admin shack. I had to make this brief, and my effusive gratitude surprised him.

'I'm pleased to hear it,' he said, 'and how did your father arrive?'

I looked non-plussed. 'He said someone from Permilovo brought him on a sleigh. He would never have made it on foot; he's far too frail to work. The Kommendant at Permilovo knew that; I told him the last time I was there.'

There was no doubt in my mind that Ivanov did not believe a word of it by the way he stared at me, but I held my ground. 'I won't keep you; I just wanted to thank you from our whole family. Oh, and how do I get my father's rations here reinstated?'

With a raised brow, Ivanov was already making for the steps. 'Leave it with me, young lady; I'll make sure Vice-Kommendant Smirnov sees to it.'

27

Our first Christmas in bondage arrived.

A scrap of paper nailed to the shop door announced: Carp and reindeer meat will be available for purchase on 23rd December.

With those sparse words, Szefczuk had managed to elevate everyone's gastronomic expectations to such euphoric levels that Gerhard and Karol decided it wasn't worth going to bed – they would be first in the queue.

'Don't be daft.' Father called after them when they set off for the shop just before midnight, 'It's snowing. You'll freeze to death standing around.'

'Your father's right,' Mother said. 'There will be plenty for everyone; go with Lodzia in the morning when she fetches the bread.'

'You won't be saying that when we return with reindeer meat,' Karol laughed.

Lodzia and I agreed to take over at two a.m. but overslept. I wouldn't have got out of bed for anything – except for meat – any meat was worth the effort.

Mother said Szefczuk should have allowed us to collect it earlier; it would need a good soaking before cooking.

I wrapped my feet in woollen leg bands,

stuffed them into my valenki, and accepted the shawl Mama insisted I throw over my coat for good measure.

Lodzia bent over the lamp and squinted at her wristwatch. 'It's just after three-thirty. 'Gerhard and Karol will never forgive us.'

I was at the window now, peering through the swirling white curtain of snow, hoping it might have abated, but it looked as if it was snowing harder than when my brothers left.

Opening the outside door, half the powdery stuff that had drifted against the wall fell in on me, spilling into the hallway. Walking was difficult, but we put our heads down and fought against the blizzard. Most of Vodopad must have assembled outside the shop because the queue snaked up from the river almost to the administration shack.

We trudged along the line, searching out Gerhard and Karol's faces, but it was hard when everyone was stomping around, covered in snow, their bodies turned away from the wind.

I was tempted to give up and go back to bed then, but the thought of us all eating carp on Christmas Eve, and venison on Christmas Day spurred me on.

'I see the NKVD aren't losing any sleep waiting for their measly bit of meat,' Lodzia said.

We found my brothers right near the front, stamping their feet, thrashing themselves with their arms. Here was the right spot; we would get the best cuts.

A light flickered inside the shop and Szefczuk, holding his lamp aloft, unbolted the door. The crowd stampeded forwards, nearly trampling us underfoot in their enthusiasm to get into the building.

'Hey!' I elbowed someone out of the way, 'we were here before you!'

'Form two queues,' Mrs Szefczuk's voice was almost inaudible amidst the furore.

'Form two queues!' Szefczuk yelled. 'No one will get served until you do. It's up to you.'

Everyone fell into line, and I realised that we were no longer near the front, but about twelve people back. Everyone was craning their necks for a glimpse of the meat when those at the counter started complaining it was such a stingy portion.

'It was never intended to be a feast,' Szefczuk insisted. 'It's plenty big enough for soup.'

When the four of us reached the counter, all the reindeer meat had gone.

'What do you mean gone?' Gerhard was incensed. 'What was it, a calf, because it certainly wasn't a bull?'

'What did you expect,' Szefczuk yelled back, 'that the Nenets slaughter their entire herd just for you?'

'We've been waiting out there since before midnight! You try standing in a blizzard for four hours!'

'I'm sorry. I'm sorry. There were only half a dozen pieces left anyway,' Szefczuk looked like a man terrified for his life. 'We Ukrainians had first pick, but we have plenty of carp. Enough for everyone.'

Through gritted teeth, Gerhard said, 'Good. I'll take seven.'

Christmas Eve arrived, but there was no excitement – not like back home.

Mother invited Sasha because she would have been alone, and our little room was full of bodies.

'I remember embroidering this.' She pulled the crochet-trimmed cloth from the pile in the corner. At home, it only came out on special occasions. 'It was part of my bottom drawer; it was a labour of love.' She sighed then. 'Seems like a lifetime ago now– it *was* a lifetime ago.' There was no point laying the table yet; it was covered in pots and pans while she and Lodzia prepared the meal.

Father delved into his box of shoemaking paraphernalia and brought out three beeswax candles. 'These are the last three.' He placed them on the windowsill, where they melted the frostwork tracery of leaves that adorned the panes and infused the room with the delicate scent of sweet honey.

Lodzia lifted the knife and beheaded the carp as if she were decapitating Sczefczuk. She threw their heads into the soup pan and enriched it with pearl barley, before placing the carp into another container to simmer. 'He can stick his reindeer meat. We have carp – and noodles, thanks to Sasha here.'

We all made appreciative noises. Dried noodles were a rarity.

Sasha was just grateful she could contribute something to the evening and was thankful when Mother invited her to join us.

'Marishu, take this soup next door and put it on my stove to cook,' Lodzia said, and I obliged. Stefan and I were spending Christmas Eve apart – he shared Wigilia with his own family, but I would have him all to myself tomorrow, and I couldn't wait.

There was no room around the tiny table, and we sat eating our meal from plates on our laps. What we lacked in food and space, we made up for with memories of past Wigilia's when food was plentiful, the cherry vodka flowed and St. Nicholas had already left his gifts for the children beneath their pillows on the 6th December.

Poor little Ella. I realised she hasn't received a single gift. We have nothing to give her. However, I was wrong; Mother had one last treat – a small packet of Halva for Ella, and another to share between us all.

'This is from Boris and Roza. They gave it to me when I sold them my clock, but only if I promised them, I would save it for Christmas.'

* * *

The New Year roared in on a blizzard, the two

days of Christmas already a distant memory – one best forgotten. Karol was back at the camp in Volosne, and Gerhard left for the forest at five o'clock each morning. They were now the sole breadwinners.

I should also have been out there working, but I inspected my leg ulcers, and while they were no better – neither were they any worse. Perhaps the candle wax was working after all. Hmm, perhaps the quack wasn't such a charlatan.

'Don't even think it, Marishu,' Mother read my thoughts. 'We'll manage somehow.'

I didn't see how we could. God, I was depressed. Suddenly the Soviet tenet of, 'He who does not work, does not eat', began to clang. I *had* to resume work. Tatta was still coughing, his lungs rasping with phlegm, and he was deathly thin. The quack pronounced him unfit to work, but at least he was now recognisable as Ignacy Glenz.

Standing in the queue with Lodzia to collect bread and soup this morning, I wondered how much longer we could exist like this. Back home there was always a chicken for the pot; a pig to slaughter; cured meats from its proceeds and plenty of fruit and vegetables. Oh, and the eggs and the milk, so rich and creamy. I hadn't tasted milk since last year in Boris and Roza's shack, and all I could do was live on the memories.

This bloody snow, this bloody place; this constant queuing; everything irritated me today to the point I could scream. Not only was there barely anything to eat, but the worst of it was that the Soviets had deprived us of the only thing we had left in this world – hope. Tatta kept repeating his mantra of, 'Have hope child, have hope; something always turns up', to the point I thought, yeah, yeah whatever. How could I hope - and for what? I neither believed in miracles nor in fairy tales. The irrefutable fact was that we had been brought here to die – and that day was drawing nearer, given the huge numbers who had already perished. Their make-shift graves beside the shacks where they once lived were a poignant reminder lest we tried to forget.

Returning with our rations three hours later, I found my father sat at the table, its top strewn with the contents of his shoe-making paraphernalia box. Mother was boiling woollen cloth in the pan on the stove, prodding it with the handle of her wooden spoon.

'Novak sent a customer for a pair of boots. He reckons there may be more. He said people's feet are in a pathetic state; their valenki are worn out.'

I sat down beside him. 'Will you have enough felt, Tatta?'

'At the moment, yes. This customer brought a blanket for Mama to boil down. But I can see it becoming a problem if the word spreads and we get a rush of orders – unless they all do the same. I still have plenty of everything else I need.'

'Will he pay you?'

'I suppose I shall have to make a small charge to cover my costs – and we have to live – but I don't want to fleece anyone.'

'No Tatta, you must charge a reasonable price. If Stefan's father said there might be more, you have to look at it as a business. They need boots to be able to work and earn money; we need money to buy food. Simple as that.'

I saw admiration in the way he stared at me, and the traces of a smile played about his lips. 'When did you develop such a business brain? I never knew you had it in you.'

Neither did I. 'Look, Tatta, we could make a go of this. I could help you. Stefan always said that we could have a good thing going. It beats chopping down their blessed trees. You thought I made a good job of those three pairs I made when we first arrived, didn't you?'

'I did indeed, child. I couldn't fault them.'

Word spread, and the orders for valenki multiplied to the point where my father began to worry there might not be enough tar and hogs' hair to coat the twine. People didn't seem to care; all they wanted was a pair of boots that would protect their feet and keep them warm.

My hands were stained again from coating the hogs' hair with tar and stitching the soles, but there was too much work for my father to manage alone. We were not out to make a fortune, but every rouble went into the family coffers, and we no longer had to worry about meeting 'norms'. Spring was on its way, Mother was able to afford an extra bag of flour, and the odd piece of Halva that appeared in the shop.

When the orders dried up, my father went to help Novak in the Artel and earned a few more roubles.

In truth, we were destitute, but rich beyond belief because unlike some families; we had each other. Best of all I had Stefan. Without him, this place would have been hell on earth. However, when there was nothing in the shop left to buy, we fell back on the soup rations from the cantina and starved for the rest of the time.

Sometimes I used to stop mid-stitch, to gaze out of the window and imagine that Stefan and I were not people at all, but flamingos. We were happy and well-nourished, soaring and whirling in an infinite sky, while below us thousands of kilometres of forest carpeted the earth.

Searching for food, we might have swooped lower, and now the mighty Northern Dvina came into view, its estuary a cacophony of birds feasting on the abundant marine life. However, we were looking for more than just food; we were searching for suitable habitat, somewhere to nest, to rear our young where flora and fauna were beautiful, where there was plenty to eat, and we were safe; somewhere we could live out our days in love, peace and harmony.

Flying over Kholmogorki, we altered direction as a dense band of green on the horizon beckoned. Reaching the forest edge, we swooped and whirled over endless kilometres of woodland, where little light penetrated the thick canopy of trees. Coming to rest on the uppermost branches of a larch, we could now see the forest floor where, because of the gloom, only ferns and a few herbaceous plants grew. Mosses, liverworts and lichens grew on tree trunks and their branches, and sable, ermines and martens scurried around at their leisure.

Having found our Shangri-La, we soared and dipped once more, flying higher and higher until – wait a minute, what was that in the clearing below beside the Vaymuga River?

It was a camp full of misery where people were toiling. No, they were not people, they were walking skeletons. How did they get there? Surely no one could have known they were there; otherwise, they would have rescued them. Their unblinking eyes were staring ahead; exhaustion etched into their haggard faces. No one smiled. This was not the happy place we birds thought it was. Alarmed, we circled over the camp once more, before flying away as fast as we could, leaving the forgotten people of Vodopad to their fate, thankful we were birds and not human beings.

PART TWO

28

Late August 1941.

Sleep eluded me. I thrashed around on my slats, swatting away bark beetles, willing morning to arrive, but time dragged.

It was Monday, and Kommendant Ivanov cancelled all the work today. It felt odd. Yesterday had felt even more odd. Never, in a year and a half, could I remember anything like this happening. The piece of paper, nailed to the community centre door, had been attracting speculating crowds all day and well into the evening. Stefan and I kept strolling past to see if it was still there, wondering if the wording might have changed, but it hadn't. There it hung, and people hung around it, so it had to be something serious. Like many people here, I could speak but not read Russian, and now wished I'd taken the time to learn the Cyrillic alphabet.

According to those who could, the message was simple; everyone was to assemble outside the Admin office at 10.00 a.m. when Kommendant Ivanov would address us.

Stefan and his family were already there when

we arrived, and I waved. He came over, slipped his arm around my waist and kissed my forehead. 'Let's hope this isn't someone's sick joke.'

I smiled at him. I so wanted whatever it was, to be pleasant news for us, but knew well in this hellhole of life versus death; the outcome might be dire. There was no point speculating, but the murmuring crowd was restless with anxious looks on many faces.

Kommendant Ivanov appeared on the step and waited for the crowd to settle. He held a piece of paper from which he read.

'In a pre-dawn offensive, on the 22nd June, Hitler's troops invaded the USSR and the Soviet Union is now at war with Germany.

As a result, your Prime Minister, Wladyslaw Sikorski, has been in negotiations with Ivan Mayski, the Soviet Ambassador to the United Kingdom. I can now report that we will free all Poles to join a new Polish army, which will form in the southern states of the Soviet Union. Or you can enter the Soviet Army if you prefer.

Therefore, Comrade Stalin has granted amnesty to all Poles as of 12th August 1941. All work ceases as of today, and you are all free to leave.'

Following a momentary silence, an enormous cheer erupted. People started hugging and kissing. Stefan and I were laughing and crying in disbelief. Giddy with joy and excitement, I flung my arms around his neck, and we kissed and kissed. We were free!

The furore continued until Smirnov fired a shot in the air and restored order.

'Identity papers,' Kommendant Ivanov continued, 'which will serve as a family travel document – I stress – a *family* travel document – and a *one-way* travel permit to a destination of your choice will be issued to heads of families as soon as we receive them.

'I ask you to be patient. However, there is to be no return to your former homeland. I repeat, return to Eastern Poland is not allowed under *any* circumstances. You will be free to leave as soon as you wish. No one will stand in your way. If you require help, Vice Kommendant Smirnov will do all he can to assist. However, it is your responsibility to cover the cost of your train fares and provide yourselves with food.'

The crowd sent up a collective howl, some shouting, 'How do you expect us to do that? We can't afford the food here!'

'You can always reapply for your old jobs as Polish Free Workers, until your papers arrive,' the Kommendant suggested.

A woman shouted, 'Where shall we get the money if we are travelling instead of working? None of us have savings. We can't do both! We'll starve before we reach this new army.'

He ignored her question, saying instead,

'Food rations will be available for you to buy as usual from the cantina or the settlement shop for as long as stocks last.' A nano-second elapsed, there were no further questions, and he vanished inside. Announcement over.

'He's weaselled out of all responsibility for us.' Karol shook his head in disgust. 'These Soviets are just a shower of shit.'

'It'll be alright. We shall manage.' Tatta squeezed my shoulder, 'Didn't I tell you always to have hope, child?' He lifted my chin and gazed into my eyes. 'Well?'

I laid my head against his chest and hugged him. 'I know, Tatta, I should have believed you.'

Karol was looking despondent. Perhaps he was thinking about Natasha. Had she waited six months longer, and stood up to her mother, they would be free to leave together.

Stefan gazed at me in disbelief. 'Hey, why the glum face? We have a future. We can marry, live a normal life anywhere we please – well, apart from Poland.'

He was right, but there were obstacles. Why wasn't life straightforward? 'Stefan, how can we marry? You heard him; first, we have to join the army and fight to save Stalin's miserable skin.'

'Then we shall fight. Our families will travel together, and we shall enlist together. It will be alright. Don't worry.'

I took a deep breath of freedom. Even the walk back to our shack felt different without the yoke of slavery hanging over us. Jumbled thoughts of what lay ahead demanded answers: what would it mean to enlist? What would they expect us to do? Could Stefan and I stay together in this newly formed Polish Army? Where would we fight? I hadn't a clue what went on in armies, and my ignorance alarmed me.

Father was thinking ahead too. 'If we have to stump up the rail fare, we had better sell off what we have left.'

Mother agreed. 'We'll sell it all, my sewing machine, the pots and pans. The lot! What's the point of lumbering ourselves with possessions?'

Lodzia looked pensive. 'Gerhard and I have nothing left. All we have is what he earns, apart from my wristwatch; but it was his wedding present to me, and I cherish it. The Soviets have reduced us to vagrants.'

'Then take my embroidered tablecloth,' Mother said. 'You could sell it.'

I said, 'No Mama, please don't part with that. It's priceless; I love it. It took you so long to make.'

'Ahh, it's only worth what someone will pay for it; and the Ukrainians will give us next to nothing.'

'Then keep it, Mama, please. It's all we have left to remind us of home. Instead, why don't we nail a notice to the Community Centre door advertising Tatta's boot-making service for those in need? Look, some people have bound their feet in rags.'

'Only if they provide the cloth,' Father

insisted, then added, 'They won't be waterproof; I've no more hogs' hair nor tar, but I don't suppose it stops me making ordinary boots. There's plenty of tree bark for insoles. Not that I'll be making many as we'll be out of here the moment my documents arrive.'

'So that means we can't get rid of the pans or the sewing machine yet,' Lodzia said.

A week passed, and the entire camp was still waiting for their family travel documents to arrive. Little by little frustration replaced euphoria.

Two weeks passed, and I was growing impatient. 'Tatta, when do you think our papers will arrive? I want to get out of here.'

'Soon. They'll be here soon.'

'Yes, but how soon? Why's it taking so long?' I hated this lack of control over our situation, annoyed and frustrated by the lack of progress. We were free, for goodness sakes.

Tatta was working on a pair of valenki for a family who had no shoes at all. 'Be patient, child. Stamping your foot won't get them here any quicker. Thread this needle for me, would you; my eyesight's worsening.'

Even I had to go and stand by the window to see the eye of the needle.

Fuming, Karol returned from the Admin shack, having gone in search of his confiscated bike. 'So much for asking Smirnov for help; the bastard's sold it! He had no right to take it. I could have sold it myself, now we need the money.'

'If our papers aren't here soon,' Gerhard said, 'I'm going to reapply for my old job. We still need to eat. Plenty already have.'

Later, Lodzia returned from the shop enraged. 'Szefczuk's cut our rations. He said the boat from the magazine has stopped visiting Vodopad. We're no longer the Soviet's responsibility, so he's cut our daily rations to 800 grams of bread for workers and 400 grams for everyone else.'

'That's decided it; I'm returning to work.'

'Me too,' Karol added, 'or we'll never get out of here.'

By the third week, those overwhelming emotions of elation and joy had fizzled out, replaced by fear. Nothing at all was happening. No one had seen Kommendant Ivanov for days, and rumour spread he had already left Vodopad; his services were needed elsewhere, although Smirnov was still here.

Swiping the basket off the floor, I paused at the door. 'I'm going berry picking because I have another leg ulcer forming.'

Mother examined the sore. 'Jesús María! We had better get you to the doctor.'

'Forget it,' Lodzia said. 'No one has seen him either. Wait for me, Marishu, I'll come with you.'

'Bring nettles,' mother called after us, 'and mushrooms if you can. I'll make soup.'

*

At last, the news arrived. They would issue family travel documents the following day, starting with A-D, then E-H on the next morning, and so on. All heads of the family should present themselves on the required days. Everyone gave up work to be ready to leave at the first available moment.

The NKVD Regional Commander Ogarkov came to Vodopad and proposed four likely destinations: Czymkient, Akmolinsk, Aktyubinsk and Uralsk. Most chose Aktyubinsk – all in Soviet Kazakhstan. However, we were told to be clear in stating our choice; otherwise, our papers would be invalid.

Patience was not my virtue. I hardly dared allow myself the pleasure of excitement, but with our surname beginning with G, we had to wait until Monday. 'Tatta, may I come with you and Gerhard when you go?' I wanted to savour every moment of our impending freedom.

'Try to curb your enthusiasm, child. We'll be out of here soon enough. It allows only heads of families.'

Monday arrived, and I urged Father and Gerhard to go early. I almost pushed them out of the shack. They needed to be first in the queue.

'We can never be first in the queue,' Tatta laughed, 'E and F come before G remember?' He and Gerhard set off for the Admin shack; their eyes bright with joy.

They returned in less than an hour, but they were no longer smiling.

Gerhard announced the news, since Father was too distraught. 'I've got our papers, Lodziu, but there's a problem with Tatta's.'

The impact of his words had me spinning down into a black chasm of desolation.

'Did they say why?' Mother asked.

Karol paced about the room. 'Well, there has to be some mistake. A mix-up. Glenz is not a common name. They couldn't have given our papers to anyone else.'

Father said, 'Smirnov told me they'd arrive later or might be mixed up in one of the other boxes. He suggested I go mid-afternoon when they've finished handing out the others.'

We waited and waited, but by late afternoon, our papers had still not arrived.

Those who had already received their family travel documents, and could afford the train fare, immediately left, setting off on foot through the forest to Kholmogorki. Gerhard and Lodzia stayed behind, refusing to leave without the rest of our family. Lodzia sold her wristwatch to Roza to raise money for their train fare.

Stefan, whose family had received their travel document, kept stalling them, begging them to hang on a few more days – another week, two weeks. Unable to wait any longer, his father overrode him, leaving him with no say in the matter. Their identity papers doubled up as a family travel document requiring them *all* to travel together – and they were going. *Him* included!

I was mortified. 'What are we going to do, Stefan? We might never meet up again.'

He gazed into my eyes, and he was helpless. 'What *can* we do? I have no choice but to go. If I stayed behind, I'd have no papers at all, and then I wouldn't be able to travel anywhere with you when your father got his. You would have to go with them, and I'd be stuck here forever without you. Look, it'll be alright. Our fathers have both agreed that we meet up at Aktyubinsk. I'm sure your papers will be here soon. There are lots of other families in the same situation, and I mean lots. Don't you worry; I shall be there waiting for you at the railway station. I promise. You don't get rid of me that quickly.'

'That's what I mean, Stefan. There are *too* many families without papers; there can't be a mix-up over them all! Something's wrong. We'll never be free, and then you'll be gone.'

29

Stefan and I spent our last few hours together, our arms entwined in each other's warmth, wandering along the banks of the Vaymuga because when I awoke tomorrow morning, he would be gone.

I cried freely; couldn't stop; I missed him already. Instead of living each last moment, unbidden cameos kept appearing of him, eyes smiling, striding into our room to collect me after work, and later our shared private moments saying goodnight on the porch outside our shack until Mama came out and almost dragged me inside.

When it was time for us to part, I still clung to him. As our lips brushed apart, another flood of tears blurred my sight, and he left me. I couldn't bear it.

* * *

Another brutal Russian winter took hold.

When Stefan was here, he used to leave an energy behind him as if things could happen, but nothing was happening now; nothing but emptiness resonating throughout the camp.

Gerhard, Lodzia and Ella no longer occupied the room next door. They left Vodopad two weeks ago because Lodzia worried they might still not afford both food and train tickets. Their leaving tore the family apart, but Tatta urged them to go. We agreed to meet up at Aktyubinsk, and that was an end of it. At least part of the family was free.

His sentiment shocked me and caused me to question his logic. Did staying here mean we were all doomed? Had he lost hope and given up?

Everything had changed since we were no longer prisoners, yet in many ways everything remained the same. In between helping my father stitch valenki, which people begged him to make, I collected our tiny bread rations, often pausing on the banks of the river, wondering where Stefan was right now. I imagined it was sweltering and he would be sweating. Was he thinking of me, as often as I thought of him? At the back of my mind was this constant, terrifying thought of being trapped here forever because father's papers had still not arrived. How would I ever cope without him? From day to day I shuffled around feeling out of balance – waylaid somehow. Time dragged and the drudgery increased.

By the middle of December Karol had run out of patience, and taking matters in hand, asked Father if he might take some money he was saving for travel, and visit the Polish Consulate in Archangelsk to see what was holding things up.

Father doubted it would do any good, reasoning, 'What if you fail, son? Then we'll have lost our money?'

'But, Tatta, what good's the money without the travel document? Please let him try. They've had plenty of time to find our papers; something must be wrong.' I thought it a fantastic idea.

Father glanced at Mother.

Mother shrugged and nodded. 'Marisha's right.'

A week later, Karol walked through the door, triumphantly shaking our travel document. He had all three of us instantly on our feet. 'They had no intention of freeing us,' he said.

'Karol, this is brilliant!' Father took the paper and scanned it. 'Well done, son!'

Mother ran to hug him. '*Kohanie*, this is *such* a relief. *Thank* you, thank you so much.'

Overjoyed, I snatched it from Tatta. 'Let me see it. When can we leave?'

Karol warmed his hands by the stove. 'Well, we might have a problem. I've spent all the money.'

I stared at him in disbelief. 'Spent it on what?'

'Train fares, accommodation, food – what do you think I've spent it on?'

'So, we're still stuck here?' Slapping the

document back at Karol, I sat down. Why did everything always conspire against us?

'Listen – there might be hope. When I described the situation to Jozef Gruja, the delegate at the Consulate, and told him there were over 650 people left stranded here, he told me he'd try to persuade the Soviets to organise transport, but I've no idea when, or even *if* they will. And it's not only the Germans fighting the Ruskies; the entire world's at war.'

'Dear God,' Mother wailed, 'to what sort of hell have Gerhard and Lodzia fled?'

1942

Christmas came and went.

There was no carp, no noodles – just fish head soup and a stingy portion of bread. Tatta, his eyesight poor, his fingers gnarled and stiff, vowed not to make any more valenki, yet still, people kept begging. There was no point charging them – no one had money to spare, but he couldn't see children go barefoot.

On 6th of January, things began happening.

Staff from the Polish Consulate arrived at Vodopad with welcome supplies. There were enough socks for everyone: Seven ladies' coats, 20 blankets and 20 eiderdowns; several pairs of shoes, scarves and sweaters, 80 cans of condensed milk and some jars of Bovril, 50kgs of sugar, 70 bars of chocolate – and a small first aid kit to distribute amongst 650 inhabitants!

In the event, my parents, Karol and I, each received a pair of socks.

Spread out on the community centre floor, it looked a lot, but once distributed amongst the neediest – which was all of us – none of it stretched far.

The Polish Consulate also donated 4000 roubles to assist welfare at the camp, since most people were now too frail to work.

It was the end of January when Karol rushed through the door shouting, 'There's a notice nailed to the community centre door. The free train is due at Permilovo Station imminently. There's no sign of any NKVD, nor of Smirnov; they've abandoned us to make our own arrangements to get to the station. People are already leaving; they have been since yesterday.

'So, who's in charge of Vodopad?' I asked.

'Who cares? What's the point of them staying? The Ukrainians have served their time, we're leaving. I'm off to the Ukrainian quarter to arrange a lift to the station, if all the sleighs haven't already gone.'

Out of habit, I automatically glanced at the empty place where the clock once stood. Karol left some time ago. I was no longer happy, but worried. Tatta's cough had worsened – how would he survive the journey to Permilovo exposed for so many hours to this crippling cold?

Mama looked equally poorly, having shared her rations for so long in order that little Ella could have more. Now she stood like a reed in the wind.

I packed what remained of our few possessions: photographs, Mama's table cloth, two pans, my father's iron last, and a hammer no one wanted. The Ukrainians had satiated their desires on everyone's cast-offs. Even Mama's sewing machine went for a few roubles. What remained fitted into my trusty red holdall.

'Tatta, do we need to take this iron last and the hammer; they're heavy?'

He took the hobbing foot from me and ran his hand over it. 'Without this, we wouldn't have been able to make valenki, and without the extra money, we wouldn't have been able to eat.' He returned it to me and kissed the top of my head. 'These are the only possessions I have to show for a lifetime of toil; a hammer and a piece of iron. Not much, is it?'

I stuffed them back into the holdall.

Karol returned in a great flap. 'Mama, I got the last horse and sleigh, but it only holds two people. Even then, her father said she can't collect you until tomorrow morning.

'Marishu, I suggest you and I leave right away if we're to stand any chance of finding a room near the station. No one seems to know when this train will arrive or leave. Knowing the Soviets, it might already have been and gone. We can't risk being left out in the open; that's providing all the Poles from the sawmills haven't already snapped up everything; they're on the doorstep. So are the people at Volosne, and other camps in the vicinity of Permilovo.

I clasped my hands over her head, my eyelids blinking and bit my lip, 'But Karol, we can't just leave Mama and Tatta behind.'

'What choice have we? I have the Ukrainian's word his daughter will be back from Permilovo tonight. He's after the money. This way, at least they won't have to walk – well, they can't; they'd perish.'

'Yes, yes, you go,' Father said. 'He slapped Karol's back. 'Thank you, son. Don't worry, we'll be alright.'

So, it was happening! The entire camp was on the move and not before time. The weather was deteriorating daily, and heavy snow fell again yesterday. Violent eddies of air swept along the banks of the Vaymuga, throwing great drifts against the bakery, the shop and the artel, almost concealing the shacks as it gathered and grew. Today there was no snowfall – so far. The sky was a clear and icy blue, but the weather was so capricious; we could never be sure that a white purga wouldn't catch us before we reached Permilovo as it had when we first arrived.

With our bedding strapped to our backs, we kissed and hugged our parents goodbye and abandoned them, two wraith-like souls waving after us from the window. We each left them our bread rations, because it was doubtful if Szefczuk would bake again.

Father felt sure there would be a soup kitchen somewhere close to the station, and we agreed to meet up there.

We took the Kenga route out of the camp, past the shop and community centre – with its memories of where Stefan and I met. People everywhere were fleeing their bug-infested abodes, and on we hurried past the Ukrainians' shacks and their petrified Kolkhoz, the call of freedom so loud there was no time to bid farewell to Boris, Roza and Vasily.

Isn't it strange, I thought, how familiar we have become with the rivers and woodland trails surrounding our prison, and how alien it all seemed two years ago?

Horses and sleighs carrying passengers passed us; others trudged on foot. Ahead and behind us, everyone was leaving.

The wind whipped against our backs and pushed us along, but once we reached the Kenga River, walking became easier; we were no longer half walking, half running, the track was well flattened by those who had gone before.

'How long do you think it will take us to get to Aktyubinsk, Karol?' I wished I still had my atlas, since I was clueless as to where we were heading.

'Depends on how often the train stops. I suspect it'll pick up others along the way.'

'Do you think Gerhard and Lodzia will still be waiting after all this time?'

'Honestly? No. The authorities would have moved them on to the Army Recruitment Centre as soon as they arrived. Perhaps we'll never see them again. I can't envisage how it will be. Any of it.'

'So, what would have happened to Lodzia and Ella, because they can't fight?' I couldn't imagine any of it either.

My brother, always so aware, seemed as clueless as I was.

Visions of Stefan waiting at the station had sustained me these past months, but now I had to face reality – the authorities would have moved him on too. How would *we* find each other again?

Another horse and sleigh passed us, and we waved.

'Karol, how did you get our travel document? Why didn't they give it to us right away?'

'I didn't. Josef Gruja the delegate at the Consulate did. The reason was that Tatta fought in the Polish/Bolshevik War. He was a political settler, like most of the farmers in eastern Poland. That's why the Soviets called us 'enemies of the people'. Gruja told me stuff I didn't know.'

'An enemy? In our own country!'

'Which happened to be full of other ethnic minorities with grudges. The Polish Government gave Tatta that land free of charge because he received medals for bravery. The rest had to buy theirs. Now the Soviets are hell-bent on revenge. Pathetic, small-minded little shits.'

'But Tatta's a peace-loving man. What made him fight in this Bolshevik War?'

'How should I know? Something about Lenin using Poland as a bridge to expand Communism across the rest of Europe. Don't underestimate our father, Marishu. He might be peace-loving, but he's an ethical man and he's not scared to fight for what he believes in; and he most certainly does *not* believe in communism.'

I imagined Tatta's feelings when he realised his decency and his desire to keep Poland free had caused the Soviets to wreak revenge on our family. 'Never tell him,' I said. 'It would mortify him.'

'I think he already suspected.'

'Karol, do you remember those hollow bricks we made when Tatta built the cowshed, and we were dreading him rebuilding the house?'

'How can I forget? My hands were sore for weeks.'

'Why did he build his war medals into the wall?'

'Because Mama told me that cowshed was his cenotaph in memory of fallen colleagues. He couldn't understand why he lived when so many better men died.'

'I don't understand grown-ups. So, why do you think the Germans invaded Russia?'

'No idea. Serves them right. Let them taste their own poison. They were quick enough to dispense it.'

'Yes, but why are they fighting? Why did the

World War start?'

'For goodness sake, Marishu, you do ask some questions. Who knows? They're all despots; like I said, pathetic little men with ideas bigger than their rodent-sized brains. I despise them all. They've ruined our lives and robbed us of our place on earth.'

'What do you mean?'

'Precisely that. We can never return to Eastern Poland, and the rest of the country is overrun by Germans. So where *can* we go? Nowhere. We've been displaced.'

We reached the edge of the forest and stepped out onto the caribou plain. I knew this route so well, but I had never experienced what awaited us. Ahead, and to either side of us, hundreds of reindeer with their candelabrum-headed horns were foraging for moss beneath the snow, digging it out with their hooves and antlers.

Karol said, 'Oh, this is excellent. It means the Nenets are close by.' His step quickened, lest they up and left before we reached them. 'Come on; they'll have raw meat we can buy.'

They were resting nearby with their dogs. Karol gestured in sign language as he approached so as not to alarm them, and held out a few roubles while I waited in silence.

'Reindeer meat! We didn't get any at Christmas, now we have lots. Tatta always said: never lament over what you haven't got because you can always get it, and never brag about what you have, because you can always lose it. Gerhard will be so envious when we tell him he's missed out on a feast. All we need now is somewhere to cook it.'

I hadn't a clue how to cook venison; we might even have to eat it raw. We were certainly hungry enough.

Onwards we ploughed, the sky behind us now daubed with streaks of blood. How many times had I followed this route? Thank God, I would never have to do it again.

30

Flames illuminated the night sky when we approached Permilovo.

Encamped around a mammoth fire were hundreds of refugees. More staggered in, desperate to get close to the blaze. A non-stop stream of youths dragged fallen trees from the forest and heaved them onto the pyre; the savage flames gobbling them up and sending up sparks to die in the air.

How many of these encamped had tried to find rooms? What chance did we have? We had arrived too late. There was no sign of the train. Perhaps there would never be a train. Perhaps this was just a ploy by the Soviets to clear us out of Vodopad, relinquish all responsibility and to hell with us. What began as a contortion of my stomach turned into panic.

'We'll freeze out here if we can't get nearer the heat,' I said to Karol. 'What are we going to do?'

'Try knocking the shacks again.'

'You're wasting your time.' I hurried after him and watched his clenched fist pounding on doors. So determined was he that he didn't listen to me? Then he struck lucky, turned and beckoned.

'The Russians are taking a colossal risk. They've been told they're not to help the Poles, but they couldn't resist the money.'

'How much did you offer?'

'As much as it took.'

The room was adequate, and the lamp illuminated two beds, two straight-backed chairs and a washstand. A pile of dry logs sat beside the stove, and an age-speckled mirror hung on the wall in place of a picture.

The babushka of the house wasted no time in pocketing our money but was reluctant to lend me a pan in which to cook our meat. 'I think she wants more, Karol.'

He dug into his pocket and produced two roubles. 'Here,' he said, 'and bring me tea and sugar.'

She looked at the money, held out her hand again.

Karol plied her with more.

She arrived with both, plus a ladle for the stock, two bowls, a knife and a tin can for boiling water.

It was late and sleep beckoned, but we were so hungry that soon the aroma of cooking meat infused the entire house! Just inhaling it was a luxury.

Settling into a chair opposite the fire, Karol sipped his tea. 'Isn't it done yet?'

Hungry as we were, we couldn't eat as much as we thought we would. It was very salty, and I put it aside for our parents, hoping it would mellow overnight. When my head hit the pillow, my thoughts turned to Stefan.

I slept well. The paillasse was thick; bark beetles didn't bother me, and I awoke refreshed. The glass at the window was frosted solid as winter held the land in its grip and I wondered how many people had perished during the night sitting around that fire; their lives snuffed out, a breath away from freedom.

The stove was out when Karol got up to stoke it, though the embers still glowed. 'We must have overslept. I've no idea of the time,' he said.

Rubbing a hole in the ice, I peered through the glass, my view obscured by flurries of snow. Beyond the shacks, smoke from the fire swirled upwards and curled away into nothingness. 'It's snowing, Karol. When do you think Mama and Tatta will arrive?'

'No idea. Depends when the Ukrainian collects them, and the weather. We'll go and see when this train's due as soon as we've eaten.'

'Do you want me to warm it; there's plenty?'

'We'll eat it cold. Warm it up when Mama and Tatta arrive. At least we have plenty to take with us; *our* family won't be going hungry.'

It was such a luxury to have food in stock. I never appreciated Karol's resourcefulness, but each day he surprised me. As children, we were always too busy squabbling over nothing, but Natasha had changed him for the better, as Stefan had changed me.

We ate and washed it down with sweet tea. It tasted awful, but neither of us complained.

Karol grabbed his sheepskin. 'We'd better go and find the soup kitchen and look around the station buildings. I need to find out when this train's arriving.'

'I'm more interested in when it's leaving. Do you think it will wait for Mama and Tatta if they're delayed?'

'They'll be here. Stop worrying.'

An old barn housed the soup kitchen, where a lengthy queue already meandered out of the door. Since Karol was eager to check out the train's timetable, we made for the station building, a single storey shack standing beside the tracks. But it was the small shed beside it with its gaping doors, which had me recoiling in horror. 'Oh God, it's a mortuary.'

Inside, the bodies, many stripped of their clothing, piled to the roof. We stood rooted to the spot. Neither of us spoke; there was nothing to say.

It was impossible to get anywhere near the bonfire, surrounded as it was with hundreds more people, but on the periphery lay the corpses of those who had frozen to death. With the mortuary full, there was nowhere else to put them. I tried not to look at their faces as I stepped over them, but I couldn't avert my gaze. Some of these people were from our camp, even our neighbours, their eyes and noses eaten by rats. They had left Vodopad yesterday full of hope, and now they were dead. It occurred to me with a jolt if they were our parents lying here with their faces bloodied and eaten away – how would we ever find them?

I felt it was time they were here. Neither Karol nor I had watches, nor did anyone else, having traded them for food. Given the station and its surrounds were just an insignificant outpost in this wilderness, finding them was proving more difficult than Karol and I imagined.

We headed to the soup kitchen, where the fetid stench of fish hung around the entrance, a potent reminder of our captivity, and in a flash, I was back at Vodopad. I called our parents' names, and a sea of sunken eyes stared back. Shaking myself out of the memory, I turned away.

Another search of the site around the bonfire proved futile. Hordes of people crammed near the flames, warming themselves. Heads bowed and covered against the cold, their ragged clothing of browns and greys amid a sea of blankets and filthy eiderdowns. It was difficult to distinguish faces, even when moving amongst them.

Karol said, 'Don't you think we'd be better standing where we first arrived, so we can spot them before they get mixed in with the crowds?'

After stamping our feet for an hour, Karol was growing anxious. 'What if they don't arrive before the train?'

'Yes, but didn't the Station Master say it would be here sometime today or early tomorrow?' Fear gnawed at the mention of it. 'I knew we shouldn't have left them. Shall we have another look in the soup kitchen?'

'No. I think we should have a closer look around the bonfire.'

'But we've already looked, Karol.'

'Not at the corpses. Not a thorough look.'

'The corpses?'

Blinking against the icy wind, we returned, needing to look, yet not wanting to see. I came across two bodies, wrapped in filthy eiderdowns. My stomach lurched and my breath caught in my chest. There was something familiar about their closeness. One lay face down in the snow, the other's body was on its side. Its arm cradling the other, face buried in its partner's back. I imagined Mama and Tatta dying in such a position – protecting each other to the end.

'Oh God, Karol, look.' My hand went straight to my midriff, and I felt a sense of impending doom. 'I think it's them.' I covered my mouth with my other hand.

Karol halted, turning his head to look deep into my eyes, the anguish in his own, mirroring mine, and he crouched down.

A sudden feeling of terror overwhelmed me. Sweating, shaking, I plucked at the ragged cuff of my coat, as it seemed to take forever for him to reach out.

He placed his hand on the shoulder and rolled the corpse over, stared at the man for a moment, before his shoulders slumped, the word, 'No' barely a breath.

I threw back my head, exhaled and closed my eyes in gratitude, nausea washing over me in waves. Oh God, what if it had been them? Another surge, this time euphoria, but looking at the two unfortunate souls lying at my feet, I realised they must be someone else's parents and felt such a stab of shame for rejoicing.

Karol covered their faces with the end of the eiderdown. 'Come on, they have to be in the soup kitchen by now. Tatta said it's where we should meet. Why are we wandering around here?'

'Because they weren't in there!' I was becoming more agitated with every step, a gamut of emotions racing around my entire body. We called out their surname in each direction as we walked, but I was losing hope.

When we reached the door, those who had been waiting for hours for soup barred us. I was undeterred; standing on tiptoe, I began shouting, 'Mama, Tatta, it's Marisha and Karol. Are you there?'

Marisha!' A faint wail came back from somewhere inside, growing louder, until our parents emerged, pushing through the starving as best they could.

I fell into my father's arms, my eyes sightless with hot tears. Swaddled in their eiderdowns against the arena of the great outdoors – they looked even more shrivelled than I could ever remember. 'Where've you been?'

'We arrived earlier,' Mother said, 'but we were so cold, we had to force our way to the fire to thaw out first. My God, I hope this train's a lengthy one.'

Tatta said, 'Did you find out when it's leaving, son?'

'The Station Master was vague. Late tonight or tomorrow, sometime. Have you eaten?'

'Only a plate of soup.'

'Come on then. We have a room.' Karol put his arm around Mama's shoulders. 'It's warm too – and tonight you shall both sleep on a comfy paillasse!'

'Karol, you are a miracle-worker!' Mama freed her hand, clasped his cheek and kissed it.

The unpleasant emotions drained away and something akin to rapture replaced them. We were halfway to freedom, and our little family was as complete as it could be – without Gerhard, Lodzia and Ella.

Expecting their surprise, I flashed a beaming smile. 'And we have reindeer meat,' I put my arm around my father's waist. 'I cooked it myself, Tatta. It's salty, but it's edible.'

'Ahh, kohanie, it needed soaking first.'

'I know, but we were so hungry that I just boiled it.'

'Couldn't be any worse than that stinking fish soup your mother made when we first arrived at Vodopad. Do you remember it?'

'How could I forget?' Karol laughed. 'I had to eat it!' We all laughed together, and it was good we were laughing. We had never laughed since arriving in Russia, and now we were laughing so hard we cried, but I didn't know if we were crying because we were happy, or because of what the Soviets had done to us.

Tatta looked into my eyes. 'I told you it would be alright, child. Never lose hope. I'm looking forward to this reindeer meat, salty or not.'

There was no reindeer meat; our landlords had eaten it without asking, while we were out.

'Listen, if we make a fuss, they will ask us to leave,' Karol said. 'Pretend it's fine; we don't mind.'

'But it's not fine, Karol. Mama and Tatta are starving – so are we. Now, what are we supposed to eat on the train – the greedy swine? They had no right!'

Two years of practice had us all awake at four-thirty in the morning.

Tatta swung his legs off the bed and had a coughing fit, but he was in wonderful spirits. Once he'd composed himself, he said, 'I was about to say, that's the finest night's sleep I've had in two years. And now – I shall wash, brush my hair and shave off my whiskers so I can face freedom clean-shaven.'

Mama and I stood at the window watching the flames flaring from the bonfire; the wind carrying sparks high and away.

'I wonder how many poor souls never made it through the night?' She placed her arm around my shoulder and hugged me as if I were the most precious thing on earth. 'I'm just thankful we are out of that place; that this nightmare's over. Now we have to find Gerhard, Lodzia and Ella. I want my family back, Marishu. I've never asked God for anything, but I'm asking now.'

Karol and I exchanged glances, but said nothing. Yet being the eternal optimist, I still hoped somehow they had wangled it and were waiting.

I sat on the edge of the bed and watched Karol working away with his cut-throat razor. He was humming to himself in the tiny speckled mirror and I wondered who he was hoping to impress. Did he have some crazy notion of bumping into Natasha if our transport stopped at Vologda and he went in search of bread? Then what would he do with her; snatch her and drag her back to the train? I had to admit, clean-shaven, he was good looking – if you liked that sort of thing.

At home, he was never short of female company, but he had never taken to anyone as he had to Natasha.

31

It was barely light when the monster of a locomotive emerged out of the blizzard, its plough spewing two plumes of snow into the air on either side of it. Our transport had arrived, and we were waiting. With a grating, metallic shriek, it ground to a halt. This might have been the same decrepit cattle train that brought us here, but given the numbers murdered at Stalin's pleasure, its length was much shorter.

Instant mayhem. Everyone scrambled to get on, shouting to parents, children, siblings, who were not so swift off the mark.

'I think we'll stand a better chance of finding a place if we moved towards the front,' Karol grabbed the two pails and my holdall, and we slithered with as much speed as we could muster along the wooden platform, me in the centre trying to hold both my parents upright.

We found space for four on the bottom shelf of the second wagon, beside the Oleszkiewicz's and their sickly child — our neighbours from Vodopad. The wagon was missing a stove, but there was a hole cut into the floor for sanitation; a source of ventilation, until it became clogged with frozen excrement, just as before.

'The other wagons are already full by now,' Father said. 'We may as well stay put. We travelled here with no heat at all for most of the journey. Now we shall head for the sun.'

Head for the sun; it sounded terrific. A strange sensation that began in my scalp instantly spread to the back of my neck and my hairs stood on end. We had survived this hellhole, and now we were heading for the sun – for the unknown. I could barely believe it, but it was happening, and it was happening now!

Karol stowed the holdall and the pails beneath the shelf, shrugged out of his shearling coat and handed it to our father, 'Here, Tatta, you need this more than me. I'll take yours.'

'But what about you, son?'

'Never mind me. Have you seen the ice on the insides of these walls?'

Our father squashed himself onto the bottom corner shelf, his head touching the one above it. 'Utter comfort,' he said when I tucked in his eiderdown around him. I did the same for Mother and – covered in our bedding – we sat it out, watching as people barrelled on board, their luggage banging against the walls. Soon, our wagon was so full to the point we were as crammed in as on our journey here.

Much to our dismay, our transport remained stationary.

'Oh Lord, no. Don't say they will keep us here for four days as they did in Zhabinka.' I pushed my way to the door to see if more people were still arriving and causing the holdup, but no. Apart from the NKVD, there were a few refugees staggering into wagons further back, carrying stoves. I climbed back onto our shelf. 'Perhaps we'll get a stove.'

'Forget it, we don't have a chimney flue,' Father said.

The train left in the night.

I heard the WHUMPH, WHUMPH, and the hairs on my neck stood on end again as we pulled out of Permilovo Station. We were on our way; there was no turning back now; we were heading for the sun.

No one slept. Most cried softly, others coughed. It was difficult not to be emotional. I kept swallowing the lump in my throat, listening as the WHUMPHING gave way to chugging, slowly at first and then gaining speed.

Tatta's cough kept me awake, but I didn't want to sleep. I wanted to keep listening, savouring freedom, lulled by the train's rhythmic shaking motion; to the chuckuty-chuck, chuckuty-chuck, as the wheels passed over the tracks, swallowing up the kilometres, speeding me to Stefan, wherever he might be.

I must have fallen asleep because the grey dawn was visible through the iron grilles when I awoke, cold and thirsty. It was impossible to reach to scoop snow from the sills without disturbing those sleeping on the shelf above, and

I had to leave it.

Then, with the thrust of the train slowing; we were approaching a station.

'Good,' Karol reached for a pail, 'I'm off to get food and water.'

I worried he wouldn't get any if our wagon stopped beyond the station building, and the others got there first.

Preparing to move to give himself a fighting chance of being near the front of the queue the moment it halted, our mother's hand on his arm stopped him. An indescribable noise caught in her throat. Tatta lay on the shelf, his hair frozen to the wagon wall. 'He's dead,' she said, her voice so quiet, barely audible to bear the weight of what she had to say.

Staring at my father's body, I shook him. 'No, no. No! Tatta, wake up!'

Mother was sitting with her fist to her lips, her body rigid, her face contorted. Karol pulled her into his arms.

Everything would be fine if I could free Tatta's hair, but it held fast. Placing my bare hands on the ice hoping to melt it as if releasing his hair would bring him back to life, my flesh stuck to the wall. I crumpled into a heap on the floor in pain.

The train stopped with a jolt and guards walked the length of the platform, rolling back the doors. 'If you have any dead, bring them out now. And be quick about it; the train won't wait. You can leave them in the shed beyond the station building.'

'Come on, son; I'll give you a hand,' Oleszkiewicz offered. But Tatta's hair wouldn't budge.

His wife, Stasia, produced a pair of scissors and handed them to me.

I didn't want to defile Tatta's image. When he awoke yesterday, he so wanted to brush his hair and shave off his whiskers so he could 'face freedom clean-shaven'. I hesitated, but Stasia gave me an urging nod. Fighting back the tears, I severed his hair, leaving a tuft embedded in the ice.

Karol slid out of the wagon, arms outstretched, ready to receive our father's body from Oleszkiewicz. There seemed nothing left of him.

The brief walk to the makeshift mortuary gave us too little time to think; too little time to say goodbye. What could we do but leave our father's body where so many had left their dead?

Karol reclaimed his shearling, and with no time for wondering how this tragedy could have befallen us, we left him there. Returning to the wagon, we sat in silence, too stunned to speak, and the train pulled away.

Daylight faded beyond the grilles, and our first day without Tatta ended. We were on our way to the sun without him; he was on his way to heaven; wherever that was. I wondered if I were to throw a stone at the sky, in which direction should I throw it to find heaven – to the left, to the right, straight up or in between somewhere? Or was it below on the opposite side of the earth – because infinity existed all around us?

Karol said, 'I wonder what will become of Tatta's body? We can never visit him to lay flowers and light a candle because we won't know where he is.'

Murk and shadow filled the cattle truck and my breath came in ragged, shallow gasps as I listened to the agonised sounds of the sick clinging to life by a wisp. They lay curled and stiff, unable to move with scurvy, unable to reach the toilet hole in time to defecate. Mother stared into space; she hadn't spoken since Tatta died.

Stunned to my core, I tried to make sense of what had happened. Pictures whirled in my mind, scenes of the past two years; a kaleidoscope of suffering, of grey.

Onwards we travelled without stopping until we reached Nyadoma.

Karol roused himself, 'I'll go and see if I can get some bread.' He had little time. Our outward journey taught us not to trust the time the train remained stationary.

I watched him go; his shoulders slumped. How could either of us reclaim our lives now Tatta was dead?

Sliding off the train after him, I gathered snow from beside the tracks, then offered some to Mother, but she refused it. Eating some myself, I put the pan down and stared at the place where my father once lay. He had gone out with Karol to find food. Yes, yes, that must be it. He'll be back shortly, but then I saw the tuft of brown hair still embedded in the ice and knew he hadn't gone anywhere.

Our transport was about to leave, but Karol had not yet returned. I watched from the open door and saw him in the distance. The engine gave a whoosh of steam, a whistle – and began pulling away as he started running.

I wedged myself in the gap between the doors. 'Karol! Hurry!' But it was moving faster and faster until a cloud of billowing smoke obliterated my view and I knew he would not make it.

The magnitude of what had just happened robbed me of breath. I returned to my place beside Mother, sat down and said nothing. What could I say?

'Jesus Maria, we're moving. Where's Karol?' She knew. 'He didn't get on, did he? Tell me the truth.'

'I don't know, Mama; I saw him running, but he got lost in the smoke from the engine.'

'So, he's missed the train.'

'He'll jump on the next one.' I tried to quell my fear as much as hers, but I could see Mama didn't believe me. 'He'll catch us up somewhere; you'll see.'

'What train will he catch? Where?'

'There must be more transport for all these

people.' Even this, I knew, was a false hope.

Mama stared at the other passengers. 'He'll never catch us up; he has no papers.'

The family travel document – that elusive piece of paper he went all the way to Archangelsk to prise out of the clutches of the Soviets, so we could all be free; it was in my holdall. I listened to the clattering wheels stretching out the distance between us, and thought of him out there, terrified and alone, clutching his pail as the back end of the train disappeared in an aura of smoke and steam. Whatever will he do? What would I do if it happened to me? My instinct would be to catch the next train – but what if it took me in another direction? Worse, what if the NKVD discovered I was travelling without papers? They would lock me up forever.

Mother sobbed quietly beside me, and I placed my arm around her shoulders, drew her frail body closer until she stopped weeping and fell asleep.

Two hours later, our transport began slowing again.

'It's a siding,' someone called from the top shelf, destroying everyone's hope of finding food, although they all reached into their luggage for pans to scoop snow.

The doors slid open to reveal two men standing outside looking in. One said, 'Does this one belong to anyone here? I found him hanging onto the back of the train.'

I stared aghast at Karol, snow swirling about his bare head, icicles in his matted hair, but sweat running down his face. 'Mama, wake up! It's Karol – Karol's here.'

He seemed to have great difficulty climbing on board, and two men beside the door took each of his arms and dragged him inside.

Mama climbed off the shelf and threw wide her arms, blubbering through tears of joy. 'Ahh, Karol, my boy, what happened to you?'

The man who brought him said, 'He's lucky to be alive. It was a job prising his hands off the crossbar.'

Karol wasn't right; I could see that.

'I ran after it,' he said. 'It was going too fast, but I grabbed the crosspiece on the end wagon and jumped on, but I couldn't get inside.'

'Oh, Karol, that was hours ago. Where's your hat?'

'It blew off.' He clasped his head with claw-like fingers, 'I've got a headache, Mama. Let me lie down.'

'What's wrong with your hands?' I took one and tried to prise back his fingers.

'I don't know? Why can't I straighten them, Mama? What's wrong with me?'

We took each of his hands, massaging his locked fingers and palms until he fell asleep in Mama's arms. She stroked his damp hair away from his forehead, anxiety etched into her face. 'He has a temperature.'

At least we have him back, I thought; at least

we are still a family – what's left of us. We had to get him right.

Everything was down to me now. I was already thinking ahead, wishing the train would get going. At the next station, I would hurry off and go in search of food. None of us had eaten since leaving Permilovo. At least I still had the strength.

When Karol awoke, he was clutching his head. I had assumed he needed sleep, but Mama was wiping the sweat from his face with her shawl. 'He's burning up,' she said. 'We need water.'

Thank goodness we were still stationary. In that eerie hour, I reached for our only remaining bucket, pulled open the door, the sound of it disturbing everyone, and jumped out of the wagon. Grey dawn was breaking on the far horizon, and I stood for a few moments filling my lungs with pure freezing air. I filled the bucket with snow and positioned it on the floor.

'Help me please, somebody.' A pair of obliging arms hauled me back into the fetid wagon.

Karol ate some snow and rested his head back into Mother's lap. I tore a piece of fabric from the hem of my dress and made a compress.

Somewhere in the wagon, another anguished cry told me someone else had died – the fifth since leaving Permilovo, including Tatta.

A little later in the day, the rumble outside heralded a passing train on the main tracks, giving us hope we would soon be on our way. Far from feeling better, Karol's condition worsened. He unbuttoned his coat as if it was stifling him; then pulled it closer. He was hot; he was cold; he didn't know how he felt.

A hoot, the wagon shook, and we were moving.

'I'm thirsty,' he said. He had already drunk all the water I had collected in the siding. Stasia Oleszkiewicz, sitting beside us, handed an empty pan to the boy on the top shelf and asked him to gather snow from the sills.

Karol raised himself onto his elbows and drank greedily, Mother holding the pan to his lips.

Irena, the nurse from Vodopad, placed a thermometer beneath his tongue, as I asked for more snow. From Karol's nuanced expression it seemed he was deriving some relief from the cold compresses, and I continued applying them.

Irena retook his temperature. It was high before, but now it had risen to 45 degrees. He threw up – a projectile of yellow bile.

He seemed to drift in and out of consciousness. In his lucid moments, he was gibbering, uncoordinated, flaying his arms.

The day wore on, and Mother ran her fingers through his matted hair. His lips had turned blue, and Irena massaged his arms.

Helpless to do more, I watched as his thrashing hands, which had been so eloquent in his distress, fell to his sides.

Irena took his limp arm, felt for a pulse but not finding one shook her head. And I knew Karol had gone.

I sat paralysed while Mama cradled his body in her arms. It all happened so fast.

'Vologda,' someone called from the top shelf, as the train rolled into the station.

I was stiff. Mother was still cradling Karol's body beside her, and beyond the open door, I saw someone carrying a corpse. It could only be from the first wagon, I realised, then another, and yet another; it looked like a child's.

Guards stepped on board to clear out any dead left with no one to do it for them, heaping them unceremoniously onto the cart brought to the station for the purpose, prompting those capable of removing their dead to get on with it.

The nearest passengers suggested removing Karol's body, and I gazed at their insensitive faces not knowing what to do. Couldn't they see Mama wouldn't let him go?

Oleszkiewicz said, 'Come on, Marishu; I'll give you a hand with him.'

It seemed passengers were wailing all around me, as they carried out their own, but Mama's eyes were imploring me not to take him. I realised it was up to me now, but how could I?

Quietly, Oleszkiewicz said, 'Come on, child.'

I reached out to my brother, but Mama tightened her grip, shaking her head.

'Mama, please,' I begged.

'No! Don't take him.'

I steeled myself, grabbed Karol about the waist and wrestled him out of her grip, as she let out an anguished wail, 'No, my boy, my child.'

Stasia took her into her arms, to allow her husband to take over. Having left his baby son buried in an unmarked grave back in Vodopad, I could see he was having trouble coping with this, especially since the remaining one was so ill.

Mama held out his shearling. 'Karol will be cold.'

With trembling hands, I got my brother into his coat, and prepared to help Oleszkiewicz get him off the train; the dreadful sound of Mother's wailing ringing in my ears. I swung down from the handle of the door, and as my feet sought purchase on the ground, far from the snow and ice I was expecting, I contacted a more malleable substance. As I let go of the handle, I lost my footing altogether and landed on my back. Trying to push myself upright with my arms, my eyes drank in the horror of falling on a corpse.

The station was an orchard floor strewn with wind-fallen bodies. They lay everywhere, beside the tracks, one on top of another. The ones in their last throws of life, like twitching fish at the bottom of a near empty stream, could not take that one last step to reach the train. A passer-by said, 'The Ruskies are emptying their jails and penal colonies; these are in a worse state than us.'

Unable to wait until I collected myself,

Oleszkiewicz dragged Karol's body off the wagon floor and onto his shoulder. I followed, clambering over the remains of what were once robust men.

He spun half around, 'Well, go and find the mortuary. There has to be one somewhere.'

With blurred, unseeing eyes, I stumbled ahead, thankful Karol wasn't one of those abandoned bodies carted off and dumped by the guards like a sack of potatoes.

Inside the wooden shed, a pyramid of naked and semi-naked bodies reached towards the roof, like at Permilovo. There was a queue, and I watched those in front holding their loved ones by their arms and legs, swinging them back and forth before flinging them to the top of the heap.

Oleszkiewicz followed me in, laid Karol on the floor and removed his shearling. 'Come on then, grab an arm and leg,' he snapped.

'No, I can't. I can't do that to him. Let's leave him here. I don't want him squashed.' Karol so wanted to come to Vologda to find his darling Natasha. He was here now, but she would never know. And what of his child? It would be a new born now.

'Oh, please yourself.' He was running out of patience. 'Here, take this.' He picked up Karol's coat, threw it at me, and turned for the train.

I held it close, and stared at the heap, while many unseeing eyes stared back. I longed to run away from it all; to pretend it wasn't happening, but I couldn't move.

Oleszkiewicz returned and grabbed my arm, 'Are you coming then? The train won't wait forever.'

I blinked and followed. Passing lengthy queues waiting for food and boiling water, the gnawing pain in my stomach reminded me I ought to get some. I no longer cared about myself, but Mama was in a bad way. I searched the pockets of Karol's shearling for money; there wasn't much – a few roubles, but first, I had to return to fetch our pail.

The stench from each open wagon door revealed the same misery within, and guards were busy clearing away the corpses from the platform which broke my earlier fall. My eyes went straight to my mother the moment I clambered aboard. A beat of alarm and my stomach lurched. She lay motionless on the shelf where I left her – eyes closed, and for a terrifying moment I thought she was dead. I reached out and grabbed her shoulder. 'Mama!'

She opened her eyes, and her smile held a hint of relief. 'Thank God you're back; but his coat, kohanie?'

'Karol doesn't need it now, but you do.' I draped it over her tiny frame.

'Where did you leave him, child?'

'In the mortuary,' my voice wobbled. 'We left him in a special place; the best place.'

'Such a waste.' She swiped away her tears with the back of her hand. 'He had no life. He was such a handsome boy.'

'But Mama,' I blurted before I could stop myself betraying his promise, 'Karol had a life. Natasha was expecting his child when she left Vodopad. I'd have told you before, but he swore me to secrecy.'

'A child?' But the spark that glimmered in her eyes soon faded, 'No wonder her mother was in such a hurry to marry her off.'

'I'm sorry, Mama, I should have told you sooner.' But she gave me a strange unfocused stare as if she was looking beyond me, to some half-formed future that excluded me. I gazed at her for a moment. 'I'm sorry, alright?' I wanted to say more, but I said nothing. Letting this pass, I picked up the pail, 'I will fetch food and water now.'

'No!' she said with sudden fervour. 'Don't go, they'll leave you behind.'

'I have to, Mama. I don't think the train will leave soon. Too many people are bringing out their dead.'

She grabbed my arm, 'But you don't know that.'

'I'll be as quick as I can.' I hurried into the station building, aware as always of the capriciousness of the train drivers who seemed to delight in some cruel game of leaving whenever the fancy took them; shattering families – adding to their heartache. They were sick in the head. I shuffled forwards with the queue, my ears straining for the first hiss of the locomotive, wishing everyone would hurry.

It surprised me to see a variety of foods for sale. Mindful of the few roubles in my pocket, which would have to last the duration of our journey, I purchased some bread and sunflower seeds, before hurrying to the boiling water queue, pushing against the tide of those returning to the wagons with theirs.

The train driver had to be feeling benevolent, I decided, because I filled my pail, and the moment I left the station building, I heard the whoosh of steam and the shrill whistle. Crowds surged. I threw my bread into the pail of water, and with adrenalin pushing me along the platform I jumped over those corpses still in my path, the boiling water sloshing against my legs. People were shouting, screaming, jumping on board.

The train jerked and began moving as I reached the opening to our wagon. I threw the pail onto the floor, and grabbed hold of the protruding handle, as the momentum swept me off my feet. I was half running, half being dragged along, aware someone was clutching my free arm, pulling me inside.

I landed on the floor, the now half-empty pail beside me, and rested for a moment to catch a breath.

The arm, which hauled me in belonged to Oleszkiewicz. 'Thank you,' I said.

'Hmm. Next time, perhaps you'll listen.'

32

I thought my mother would relish the bread. Softened with water, and squeezed out, it was easy to eat, but she refused it. For days she kept complaining of stomach pains, needing to empty her bowels, yet what remained inside her to purge? At my wits end, I searched out nurse Irena, busy somewhere in the wagon with people needing her help.

She came right away.

'How can Mama not eat?' I wailed. 'She hasn't had a crumb since we left Permilovo.'

'Marishu, we have dysentery in the wagon and she may have caught it. Get her to drink as much as possible.'

When Irena patted my arm, I felt even more helpless. I wanted to ask if people recovered from dysentery, but didn't want to hear the truth.

Midway between Danilov and our next stop, our transport pulled into a siding to allow another train to pass on the main line. Apart from drinking what remained in the pail, my mother was maddening me by refusing food, and I ended up eating all the soggy bread and sunflower seeds myself.

Needing more and more water, I worried how we would survive if stuck in a siding when all the snow had melted – as it would – the further south we travelled. As my darling father said, 'We were heading for the sun'.

With the signs of wakefulness all around me now, I slid open the door and jumped out of the wagon with my pail. Packing it with snow, I paused for a moment to take in deep lungsful of crisp dawn air, aware the landscape was less wooded now, but the hamlets no less decrepit. Yet I couldn't quell my mounting anxiety. What was this dysentery? It was so contagious that it was scaring me.

In the wagon, people were defecating where they lay, and the stench was gagging. Many were vomiting blood. Less than two weeks into our journey, the conditions on board were much worse than those on the way out.

I remained outside for as long as I could, before returning, but saw only Mother's pillow, and her rumpled eiderdown. She was heading yet again for the hole in the corner. Beside her, Oleszkiewicz's little boy lay crying. 'How is he today, I asked?'

Stasia shook her head. 'Look at him; he's just skin and bone.'

'Mama's no better either. I feel so useless; I don't know what else to do to help her.'

'What can you do? What can anyone do?' Stasia was washing away her son's bloodied diarrhoea, trying to keep him clean, but it was impossible.

I fluffed up Tatta's and Karol's flattened eiderdowns on which Mother had been lying to cushion her bones from the hard shelf beneath, and folded them into a comfy mattress.

She returned and lay down, exhausted. 'You folded the eiderdowns. Thank you, child, thank you.'

'Mama, I am so worried about you. I wish you would eat.'

Ignoring my comment, she pulled her eiderdown closer. 'I'm cold.'

I felt her forehead, but her temperature seemed normal. Perhaps she didn't have dysentery after all; maybe it was something else. I covered her with Karol's shearling and sat watching to see if her condition improved.

After a while, I heard her moan and checked on her again. Her eyes were still closed, but I couldn't tell whether she was sleeping. 'Mama,' I whispered, but receiving no answer, assumed she was happier in her little world with her eyes shut.

I took myself off to sit on the floor by the door, my legs dangling over the edge of the wagon. A freight train was lumbering towards us from my right, while youths loitered outside our transport, watching.

They moved towards the tracks as it drew closer, then as quick as mice, they grabbed the handles and clambered onto the roof. Their hands began jimmying the oilcloth from its anchor, yanking, gouging, leaving the freed tarpaulin flapping in the wind. One of them fell off, but the remaining looters kept working, throwing the spoils overboard. Some sacks and crates burst and splintered, spilling their contents. Vigilant passengers jumped out of their wagons with their pans and pails, limping, walking, some running, and cleared up the food.

Mustering latent energy, I joined them. It was exhilarating! Grabbing a bag of what I thought was flour, I reached for some dried potatoes, but another passenger snatched it first. Within moments of the heist, every scrap of food had disappeared into our transport, leaving nothing but brown patches of spelt staining the snow.

Watching us was our Russian train driver, who threatened reprisals at the next station, but I couldn't care less; my bag contained not flour, but sugar cubes. I offered some to Mother, thinking she wouldn't refuse sugar, but to my dismay she turned away. With both Tatta and Karol gone, it was as if she had given up, and if she wouldn't eat – oh God – the enormity of the potential chasm of loneliness, hit me like a telling punch.

'Come on Mama, please – one sugar cube – please, for me, please.' But she pushed my hand away from her lips, while my eyes welled with tears.

'I'm not hungry,' she said again. 'I have no

appetite. You eat them, kohanie.'

One of the other passengers offered some dried potatoes, and I gave him some of my sugar cubes in exchange.

Even well soaked, Mother still refused to eat the potatoes, and I realised with a shocking jolt that she was ensuring her one remaining child survived. In the filth and the gloom of the wagon, I knelt on the floor beside her, stroking her hair from her forehead, her bones pushing up under pale skin. Her limbs seemed swollen, and to me, she appeared like some dreadful caricature of a human being.

'Mama, if you ate a bit of potato I'm sure you'd feel better.'

She stretched out her arm and placed her hand on mine. Her voice was only breath when she slipped off her wedding ring. 'Here, child, take this.' She wrapped my fingers around it and gave them a gentle squeeze.

I opened my hand and stared at the gold band. I didn't know what to say. My parents had loved each other so much that I felt almost like an intruder gazing at what they meant to one another.

'Keep it safe,' Mother closed my hand around it once more.

'Only if you eat some potatoes.'

'You eat them, child, you eat them.'

'I can't,' I said, but Mama didn't reply. I stared at the sliver of potato for a long time, then put it into my mouth, but it was almost impossible to swallow. When I looked at her again, I thought I detected the smallest of smiles. The smile faded, and after a while, I detected no life at all.

Morning brought our transport to a stop at Penza Station, southeast of Moscow.

I awoke, and there were three or four seconds when I forgot it had happened, then I remembered. My Mama was dead. Tatta and Karol were dead. Disbelief followed emptiness and the terrible, dawning realisation I would have to let my mother go. What was happening to me? I glanced at poor Jan and Stasia Oleszkiewicz, and knew it was about to happen to them too.

The drill was now familiar. No way would filthy Soviet hands be touching Mama's body. Gathering myself off the shelf, I prepared to face this one last deed.

With swollen eyes and a stuffed nose, I turned once more to Oleszkiewicz for help, but he was too pre-occupied with his dying son. 'Well, don't look at me,' he rasped. 'What do you think I am – just here to take out your dead?'

'No, I am so sorry; I should have thought.' Choking back the words, I dragged Mama's body to the door and jumped down.

It was Stasia who helped heave Mama's body onto my shoulder, and arrange her until she was hanging like a shawl that I could manage without toppling over. 'Please forgive him; Jan didn't mean it. He can't cope with all this death.'

'There's nothing to forgive. I understand.'

The platform at Penza was no longer white with snow; hundreds of shuffling feet had left great globs and trails of frozen slush, making it hard for my feet to find solid purchase. I staggered along the platform looking for somewhere to lay my mother, until what little strength I had, gave out. I felt the eyes of onlookers watching me from inside the arched windows of the station building; scrawny old biddies, swaddled in shawls, their menfolk in their trapper-style hats, scarves around their scraggy necks, but no one came out to help me. What was Mama to them – another corpse?

Unable to carry her any further, I slid her off my shoulder, and propped her body against the station steps, as if she were still alive, but resting. I rearranged her shawls and fastened her headscarves tightly beneath her chin so they wouldn't blow away, leaving her head exposed in this weather.

An ethereal emptiness settled about me then, and I neither heard nor saw anything else. It was like I was going through the motions, but looking down at myself from above.

The setting sun had left behind the redness of a heavenly slaughter as I pushed myself to my feet. The wind moaned, whipping the untrammelled surface from the snow beyond the tracks, blowing it in our direction, smothering my mother in a white shroud. It didn't seem right leaving her here, surrounded by this callous landscape.

After what seemed like an eternity, I said, 'Mama, I have to leave you now.' I kissed her goodbye, but her cheek was a slab of ice, her unseeing eyes staring straight ahead beyond my shoulder – perhaps even to heaven – if there were such a place, which I doubted, but hoped for the sake of her soul there was.

Turning, I made my way back to the wagon, my body as fragile as a shrivelled leaf which the wind threatened to blow away, buffeting me along the platform. Everything was meaningless, and the look in my mother's eyes would stay with me forever; I hadn't the heart to close them.

33

I sat on the bunk staring, staring, twisting my mother's wedding ring around my middle finger until the rhythm of the pounding wheels put me out of my misery, and I fell asleep.

When I awoke, I lay still for a moment before a nauseous sensation welled up from my gut – a dawning realisation that *my family was dead!* I was alone. I had no food, no money and no idea where to go. Anders Army was out of the question; I was barely seventeen and had seen enough death to last me a lifetime.

Stasia urged me to cling to memories of happier times, but it was hard to invoke joy when my heart was dead. My one hope was to find Gerhard and Stefan, but where was I to look? It was akin to searching for a pine needle in a forest.

Jan and Stasia's child died. They carried his body off the train when it stopped at some nameless station, but never returned.

I stood at the open door watching and waiting, trying to quell the mounting panic. The train pulled away, leaving me abandoned when I was relying on them to show me where to go once we'd reached Aktyubinsk. Stasia promised. She said, 'Stick with Jan and me. Don't worry, we will look after you; you'll never be alone again.'

Returning to my place on the bottom shelf I drank sparingly of my water, hoping to appease my twisting gut. My body needed food, yet I had no desire to eat. Worse, a fellow passenger told me he was sure there was no army muster point at Aktyubinsk. So why was it suggested to us at Vodopad by the NKVD? Spite? I now wondered if I ought to carry on, or return – but return to what – the corpses of my family? But if neither Gerhard nor Stefan had enlisted here, then where was I to go?

The ice was now fast melting from the wagon walls, and I found it easy to remove Tatta's hair. Inhaling his scent, I arranged it with care in the scrap of fabric I had torn from my dress to make Karol's compresses. The fabric was dry now and I folded it over with care to ensure not one precious strand escaped. His hair, my mother's wedding ring and her goose down pillow, together with Karol's shearling coat, were the only personal things I had left of my family. I wished now I had cut a lock of my mother's hair, and wondered if she was still leaning against the station steps, but felt the authorities would have removed her body.

Our transport veered east at this point. Kuybyshev Station was one of the more extended stops. I remained in my place on the top shelf, which I had occupied since the moment its occupants vacated it, listening to the buzz of strangers boarding. They were apologising for intruding on someone's personal space, introducing their names and the places they'd come from and complaining that it wasn't fair that the free food at the station was available only for those passengers travelling from Permilovo, thanks to someone called Alfred Powiecki.

I thought I had misheard. Alfred Powiecki? Dear God! I snatched my bag, and pushed through the crowds like someone unbalanced. Alfred was Zygmunt's brother. No doubt the entire Powiecki clan would be with him. I longed to travel with people I knew, especially Zygmunt. He was kind and always had a soft spot for me, and it was his mother, Albina, who delivered me into the world.

Flashing my family travel document at the canteen entrance, it allowed me in. I cast about for our neighbours, refusing to believe they couldn't be here, but they must have been and gone. My sights settled on the glass buffet, behind which was a mountain of dark brown loaves, smoked fish, and a variety of cured, dried and smoked sausages. The pungent aroma of black pepper and garlic filled my mouth with saliva and longing. I yearned to taste Kielbasa again – how long was it since I last ate Polish sausage? I had no desire to keep living – yet the sight of it made me so hungry that a stronger instinct urged me to throw in my lot and opt for survival.

Inching forwards in the queue, I took the rations as if accepting the communion host at Mass. Once out on the platform, I tore into the bread and stuffed my mouth with sausage. Oh, it was indescribably delicious, but I couldn't eat much; my stomach couldn't handle it. I stood as I chewed and thought I was hallucinating – the train had more than doubled with nine additional wagons added.

I stowed the rest of my food in my bag and went in search of our neighbours. As I peered into the trucks; gaunt faces gazed back at me. There was a glimpse of a half-familiar face, but it was someone I might have seen somewhere in a bread queue or maybe even from Vodopad – they weren't friends but helpless people like me, far from home.

Damn, the Powiecki's were impossible to find. They could have been in any of the now seventeen cattle wagons – or even left the transport altogether having eaten their fill.

A delegate from the Polish Embassy, who was staffing the information desk, told me the family were unknown to him. All he knew was that someone called Alfred Powiecki had contacted the Polish Embassy from Yaroslavl Station, begging they make food available to the train arriving from Permilovo because of the perilous state of its passengers.

The envoy was about Gerhard's age. He had kind eyes, someone I felt I could trust, someone who would understand. 'I need to reach Aktyubinsk,' I said. 'My brother left Vodopad two months before us to join the army, and he'll be waiting for me.'

'You're travelling alone?'

Nodding, and hating having to acknowledge the truth of it, I explained. 'My family perished in Arctic Russia – within two weeks of each other. I lost them all apart from Gerhard.' Lost them; it sounded as if I had misplaced them somewhere.

'If you say he left Vodopad two months ago, then I'd say it is doubtful he would wait for you after so long. I think it is more likely that he's already joined up elsewhere.'

'Then I shall go to the enrolment centre. Where is it?'

'There are so many now scattered all over vast areas of central Asia. The headquarters are at Buzuluk but the principal enrolment centres are at Totskoye and Kermine. More are being set up in surrounding areas because of the huge influx of refugees.'

'So where could my brother be?'

'I have no idea. The only certainty is that Stalin's refusal to provide recruits with sufficient food, let alone feed their families, means our troops are being evacuated out of the Soviet Union with all speed through Persia. Then it's on to Iraq and Palestine for training. From there, they will send them to the front line in the war zone.'

I felt the blood pump in my ears. Would I ever see them again?

'Have you considered enlisting?' the envoy asked.

'I'm too young. I'm only seventeen.'

'Then lie about it – they would accept you – it would mean the difference between starvation and salvation.

Gazing into his eyes, I realised he wasn't joking.

'Food is guaranteed because the British Army is in control in Persia and Iraq. They would give you a uniform,' he looked down at my feet and tattered valenki, 'and sturdy boots.'

In my bereaved and fragile state of mind, I was not fit to decide what to do with myself and felt I was being coerced along a path upon which I was not ready to embark.

'I wouldn't be any good.' A sudden rush of tears spilled down my cheeks. 'I couldn't kill anyone; I just want to find my brother.' Then thought of adding, 'And the boy I love,' but realised how silly it must sound.

'Then I wish you well. Your brother may still be in Persia when you arrive.'

Staring at him then, open-lipped, I said, 'You mean I'm going to Persia?'

'You will be if you remain on this train.'

'But our transport is heading east – Persia is in the opposite direction.'

'It's heading almost to the Chinese border to collect as many of our soldiers and refugees as possible. From Alma Ata, it will head back to the Caspian Sea via Tashkent to pick up more troops, so if you reconsider enlisting – that's the place to do it – or even in Totskoye later on – it's never too late.'

'And if I didn't enlist, would I still be able to travel to Persia?'

'You wouldn't be the only orphan, providing Stalin hasn't already put a stop to it. Stay on the train and make sure your boxcar doesn't become detached from the main transport. The NKVD are fond of their sick petty tricks.'

I collected water and returned to my wagon. It was full of newly arrived refugees. My place and bedding had gone, but I couldn't point an accusing finger at anyone; one filthy eiderdown looked the same as any other. Thank goodness for my shearling, and my mother's pillow stuffed into my holdall. I meandered along the platform, peering into each wagon. The recently added trucks were less cramped, and I climbed aboard.

The first blessing was that the stench was less pungent. The second that there was enough space for me on the top shelf beside the iron grilles. I plumped up mother's pillow, wrapped my coat closer, and kept myself to myself.

The hours slipped by. Only when stars freckled the sky did I feel safe enough to reach into my holdall for a couple more slices of sausage, and a crust of bread, terrified the others might notice I had food and steal it while I slept.

By morning, our transport was well on its way. I sat with my head resting back against the wall; the breeze blowing in through the grilles. It offered a comfortable relief from the stale air of the wagon where everyone was wheezing and sick. While I dozed, the kilometres sped by; my head lolling in rhythm with the motion of the train.

Eleven hours later we arrived at Uralsk. There was the usual rush of refugees surging for spaces in wagons, impeding those trying to leave.

My desperation for water overcame my desire to hold on to my place on the top shelf and I grabbed my pail and bag. With Karol's jacket hanging below my knees, my boots ripped, my scalp itching, I staggered through the mud and slush of the platform like a drunken vagrant. By the time I found a tap, filled my pail and returned to the wagon, someone was in my seat.

With ghostly whistles shrieking into the night, our transport swallowed up the kilometres. Another morning dawned – another station – guards helping grieving families to remove their dead – the usual ghastly routine. The moment someone got off, I transferred myself to the upper shelf. The niceties of respectful manners no longer bothered me; I had learned to look out for myself.

Despite what the envoy had told me, I knew

I would do whatever it took to find Stefan and Gerhard – and that meant searching for them in Aktyubinsk – just in case. Beyond that, my mind and my fate were a blank. Without them, I had no future – too old for an orphanage and no appetite for a fight. What would I do with myself if I couldn't find them?

Turning my face to the iron gratings, I watched the passing countryside. There wasn't much to see – kilometre after kilometre of endless steppes, sparsely populated with few trees, grasslands and abundant sandy areas.

I vaguely remembered learning about this part of the world at school and felt sure I was following the Silk Route. I'm like a tramp following in the footsteps of Alexander the Great and Marco Polo, and there was that unexpected urge – the word 'Mama' instantly on my lips, ready to tell her, and for a moment I let my guard drop when I realised there was no one to tell.

* * *

At last – Aktyubinsk.

Ever since Stefan and I parted at Vodopad, I had fantasised over how it might be once I arrived here. I would fly along the platform straight into his arms, leaving Mama, Tatta and Karol to greet Gerhard and Lodzia first. I knew, without doubt, they would all be waiting together for us, but Karol already killed that notion dead in its tracks. However, I couldn't help hoping.

Tatta told me to always have hope.

As our transport drew into the station, and the steam enveloping us evaporated, reality bore no resemblance to my fantasy. Yet still I couldn't help myself and held onto the iron bars, scanning the burgeoning crowds, my anticipation mounting – just in case. My disappointment was doubly crushing.

The reality was nothing like my dream. The platform – as everywhere else – teamed with sick, bedraggled refugees, desperate to board impeding the sick and bedraggled passengers trying to get off. The carts for the dead – it was all here.

Reaching for my holdall, l pushed my way off the train and stood at the back of the platform beside an empty wooden bench, my eyes alert. How naïve and stupid was I? When it became apparent there was no one waiting for me, I stood on the periphery of the crowd assembled around a Polish information centre and listened. There was no army muster point here.

I ventured outside the station – that niggling little voice still suggesting they might be waiting outside, even though I knew it was futile.

A sharp wind blew, and I pulled my coat tighter about me, inhaling the fresh air. I walked a short distance – no further than the end of the station building. Ukrainians, Georgians, Turkmens and Jews passed me by, and I wondered what life was like for people living here.

The town looked pleasant enough with lots of significant recent buildings. The streets were of asphalt, adorned with trees and shrubs, and I could imagine this might be a safe place to live. But then two Black Crows – Soviet Police vehicles – screeched to a stop ahead, arrested a group of innocent-looking men, and took them off to prison. Was there nowhere on earth where the long tentacles of the NKVD didn't reach? In fright, I flew back to the train. Flashing my family travel document at the official, I ran onto the platform and clambered up to the safety of the top shelf of the wagon.

34

A week later, our transport arrived in Alma Ata, in southern Kazakhstan. The crew disembarked, disappeared into the station buildings, and I looked down at the platform in dismay – no quick turnaround here then. I needed to get to Persia with all speed if I were to stand any chance of finding Gerhard and Stefan before they moved on.

I had eaten all my smoked sausage, and only a puddle of drinking water remained in my pail. People were getting off the train in search of food. I did too.

The Russian at the Information Desk said the train would remain for three days and suggested everyone use their time to visit Zenkov's Cathedral and the Zelyony Bazaar – we should explore the many delights Alma Ata offered. A large framed city map hung on the wall beside him with directions.

Lost and hungry, I was in no mind to explore anything. Out of the confines of the station, a stiff breeze blew from the Zailysky Alatau Mountains and whipped about my legs. The sky threatened rain.

I followed the crowd trudging down

Furmanov and along Zhybek Zholy to the bazaar. The place was abuzz with Russian and Kazakh voices, the air redolent with the aromas of cinnamon and turmeric. People were going about their daily business, getting on with their lives, unlike me. On the far side, Kazakh farmers were bringing their cattle to sell, and the similarities between this place and Zhabinka market on a Saturday morning were a stab to my heart.

Seeing so much food, none of which I could afford, was pure torture; dried and candied fruits and large luscious red apples. I saw cheeses in varieties I could only dream about, and nuts and honey, and meat stalls where women prepared sausages in front of my eyes. There were stands selling horsemeat, lamb, goat and real pig body parts, and the whole market was a sweet mix of noise and aromas.

Only three items remained in my bag. Standing between me and starvation were my father's iron hobbing foot, his hammer, and mother's beautifully embroidered tablecloth.

The tablecloth was no problem; I hated parting with it, but out of hunger swapped it for a sizeable Kazy sausage. With care, I could eke it out for two weeks, providing I had something else with which to augment it.

Bartering the hammer and iron last was difficult. No one was interested. When a trader tried to sell me some of his amazing red apples, I cried, 'Don't you understand, I have no money?

Look, this is a hobbing foot. Everyone should have one. It's for mending shoes.'

He replied with a toothless grin, shook his head and nodded at the same time.

I waded further. 'It's suitable for use with a range of shoe sizes. See,' I rotated it to show, 'I promise you'll get your use out of it.' I remembered how Tatta used to sit on his comfy armless chair, mending our boots, pulling each one over the last, the whole hobbing foot clamped between his knees, small tacks in his mouth, the hammer in his hand, while he worked on the repair. When the hobbing foot blurred in front of my eyes, I straightened up and added, 'I'll throw in the hammer too, if it helps.'

He hadn't a clue about what I was talking. No money exchanged hands, but he took pity. I swapped the tools for an apple, the size of a large grapefruit, honey, nuts and dried golden fruits. It was only later when I passed a stall selling shoes that I realised, had I tried here first, I could have easily swapped the last and hammer for a fresh pair of boots. But then I couldn't eat them, could I?

Leaving the bazaar, I bit greedily into my apple, gazing for a moment at Zenkov's beautiful Cathedral looming over the town in Panilov Park, but I had no desire to explore; the apple consumed my concentration, and I devoured it complete with pips and core.

At the station, I filled my pail with boiling water and returned to the wagon to sit out the next two days. My fruit and sausage were out of sight in my holdall, which I kept beside me at all times. It seemed pointless lugging it around now since it only contained my box of photographs and my mother's pillow, but my fingers kept sneaking into my bag, picking off the nuts and dried golden fruits one by one, until I got a grip. I knew if I didn't show some restraint, I would starve later.

To take my mind off my continually grumbling tummy, I reached for my box of photographs, opened it, and a picture of Jusio stared up at me. 'Hello you,' I sighed. 'You once monopolised my every waking thought, but now I have Stefan – and I love him.' I relegated his photograph to the back of the pile. Then I remembered the first time I saw Stefan and how my life had changed in that instant. My recollection of that moment when he came over, and I thought he would ask me to dance, but he lost his nerve and instead turned off the record player because the needle had got stuck in the groove. I felt utterly crushed, and now, separation from him was like a dull perpetual ache; I had to find him again.

I fingered through the remaining happy snaps – Gerhard and Lodzia's wedding. Gerhard looking elated, Lodzia radiant in her white gown with Mama and Tatta on either side of them. Tatta was wearing mud-covered boots, having arrived late at the church because he'd been up all night helping his heifer through a breech birth, and had refused to leave her. Mama was so mad at the state of him. Then there was Ella's baptism. One of myself, hands clasped at my first Holy Communion. Who took this one of Karol sitting on the step outside his little shop, one leg extended, playing his accordion, his gold tooth glinting beneath his dark moustache, the usual mischievous look in his eyes? And this one I took of Mama and Tatta outside our overflowing granary before Stalin's henchmen arrived and destroyed our lives. How precious were our lives – how happy, how pure!

What would Mama and Tatta think if they saw what had become of their daughter; an orphan in a filthy cattle truck somewhere near the Chinese border? Could they see all these decent people here, ill people doubled up in pain? Some were lolling, others sprawling, their heads drooping forwards or backwards, toothless mouths open in sleep, everyone covered in sweat, not from the heat – because there was none – but from diseases. The Soviets had reduced us all to this.

No one spoke to me. Why can't I shake off this never-ending evil, I wondered? It just goes on, getting worse and worse. Why has this happened to *me*? What did I do that was so wrong that God had to punish me like this because it's me he's punishing. Mama, Tatta and Karol are out of it – thank God, and Gerhard, Lodzia and Ella have probably starved to death somewhere too.

The sun was setting, throwing the mountains into relief, as it must have done since time immemorial. As darkness fell, the silence closed in and the wind sighed. I was with people, yet I was alone. All I wanted was to die, but my stubborn body kept living. I wept.

35

The train jerked.

I awoke, stiff. It was light and we were on the move again. My first thoughts were of food – food, food, always of food. I was so hungry. If I wasn't thinking about food, my fellow travellers spoke of nothing else.

I slid my hand into my bag for the sausage, ripped off a tiny piece, and slipped it into my mouth. Chewing, I savoured each delicious smidgeon, relishing the saliva it created around my mouth and craved more. How far is Persia, I wondered? Why did I part with my atlas? It was all for nothing now. I rested my head against the wagon wall and watched the view through the iron gratings.

We passed vast piles of snow-white cotton picked and delivered to the collection point, but with no protection against the elements the cotton fibres had rotted. Close by stood several enormous trucks, their tyres missing, rusting away to the complete indifference by the Kazaks. What wastefulness, what apathy, I thought, when we have so little, and they can afford to allow things to decay.

This last journey was as awful as all the rest,

but what made it more bearable was the knowledge that perhaps I was getting closer to freedom; out of the Soviet Union.

One by one, the stations rolled by: Bishkek – Taraz – Tashkent. Tashkent was another longer stop, and the platform heaved with soldiers wearing battledress, surrounded by their families. Some climbed aboard my wagon and I watched with envy how excited and happy they were to leave – but they had each other.

Was my entire life destined to be like this; coming and going, one blurry station after another, cold, hungry, covered in lice and a worsening ulcerated leg – no present, no future, just heart-breaking memories following me around?

We were off again, collecting troops and rescuing refugees – Samarkand – Bukhara – Turkmenabad – Ashgabat.

The transport was slowing again. Awake now, I gazed through the grilles as we passed through the insignificant town of Dzhanga, and stopped in a field beyond it.

All at once Polish soldiers appeared and ran along the length of the train, sliding open doors. 'All out! Everybody out! Ships are waiting for you at the port.'

What started as a buzz of excitement soon grew into full-blown exhilaration. The soldiers began helping those too sick or unable to remove their bags – women, little children and older adults.

Reaching for my pail and bag, I jumped from the wagon and looked around but could see neither ships nor water. The sandy field in which I stood was empty, grassed, with clumps of bushes growing here and there.

A soldier who saw me looking bemused drew up and explained, 'Sorry there's no transport to take you to the holding point, but we have to clear this field. We are expecting another train within the hour; and many more after that. Please collect your things and hurry.'

'So where is this port?' I asked.

He pointed toward a knoll.

I trudged to the top of the hillock and there, in the far distance, lay the gleaming water of an enormous bay with a town stretching either side along the shore.

'On the other side lies Persia. Freedom,' said a woman's voice.

I spun around; it was Irena, the nurse who left with us from Permilovo, and helped me comfort Karol and my mother. 'Irena! My God, how are you? I've been so lonely and frightened.'

She wrapped me in her arms, 'Don't be; we shall sail together. Isn't it a wonderful sight?'

'But water terrifies me.'

'You're not being asked to swim across. You'll be fine.'

A group of Polish soldiers approached on the track from the port. They circulated amongst us, and people formed into groups to listen to what they had to say. The young NCO in our group explained the situation. 'Once again, apologies for the transport, but it's not too far to walk to the holding point. Take just what you can carry. There won't be enough room to take more on the boat. Sorry,' he held up a defensive hand, 'General Anders instructions.'

It amazed everyone who had clung to their cases and bundles. Compared with life, they were worthless, but their contents were precious to them. They had lugged them for thousands of kilometres, protected them from theft and now had to abandon them in a field.

'They will search you on embarkation. You may not take roubles out of the country. The NKVD will do the searching, will arrest anyone who tries to smuggle out money, and will turn his or her family back and stop them from leaving. Is that understood? They can even prevent entire transports from leaving port.

'The NKVD will come around with bags.' He left before anyone protested.

Everyone fell on bags and bundles, turning out suitcases, tearing open wrappings. It amazed me some people still had their bedding and kitchen utensils, clothes, even. Their less dishevelled appearances told me they had been lucky enough not to have spent much time in Stalin's paradise – unlike me.

In a frenzy of terror in case the NKVD denied me freedom, I pulled my mother's pillow from my bag. Burying my face in its softness, I inhaled Mama's hair, sweaty as it might have been. I had vowed never to part with it, but the soldier left me no choice. Imagining my mother's lips against it, I pressed my own into the soiled linen before propping it up against a clump of grass.

Irena said, 'I'm sure he didn't mean your mother's pillow; it doesn't take up much space. Fetch it, kohanie – it's all you have left. I'm sure he was referring to all those who still have sacks and suitcases full of excessive baggage.'

I was unsure. 'But what if they stop me from leaving?'

'So, take it out then. Just say, 'sorry,' and leave it behind.'

Soviet functionaries came around with canvass bags, and people threw in whatever they had before they joined the others and followed a lead towards the holding area. Abandoned luggage littered the field beside the railway line for as far as I could see. Containers of every sort, suitcases almost full, lay scattered. Some had even set fire to theirs to stop anyone profiting from their loss.

'Oh, God, now it's raining.' I set down my bag and pail, pulled my coat over my head, and caught up with Irena. Onwards we trudged – sick mothers, clutching their even sicklier children, the elderly with sticks.

We reached the makeshift civilian transit camp. It was about half a kilometre from the port where two ships were already heading for Persia.

Black clouds hung over the sea, and white caps crowned the waves. There must have been a thousand refugees here already, all waiting in nervous anticipation.

I pulled my shearling further over my forehead and sat down on the ground beside Irena, the wet suede of my coat weighing me down.

There was a bit of a rebellion brewing nearby. The newcomers were complaining of being tricked into leaving their precious possessions behind by Polish soldiers – of all people! Whatever happened to honesty – robbing us when we already had so little?

A man in the crowd shouted back, 'Rubbish, nobody's robbed you of anything! The reason they have asked you to take just what you can carry is that General Anders wants to evacuate as many civilians as possible. He's worried Stalin will put a stop to any more ships leaving. Surely human life's worth more than your piles of worthless rubbish!' He shook his head, wafting his hand as if they were all stupid.

'How come you're such a know-all?' someone shouted back.

'Oh, I have it on good authority. My son's an officer in the army. Stalin has no intention of liberating civilians, so think yourselves lucky you're on the next ship out. They might even cancel that, or recall it when you're out at sea.'

I turned to Irena in alarm. 'Is this true? What if that man's right and Stalin changes his mind?

What will happen to us? Where will we go? I haven't any food or money; we'll starve here.'

'You are a little worrier, aren't you?'

Everyone spent the night huddled together beneath the open skies, and spoke of nothing else but whether the Soviets would let us go. More refugees kept arriving so that by morning we were cramped beyond capacity. It was cold; the rain had stopped, but the sea looked rough.

'I need a pee.'

Irena pointed to some distant bushes. 'Be quick; you don't want leaving behind. In fact, we'll both go. We might not get the chance later.'

Clambering to our feet, we were careful to avoid the uncontrolled stools from the dysentery of the ill, who had defecated wherever they lay.

It proved to be a long wait with everyone else queuing for the same purpose, but we waited, crossing and uncrossing our legs, tolerating the discomfort in our tummies.

Just as we were crouching down, the hum of voices grew louder, and as a wave of undulating geese taking flight, the crowd began rising to its feet.

'Hurry!' I was half walking, half running, the puddle of remaining drinking water sloshing around in my pail. 'There might not be room for us.'

36

Irena and I tagged onto the end of the queue and shuffled along.

Crawling with lice, we endured our fate with stoicism. Our clothes and shoes were in tatters. Some had feet bound in rags, yet everyone clung to that one intangible thing – hope.

A flat-topped corrugated shack at the far end acted as the checkpoint. The NKVD and Polish soldiers stood checking lists of names and permits before they allowed passengers onto the quay. Once in a while, the NKVD asked somebody to step aside, where a Polish soldier would explain the problem, and that person and his family couldn't sail.

'Dear God,' said Irena, 'to be so close and then refused. I wonder what they've done wrong?'

Everyone was being allowed through – ill or not. 'Perhaps I should leave Mama's pillow...'

'Don't be silly.'

When it became clear the NKVD were not searching anybody, and the man in front could pass through, he began protesting, 'Search my bag,' he cried, 'go on, search it! Everything I owned, I left behind! For what? For you to pick up later, you swindling bastards! Don't you think we've been through enough?'

We arrived on the wharf at two in the afternoon. 'Told you no one would search us,' Irena said, 'but I'm surprised they've allowed so many sick people through. I don't suppose the Soviets care; we're taking *their* diseases with us.'

The excitement and euphoria of arriving at the quayside was contagious. Everyone was glad to see the ships, the surrounding activity – knowing that soon, oh so soon, we would get out of Russia forever. Words could never express the sensation.

A sharp wind blew off the sea and brought with it the smell of oil from the nearby refineries. It settled in my stomach and made me feel queasy. Embarkation was slow, and all the while the greasy, polluted brine slapped against the ship's hull.

Our transport was a massive Soviet freighter, its sides streaked with far more rust than paint to inspire confidence. Polish troops, their kit strapped to their backs, boarded first. They marched up the gangplank, and one by one disappeared below deck into the innards of the monster. When it was our turn, I held onto Irena's arm and tried not to look down. There was so much space up here that it was difficult to decide where to sit. The hundreds who had boarded before were as mere ants.

I looked around at the filthy floor where thousands of previous passengers had left their mark. It was awash with the remains of bloodied excrement, and the stench would have been unbearable, had it not been for the westerly wind.

The few quickly rigged toilets hung out over the sea on the other side of the guardrails – planks of wood crudely fettered together to form a box with a hole in the bottom and a ledge on which to stand. They were lashed to the rails with rope.

'I won't be risking my life in one of *those* things,' Irena said, 'one slip, and you'd be in the water. Is there anywhere sheltered to sit? The sky threatens rain.'

'I'll see if there's space down here.' I was already heading for the lower deck, but the guard barred my way. 'Sorry, military units only.'

'No luck – troops only.

We headed for the prow. Irena emptied the contents of her drinking water into my pail. 'We'll use mine instead of those hanging latrines.'

After a few hours, we were feeling penned in as more and more people kept boarding. They filled the areas where anyone could stretch or sit, turning the deck into a menagerie of noise, and moving arms and legs.

The ship was full, the waves ramming it against the buffers, but still they kept coming. Soon human bodies clogged the decks, the stairs, the hold and gangways. I had to sit with my holdall on my lap to make more space, but still they came.

'What are they thinking,' Irena said. 'What's wrong with them? Enough!'

I wondered how long it would take to drown. My only option now was to get off this floating catastrophe waiting to happen, but that would mean typhus, twisting bowels, a brief stay in Stalin's Paradise and then eternal rest.

Nearby, another massive freighter had docked, filled with war supplies from America. As it grew darker, lights glowed along the quayside. Our ship was full, yet a sizeable crowd remained on the wharf.

From down on the docks came the sounds of clanking chains, as our vessel prepared to sail and they hoisted the anchor. I felt it shunt away from the pier and we were on our way.

Realising it was about to leave without them, the crowds below made a desperate surge towards it. Soldiers barred their way. Everyone could hear the commotion; the pitiful cries, the soldiers shouting, 'Stand back; you'll be boarding the next ship.'

The noise on board died down, as everyone imagined those poor souls' plights, how we would feel if it happened to us, and thanked God for our wonderful fortune. The thundering ship's stack charged the air as the old wreck crawled out into the Caspian Sea and headed off into the night.

We knew the dead wouldn't hurt us – but we

were sitting next to a corpse. At least it wouldn't shit. By morning many were dead.

Some passengers had grouped nearer the rails for the burials, treading on others to get there. A priest, in his tattered cassock began his liturgy, but the wind meant prayers were almost impossible to follow. When he crossed himself, they did it too. When he paused, they took it as a cue to chant, 'Amen.'

At each interval, the living let the dead slip from them. Sometimes the passengers heard a splash as each uttered their prayer for their own grave – that it would be on land, on their new soil – their heaven would be on the new earth.

The priest opened his arms so that the sea may receive death more generously. Then he looked upwards at the scudding clouds.

'Poor souls,' I murmured, crossed myself, and turned away. I might have been one of those cast overboard; an orphan like me, travelling alone with no relatives to ensure I received a proper burial in Persia – if we ever made it that far.

Irena was off somewhere tending to the sick, and I sat alone all day, not speaking to anyone. She returned once the sun dipped, and I asked her if she still believed in God. Her answer was, 'Of course I do! Why wouldn't I?'

Night fell again and I, like most others, kept silent watch; my eyes darting from the deck to the sea, listening as it thrashed against the hull. I felt the vessel heave and pitch and hoped the waves wouldn't swamp it and wash everyone overboard. The sky was a vast orb adorned with stars so distant they added to my fear and isolation. A cough here, a whisper there – everyone was alert to the slightest unusual movement that might herald disaster.

The night seemed endless, but on the third day the dawn wind stirred, and the unbroken gloom gave up a single solitary offering. Land.

I saw we were getting closer. I could see crane jibs thrusting into the sky, tiny at first, but growing larger. Like many others, I stood and started forwards towards the rails. Cracked voices rose in gratitude and celebration. The ship swayed. Perhaps Stefan was there waiting for me.

We neared the port and I could see ships at anchor, all bearing the Persian flag of the Lion and Sun. I drew a massive lungful of air when I realised I couldn't see a Hammer and Sickle anywhere. Everyone was eager to disembark in case we sank before we got off, but we would have to wait. Another transport was already lying off the harbour waiting to land refugees.

We stood about a kilometre off the harbour mouth, but the port authorities sent out smaller ships for the evacuees on the neighbouring tanker to transfer over. To my surprise, they landed the entire contingent on two trips and returned immediately to get us off.

My legs wobbled when I stepped onto land and didn't stop trembling until I reached the beach. Passengers cried, fell to their knees, kissed the sands and gave praise; others sat and wept for joy. It was Easter Sunday.

To my dismay, our ordeal wasn't over. First, we had to pass through a medical tent erected on the pier. A copious amount of hot tea was available, and a flurry of activity kept the massive kettles topped up. Harassed staff dealt with both dockings and the subdued queues hacked and coughed as they shuffled forwards; small children cried.

'Typhus,' whispered Irena, turning away from the small boy wriggling in his mother's arms in front of us. Poor soul.'

I stepped back, 'How can you tell?'

'The rash. And the fever – the poor mite's burning up.'

We reached the checkpoint and the duty medical officer who, to our surprise, was Polish, removed the child from its mother and handed him straight to a gowned woman in a facemask who carried him away. 'Please don't worry; we're putting him into quarantine – for everyone's sake. It will only be for a few days, unless he deteriorates, in which case we'll admit him to hospital.'

'But I can take care of him,' the mother wailed. 'Please.'

'It may not come to it. Don't worry; the hospital is just over there. It's for everyone's safety.'

Irena and I, although we were just skin and

bone, had somehow survived these life-threatening diseases, with little more than leg ulcers, lice, exhaustion and starvation. We could continue to the Reception point, where an Establishment Officer, again from the Polish military, registered newcomers and gave out instructions.

He recorded our names, looked up, smiled, but offered no platitudes. 'This is what will happen next. After delousing and bathing, we will take you to Camp 3, to a shared tent. It is on the Kazian side of the harbour. There are four camps here. The military one is separate.'

It delighted me to hear this. If Stefan had already enlisted, this is where I would find him, and my excitement soared; I could barely contain myself. He was so close now. I could imagine his expression when he saw me; his joy. I was so happy my chin wobbled and my tears stung.

'Each camp has its own field kitchens and canteens,' he continued. 'Don't use other camps; we have clean camps, dirty camps and quarantine areas. The Soviets at Krasnovodsk were too lax in allowing sick people to travel.

'Your stay in Pahlevi is temporary. We will evacuate you to camps in Tehran with all speed. The convoys leave daily from behind Camp 3 on the Rasht Road. We will notify you when it's your turn. There are notice boards surrounding the Polish Headquarters tent, and you need to check daily. When you see your name, it means you will leave the following morning. If you don't turn up, the convoy will leave without you. Be prompt, it leaves on time.'

'Are there many refugees here?' I asked. I needed to know, so I had some idea of the size of my task in finding my loved ones.

'Tens of thousands, and more are on the way; they arrive unannounced day and night. We haven't enough tents, and our sappers are building temporary shelters along the beach – unsatisfactory in this weather, I know, but what can we do?'

'Is that why you're in such a hurry to move us to Tehran?' Irena asked.

'No, it's because the Germans are shelling Stalingrad, and we're expecting them to cross the Caspian Sea any day soon.' He gave us a brief smile which in no way deflected the sudden fear which consumed me.

'Right now you need to get on that truck. It will take you to the sanitation area.'

We climbed on board and settled ourselves on the wooden bench.

The truck filled up, and immediately the last refugee climbed on board, an empty truck drew up behind it. It conveyed us to the Boulevard on the Pahlevi side of the harbour via the Ghazian Bridge, crossing the Sefid River at its narrowest point. The Tent Unit was a series of large-scale improvised bathing and disinfection tents that covered the cemented floor. Enormous barrels, in open brick fireplaces, provided constant hot water for bathers from the many wells along the Boulevard's length.

I shed my rags, threw them on the heap for burning, and handed over Karol's shearling and my mother's pillow for delousing. Watching what remained of my hair falling to the floor, I hadn't realised how much it mattered; it was my identity. Now I ran my hand over my bald scalp, and instead of feeling liberated, I felt invisible. Following the other women through the interconnected tents to the mobile bath unit, I gasped with shock as the hot shower hit my flesh, before I luxuriated in its warmth, rubbing myself all over with sharp disinfectant soap.

A pale blue brocade dress, from clothes donated by the American Red Cross, caught my eye and I held it against me. It was a little large, but I loved blue. My shearling had been heat treated to kill the lice, and was still warm when I slipped it on. It was a bitter day and I was glad of it. Stretching out my arms, I couldn't see my fingertips, and was dismayed I hadn't grown a millimetre since leaving Poland; the coat still swamped me. All I needed now was food.

Camp 3 known as the 'Clean Camp' – was back on the Kazian side of the harbour. Sheltered by dunes from the sea, it sprawled along the beach. A barbed wire fence divided it from Camp 4 – the quarantine area, which they called the 'Dirty Camp'. Polish guards maintained that one.

'Thank goodness for the British Army,' Irena

said, 'this must have taken some organising. It's good they're allowing our boys to help, although I suppose it's obvious – they speak our language.'

The camp was huge with tents in every direction. 'How will we find our way back?' I asked her.

'Just remember, we're in the second row from the dunes, with a side view of the sea.'

The smell of food cooking led us to the field kitchen, the aromas growing richer as we drew closer, our tummies rumbling at the thought of what awaited.

Irena and I squeezed onto a bench at the end of a trestle table beneath an enormous tarpaulin supported with metal poles. We sat facing each other before the person beside us told us we had to queue at the counter for our food.

A feast awaited: mutton stew and rice, corned beef hash and fatty soup; all British luxuries – we didn't know what to choose. The aroma was unbelievable, and we salivated – but our stomachs were so shrunken; we couldn't eat much of what we received.

Exhaustion was taking its toll. With just enough strength to make it back to our tent, I flopped to my knees and formed the sand beneath my rush matting into a bolster. Snuggling down in Karol's shearling, I buried my face in my mother's pillow, and for the first night since Permilovo, succumbed to blissful sleep.

37

The rhythmic swash and backwash of breaking waves woke me.

I raised myself onto my elbows, and from the limited view of the beach beyond the upturned flap of our tent, I saw laughing children playing with a ball made of rags, and collecting shells. It took a moment until I was fully awake and able to savour the taste of freedom. Then it welled up again, that gut-punching realisation that Mama, Tatta and Karol were dead.

I heard Irena stir awake on the mat beside me, the clatter of mugs and mess tins as people left for breakfast.

'We'll have a look around later; get our bearings and see what's here,' Irena said, reaching for her mess tin, mug and spoon, 'But food first.'

I reminded her that I was desperate to ask someone in authority whether Gerhard and Lodzia, and Stefan and his family had arrived.

She said, 'I haven't forgotten. I'll come with you, but first let's familiarise ourselves with the place so we don't get lost.'

I was impatient to start searching, but reluctantly agreed.

How could I have forgotten that a boiled egg could taste so delicious? But the British bread was strange – it was white, as opposed to the heavy black Russian sort – and the tea was not nearly so sweet.

Replete after breakfast, we made for the beach where Polish sappers were hurriedly erecting shelters and digging sanitation trenches. There was nothing more than tents over here, so we turned in the opposite direction and found the hospital on the Kazian side of the harbour.

'Wait here a minute,' said Irena as she disappeared inside.

She appeared a little while after. 'They're desperate for help in there. The Iranians have made over the hospital to the British, and there are just a handful of British military nursing sisters almost on their knees with exhaustion.'

'Aren't there any Polish nurses helping?'

'A few, but some are in as bad a state as their patients. I've offered my help. You don't mind, do you?'

How could I mind? Irena said she would help me search, but I didn't let my disappointment show.

'Listen, Marishu. You should volunteer too. They're overwhelmed.'

'But I'm not a nurse.'

'You don't have to be to help feed the sick and stuff bags with straw for mattresses.'

I thought, 'Oh, no, please don't do this to me,' but then if Stefan, Gerhard or Lodzia were sick, I would be in the right place to find them. I agreed.

We started right away; the gnawing urge to find my loved ones at times overwhelming me. When the straw ran out, they roped me into feeding duties and I willingly did that too. We were not alone. Amongst the recent arrivals came Polish medical officers, trained matrons, and nurses from the large hospitals in Poland, offering their services. All day long, the sick kept arriving. They sent the severest cases over the mountains to the hospitals at Qazvin, or Dosham Tapu in Tehran.

However, much as I wanted to help, desperation got the better of my good intentions. The moment someone else offered to take my place, I hurried off across the Ghazian Bridge in search of the Polish Army headquarters. The tent was hard to miss with so many crowding the notice boards searching for their names.

Giddy with excitement, I sought out the officer staffing the desk. 'I'm trying to find my brother Gerhard, his wife, Lodzia and their daughter, and also the Novak family. They left the labour camp at the end of 1941. Would you know if they're here?'

'That's a fair while ago. Best you try Q Tent across the road. Ask for a Transport Officer; they may have been and gone.'

Filled with nervous anticipation, I hurried across the road, and asked there. The Officer reached for a thick log with a large G written in black ink on the cover and his finger drifted down the names before he turned the page; then his finger moved slower still.

'Glenz, you say? Ah yes, here it is. We evacuated the Glenz family to one of the refugee camps in Tehran at the beginning of March.'

March? That was over a month ago. My brain went into pause; I wasn't expecting them to have survived, but his news brought forth a torrent of tears, fuelled by uncontrolled joy. 'Thank God they're still alive. Thank you, thank you.' I brushed them away with the heel of my hand. 'You say one of the camps. Which one?'

'Ah, we don't keep a record of that here. We have no way of knowing at what time they arrived at the vehicle park on the day of departure. The first and last would go to different camps.'

'And what about the Novak family?'

He reached for another fat log with a 'N' on the front. I could hardly wait; I wished he would make haste.

'Ah yes, here we are. The Novak's are being evacuated tomorrow. It's on the notice board.' He looked up at me and smiled.

They were here! Oh God, I had found them! Stefan was here. But tomorrow – they were leaving tomorrow.

'I need to find them. Where's their tent?' I realised it was a pointless question the moment I opened my mouth – there were hundreds of tents and thousands of people.

'Sorry, can't help you there. I'm in charge of transport.'

'Then can you tell me in which truck they will travel?'

He smiled at my naivety. 'Trucks, buses – the British have commandeered anything that's fit to travel – short of camels; there are over a hundred vehicles in each convoy.'

'How many camps are there in Tehran?' I felt myself floundering amidst the bureaucracy.

He stared at me and said, 'Five – including the orphanage at Isfahan, but that's much further out. You must ask again when you arrive. Our job is to evacuate as many people from Pahlevi as fast as we can.'

'When will it be my turn to leave?'

'Impossible to say; over 43,000 people arrived in Pahlevi in the past nine days, 19,000 of which we will have evacuated as of tomorrow. I doubt you'll be leaving soon – there are others before you. My guess would be in two weeks, maybe three. Keep checking the notice board.'

I was near to tears again. Each time I got closer to finding my loved ones, they moved them further away from me.

'But the Germans are coming.'

'Why don't you get up early tomorrow morning, go to the vehicle park and see if you can spot your friends? You never know – you might be lucky. You'll find it at the back of Camp 3. They leave at 0800 hours.'

Yes, yes, I would. I thanked him and left.

That evening, Irena and I walked over to the convoy rendezvous point. And what a shock it was. Lorries and buses of every shape and size, some of dubious roadworthiness, lined up in rows of ten with a Polish guard mounted at each group to prevent the vehicles moving without orders. Clustered together were a group of Iranian and Armenian drivers deep in conversation. They looked up as we passed, but made no comment. Others slept inside their vehicles.

Sleep eluded me; the excitement proved too much because tomorrow I would see Stefan. I would find him, even if it meant lying in the road in front of the convoy and yelling his name for all to hear.

Rain thundered down on our tent roof. It was still barely light when I reached the vehicle park the next morning, but well lit. People were arriving in a steady stream, hurrying to get out of the weather. I pulled the collar of my sheepskin closer, my eyes everywhere, trying not to miss a thing.

The troops were already waiting in their lorries. Some had their backs to me, so I couldn't see their faces. When I called Stefan's name, some turned to look but no one answered, and they resumed their conversations.

The wind beat across the vehicle park, driving the rain through my thin headscarf and chilling my scalp. I walked up and down the individual lanes, which revealed hundreds of passengers already sitting in their vehicles surrounded by bundles, obscuring their faces. So many times throughout the interminable night, I'd imagined throwing myself into Stefan's arms, but I hadn't factored for people boarding various trucks simultaneously. I couldn't be everywhere at once. Nor did I envisage that some trucks would be open-topped, others covered in tarpaulin, and others high-sided with slats obscuring their occupants.

Then there were the stretchers with the lying sick and the sitting sick transferring from the local hospital onto buses, trucks or army ambulance, not to mention the guides, loaders and luggage porters rushing back and forth.

The storm passed over leaving me wet and weary, but the sky was growing lighter. Engines burst into life and vehicles disappeared behind veils of belching fumes. The convoy pulled slowly away, forcing me to break into a trot alongside, jumping up and down to see through bus windows, shouting Stefan's name.

A truck ahead stalled, holding up the others, then leap-frogged off down the road and stalled again. It was then I heard someone calling my name – a woman's voice from the truck in front of the bus. I caught up and ran alongside. It was Olga, Stefan's sister. Both his parents and his four sisters were there – but there was no sign of him.

Their truck was gaining speed now, and I was becoming out of breath. 'Where's Stefan?' I yelled.

'In the military field hospital outside Tehran – he's got typhus. They took him straight there as soon as we arrived. Please go to him, Marishu. He was so insistent that you go...' Olga's words trailed away in a cloud of exhaust smoke.

I doubled over with a stitch as the convoy rumbled past me. Exhausted, I dropped to my knees and wept.

* * *

I couldn't wait to get out of Pahlevi, but until that happened I devoted myself to my voluntary work at the hospital. I checked the many notices boards each day to see if my name was on them, but it never was.

If I wasn't stuffing mattresses, I spent hours encouraging little children to eat. Their little tummies were all blown up, their skin embedded with lice. Bones protruded from their shrivelled faces and their enormous eyes stared into space. They were so ill they were too weak to cry, and I wondered if Stalin would feel any remorse if he saw what he had created.

Irena returned at night with horror stories of refugees arriving daily with malaria, dysentery, tuberculosis and frostbite – some with limbs almost dropping off with the disease, and typhus. She said typhus was now at its worst amongst children under four years old and the latest news was that sea crossings from Krasnovodsk to Pahlevi had ceased.

To my surprise, I enjoyed volunteering; my life had meaning again. The hospital was now my new family; it was somewhere I belonged.

38

It was 16th April – evacuation day for Irena and me, and we were waiting to board.

Lanes had been delineated with ropes on each side of the vehicle park, and as civilians arrived from the camps they were being formed up into groups of threes in each of these lanes and then led forwards in parties according to the size and capacity of individual vehicles. I was the last of one party – Irena was the first of the next.

'We want to travel together,' I protested, as they marched her off to towards a bus with a load of strangers.

'Don't worry,' Irena called back, 'we'll meet up in Qazvin.'

The only remaining seat was at the front, besides the Polish guard. He was a man who gallantly suggested I take the window seat, then shattered the illusion by admitting it was because he had to monitor our Armenian driver, who was not very reliable and prone to speeding. He introduced himself as Pawel and said he came from Brest.

This constant talk of the Germans advancing towards us had been like a yoke of terror, but now we were being moved into the interior, there was nothing but relief. How was this young man feeling knowing he would soon face the deadliest peril somewhere on the front line?

There was a buzz of excitement on board as children jostled for places next to windows, their noses already pressed to the glass. Adults settled in their seats with their few packages and shouted to their offspring to behave, but everyone was optimistic.

The convoy set off at 0800 hours and clung to the coast for some time, before it veered inland and headed for Rasht. In the distance, the Elburz Mountains loomed bleak and daunting.

I took one last glance back at Pahlevi as it receded into the distance and thanked God for the British military. They came to our rescue when we were at our most helpless; they fed us, clothed us, built up our strength, and restored our faith in humanity and in ourselves.

With the town of Rasht behind us, we headed through arable land towards the mountains, and the convoy made a comfort stop when the greenery became scanty, so people could relieve themselves amongst the few bushes that still grew there.

The gradient increased, gently at first, but soon the driver had his foot down.

I gripped my seat, and my dry rations fell to the floor. We had all heard about the recent fatal accident caused by an overtaking bus where the truck ended up at the bottom of a ravine and burst into flames.

We followed the Hamadan Route along the most dangerous road imaginable. On one side of us, the steep rock face obliterated all sunlight. Shale and rubble covered the slopes, and I realised there was nothing to stop avalanches running down into the valleys on the other side of the road – with our transport caught in the middle.

Stefan would have passed this way too. I wondered if he was one of the 'lying sick' or the 'sitting sick' aboard his ambulance vehicle. Mercifully, he might have been lying down and spared this heart-stopping experience.

The gradient grew steeper, and the ledge on which we travelled appeared narrower. The driver changed down a gear to gather speed, but the gears crunched, failed to engage, and the vehicle slowed. He tried again and again, but now our bus was slipping backwards. The noise of grinding gears silenced even the noisiest passengers as everyone prayed and willed him to correct the situation because another truck was making up ground behind us, sounding its horn. Passengers began shouting it would crash into us when just in time he hit the right gear and continued at a slower pace.

I saw fear in Pawel's eyes. 'Let's hope he doesn't try that trick again.'

My mouth was dry. I peered over the edge to see where we might have landed. It was a very long way down. Many of the streams had caused deep gorges, and only the valley bottoms were lush. It was a harsh landscape of sublime beauty. However, when I looked up, I occasionally caught sight of another transport above us on a hairpin bend so steep that it looked as if it were travelling almost vertically.

We reached Qazvin at dusk and stopped outside a sizeable building. Everyone started chattering at once while getting out of their seats.

Pawel stood. 'Everyone, could I please have your attention for a moment. This is a school building, and the Iranian authorities have allowed us to use it overnight. We ask that no one leave the building as we need to make a very early start in the morning. The children will use the school an hour after we vacate it, so please leave the place as you found it. There are plenty of latrines and washbasins, so use them. It might help if you left your baggage on the bus. It's locked and guarded overnight.'

I climbed off the bus and milled about, hoping to find Irena disembarking from another vehicle, but I must have missed her. When I asked Pawel, what could have happened to her, he told me there wasn't enough space at the school for the entire convoy and the others had gone to different destinations.

Over our evening meal of spicy soup, and lamb with paprika and raisins, everyone learned to which camp they were being transferred. For me, it was Camp One. All those heading to Camp One had to remain in the school hall.

I asked Pawel if Irena would also come to Camp One, but he was vague. 'It's beyond my control,' he said.

They turned off the lights later, and I lay in the darkness on the concrete floor, wondering if I would ever see my friend again. But such was life. Everything and everyone was fleeting.

At daybreak, half asleep, everyone crawled back on board their transport for the last leg of our journey.

Descending from the foothills, the driver took us through villages surrounded by date and olive trees, occasionally swerving to avoid animals that roamed the streets amid houses made of mud bricks, while the Persian people threw gifts of fruit and flowers into the passing trucks.

Further south, the land became drier, making travelling in a convoy of dust cloud an ordeal. Everyone was wide awake by the time we reached the outskirts of Tehran – with its skyline of minarets, domes and mosques.

Camp One was on the outskirts, and according to Pawel, it once belonged to the Iranian Air Force. Approaching the high yellow daub wall which surrounded it, I could see two substantial brown brick buildings. As our convoy passed through the gates and ended its journey inside the compound, I could see other buildings and many tents. Below us, civilians began surging towards the trucks and buses in search of their loved ones, and those on board pushed and shoved to be first off.

I sat for a while, watching their joy, their unfettered exhilaration when family members found each other again – hugging and kissing multiple times over. When the bus was empty, I scooped up my holdall, and climbed off, my limbs stiff from having sat for so long.

I didn't see them at first, but there, waiting for the convoy were Gerhard, Lodzia and Ella!

They rushed towards me, and my brother crushed me to him. 'Ahh, Marishu we've been waiting here for the convoys every day since we arrived. We've been checking at all the other camps too. What's taken you so long?'

A nerve ticked below my eye. I knew I should answer but couldn't.

He looked over my shoulder. 'Where's Mama, Tatta, and Karol?'

Another moment passed.

'Dead!' I cried. Then the dam burst and I sobbed in his arms.

'You poor child.' Lodzia joined us, slipped her arm around my waist, looked up at Gerhard, and they led me away.

Gerhard barely uttered a word until later in the afternoon, when we left the tent and they took me to the field kitchen for dinner. Over the meal of baked brown stew and macaroni, he shook his head countless times; his food left untouched. 'I knew something was wrong when I saw you wearing Karol's coat.'

'What happened?' Lodzia asked.

Gerhard continued staring at the food, 'I knew we shouldn't have left you at Vodopad. If I'd had any idea... Marisha, I am so sorry.'

I slipped my arm around Ella and planted a gentle, lingering kiss on top of my niece's head.

'I can't imagine how you felt.'

'Can't you?' I gazed into his eyes and felt my rage mounting. 'I had to cut Tatta's hair from the wagon wall. Ice – two inches thick. We couldn't move him. We left him there... at Plesetsk... at some mortuary... a wooden shack with bodies piled up to the roof. Two days later, I had to carry Karol's body. Another makeshift mortuary. And soon after, Mama. All on my own because no one would help me. Everyone feared dysentery. I left her body on the station steps at Penza, Gerhard. Left her because I hadn't the strength to carry her any further. I deserted her. Can you imagine how that feels, Gerhard – can you? And where were you when I needed help? Where were any of you? I felt so guilty for deserting her like that; she deserved better.' I thumped my chest with my fist, and my tears gushed unchecked.

'Dear God, none of this is your fault.'

'No one's saying it is my fault. But it's how I feel – it's how I shall always feel.'

After a pause, he asked, 'Where did you leave Karol's body?

I composed myself. 'In Vologda. At least he's

near Natasha and their baby.'

'What baby?'

'Didn't you know? She was pregnant; that's why her mother wanted to get her married off to that Valerik and out of Vodopad – away from Karol – before it showed. But he knew – oh, Karol knew.'

All Lodzia could manage was, 'Dear God.'

Gerhard kept repeating, 'I am so sorry.'

I closed my eyes and exhaled. 'Enough.' Now I had blood let my sorrow; I felt relieved. I swiped away my tears. 'It is as it is.'

After the meal, Gerhard had to return to the military camp. They kept the men and women segregated.

'They're moving him out tomorrow,' Lodzia said. 'This was our last day together.'

'Tomorrow! So soon?'

'We were despairing you wouldn't arrive in time.'

I had given up railing against what happened to us. That was the way of it – everything was short-lived; life was short-lived. 'I spoke with Stefan's sister just as they were leaving Pahlevi. He's ill with typhus in the military hospital. He wants me to visit him. When Gerhard leaves, will you come with me, Lodziu? I need to know for sure if he's dead or alive; I won't rest until I find him.'

She squeezed my hand. 'You poor child, you don't have to ask. It's close to here.'

I looked at my brother, withdrawn, subdued and distant and felt sorry for him. 'Do you know yet where they're taking you, Gerhard?'

He shrugged as if he didn't care. I had lived with the death of our family for the past four months, but he had to go and fight with this burden.

'Somewhere in Iraq to start with – we have to guard some strategic oil fields. Then we're being moved to Palestine for training. After that, I suppose they'll send us to the front line – either in Italy or North Africa.'

'I'm sorry. Gerhard, please don't go yet.'

'I have no choice; I'm not the first. Thousands have already left. I'm lucky they've allowed me to stay behind this long. But at least I know you're safe. You have no idea what that means, Marishu.'

39

The field Hospital at Dosham Tapu – or the 34th British Commonwealth General Hospital – as they knew it, lay on a salty plain beneath the shadow of the Caucasus.

I was hoping for the best, but prepared myself for the worst. What a sight greeted us. Hundreds of sick and dying people lay on folded blankets outside, as there were insufficient beds. The fatigue party were working non-stop, putting up more tents over them, and all the while more army ambulances were arriving from Pahlevi with the very sick and the dying.

We wandered inside and soon learned that it was an all-Indian staff, and we didn't understand their language. Lodzia wrote Stefan's name in capital letters on a slip of paper, but they couldn't read that either. The only white people we saw – apart from the patients – were the sisters from Queen Alexandra's Nursing Service who were so rushed off their feet, they couldn't spare the time and spoke only in English. We asked some nursing sepoys, but none of them understood Polish. It was hopeless.

'There must be someone in this hospital who can tell us what's become of him.' My nerves were so coiled they were at snapping point. Faced with defeat, we left, not knowing if Stefan was dead or alive.

Back at Camp One, a friend of Lodzia's tactfully suggested we try the cemetery. 'Few with typhus survive,' she said.

We lingered in the shade of the pine and plantain trees in Doulab Cemetery, grateful for a fleeting respite from the sun. Beneath them lay the slabs and monuments each marking a dwelling place in which no one was home.

There were no shrines for the Poles. A simple cross bearing a name and a date identified our freshly dug graves; so many of them children's. Candles burned on some; flowers lay on others. How I wished I could have given my parents and Karol such a burial in a tranquil and beautiful place such as this. Everyone deserved an engraved marble slab or a stone angel to say they had passed this way, but a wooden cross would have sufficed. Instead, the Soviets would throw their bodies into some anonymous pit with thousands of others and no one would ever discover their barbaric secrets.

Lodzia and I visited each grave, walking up and down on opposite sides, while little Ella complained her legs ached, and she had had enough.

'Well, Stefan's not here,' I said with a sigh of relief. 'So that must mean they have already transferred him to Palestine for training, or even to the front line.

'Or he might still be at the hospital. We'll try again tomorrow.' said Lodzia.

A second visit to the hospital proved futile. I convinced myself that like Gerhard, Stefan had been moved to the war zone somewhere. I refused to accept he was dead.

Without the men visiting their families, life at the camp went on as usual. Women washed the clothes, hung them against the barbed wire to dry and children played.

There was an airport close by, and I often sat alone, watching the military planes taking off and landing, fascinated how such enormous things could remain airborne.

The camp was large, taking up a full ten minutes to cross. The vast influx of refugees meant that a massive tented city had spilt out beyond the perimeter walls, protected by barbed wire fencing. Washrooms and showers were under open skies and the smelly latrines on the periphery of the camp were being treated non-stop with quicklime, but dysentery was rife.

'I wonder where Gerhard is,' Lodzia said. 'It's been eight weeks since the troops left for Iraq. I no longer feel safe here without the men to protect us.'

Rumours were rife again: German paratroopers were coming down in the north; some already captured in the Caucasus. Whether this was true, British and American troops began arriving in huge numbers to meet what everyone thought would be a grave situation. That was tangible proof that it wasn't hearsay, wasn't it? Some even claimed they'd heard the distant sound of guns echoing across the mountains from the north.

'A new school's opened,' Lodzia said. 'I was planning to enrol Ella if we would stay, but now there's the talk of the British wanting to evacuate us to their colonies right away.'

'Because of the danger?'

'No. As I understand it, Persia was only ever going to be a temporary landing point for our army. The British never expected so many civilians – I don't think they expected any civilians at all.'

'So where are they sending us?'

'Who knows: New Zealand, Canada, India... British Central Africa. I think if we're given a choice, we should opt for Africa – it's nearer Poland.'

'It's nowhere near Poland.'

With patience, 'Well, it's nearer than Canada or New Zealand.'

We agreed on Africa.

'Let's see if we can get another change of clothes and underwear.' Lodzia discovered a new consignment had recently arrived from the Red Cross. She had some money left, but not enough to waste on frivolous garments – and not at Tehran's prices.

I wasn't interested in clothes; I had all I needed. Who cared about clothes?

She returned soon after, having done pretty badly out of what they left. 'I brought you a hat.' With a swift backhand, she propelled it across the tent, and I caught it by the rim.

'Put it on then.'

Dragging off my headscarf, I drew my hand across the soft black down already sprouting from my scalp, and donned the hat.

'Perfect,' Lodzia held up a rather large nightdress. 'With a little imagination, I'm sure I can make something out of this.'

Yesterday she dragged me into Tehran city centre, but I wasn't interested in sightseeing; I wasn't interested in anything. The finely clothed women and the beautifully dressed shop windows held no appeal. Even the wide streets, which cut through the urban fabric of the city, depressed me further; everything was so modern that I felt intimidated.

I yearned for the simple meadows of home, filled with clover, daisies and corn poppies. I wanted for Mama and Tatta to be going about their daily chores. I yearned for my cows, for my darling Bookiet rounding them up at milking time.

I knew Lodzia was becoming exasperated with me. She said she felt as if I had put up my walls and didn't want anyone near me. She was right. I couldn't bear to relive what had happened to me, but she wanted me to open up and talk; to share my emotions. She said it was the only way of letting go. I knew she meant well, but couldn't she understand I was numb inside?

It was kind of her to help me, but she had worries of her own. She, like other wives at the camp anxious about their husbands, was waiting for word from Gerhard. Worrying about my well-being was the last thing she needed.

It had been five months since the death of my family, and at last, I felt less like an ethereal observer viewing these ghastly happenings, and more of a victim. This was far worse. Reality hurt so badly. All around me there were mothers and daughters, and children with grandparents, with siblings. I couldn't bear to be near them; they were emphasising what I had lost. The only way I could cope with life was to blot the whole ghastly nightmare permanently from my mind and not discuss it. I wished I were dead. But Lodzia refused to give up on me.

'And all this has happened because the Soviets wouldn't give Tatta his travel documents,' she droned on again, trying to break through my defences.

This time she had hit the one button that caused me the most pain. Oh God, why couldn't she let the matter rest?

'You could all have come with us, and they would still be alive now.'

'Yes! Yes,' I shouted, 'they would be alive!' This was the tragedy of it all. I couldn't get my head around this one thing because, at the time of everyone else receiving their travel documents, we had sufficient funds to support ourselves to leave Vodopad without starving. Had the Soviets given us our papers, we could have left with Lodzia and Gerhard, and I would have been on the same transport as Stefan and his family. In my mind, I had been over and over this scenario countless times – and it was this feeling of impotence – of helplessness – it crucified me. 'Yes, I believe they would have lived,' I cried. 'They should have lived, Lodziu. They were fifty four years old. Karol was twenty one; they had done nothing wrong. Why couldn't I have died with them? I have nothing left to live for.'

She watched me force my fist into my mouth and sob. Huge rasping sobs wracked my body, and I felt ashamed. 'I don't know how to live, Lodziu; they were everything to me.'

She pulled me into her arms. 'There, there – let it all go; that's the way.' After a while, she gave me a gentle shake to ensure I was listening. 'We'll speak no more of it. None of this is your fault. You have your path in life to follow now. You mustn't give up. You've got to keep going.'

※ ※ ※

Vivid fields of yellow rape glinted at me.

I rested my head against the carriage seat and watched idly as the countryside sped by the train window. But it was not my countryside, not Szpitali; it was some foreign land.

It was now September, and we were once again on the move. This time we were en route to the transit camp at Ahwaz in southern Iran.

My thoughts once more turned to Stefan, as they always did. I now felt sure we had lost each other forever. I felt odd today. My legs swelled; it was hot, yet I felt cold, and all at once I shivered and sweated.

Two days ago, Lodzia received the long-awaited letter from Gerhard. He was in Bagdad and complaining it was too hot. Six months ago, he would have given anything for a little heat.

The next thing I saw was Lodzia leaning over me as I came to, and Ella shaking my arm, urging me to wake up.

I was lying in a bed with spotless white sheets, in a proper building with electricity. There were nurses, wearing starched uniforms and everywhere looked so clean. 'Where am I? What's happened to me?'

'You're in the hospital in Ahwaz. You've had malaria.'

'How long have I been here? Am I going to die?'

'No, kohanie, sorry to disappoint you; you're on the mend now. I've been so worried about you.'

'But how'... I tried to raise myself onto my elbows, failed and flopped back in exhaustion.

'Shh, is it any wonder after all you've been through? Your body couldn't cope and gave up.'

'What are we doing in Ahwaz?'

'Don't you remember? They're taking us to Africa. We have to go via Karachi and try to avoid German submarines. And from there, kohanie, we sail to Africa.'

'Did you miss the other ship because of me?'

'Yes, we did.'

'Lodziu, why didn't you leave me here and go on without me?'

'Ahh, Marishu, don't be so silly. My God, we couldn't leave you behind. And I have a surprise for you – we shall sail on the MS Batory.' She smiled then. 'Ah, do I see a flicker of interest in your eyes?'

This time I managed to raise myself onto my elbows. 'The Polish ship, Stefan Batory?'

They named the MS Batory after the 16th century Polish King, Stefan Batory.

From the moment I stepped on board I felt secure; it was like a piece of Poland. We were sailing on a Polish ship crewed by Polish seamen.

Escorted by two frigates, we passed through the Strait of Hormuz into the Gulf of Oman, and sailed south for two days.

The temperature was rising as we navigated what looked like a vast canal with mangrove swamps accompanying us for some ten kilometres or more before the Batory entered a wide bay and docked in Port Karachi.

Our connecting ship hadn't yet docked and wasn't due for another week. Meanwhile, we were to await its departure in a tented part of the city – The Country Club near University Road.

The evening temperature was insufferable as the day's surplus heat continued quivering off the scorched earth, which hurled it back to the heavens. After our frantic arrival in Pahlevi, our anxious journey through the mountains, the well-ordered manner of being processed through and out of Iran, Karachi seemed a million miles removed. It was also all things British.

Noise beset us from all directions. Amid the fretwork of shadows, the dense aromas of spices mingled with the fragrance of patchouli, and did battle with the foetid stench of sewers. For a British penny, street sellers offered rags dipped in water from leather buckets, to refresh us while we fought of flies and mosquitos. There were horses with rickshaws, and women sweeping streets with wide straw brooms. A performing bear and his owner turned tricks for onlookers, while camels pulled a cart full of pipes to some construction project. There were beggars and shoeshine boys, and it seemed as if all life was here.

All life was here. We spent the night in a tent crawling with bugs and insects, thankful when morning arrived and we could get into the open air. We were even more grateful when it was time to board the ship to Africa.

40

We sailed west across the Arabian Sea.

Each day, as the sun set molten bronze and the evening clouds descended, I sat by myself at the back of the ship. Alone with my sorrow, my trail of dreams unfulfilled, its soporific motion hypnotised me as it ploughed up and down through the waves. It soothed me, anaesthetised my pain. After the day was spent, and when only a thread of light remained on the horizon, did I rejoin Lodzia and Ella before climbing into my bunk bed, the tears always there behind my eyes.

Eight days later, the port of Dar-es-Salaam came into view, but something was wrong.

Lodzia was panicking. The insect bites on Ella's leg which she had received in Karachi, had turned nasty. 'Look at these livid purple streaks,' she wailed.

Ella was shaking, and her entire persona had changed.

I felt her forehead. 'She's feverish.'

Then Ella threw up.

A concerned fellow passenger said she would get Ella to the hospital with that – and fast.

The tugboat drew our ship into harbour and

passengers gathered at the rails to watch. Lodzia was now desperate to get her daughter off and to seek medical help since there was no one on board and nothing was moving fast enough for her.

While Ella was slipping in and out of delirium down on the dock, Africans were awaiting our arrival with baskets of oranges, calling up to us with broad smiles and 'Jambo mzungu' (Hello white people). Everyone smiled back and waved. They were friendly, joyful people. Neither Lodzia nor I waved back; we were too busy applying streams of cold compresses to Ella's chest and forehead.

Everything to Lodzia must have been passing in a blur, but I had arranged we received priority to leave the ship. While the other passengers were being sorted into groups for their onward journeys to the various refugee camps in the interior, Lodzia, Ella and I were rushed to the Sewa Haji hospital in the port area.

Ella had septicaemia.

As if to re-emphasise that someone 'up there' was looking after us, a Polish-speaking nurse passed on the doctor's message. 'The doctor said it would be best to prepare for the worst, because half of those who have blood poisoning die.'

We both stared at her in disbelief, because she was so matter-of-fact about it all.

Die! How could she die? Ella was perfectly fine yesterday, wasn't she? Or was she? How long had she had this bacterium coursing through her veins?

'Tell me what to do,' Lodzia begged her. 'I'll do anything, just tell me what.' Her entire world had come to a stop.

'Pray,' the nursed squeezed her shoulder, 'and hope for the best.'

Day and night Lodzia sat beside Ella's bed, watching her dying child clinging to life.

I strolled around the hospital grounds to get some air and to stretch my legs. It was only when I glanced up at the hospital window behind which my young niece had been fighting for her life for the past three weeks, did I realise how ill she was, and might not survive.

Nothing catastrophic had befallen Lodzia or Ella so far – and now this. Who or what determined who was to live or to die, I wondered. What did people have to do to survive? At Vodopad, 43 souls lost their lives, but they were no different from our family. Everyone had the same amount of food and endured the same hardships.

I realised then it was Mama and Tatta who had made that difference. It was their self-sacrificing attitudes that kept us all alive. Mama not only cared for us, but she helped others, sharing our precious food when Sasha's little boy was ill. Even then, disease and hunger got them.

I had long since given up praying to God to spare Ella. Now, I *willed* her to live. She was such a darling child. Gerhard was out there somewhere preparing to give his all for Poland and his family; with no idea that his daughter's life was already ebbing away.

I returned to the hospital carrying water and fruit the nurse had given me.

'How is she?' I set down a glass of water on the cabinet beside Lodzia.

We both stared at the panting, sweating child and Lodzia shook her head.

'The nurse gave me these.' I handed her some bananas. 'She said you have to eat.'

Lodzia pushed away my hand. 'I'm not hungry.'

I was angry. This is just what Mama said, refusing the slither of soaked potato I tried to give her. 'Eat them, Lodzia! You'll need all your strength for when Ella gets better. What use will you be to her when you're dead?'

She took a banana and ate it. It was a start. Ten days later, Ella's eyes flickered open. She had survived.

The flamboyant trees of Dar-es-Salaam blazed with blood-red blossom, the humidity was relentless, and the air hung with the pulsating drone of cicadas.

Ella and I sat in the shade of an Acacia tree on the long dusty road that stretched into the distance on either side of us. Indian traders stood in their shop doorways, and black and brown-skinned tailors worked on their treadle machines.

Lodzia stepped out of the station building clutching the tickets. 'There's a train leaving in under an hour that will take us as far as Dodoma. From there we have to organise passage to take us north to Kondoa.' Having missed the pre-arranged transport when we first arrived, we had to make our way into the interior.

The sun beat down and there was not even a wisp of cloud as the wood-burning Garrett locomotive towed us along the metre-wide track at a leisurely pace.

We followed the old caravan route, from the Indian Ocean to Lake Tanganyika, an eight-hour journey. It was so hot that even the lizards took shelter in the shadows of rocks where the parched earth threatened to bake them alive.

Lodzia coped with everything calmly, did what needed to be done. When the train approached each of the many little stations, hustling and shouting Africans ran alongside the carriages, pushing their bags and their wares through the open windows, even before it had stopped. She used the opportunity to step out, collect water and buy bananas. The stops were not long, yet the train never left until everyone was aboard, and continued at its unhurried pace. The African people were kind and relaxed – unlike the angst-riddled and fearful citizens of the Soviet Union.

Vast herds of game turned and sped in the

opposite direction as our train approached. A line of low blue hills appeared, turned brown and receded into blue again. Everywhere else was brown; brown cattle, men and houses. About 175 kilometres from Dar-es-Salaam, we passed the Uluguru Mountains, brooding in the mounting dusk against an enormous sky; Africa was vast.

Dodoma was the end of the line for us, and Lodzia rented a room at a clean but basic lodging house. Before retiring to bed, we ate a wholesome meal of Ugali and lamb stew. Watching closely how the locals ate theirs, Ella copied, clumsily rolling the Ugali into a ball with her right hand, denting it with her thumb, and using it as a scoop to wrap around pieces of meat and to soak up the sauce. Looking pleased with herself when she had mastered it, she cleared her plate of food.

The next morning saw us climb aboard a covered truck Lodzia had hired to complete the last of our journey to Kondoa.

The temperature was already rising, and the cicadas were in full voice. While Ella stayed well out of the sun, Lodzia and I sat fanning ourselves in the canopy's shade, grateful for the passing breeze.

Deeper into the interior, away from civilisation, the countryside was harsh – a sunburnt landscape of bleached pale yellows and tawny browns. There was little to see, but outcrops of rock, a scattering of thorn bush, the occasional patch of withered millet and the odd tree.

Lodzia pointed to a pride of lions sheltering beneath a baobab tree. Sand rivers crossed our path and in the distance a herd of giraffe fed on the leaves of an Acacia, before the engine's noise disturbed them and they loped off in the opposite direction.

The late afternoon was a listless stream that had lost its torrent by the time we arrived at the old Italian mission, three hours later.

A rosy-faced nun appeared, her crucifix bouncing against her bosom as she hurried to greet us.

'Welcome.' Her arms were already outstretched to help us down from the truck. 'We've been expecting you for the past month. Praise the Lord you are all well.' She clutched Ella's hand and led us to our quarters. 'You've arrived just in time for afternoon tea.' She walked and talked. 'We have bread and runny butter delivered to the huts at about this time; a vat of soup for your breakfast, and you go to the canteen for your mid-day meals. Work finishes at twelve.'

'Home,' she announced and led us into a wattle and daub hut covered with banana leaves.

There were eighteen beds, and fifteen lounging bodies lifted themselves to their elbows when we walked in.

'Everyone, this is...' She turned to Lodzia for

support.

Lodzia pointed, 'Marisha, Ella and I'm Leokadia, but everyone calls me Lodzia.'

The nun whispered, 'They're all waiting for their teas.' Then louder, 'Can I leave these wonderful people in your capable hands ladies? They have just navigated their own way from Dar-es-Salaam – how amazing is that – so they're tired and hungry?' With the introductions over, the nun disappeared.

A young woman called Danuta seemed in charge. Her bed was furthest from the door at the end of the hut. She swung her legs to the floor and joined us. 'Sorry, these are the only beds left. Chose which you want, and I'll take you to the wash-house; I'm sure you'd like to freshen up before we eat.'

When we returned, Danuta was already divvying out the bread and runny butter. I noticed our three portions were smaller than the others, but you notice these things, don't you? They were used to the larger ones in our absence, and I still felt hungry.

I ended up with the worst bed – it was opposite the open doorway, but there was no door. Neither was there any glass at the windows – just blinds. Lifting the mosquito net, I lay down on the bed, surprised to find it comfortable; the mattress stuffed with banana leaves.

At night, Danuta placed a candle in the door opening to ward off snakes and hyenas, and I prayed it worked because I would be first in line to make a tasty meal for a voracious animal.

Exhausted as I was, sleep eluded me. Strange and disturbing sounds drifted into the night; the occasional chanting in an unfamiliar tongue accompanied by rhythmic drumming from somewhere beyond. It had to be the natives, but why so late?

'Did you sleep well?' Lodzia threw her legs over the side of the bed in the morning and disentangled herself from the mosquito net. Ella was already awake and sitting in the doorway; the candle gone. So had all the girls.'

I propped myself onto my elbows and looked around. 'Did you hear that drumming in the night? It kept me awake.'

'Must be the natives.'

The rest of the girls returned just after eight, in time for the kettle of soup brought to our hut from the kitchen.

'We've been to Mass,' the one called Stefcha told us. 'It starts at seven. Danuta wanted to wake you; she insisted you wouldn't want to miss Mass, but I told her to let you sleep in.'

'Thank you,' I said. I didn't know why, but already I was disliking this Danuta.

'If you like,' Stefcha offered, 'after breakfast I'll take you and show you around the camp. It's not huge. We're two kilometres outside of Kondoa town, and there are some nice little cafes there.'

I liked her; she was a little chatterbox.

'According to the nuns, these huts used to house Italian prisoners of war. There aren't any now. Ah, here comes the soup.'

Danuta dished it out, and it wasn't just me who noticed we received less again.

'Oi,' Stefcha said, 'these three have less than us.'

'Have they?' Danuta looked embarrassed, 'I've served it now.'

'Tell you what then, we'll give them ours, and we can have theirs? How about that?'

'I'll see if I can get you all cork hats,' Stefcha said. 'We're just below the equator, so you must wear them at all times when you're outside. The nuns are very strict about that.'

'Not just when it's raining?' Ella said.

Lodzia clipped her gently under the chin. 'Sign she's recovering,'

'They say there has been no rain for months.' Stefcha led us to the rear of the huts where a narrow mango-lined lane separated our settlement from the Bubu River. 'That's why this one's arid. The nuns told us that during the rainy season, it turns violent. It's even washed away the largest trucks, so it's best not to swim.'

'When is the rainy season,' I asked?

'December to March. It's mostly dry till then. It's not rained since we arrived.'

We stood for a while watching the local black

children scrape away at the sandy river bed with their bare hands until they reached water beneath. They scooped it up into dried melon skins, which they had fashioned into kitchen utensils and then set about washing. Ella moved closer and crouched down beside them; they were about the same age, and she was ready to muck in with them.

'Ingenious,' Lodzia remarked. 'Who would have thought of using melon skins!'

I too shook my head and smiled.

'You smiled!' Lodzia hugged me. 'It's the first time I've seen you smile since we left Szpitali. Hallelujah! Kohanie, as tragic as everything is, never allow what's happened to you to destroy your spirit.'

Stefcha led the way to the church, which stood across the road from our huts. Dense clumps of elephant grass sprouted here and there, but on the whole the area was arid with sparse vegetation. I thought it had a melancholy air about it.

'Mass starts at 7 a.m. each morning. They say it gets greener around Lake Babati,' she said, reading my mind. 'There's also some rock art around here – if you're interested in that sort of thing.'

'How many refugees are there here?' Lodzia asked.

'Four hundred – excluding the clergy – most are women and children; all the younger and more able men have gone off to fight.'

'What about school?' Lodzia asked. Ella was already six years old, and she did not want her to miss out.

'Yes, we have set up a Grade School since we arrived, but secondary-school children have to travel to Tengeru. Danuta takes the lessons here; she's a teacher back home.'

'We have seamstresses who can make clothes if you supply the fabric. There's an Arab in Kondoa who has a shop. What else? Oh yes, we have a theatre group, embroidery classes, and we've also started a scout group. The few men here run that. That's about it. I think we've done about everything to create normality, given we will be living here – well – forever.'

As in all tropical countries, darkness fell swiftly. The heavens were so black yet alive with a raw energy. They reminded me of the last time I gazed at the majestic beauty of the night sky, through the gratings of my prison wagon in Arctic Russia. The sight of it gladdened my heart in a world so cruel yet able to retain its serenity.

I liked to imagine stars were the souls of the dead keeping watch over their loved ones still trapped on earth. The ones that glowed most brightly were Mama and Tatta guiding me in that way which ancient mariners used for navigation. If only I could understand what they were trying to tell me.

Dawn brought shimmering rays through the

open door to the foot of my bed as if mocking me for not getting up and giving thanks that I was one of the fortunate ones to have survived the slaughter of our finest at the devil's command.

The hut was empty, the faithful already giving praise across the road. High notes drifted through the windows and soared on the breeze.

I swung my legs out of bed and stood on a cockroach whose hard shell crunched beneath my bare foot and its squelched body stuck to my flesh. 'Ugh.'

Making my way to the church, I loitered outside; still mad with God for robbing me of everyone I loved. Yet it wasn't God's fault. Only one man was responsible for their deaths – Stalin. As the chant of prayer mixed with incense, I could once more feel elevated towards some higher being. I yearned to belong to something or someone and I prayed He would find me a mission in life. Something where I could make a meaningful difference.

The natives were already congregating for their ceremony, held in the same building. The rosy-cheeked nun told us that they believed in a single deity, yet still practised traditional African religion.

Their women were dressed in red fabric no larger than a tablecloth tied in a knot above their left breast, and the men wore anything red or rust coloured. All were barefoot, and I couldn't help looking at their ugly feet, shaped by their environment. Their skin was hard and burnt, their heels cracked and their toenails long and bent over where they gripped the bare earth.

No sooner had the Catholics vacated the church, than we heard the sound of their monotonous, rhythmic chanting wafting out through the open windows. These people were dirt poor, stank of body odour and wood smoke, but all was well with their world.

I approached a nun and asked if she knew anything of the drumming and chanting I heard again last night.

'Just ignore it; it's the Valangi practising their black magic. What you heard was their rain ritual. They purport to be bringing rain to the land belonging to the chieftain so that no one else gets it. Anyway, it always rains a few weeks into January, but they think it's down to them.'

41

God answered my prayers sooner than I expected; the next morning, I received a shovel. My mission was to grow beans and corn.

Mr Baranowski inspected us to ensure we were all wearing our cork helmets – he didn't want anyone to suffer sunstroke – before he took us along to our place of work on the road leading to Kondoa town. Lodzia stayed behind to settle Ella into school.

Our working day began at eight in the morning and ended at noon when temperatures soared. The land belonging to the Mission was rich and gave forth its fullness in food and flowers, unlike the surrounding ground, which was rock hard, and I found I was enjoying contributing to the greater good of our little community.

The temperature rose with each passing hour, and at 12 o'clock Mr Baranowski walked around with a giant alarm clock tied to a piece of string slung over his shoulder, banging a saucepan and shouting, 'Lunch!'

Work stopped, everyone straightened and ran their forearms across their brows. It was the end of our workday.

Our meal comprised one portion of boiled rice together with meatballs and beans or corn. It was always beans, or corn.

'These meatballs are delicious,' I said to Lodzia, who joined us at the table. 'Did you get Ella settled at school?'

'I did. Listen, that Danuta holds English lessons in the afternoons. It's only for an hour – why don't you go along?'

'What? I don't think so; she's very bossy. Anyway, who wants to learn English? Swahili maybe. English – what use is that?'

'Because it's time you did something for yourself. Don't let her intimidate you. You might enjoy it.'

I supposed it was something different, and I hadn't anything better to do than to recline on my bed and sweat until the temperatures dropped, so I went along. Other girls of my age attended the class, and I made friends with a girl called Appolonia, whom everyone called Pola for short. She was here with her younger sister, also called Leokadia and their father. Their mother died when Pola was twelve, and the role fell to her to look after the family. There was also a lovely girl called Bronia, and the two of them seemed like good pals. Pola was a decent sort; I liked her. Now I had three new friends: Stefcha, Pola and Bronia. Already my life was more interesting.

Two black boys jogging from Kondoa passed us

each morning on the way to work, an animal carcass skewered onto a pole across their shoulders, their footfalls stomping in unison to the rhythm of the chant that lingered on the breeze long after they had passed.

The food here was good, and as I recovered my health, my appetite improved. However, I found the ration of bread and runny butter we received in the afternoons was never enough to sustain me until morning, and I always felt hungry.

At the end of the week we received payment for our labours and Pola said, 'Let's go into town and buy some dress fabric. There are two seamstresses here.'

In the evening all four of us strolled to Kondoa. It was an insignificant place with dusty streets, occupied by low, flat-roofed buildings. Here they sold spiced coffee and there were sweetmeats available from the shop run by an Indian gentleman.

I felt liberated having money of my own. In another shop, we browsed through the dress fabrics and met the Arab owner. He had three wives, and he was *very, very* cheerful, *very, very* helpful and spoke *very, very* fast.

'Ladies,' he flung out his arms, 'Do not worry if you cannot find anything you like. I shall be going to Arusha next week, and I shall bring more fabrics. Silks of every hue; it will spoil you for choice!'

We all laughed, and each one of us bought

two lengths of fabric. I settled on red and a vibrant lilac and vowed I would return in two-weeks' time for the lemon shade.

Stopping at another shop, we treated ourselves to sandals, the kind that slipped between the big toe.

On our stroll back to the Mission, I caught Pola's arm. 'Wait! Look!' A fat snake slithered across the road ahead of us, and another uncoiled itself from a branch of a Baobab tree. Dangling in front of us, it fixed us with its beady stare, while all the time its forked tongue was working as if slavering after meal.

Skirting slowly around it, we made a dash for it. The four of us became vigilant, as we often found the snakes coiled up in long grass amid cactus plants. I hated them and could see no use for them.

What made me laugh aloud though, was the crane, with its comical opened fan of feathers perched on its head. It was an enormous bird about a metre tall with a wingspan of two metres. It stomped its feet as it walked, like a flat-footed angry old man, to flush out insects which it caught and gobbled up.

It didn't take long for us to fall into the unhurried life of Kondoa. Lodzia, the most gregarious person I knew, made friends with everyone, and Ella was growing up fast and had little friends of her own. I spent my morning in the fields, and after lunch lay sweating on my bed before temperatures dropped enough to attend English lessons. However, I spent my evenings sauntering into Kondoa town, with Pola, Stefcha, and Bronia; and our love of coffee and sweetmeats turned into a habit.

Settling into our novel way of life, we found fresh interests. I joined an embroidery group, and Lodzia, a theatre troupe. However, I realised that despite all the outward normality, life here held nothing for me; I had been dead inside since my parents and Karol died, going through the motions for Lodzia's sake, because she had tried so hard to help rehabilitate me. But no matter what I did, I could not purge my sorrow. The scars of Russia had scabbed over, but they were still painful if I scratched too hard, so I chose not to go there.

The mail was always slow. No one wrote to me, but Lodzia received letters from Gerhard. Why doesn't he ever write to me? I wondered, but knowing Gerhard, he would assume Lodzia would pass on his news?

In his last letter he wrote:

Moja Kohana, (My Dearest)
We've arrived in Palestine, and it is a relief to have left Iraq behind and Kizil-Ribat with its 120-degree shade temperatures. The climate in Palestine is much kinder, although we are not here on holiday. Most of the Jews defected to join their army, including one of my friends.

They have told us we are going into combat in Italy and we have been conducting large-scale exercises with the British army.

In our free time, we do some sightseeing. So far, I have visited Jerusalem and Bethlehem. It is incredible how small-scale everything is compared with how I had imagined it from the Bible. The Mount of Olives, which in my mind's eye was always a considerable escarpment extending for hectares, is tiny. I suppose I have to be thankful. Had I remained in Poland, and none of this had happened to us, I don't think I would ever have experienced anything – although I am not sure I want to experience what lies ahead.

Is my darling Ella still keeping well? No more recurrences of the blood poisoning, I hope. And how is Marisha? I worry about her all the time, and cannot forget how she coped with all the grief that befell her at so young an age – at any age.

Write again soon if you can, I miss you all. Love and hugs forever, Gerhard x-x-x

Lodzia kissed the kisses at the bottom of his letter and clutched it close to her heart. That is something I would never be able to do because the only future I had was here within the confines of this tiny Mission and I would die here, unfulfilled, growing beans and corn.

42

September 1943

Nothing much ever happened in Kondoa, but today the place was buzzing. A man had arrived at the Mission and we were all to assemble at the church after work.

Changing out of my work clothes, I asked Lodzia who he was.

'No idea; he's been with the priest since he arrived. Those who've seen him said he was wearing a cork hat, an open-neck shirt and a loose tie.'

It was a toss-up between my red dress, the vibrant lilac or they yellow one. I chose the lilac. 'That's no help – everyone here wears a cork hat. Was he black?'

'No, white – as far as I know. Perhaps he's here to tell us the war's ended.'

'Father Barbaranelli could have told us that.'

It was standing room only in church.

'You must all be wondering who I am,' the man said. 'I am an envoy from the Polish Government in exile which is now based in London, and I'm here on a mission. My task is to search out recruits for the Polish Women's Auxiliary Air Force, willing to enlist and travel to Great Britain for training, to help the British fight the Axis forces.'

That raised a buzz of excitement. The envoy stood and waited until the chatter died.

For a few of the girls, the decision was clear-cut – they needed no persuading.

I raised my hand to gain his attention. 'What would we be doing in this Air Force?'

'We need office workers, drivers, mechanics, wireless operators, meteorologist, cooks, ... in fact, auxiliary staff in every department to work alongside the men.'

Stefcha's hand shot in the air. 'May I volunteer?'

'You may.' His eyes roamed the crowd, and a few more girls added their names before his gaze returned to me. He was expecting an answer.

'How would we get there?' I asked. I had to admit the prospect sounded tantalising.

'By sea. We will take you to Mombasa, put you on a ship that will take you down to Durban, and then you will travel by troopship to England.'

'How long do we have to decide?' I asked.

'No rush; I'll be here until tomorrow lunchtime; I have other Polish refugee camps to visit throughout central Africa.'

Pola raised her hand, 'I'd love to go, but I have my elderly father and my little sister to consider.'

'Arrangements can be made to accommodate them too. England needs all the help it can get.'

Later, when the meeting disbanded, and we were walking back to our hut, Lodzia said, 'Will you go?'

'I'm tempted.' Yet I was undecided. I would have to part with her and Ella, and I wasn't sure I could do that. She and Gerhard were the only family I had left. Who else was out there for me?

'What's stopping you?'

'So long as I'm not expected to fly the aeroplanes.'

'No, Marishu, they won't expect you to do that. They have proper pilots.'

In the evening, when I joined Stefcha, Pola, and Bronia for our stroll into Kondoa town, the only topic of conversation was the Polish envoy and his proposal.

'There's nothing here for me,' Stefcha said. 'I'm off. What about you, Marishu?'

'It's parting from Lodzia and Ella that bothers me. I don't know if I can do it.'

'What about you Pola?'

'I'd love to go, but my father's the problem.'

'Yes, but the envoy said they could accommodate him.'

'That's the problem; Tatta wants to know *where*. What do they intend to do with him; he and my little sister will be on their own in 'some' foreign land. At least here, he's amongst Polish people. He's dug in his heels and refuses to budge – and in all conscience, I can't leave them behind.'

'What about you, Bronia, will you go?'

'Not if Pola doesn't. We've all been like a band of sisters, and now this envoy is tearing us apart.'

'So that's two of us for enlisting – and two against.'

It was the end of September when an open-topped truck arrived to collect us girls. We were on our way to Tengeru.

Tengeru was the largest refugee camp in the area, and the muster point for all recruits making their way from all corners of central Africa, and even as far away as India.

Unable to persuade me to remain, Lodzia said, 'Marishu, will you need those dresses? They'll give you a uniform. I could do with them myself.'

I agreed to share them. 'Which do you prefer, the lemon, the lilac or the red?'

Lodzia tried on the lemon one. 'See, a perfect fit.'

The day to leave arrived all too soon, and we all bade our farewells.

'Remember to write the minute you arrive so I know where you are,' Lodzia reminded me for the umpteenth time. 'Be safe, kohanie.' She hugged me and planted a huge, sturdy kiss on my cheek.

I hugged her back, crouched down, and kissed and hugged Ella. 'Look after Mama, kohanie.' My voice caught in my throat, and I climbed aboard with tears in my eyes; frightened that one good blink would release a torrent.

We set off along the bumpy track of the old caravan route. Those we had left behind stood waving, and we all waved back until a cloud of dust obscured our views of one another. The enduring picture I carried with me to my unknown life was of Lodzia, with her light brown hair plaited in a coronet around her head. She wore my lemon dress and beside her stood little Ella in a sweet pink dress with her fair hair tied up in two bunches and secured with white ribbons.

For some time, there was silence on board the truck as we all came to terms with our partings, of the decisions made and of what lay ahead. I would miss Lodzia so much; she had helped me through my trauma. To whom would I turn now for help?

Startled by the sound of the engine, a herd of wildebeest took flight, their hooves pounding away, and in the distance a cluster of antelope looked up from their grazing. From then on, the wildlife of the Masai Mara, the giraffes, the elephants and game animals occupied our attention; who knows perhaps as a foil to the momentous decisions we had made.

With the breeze in my hair, I felt somehow

liberated. It was the first decision I had made and whether it be right or wrong, I had only myself to blame.

Approaching Tengeru, the warm air of Mount Meru caressed our skins. We drove through sprawling banana and coffee plantations where the soil was fertile. The natives spoke to us in Swahili and we answered back, having picked up the rudiments of their language. In the distance, the snowy stack of Mount Kilimanjaro tracked our journey.

Tengeru was a large, delightful settlement vibrating with birdsong, its circular mud huts set amid tropical plants of white flowering umbrella like Acacias.

Each day a few more girls arrived from all destinations. A week later, Pola appeared, having regretted not volunteering, bringing her father and little sister. Tagging along behind was Bronia. What joy!

There was nothing to do here, no digging, and no planting. We spent our days strolling around the massive settlement, socialising and attending English lessons. God, it was a tough language to master. Sometimes we would venture to the nearby bazaar and watch local families going to market to sell their produce. The husband would stride out in front, followed by his dogs and elder children, while behind them plodded his wife, a basket loaded with fruit and vegetables on her head, lugging a baby in a sling on her back.

When the Polish envoy had rounded up about five hundred of us, they took us to Makindu, another camp closer to Mombasa, to await the ship that would take us to Durban.

Our journey to Durban was a nightmare. We sailed with the shoreline always in sight to our right. The ship was small and the currents violent. The prow of the boat went up, up, up, and then it dropped so fast it made everyone sick. Our seasickness was so severe after a few days that even the Captain worried about us. Our meals went uneaten, and when we refused his plain digestive biscuits he seemed at his wits end.

It relieved me when we docked in Durban a week later, and I wobbled off the boat, trying to regain my land legs. Now we were all worried, because if this were to be a foretaste of ocean travel, we would have been better staying behind in Africa.

The Nieuw Amsterdam was yet to arrive. It was sailing from Australia, and due to dock in Durban on 20th February, remaining one day to collect us five hundred new recruits. So, while they allowed sightseeing in the meantime, everyone had to be back here on 19th February without fail otherwise, the ship would sail without us, and we would have no means of returning to Kondoa.

Africa helped me heal. Yet the naked truth of

feelings I could never convey to anyone who had not been through what I had endured – and had no wish to recapture – would remain in my mind like an etched plaque.

Had I made the right decision to leave Africa? Perhaps – perhaps not. But the remembered contentment of my once secure and peaceful life in the meadows of Szpitali lay curled up in my heart forever. It was some mystical earthly paradise to which I yearned to return, to relive the carefree days of my childhood with my family, but Stalin's barbaric war machine had put paid to it forever. I said goodbye to Africa – and braced myself to set sail for England and an uncertain future.

THE END

ACKNOWLEDGEMENTS

I should like to extend my thanks to my dear friends, Tina Newell, Gloria-Jean Bamber and Dianne Ashton for their tireless and patient reading of each draft I produced—and there were many. To my colleagues at the Leicester Writers' Club for their patient critiquing and helpful remarks—especially to Dave Martin. To Miss Fones, Head of English, at English Martyrs Catholic School, for her invaluable critiquing and insight into the application of this book to the educational sector, and her encouragement to make it a reality. Also to her colleague Mr Kaczmar, Head of History, who contacted me later with the names of Exam Boards dealing with this curriculum.

Thanks also to my Editor, Nancy Callegari, who returned my MS with a morale-boosting note saying:

'Imperilled' was an incredibly emotive storyline to work on, and so well-written I imagined every inch of the journey and the family's battle. It made me cry, but that's the sign of perfection - being able to convey that agony, despair, and loneliness.

To Cathy Helms of Avalon Graphics LLC for painstakingly trying to convey the above sentiments within the design of the book cover. To Maureen Vincent-Northam for reading and line editing the final manuscript. Finally, to Rebecca Emin, who not only prepared the script for publication but also for constantly being on hand to help with my queries and offering advice. How blessed was I to have found such an 'A Team'? For this, I have to thank my fellow author, Madalyn Morgan.

Thanks also to Dr Mark Ostrowski for posting his family's experiences at the same hard labour camp on the Kresy-Siberia Virtual Museum News Letter of December 2013, certain facts of which enabled me to further flesh out this story.

Love and thanks to my wonderful husband, Verdun, whose television viewing I blighted for years whilst working on this book, tapping away on my laptop in the armchair beside my mother so that she wouldn't feel lonely.

Last, but not least, to my mother; a wonderful, inspirational woman who lit up every life she touched and whose smile and patience allowed this book to be.

Printed in Great Britain
by Amazon